BOOKS BY MICHAEL SCOTT
FROM TOM DOHERTY ASSOCIATES

Etruscans (with Morgan Llywelyn)
The Thirteen Hallows (with Colette Freedman)

MIRROR
IMAGE

MIRROR IMAGE

MICHAEL SCOTT

and

MELANIE RUTH ROSE

A TOM DOHERTY ASSOCIATES BOOK **TOR** NEW YORK

This is a work of fiction. All of the characters, organizations, and events portrayed in this novel are either products of the authors' imagination or are used fictitiously.

MIRROR IMAGE

A Tor Book
Published by Tom Doherty Associates, LLC
175 Fifth Avenue
New York, NY 10010

www.tor-forge.com

Tor® is a registered trademark of Tom Doherty Associates, LLC.

The Library of Congress Cataloging-in-Publication Data is available upon request.

ISBN 978-0-7653-8522-2 (hardcover)
ISBN 978-0-7653-8561-1 (e-book)

Our books may be purchased in bulk for promotional, educational, or business use. Please contact your local bookseller or the Macmillan Corporate and Premium Sales Department at 1-800-221-7945, extension 5442, or by e-mail at MacmillanSpecialMarkets@macmillan.com.

First Edition: August 2016

Printed in the United States of America

0   9   8   7   6   5   4   3   2   1

FOR BARRY

ACKNOWLEDGMENTS

The authors would like to thank the many people who helped usher this book to publication: Tom Doherty, Bob Gleason, and Elayne Becker at Tor for everything!

The dynamic duo, Barry Krost and Steve Troha.

Melanie would like to especially thank: Matt, Shelley, Sue, Paul, and Jaffee for their encouragement.

And for Jill who showed me nothing but love, support, and inspiration in my new journey.

MIRROR
IMAGE

1

THE MIRROR stood seven foot tall, four foot wide, the glass dirty and speckled, warped so that the images it showed were slightly distorted and blurred. It was quite grotesque.

And Jonathan Frazer knew he had to have it.

He stood at the back of the small crowd in the foul-smelling auction room and waited impatiently while the bored auctioneer made his way through the catalogue of the *Property of a Gentleman.*

"Lot 66, a French Gendarme's Side Arm Saw Sword, with a double edged steel blade, bronze handle and cross guards, complete with leather scabbard. The blade shows some wear . . ."

Although it was only just after one in the afternoon, Jonathan Frazer was tired. He'd been in England a week, but was still jet-lagged, a feeling not helped by London's miserable November weather which sapped his energy and left him achy and vaguely fluey. He had spent the last few days doing the rounds of the auction houses in London but had come away empty-handed. He'd been tempted to skip the quirky auction house on Lots Road in Chelsea but, like every dealer he knew, there was always the fear that the find of a lifetime was waiting in the auction you never attended. Thanksgiving, and then Christmas, were just round the corner and he needed to find some unique items. In the next few weeks Hollywood's A-listers or, more likely, their personal assistants would go looking for expensive presents for the friends they never saw.

The auction had already started when Jonathan stepped into the shadowy interior of the auction room and began to wander around amongst the larger objects piled up at the back of the room. Furniture, none of it interesting, was strewn about the premises and, at the other end of the room, a motley assortment of people faced an elderly man. The auction-eer's singsong chant drifted through the room. Frazer shook his head slightly. He hadn't been expecting to find anything: the really good stuff was usually traded amongst the dealers and collectors and rarely reached the general public. Much of what was here was trash, or the condition was so poor as to render them worthless. But one man's trash was another's treasure.

"Lot 68, a gentleman's half-hunter pocket watch . . . in need of re-pair . . ."

A sliver of silver light at the very back of the room caught his attention and he turned, squinting into the gloom. It took him a moment to make out the shape: there was a mirror behind a wood-wormed wardrobe and an early Edwardian dresser.

He squeezed between the wardrobe and the dresser, initially attracted to the sheer size of the glass. He was six foot tall and it was at least a foot taller than he was. He spread his arms, judging the width from experience: it was at least four foot wide. There was a surprisingly plain wooden frame surrounding it, complete with brass clips for securing it to a wall, although it was now mounted on an ornate stand. The stand was a later addition, he decided.

Jonathan Frazer ran his hand down the mirror, drawing long streaks on the glass; it was filthy, covered with a greasy layer of grime. He rubbed a tissue around in a circle at about head height and peered into it, but, with the dimness of the auction room and the dirt encrusted onto the glass, he could barely make out his own reflection. He licked his finger and rubbed it against the mirror, his breath catching when he felt its chill against his flesh, but even that made no impression on the grime.

Without examining the back of the mirror he had no way of accu-rately dating it, but, considering the slightly bluish tinge to the glass, the perceptible distortion around the perimeter and the curious beveling in towards the center, it was certainly old, seventeenth century, possibly earlier.

"Lot 69, a large antique wooden-framed mirror, approximately seven feet tall by four feet wide. An imposing piece."

Jonathan Frazer took a deep breath, suddenly glad he was wearing jeans and a long sleeved sweatshirt and not his regular suit. He cast an experi-enced eye over the small crowd: he couldn't spot any obvious dealer-types.

He hoped anyone looking at him would assume he was just another guy in off the street looking for a bargain.

"Now who will open the bidding at eight hundred pounds?"

Frazer could hardly believe his ears. The mirror was worth at least ten times that. But he kept his head down, not looking at the auctioneer, showing no interest.

"Seven hundred and fifty then. Come along ladies and gentlemen; it's here to be cleared. Seven hundred and fifty for a fine piece of glass like that. A handsome piece in any house."

"You'd need a bloody big house for that, mate," someone quipped in a cockney accent.

The auctioneer smiled. "Five hundred pounds, ladies and gentlemen. Five hundred pounds, or I'll have to pass."

Frazer looked up and caught the auctioneer's eye. He raised his left hand and spread his fingers wide.

The auctioneer frowned, then nodded slightly. "Five hundred pounds is bid. Any advance on five hundred pounds? Come along ladies and gentlemen, this is a real bargain. Any advance on five hundred pounds?"

No one moved.

"Fair warning at five hundred pounds. Five hundred. Going once, going twice . . ." The auctioneer slammed his gavel on the lectern. "Sold!" He looked in Frazer's direction and nodded. "Now moving on to Lot 70 . . ."

A young man wearing blue overalls made his way through the crowd and handed Frazer a slip to fill in.

"Can you ship it?"

"We can, of course, sir, shipping is extra."

"Of course." Frazer handed across his business card. "To this address."

The young man turned it over. "Frazer Interiors. In Los Angeles. I remember you, sir. We shipped you those carved Chinese lion heads."

"You've a good memory."

"I had to wrap them and ship them. I've never forgotten them. It's been a while since we've seen you."

"I know. And you're my last call of the day." Frazer glanced back at the mirror. "My lucky day."

The young man smiled. "You got a real bargain, Mr. Frazer. You're obviously the right man in the right place at the right time."

2

IT'S QUITE something." Tony Farren ran his hand appreciatively down the length of the glass. "The frame's horrific, but we'll see if we can do something about that."

Jonathan Frazer crouched down in front of the enormous mirror, pointing to the black speckling that ran around its edges. "Let's see what we can do about these, too, OK?"

Tony nodded. "That'll be no problem."

Jonathan stood up and brushed off his hands. "What do you think?"

The two men were standing in the converted garage-workshop at the back of Frazer's home in the Hollywood Hills that held the overflow from the shop. Tony Farren tucked his hands into his jean pockets. He had been with the Frazer family since James Frazer, Jonathan's father, opened an antiques business in Hollywood in the mid-sixties. When Jonathan inherited the business and turned Frazer Antiques & Curios into Frazer Interiors, selling mid-century furniture mixed with carefully selected antique pieces, Tony stayed on. Small, stout, and completely bald, his knowledge of antiques was phenomenal. When Jonathan was a boy, he spent most of his summers in the crowded, musty converted garage at his parents' home in Los Feliz watching, fascinated, as Tony worked and talked. Jonathan always claimed that everything he knew about antiques he learned from Tony Farren.

"It's a fine piece," Tony said eventually. "Very fine."

"Can you put a value on it for me?" Jonathan smiled. *Very fine* was high praise indeed.

Farren ran his hands over the glass, and then used a small flashlight to throw a light onto the mirror. He repeated the procedure with the wooden frame, and then moved behind the tall mirror to examine the back. He ducked out from behind it, peering over his horn-rimmed glasses. "It's an interesting piece, no mistake about that. The glass is Venetian, possibly late fourteenth, early fifteenth century, although it's very difficult to say. Could be even earlier for all I know. The frame looks early sixteenth century, it's in the style certainly, although the wood looks older . . . and it's a peculiar wood, too, birch or alder." He stepped back, sinking his hands into his pockets, his head tilted to one side. "On reflection . . ."

Jonathan groaned at the pun.

Tony grinned. "Sorry about that. It would seem a shame to remove the glass from the frame, unless we could put together a more ornate—but finding a frame of this size would be virtually impossible, it would have to be custom made. Let's leave it as is."

"The price, Tony," Jonathan gently reminded him.

"I'd say about twenty thousand dollars . . . give or take a few."

"What!"

Farren grinned at Jonathan's surprise. "Why, what were you going to charge for it?"

"About seven grand, seventy-eight hundred maybe . . ."

"For twenty-eight square feet of what is possibly Venetian glass with what looks like an Elizabethan frame on it! That'd be like giving it away."

"Could be a fake," Jonathan suggested.

Tony Farren snorted rudely. He tapped the glass with his knuckles. "And this, by the way, is not going to go down in price. If we store it for a couple of years, it will double in value."

Jonathan Frazer moved away from the huge mirror, looking at it in a new light. He sank down onto a badly made copy of a Chippendale and began to laugh gently. "I paid five hundred English pounds for it. So with the exchange rate and freight, approximately thirty-five hundred dollars."

Tony shook his head. "It's a once in a lifetime bargain."

"A piece of good fortune, indeed!"

Farren smiled. "Every dealer—whether he's dealing in books, stamps, coins, furniture, pictures or silver—turns up one special item in their lifetime." He rested his hand against the glass, a damp palm print forming on the surface only to disappear almost immediately. "This could very well be your special item."

Frazer checked his watch. He looked at the mirror one final time. Maybe he wouldn't sell it. Not yet anyway. With the economy tanking, this might be worth hanging onto. "I'll be at the store if you need me." He looked at Tony. "Take special care of it for me."

"I will. I'll start refurbishing it immediately. I'm quite looking forward to it," he added, rubbing his right hand across the mirror again. "Just think: if this glass could talk. What has it seen?" he wondered aloud.

"You say that about every single item I bring in here."

"Everything has a story," Tony said to Jonathan's retreating back. "You know what I've always told you . . ."

"I know, I know. I'm not selling antiques—I'm selling stories."

TONY FARREN WAS born in the Sunset District of San Francisco. His parents, post-war sweethearts, settled there after World War II. At the age of eighteen, uneducated Farren was drafted to Vietnam. He served one year before returning to the US with no skills other than how to handle and fire—with extraordinary accuracy—an M60 machine gun. Farren had moved to Los Angeles in the hope of finding a new life for himself. He drifted from trade to trade—painting, glazing, building, carpentry, plumbing and electrical—learning enough to be competent in each, but eventually finding each job remarkably boring.

James Frazer was in the process of opening an antiques store in Hollywood and he needed a handyman, someone who could fix the leg of a chair, refinish a tabletop, touch up a painting.

During his interview Tony Farren lied; he told James Frazer he could do all these things and more. And there was no one more surprised than he was, when he actually discovered that he could. He improved his basic skills by studying, and his solutions to the problems presented to him on a daily basis, whilst unorthodox, usually worked. James Frazer claimed he was a genius; Tony put it down to the fact that he was finally doing something he enjoyed. Every day was different: one day he might be working on chairs or tables, the next re-wiring a crystal chandelier or mending the hinge on an antique armoire, and the day after faux finishing a night stand.

Tony Farren had spent over forty-five years in the business working alongside James Frazer, growing the company, eventually becoming one of its master craftsmen as well as a recognized authority on the history of eighteenth century antique furniture. Over the years, he had seen just about every type of antique and artifact . . . but he had never seen anything quite like it.

He walked slowly around the mirror—certainly the largest he had ever seen. It was a sheet of glass set into a plain wooden frame, with a solid wooden back fixed to the frame. Obviously the back would have to be removed before he started work.

Tony fished into his back pocket and removed a magnifying glass, then bent to examine one of the clips which secured the back to the frame. He hissed in annoyance: the heads of two of the screws were entirely destroyed, the grooves worn smooth. He moved onto the next screw and frowned; this too had been destroyed. Moving slowly from clip to clip—there were twelve in all, two screws to a clip—he discovered that the heads of all twenty-four screws had been worn completely smooth, the grooves hacked and torn away. He rubbed a callused palm against the wooden backing. It looked deliberate.

"Whoever put you on didn't want you coming off."

However, the problem wasn't insurmountable. The trick was to cut new heads in the screws, make a groove deep enough to give him purchase for a screwdriver. There was always the danger that the screw would snap—and that would be a bitch, but he'd cross that bridge when he came to it.

Farren moved over to the long workbench. It was a chaos of tools and littered with half-completed projects. The workbench had been the despair of numerous assistants down through the years. While they searched frantically for tools, he had always been able to go exactly to the place he had last left it. He chose a small Black & Decker and fitted a circular abrading stone to it. Then he slipped a pair of tinted protective glasses over his own and pulled on a pair of gloves. And then, with infinite patience, he carefully cleaned the ragged metal off the heads of the crude screws. It took him the best part of an hour, starting with those he could easily reach and then climbing up onto a stepladder to complete the job. When he was finished, the heads gleamed silver, sparkling in the light. Returning to the bench, he replaced the Black & Decker with a diamond-tipped drill. He took a few moments to review what he was about to do and then, satisfied, knelt on the floor beside the mirror. This was the tricky bit.

"Don't try this at home kids," he murmured, as he maneuvered the drill in a reasonably straight line down the center of the first screw. Sparks flew and the soft, musty air was tainted with the sharp tang of scorched metal.

It took him about three tense minutes to cut the groove, but when he fitted the screwdriver head into the groove, it slotted neatly into place. He grunted in quiet satisfaction.

No problem.

Tony Farren had cut twenty-two of the twenty-four screws when the accident happened. He was tired; he'd been working for over an hour just cutting the grooves and his neck and shoulder muscles were bunched and his eyes felt gritty, nerves twitching in his eyelids. "God, I'm getting too old for this," he muttered under his breath. He should have stopped for lunch over an hour ago, but far better to get this bit finished, grab a bite to eat and then proceed. He moved the ladder along to the last clip and climbed up with the drill clutched in his right hand. He had just about reached the top when the stepladder shifted. Farren yelped with fright and dropped the drill, scrabbling to catch the expensive piece of equipment, missing it, hearing it crack onto the concrete floor. He toppled forward, instinctively clutching at the top of the mirror for support. He immediately realized what he was doing and attempted to push himself back, terrified that he was going to push the mirror to the ground. The stepladder swayed with the violence of his movements, metal legs screeching on the floor. Tony Farren crashed to the ground, his head cracking against the solid floor, right hip popping with the sickening force, shards of metal from the shattered drill casing digging into his flesh. Luckily the heavy metal stepladder had pushed away from him as he fell and went clattering across the floor.

Tony didn't know how long he'd lain unconscious. Ten, fifteen minutes, maybe. The angle of the sun through the window had definitely shifted. When he came to, he defiantly resisted the urge to vomit. His protective glasses now rested at an awkward angle across his face. Pulling them off, he threw them to his side, relieved that his own glasses were still intact. He felt the back of his head, wincing as he touched a warm sticky liquid oozing from an open wound. Skull laceration, maybe a concussion, he guessed, but he'd been lucky. It could have been worse, much worse. He could have snapped his neck when he'd fallen.

Every movement was agony, and his entire body was a solid mass of anguish. Paradoxically—in spite of the pain, because of the pain?—he was losing feeling in his legs, but he guessed that was just the shock, or maybe there was internal bleeding.

"Stupidstupidstupid." His voice was a strangled hiss of pain. Finally, when he decided he had come to terms with the hurt, he began the painful process of crawling across to the telephone on the wall above the workbench. All these years he had resisted getting a cell phone and now he wished he hadn't. How he was going to get the phone down was another matter, but one thing at a time. He knew Jonathan was at the store; he knew Celia—Mrs. Frazer—was still surfing in Hawaii and wouldn't be back for another few days, and Manny was staying with friends. If he could get to the phone he'd call Jonathan at the store. Fuck that! He would call the paramedics first.

Digging his fingernails into the scarred concrete floor, Farren pulled himself forward, moving awkwardly around the mirror, which was directly in front of him. Blood was pounding in his head, roaring in his skull, and he could feel it trickling warmly down the side of his face. His breathing was a loud rasp. When he got to the bench, he would . . .

Concentrate . . . one thing at a time . . .

He was going to have that engraved on his tomb: one thing at a time.

Right now he was concentrating on reaching the workbench. When he reached it he would rest.

Pressing his palms to the floor he pushed . . . and nothing happened. He couldn't feel his legs now. His shoulder muscles were aflame; his arched spine ached as he dug into his reserves, attempting to pull himself along the floor. With an almost superhuman effort he reached out, his fingertips lightly brushing against the wooden corner of the workbench. With one final effort he managed to grab a firm hold.

Something shifted.

Tony Farren turned. His left foot had become caught up in the ornate base of the mirror. He had been pulling the mirror with his every movement, and the flesh of his ankle was rubbed raw. He hadn't heard it because of the noise in his head, hadn't felt it because of the numbness in his legs. He sat up and attempted to extricate his leg using both hands, jerking it towards him.

The seven foot tall mirror shifted on the stand, the top swiveling, dipping downwards.

Tony Farren opened his mouth to scream, but no sound came. He knew what was going to happen. Trapped, unable to move, he could only watch in horror as the mirror shifted, turning on its stand. With a slow, almost ponderous movement, the entire four hundred and twenty pound weight toppled forward.

Farren managed to scream once before it crashed into him, snapping through his outstretched hands, impacting the bones deep into his body, cracking and then flattening the skull, crushing the ribs deep into the lungs and internal organs. Blood and gore spurted once—briefly—before the weight of the mirror pressed the corpse onto the ground.

IT TOOK FOUR firefighters to lift the mirror off the crushed remains of Tony Farren. There were two surprises in store for them: the mirror was intact despite the fall, and there was virtually no blood.

4

THE MAN was, Dave Watts thought, one of the biggest and, without a doubt, the ugliest, motherfucker he had ever seen. Dave had been watching the man for the past few moments peering in through the auction room's large windows, shading his eyes with his hands to see into the darkened interior. Finally, he moved in off the sidewalk and stood in the doorway, effectively blocking it. He was not the sort of guy you'd want to meet in a brightly lit alley, Dave decided, never mind the other kind.

Dave Watts moved through the bewildering assortment of furniture he was presently listing in preparation for the usual weekly auction and stopped a few feet away from the large shadowed figure. "Morning, can I help you? Auction's not 'til Wednesday, and there's no viewing until Tuesday morning."

The big man moved into the large circular room, ducking his head slightly to avoid the low beams. He was dressed entirely in black, the outfit vaguely clerical, except that he wore a black turtleneck sweater instead of a Roman collar.

Dave, who himself stood six foot and weighed a hundred and ninety-six pounds, found himself looking up at a man who topped him by at least four inches, and who had the body of a professional wrestler. The big man stopped in the center of the room, his head swiveling on a thick neck. He had a shock of snow-white hair, though his eyebrows were coal black, and much of his face was lined with a tracery of scars, which were especially evident along his cheekbones and forehead. His nose had once been broken and badly set and his chin was deeply cleft. When he finally turned to look at Dave, coal-black, stone-hard eyes stared unblinkingly at him.

"Can I help you?" Dave demanded more forcefully. As casually as possible he began to move over to a collection of umbrellas and walking sticks in an elephant's foot stand. There was a sword cane in one of them, though God alone knew which one. The auction rooms had been raided once, and on two previous occasions they had been approached and asked—no, *told*—to pay protection money. Despite repeated threats of burning they had refused to pay, and they had heard nothing further.

But the big ugly mother was an enforcer if ever there was one.

"You're auctioning a mirror," the big man said finally, his voice a rasping whisper as if his throat had once been damaged, though still revealing traces of a refined Oxford accent.

"No . . . no . . . sir, we're not. Not this week anyway."

The big man frowned. "I was told there was a large mirror coming up for auction in these rooms. I have traveled a long way to purchase this mirror. Now, is there a mirror for auction?"

"Well, no, sir," Dave said nervously, completely disconcerted by the man's sheer presence. "We did have a large mirror for sale in last week's auction . . . perhaps you got the dates wrong."

"Have you the catalog for that auction?"

"Yes sir, but I can describe the mirror to you. I actually catalogued it myself."

"Describe it."

Dave glanced nervously around the room: where were the assistants? Surely they should have been back from lunch by now?

"It was a large mirror, measuring approximately seven feet by four feet, set into a plain wooden frame, the whole lot mounted on a hinged base which allowed the mirror to be tilted back and forth. It weighed a ton," he added with a grin, which faded at the expression on the other man's face.

"That is the mirror I was looking for." He took a step forward. "It was sold." He turned the question into a statement.

"Yes sir."

"To whom?" he demanded.

"I . . . I'm afraid we're not at liberty to disclose that sort of information."

"Disclose it!"

"Now hang on a minute . . . !"

"Who bought that mirror?" Although his voice was still little more than a whisper, there was a definite menacing tone in it now.

"Sir, like I said, we guarantee client confidentially. I'm afraid I cannot disclose the purchaser of the mirror." Dave felt beads of sweat pop out on his forehead as the man stepped nearer, towering over him. The scars on his face stood out whitely against the darker tan of his flesh. He looked as if he'd gone straight through a windshield. Dave glanced longingly at one of the nearby walking sticks; he wasn't sure he'd be able to get to one before the stranger was on top of him.

"Why make trouble for yourself?" the man asked pleasantly. "I can make it worth your while." He pulled out a roll of currency and began peeling off the larger red notes, the fifties.

Dave Watts stared at him until the man had counted out four fifties.

"Frazer Interiors," he blurted out suddenly. "Los Angeles address, purchased by Jonathan Frazer for five hundred pounds and shipped by AGP International Shipping, which cost him another nine hundred pounds."

The stranger smiled thinly, and the wad of money disappeared back into his coat. "Thank you."

"Hey," Dave said, affronted, seeing his two hundred disappearing along with the rest. "What about my money?"

"I never said I'd give you money," the man said, turning away.

"We had a deal; you said you'd make it worth my while." Forgetting his earlier fears, he reached out and grabbed the bigger man by the arm.

The large man turned, grabbed Dave by the throat and shoved him up against the wall behind him. Pitiless black eyes stared into Dave's face for at least a minute, then the big man loosened his grip and smiled. Dave rubbed his hand over his throat wandering if it was covered in red marks: that smile had been the most frightening thing he had ever seen. He stepped forward and tripped over the elephant's foot, scattering umbrellas, walking sticks, and canes all over the floor. He looked down involuntarily, and when he looked back, the big man had vanished.

Dave Watts wiped his face on the sleeve of his shop coat. He felt chilled although he was bathed in sweat: for the first time in his life he realized he had experienced real fear. And then he discovered that he had wet himself.

5

THE PLACE wouldn't be the same without Tony. Jonathan Frazer wandered down the silent workroom, still wearing the black suit he had worn to the funeral. This was the first time in the past week that he'd come into the guesthouse, and the long room—even though it was crowded with furniture and antiques—now felt empty. He sat down in Tony's much battered chair and looked around the room, dust motes spiraling upwards in the afternoon stillness. He had lost a friend. He had never looked on Tony Farren as a father, but rather as an uncle or maybe a much older brother. Oh, he'd had his faults—he could be petty and spiteful, quarrelsome, and he hated to be proven wrong, and in recent years he had become far too fond of old wine and young men—but he had always been a friend.

His eyes were drawn to the tall imposing mirror and the dark red-brown stain on the floor in front of it. Christ, but what a freakish accident! There had been an autopsy, of course, and a coroner's report: accidental death had been the predictable verdict.

The sequence of events was easy enough to reconstruct. Jonathan found his eyes going up the mirror, visualizing Tony working on the screws, cleaning them all off, and then laboriously cutting new grooves in them. He'd overstretched and fallen, cracking his head, breaking his hip, damaging his spine. The mirror had tilted, shifted, and then fallen forward on top of him. The cops had estimated its weight at about four hundred and twenty pounds, but he thought it might be heavier. Tony must have been in terrible pain when he'd fallen and it was small consolation that he'd died instantly when the mirror crushed him.

Jonathan smiled bitterly. Tony always said he thought he would like to die working on something special. Well, he'd had his wish.

May God have mercy on his soul.

The door cracked open, the hinge screeching, startling him.

"Sorry Jonathan, I didn't expect to find you here." Diane Williams, Tony Farren's assistant, stepped into the long room, allowing the door to swing closed behind her. "It's not the same without him," she said quietly. She was dressed in a black suede skirt and crisp white shirt—the first time Frazer could ever remember her wearing a skirt—and her shaggy blond hair was bundled up neatly at the back of her head. She was wearing dark glasses to hide her red and swollen eyes. Although she had fought long and bitterly with Tony every day, they had been very fond of one another. "There was a good turn-out," she said numbly, the silence of the long room oppressive.

"He would have been proud." Frazer nodded. Just about every notable antiques store in Los Angeles had sent a representative, along with numerous interior designers, colleagues, and contacts Tony had built up over the years. Frazer's one regret was that his wife had categorically refused to cut short her surfing vacation to attend the funeral and Manny, his daughter, was still with friends in San Diego. Jonathan had never felt so alone.

"Jonathan . . ." Diane began tentatively. She loosened her hair clips letting her long shaggy hair fall to her shoulders. "I know this isn't the time, and this probably isn't the place . . ."

"What is it, Diane?" Frazer asked gently.

"It's that mirror, Jonathan, that . . . that fucking mirror! I'm not working on it. I couldn't!" She began crying then, the tears which flowed so freely at Tony's graveside returning again. She pulled off her glasses, wiping the tears away with the palm of her hand.

Jonathan took her in his arms, pressing her head to his chest, stroking her hair, crooning softly to her. She would be about the same age as Emmanuelle—Manny—he guessed, around eighteen, and he had soothed and salved enough tears in his twenty-year marriage to be counted an expert on the subject. "I wasn't even going to ask you," he lied. He hadn't even thought about the subject. "Now, listen to me. I want you to take a couple of days vacation—we'll call it compassionate leave. Come back to me Monday, and we'll work out something. I need you now, Diane, and I need you in top form. Only you know all of Tony's tricks. Don't even think about the mirror. I'll probably dispose of it."

"I'm not superstitious, Jonathan, you know that. But that mirror is bad luck . . ."

"Diane . . ." he began.

"Look . . ." Taking his hand, she maneuvered him in front of the mirror. "What do you see?"

"Beneath a layer of dirt, I see two unhappy people," he said gently.

"I polished that mirror four times since it arrived here. The first day I spent nearly two hours removing every speck of dirt and grease from it. Tony insisted."

"It probably got dirty when it . . . when it fell," he said reasonably.

Diane took Jonathan's arm and turned him so that he was facing her. "Please Jonathan, get rid of the mirror, break it up, throw it away, burn it, but please, don't keep it here."

Frazer took hold of both her arms, squeezing tightly. "You're over-wrought, Diane. Now please, go home, get some rest. We'll sort everything out on Monday, I promise."

"Thanks," she said meekly.

"Off you go now."

When she had gone, Jonathan Frazer walked up to the mirror and ran his fingertip down the length of the glass. It came away black with grime.

He presumed it had gotten dirty when it had fallen, but wasn't it amazing that it hadn't shattered when it had fallen on poor Tony? It had emerged from the accident completely unscratched . . . even the frame . . .

A sudden thought struck him and he knelt on the floor, unconsciously standing in exactly the same spot where Tony had been killed. He examined the edges of the wooden frame. They had been splashed with blood, they should be stained, the wood scarred where they had struck the concrete floor . . . but there was no evidence that it had ever fallen. And then he noticed something else: the black speckling around the edges of the bottom of the glass had disappeared!

6

J ONATHAN FRAZER turned his Volvo Estate into the driveway and was
surprised to find his wife's new BMW M3 convertible parked carelessly
across the double garage door, effectively blocking it. Hissing in annoyance, he pulled the Volvo onto the pathway leading to the house and then
tramped up the graveled driveway, lifting the duplicate key for the BMW
off his own key ring.

It would have taken her two minutes to park the car.

Jonathan sat in the BMW, smelling its newness and the richness of the
leather upholstery, now overlain with his wife's latest perfume, Opium. She
changed her perfumes with extraordinary regularity. Before starting the car
he took a deep breath to calm himself. She could have parked the car, or
at least not blocked the entrance . . . it was just thoughtlessness. Or maybe
it was something more than that. He suddenly grinned into the mirror.
He hadn't had an argument, hadn't felt like this in a month . . . which was
exactly how long Celia had been away.

The last time he had had an argument with Celia—which was just before she left for Hawaii, which was her third, or was it her fourth holiday
this year—he had stormed out of the house, climbed into the Volvo and
proceeded to back into one of the free-standing ornamental water features
on the lawn. The large ceramic pot had toppled off its pedestal and shattered the back taillight. He hadn't seen the bill for the repair yet, but
he knew it was going to run into thousands rather than hundreds of dollars. In some obscure way, he felt that just about summed up their relationship.

But the bitch could have parked the car properly!

When his breathing returned to normal and his heart slowed its angry pounding, he started up the BMW, carefully backed it down the drive and then tripped the garage door with the remote control. Celia had had a trick with the previous car of tripping the garage door when she was just turning in to the driveway and shooting straight into the garage without waiting for the roof to settle. Jonathan had been waiting for the day when she would either drive straight into the garage door which had refused to open or the door sticking halfway up and taking her head off.

With her car safely parked, he strolled back down the drive to his own car, breathing in the cool evening air. He had had a particularly frustrating day; a client had returned an expensive custom dining table because she didn't like the color, even though she had chosen it, and then an order of expensive crystal lamps had arrived which were completely wrong. He should have taken the day off, he realized now. Tony's tragic death and the funeral yesterday had completely unsettled him, and of course, he hadn't really had a chance to settle back into a work routine since his return from London.

Unfortunately, tomorrow was Saturday, one of the busiest days in the store, and he couldn't afford to take it off. And with Thanksgiving so close, and then Christmas, followed by the January sale, his next break was at least three months away.

He parked his own car carefully—the double car garage was just the right size for both cars, providing Celia parked her car straight. He locked down the garage and strolled around to the front door, and there his anger flared again when he put his key in the door and it immediately opened inwards. It hadn't been locked. Standing on the step, he pushed the door all the way open.

The marbled hallway was littered with Celia's luggage and numerous bags. A surfboard leaned against the Italian Rococo occasional table.

Moving through the mess, Jonathan gently pulled the board away from the table, licking his finger, rubbing it to the spot where it had scored the varnish.

Aware that an argument was almost inevitable now—recognizing the signs, feeling his shoulder and stomach muscles beginning to knot—he slowly climbed the stairs.

The master bedroom was littered with clothes, and through the closed door of the en suite bathroom, he could hear the shower drumming steadily. Frazer cracked open the door and peered inside, wincing as steam billowed out around him. He could just about make out his wife's naked form through the frosted glass.

"Hey . . ." he called. The hissing of the water lessened. "Hey, it's me . . ."

"Oh, you're home. I'll be out in a minute." The shower resumed with full force.

By the time Celia Frazer emerged from the shower and strolled, naked and dripping, into the bedroom, Jonathan had tidied up most of the scattered clothes, bundling the majority of them into the laundry basket and hanging the rest up on their hangers in the walk-in closet. She kissed him perfunctorily on the cheek, even though she hadn't seen him in a month, then walked straight in to the closet to pull out an ivory silk nightdress. It stuck to her wet body, and Jonathan found he could look at her without feeling anything. Even though they hadn't slept together in a month and hadn't made love in six months, he wasn't in the least aroused by the sight of her naked body. An ever-present diet had stolen much of the flesh off her, and constant exercise had replaced it with muscle, which gave her skin a slightly lumpy appearance. Her breasts, which had always been small, had almost vanished as she had developed her chest and shoulder muscles, and although she only stood five six—and even he didn't know what she weighed—he guessed that she was stronger than he was.

"Aren't you going to ask me how my vacation went?" she said eventually, not looking at him as she unpacked the rest of her clothes, dropping them in a pile on the floor beside the laundry basket.

"You left the front door open," he said shortly.

"Oh. I thought I'd locked it."

"There's little point in having a twenty thousand dollar security system installed, if you're going to leave the door open."

"It wasn't twenty thousand dollars sweetheart . . ."

"That's not the point," he snapped. "You left the fucking door open."

"I forgot."

"Why didn't you just hang a notice on the door, please come in and rob us, oh and take your time."

"I'll do that next time."

"Jesus, Celia!"

Celia dropped a bag onto the bed and snapped the catches. "I forgot. All right, I had a lot to carry in. I was in a hurry. I'd been on a plane for just over five and a half hours, and then I sat on the freeway for another hour. I was tired. I felt dirty. I wanted a shower, OK." They glared at one another across the expanse of the king-sized bed.

Finally, Jonathan shrugged. "OK," he said tiredly. "You could have come home for the funeral," he said softly, realizing that this was at the heart of his anger.

"It would have been awkward."

"He was an employee . . . a friend."

"He certainly wasn't my friend!" Celia snapped. Tony Farren had had little time for Celia and her fashions and moods, and hadn't bothered to hide his distaste. Their aversion was mutual. She disliked him; she detested the very thought of him working on her property and in her guesthouse. "He was an employee, in fact he was nothing more than a glorified handyman!"

Frazer allowed the rage to engulf him, paradoxically enjoying his anger. "Let me tell you something," he said icily. "Tony Farren is the reason Frazer Interiors is as successful as it is today. When my father opened the antique store, Tony Farren helped build the business, he became known for his expertise, and then when I inherited the business and turned it into a design store those clients followed Tony. I am very thankful that he stayed with me, turning the cheap antiques I bought into antiques of value so you . . . so I . . . so we . . . could send our daughter to the best schools possible, so we could afford the luxury lifestyle we have, and so you could take your fucking vacations whenever you felt like it. He is the only reason we survived!" He turned and hurried from the room before she could see the tears in his eyes, realizing he was saying to her all the things he should have said to Tony.

Everything he said had been true.

Maybe he had overemphasized the case for Celia's benefit, but it was still true. Frazer Interiors had survived because of Tony Farren's reputation, skill, and knowledge; it wasn't going to close up tomorrow because he was gone, but there would be a difference. He'd had the gift of taking trashy bits of junk and turning them into antiques—and an antique is in the eye of the beholder.

And now he was dead.

Killed by a fucking mirror.

With the rage still bubbling inside him, leaving him cold and empty, he stormed out to the guesthouse. The mirror stood in the center of the floor, outlined in the late afternoon light, the glass a milky-pale, non-reflective sheet.

Frazer grabbed a hammer from the workbench and stood before the mirror, chest heaving.

Killed by a fucking mirror. He raised the hammer and approached the glass.

It was worth twenty thousand dollars. At least.

The thought stopped him cold.

Breaking it would give him a great deal of satisfaction; help work off some of the anger he felt at Tony's needless death. But the need was there to strike out, to hit something, hurt something. OK. So perhaps he had a just reason for arguing with Celia; she'd been in the wrong. She should have come home for the funeral, three lousy days wouldn't have made much difference to her vacation. She should have parked the car properly; she should have locked the front door behind her.

But that didn't make him any more in the right.

They had been married for twenty years; he should have become used to her ways by now.

He raised the hammer again; surprised to find that he could barely see himself in the glass. He reached out and rubbed his finger down the length of the mirror: it came away encrusted with thick sooty grime.

He looked at the hammer in his hand. And then allowed it to fall to the floor.

Break the mirror and what would he achieve? It would give him a momentary satisfaction . . . and he would lose twenty thousand dollars or more. And the first person that would call him a complete fool would be Tony Farren.

He turned away and stopped at the door, glancing back at the mirror. He'd clean it up and sell it—cheaply, just to get rid of it.

As he closed the door, colors, like oil on water, ran down the surface of the glass.

7

THE INSISTENT high-pitched bleeping woke him close to three in the morning.

Jonathan Frazer rolled over, arms flailing blindly, assuming it was the alarm clock . . . and then suddenly snapped awake.

The alarm!

He sat up quickly, rubbing sleep from his eyes, then slid from the bed, naked, shivering in the early morning chill. He blinked at the white rectangular plastic box by the bedroom door, the high-pitched noise ringing in his ears. The monitoring device kept track of the sophisticated alarm system that girded the house and the guesthouse. The small LCD panel illuminated a pale green, the words "Guesthouse" blinking on the screen. It looked as if the guesthouse was in the process of being broken into. The alarm was a silent one, there were no loud, outside jangling bells—Celia didn't want that—but the alarm panel bleeped in the bedroom alerting them that there was a problem.

Jonathan punched in the distress code to turn the irritating noise off. He knew the local police department would have already been notified.

Wasting no time, he slipped on a pair of dark jogging pants and a black sweater, then pushed his feet into house slippers. Ignoring the advice of the alarm company—*if the alarm goes off, do not, under any circumstances, investigate yourself*—he raced down the stairs, heart pounding. He stepped into the kitchen and stopped. Ducking down below the level of the windows, he moved cautiously to the glass paneled back door and peered out across the tiled patio to where the guesthouse was barely visible through the trees.

Light flashed, flickered, died.

Shit: there was someone there!

At the back of his mind he had half hoped that it was a false alarm, although the alarm company guaranteed that the system was self-regulating, incapable of going off for no reason. Now, he stood in the kitchen, beginning to shiver with nerves. The cops would be—*should* be—here at any moment, but whoever was in the guesthouse could be long gone by then, taking goodness knows what from inside. And there were some very valuable pieces in there that were easily portable: gold coins, watches, silver spoons.

There was a set of kitchen knives on a rack to the left of the sink, each knife secured to the stand by a magnetic strip, naked blades gleaming dully in the gray light. He pulled off the longest, a heavy eight-inch butcher's knife, and hefted it in his hand, wondering if he would have the nerve to use it. Wondering if he would have the nerve to even open the kitchen door and step out into the night!

Realizing with a wry smile that he was merely making excuses for not going down to the guesthouse to investigate, hoping the cops would arrive, Frazer stooped down and undid the bolt at the bottom of the door. He pulled back the top bolt and quietly turned the key, and then cracked open the door. The wash of chill night air was a shock. He shivered and was unsure if it was the night or the adrenaline buzzing through his body.

Clutching the knife like a talisman, he stepped out onto the patio, the leather soles of his slippers squeaking on the path. He moved quickly onto the grass by the sprinklers. The garden was cold, and his suede slippers were quickly soaked. The chill air bit through his sweater, and by the time he reached the stand of trees that partially hid the guesthouse from the main house, he was shivering uncontrollably.

He crouched in the bushes for what seemed like a long moment, berating himself for his cowardice: his father might have been a war hero, but his son certainly hadn't inherited any of his father's characteristics. For him, something heroic was selling the most expensive chandelier in the store.

Something fell inside the guesthouse with a dull clanking, the sound abruptly spurring him into action. Switching the knife from his right hand, he wiped his sweating palm on the leg of his pants and then gripped the knife tightly again.

Keeping on the grass, he darted from bush to bush, moving up to the guesthouse, checking the windows on this side of the building. They were all screened, alarmed, and none of them had been broken. Maybe the thief had come in through the skylights . . . but as he rounded the corner he discovered that the guesthouse door was wide open.

The door was secured by three heavy mortise locks, one at top and bottom, one in the middle. The hasps were sunk into concrete and not the frame of the door, and the door itself was two and a half inches thick, an ornate Spanish colonial door that Jonathan and Tony had found at an estate sale.

The only way in was with two keys.

And the only people with keys were Tony and himself . . . and then he abruptly realized he hadn't gotten Tony's keys back yet. OK. So maybe a friend of Tony's? Maybe friend wasn't the right word. He knew Tony preferred the company of younger men. Possibly one of his men friends who knew what he was doing and where he worked had found the keys among his possessions and had just taken advantage.

Jonathan Frazer stood beside the door, listening intently, but he could only hear his own thundering heartbeat. Finally, he pushed it open with enough force for it to slam back against the wall and simultaneously slapped at the light switch.

The guesthouse blazed alight, all twenty-two recessed lights illuminating the entire length of the room.

"Who's there?" He was surprised at how calm his voice sounded.

Something fell to the floor at the far end of the room.

"I know you're there. I can see you," he lied. "Now come out."

Two lights above began buzzing, flickering annoyingly. Something moved at the corner of his vision and Jonathan whirled, knife upraised . . . and the lights above his head exploded with a bang!

Frazer screamed with fright, then pain as tiny slivers of glass rained down on top of him. And then, one-by-one, in a long series of rattling detonations, the rest of the lights exploded down the length of the room. The air was suddenly rank with acrid fumes and the brittle stench of electricity. A single light remained at the far end of the guesthouse, and it was buzzing furiously, flickering on and off, strobe-like.

Frazer staggered to his feet, turned—and screamed aloud!

There was a figure facing him: tall, pale, gaunt, hollows where the eyes should have been, a disembodied face. Frazer brought up his arm, thrusting the knife forward . . . and the figure copied him, producing a knife of his own. He waved the knife left to right, and the figure moved with him.

The wave of relief that washed over Frazer almost made him light-headed. He was facing the mirror. He was looking at himself in the fucking mirror!

He'd hardly recognized himself in the dirty glass: his face appeared positively skull-like, and he looked as if he hadn't slept for a week! With the light at the far end of the room now flickering madly, he put his back to the glass, and looked out across the clutter. It had been a mistake to come in here, he knew that now. He should have waited outside and kept the burglar trapped inside.

There!

A shape. Tall, dark, directly ahead and to his right, moving along a collection of consoles and coffee tables.

The shape moved and, in the flickering strobing light/dark reduced his movements to slow motion.

At that moment, the final light at the end of the room exploded, a hand dropped onto his left shoulder, long hard fingers biting deeply into his flesh. With a scream of absolute terror, Frazer leapt forward . . . and in a blinding flash of light found himself facing a slavering nightmare: long yellow pointed teeth, huge golden eyes, the entire face covered with long coarse hair. The creature howled at him, fetid breath washing over him, making him gag.

"Freeze . . . drop the weapon . . . I said drop the weapon."

The cool, neutral voice cut through his terror. Raising both arms Jonathan opened his right hand, the knife clattering on the concrete floor as it hit.

"Put your hands behind your head, spread your legs," the voice said more forcefully.

Jonathan Frazer opened his eyes. Strong hands gripped his arms, forcefully pulling them down and behind his back. He felt the coldness of metal on his skin as both wrists were handcuffed.

Police.

The police had arrived. He tried to form words, but his tongue felt huge in his mouth.

Jonathan was pulled outside and shoved against the exterior wall, the right side of his face pinned against the stucco as the officer patted him down. He fished something out of Jonathan's back pocket. Then he was spun around and Jonathan found himself squinting at the stark white light from the officer's flashlight.

"Sorry, Mr. Frazer." The officer handed Jonathan back his ID. "That was a stupid thing you did going in there. You could have been hurt by either them or me! And, I could arrest you for brandishing a weapon," the police officer added with a quick grin as he undid the handcuffs.

"I know, I just . . ."

Jonathan found himself looking at the impassive faces of two hefty looking officers. To the side on a short leash, panting and salivating, head cocked to one side, regarding him quizzically was an enormous German shepherd.

"We had a report that your alarm had gone off," the smaller, slightly older officer said.

"Yes . . . yes, that's right. And there was—there is—someone here, I saw them. Inside, towards the back of the room." He pointed toward the guesthouse.

"Thank you. Now, if you'll just go back to the main house, we'll take a look around."

The officer with the canine was the first to enter, his gun drawn, the dog now anxiously straining at the leash. He moved to the left while his partner, gun held in both hands moved to the right as he entered. They disappeared into the shadows.

Jonathan turned and headed back across the wet grass toward the house. He was almost at the kitchen door when he heard the scream.

The sound was high-pitched and chilling; the cry of a creature in mortal agony. It lasted a couple of seconds and the silence that followed was, if anything, even more frightening.

Jonathan turned back toward the guesthouse, adrenaline pumping through his entire body.

There was a second scream, and this time the sound descended into a recognizable whine of a dog in pain or terror.

Lights moved behind the guesthouse windows, the dancing beams of flashlights. Frazer could follow their progress as they moved from the back of the building. He had almost reached the open door when he saw a flicker from the corner of his eye. He stopped, just as the shape loomed from the doorway. Black against black, it was almost completely invisible. There was a vague oval of a face, the startling white of eye and teeth. And then the shape lunged towards him.

Frazer tried to scream, but his cry caught in his throat. There was a suggestion of movement in front of his face before the night exploded into light and pain. He sailed backwards into the bushes and sprawled on the grass. Rolling on his side, he was vividly aware of the wetness on his face, running down his nose, tasting the copper in his mouth. Then, a booted foot landed beside his head, inches from crushing his skull, and he attempted to cover his head from the kick. But it never came, and he heard the squeak of rubber soles on wet grass as the intruder disappeared into the night.

8

D EATH.
Violent bloody death.

Color in the Otherworld, the soul of a creature ripped from life. It experienced the creature's confusion, pain, anguish . . . and then the immediate fading of consciousness, of awareness.

An animal then.

The little soul of an animal.

Nothing more than a morsel.

But enough.

The memories were returning . . .

9

It was dawn by the time the police and the paramedics had left.

Frazer sat in the kitchen, his head cradled in his hands, an enormous bandage around his skull, a thick pad, already faintly stained, in the center of his forehead. He stared blankly at the two painkillers Celia had offered him, moving them to and fro with his forefinger. He disliked taking pills, but he knew if he didn't take something for this headache soon he would be sick for the rest of the day.

Celia moved quietly around the kitchen, wan and shaken after the night's events. She had awakened to hear screaming coming from the guesthouse, and she'd been horrified when she rolled over and discovered that Jonathan was missing. She was actually phoning for the police when the sirens had woken up the whole neighborhood: blue, red, and white flashing lights pulsing in the darkness beyond the window.

However, by the time Jonathan had been carried in, stunned and bleeding from a gashed forehead, her initial fear had turned to anger. Why hadn't he let the police handle it? That's what they were there for. Of course this was typical of him: hire someone to do a job and then do it himself anyway. Stupid bastard could have been killed! Anyway, maybe now he'd think about moving the contents of the guesthouse into some sort of secure storage, and she could turn the building into the home gym she'd wanted when they had first moved in. She sat down across the table from her dazed husband and pushed a mug of coffee over in front of him.

"How do you feel?"

Jonathan attempted a smile. "How do I look?"

"You look like shit."

"That's how I feel."

"Do the police know what happened?"

He shrugged, and then winced as his shoulder and neck muscles protested. "It was an attempted break-in . . . or maybe they actually stole something, I don't know, I haven't been back to the guesthouse yet. The police
want to go over it for fingerprints first. The alarm went off . . ."

"You should have waited for the police," she said coolly.

He started to nod, then stopped, blinking with darts of pain.

"You could have been killed."

"I know. Anyway . . . and this is the scary part: when I went into the
guesthouse, there was someone in there, watching me, waiting." He shivered, and then wrapped both hands around the mug to steady them. "I
was in the guesthouse when the two cops arrived, one with a German
shepherd; they were here pretty quickly. They thought I was the intruder
and cuffed me until they saw my ID. They went in, and told me to go back
to the house."

Celia nodded.

"There's some confusion about what happened next." Frazer drank
quickly, trying to take the sour taste from his mouth. "Whoever was in the
guesthouse killed the dog."

"I heard the scream," Celia whispered.

"It was awful," Frazer muttered.

"But there were two screams."

"Do you want to hear this?"

"Tell me."

Staring into the cup, he continued, his voice devoid of emotion. "From
what I can gather, the dog was shot through the back of the head with a
nail gun. And then its throat was sliced open with a box cutter. The police
think it was still alive when its neck was snapped back. The head was almost twisted off."

"Jesus Christ!"

"So whoever did it was obviously immensely powerful."

Celia pushed her mug away.

"The second officer was not far behind. Somehow the intruder slipped
past him and ran into me outside. He struck me once just here." He touched

his forehead tentatively. "The police say it was probably with the heel of his hand or some sort of martial arts punch. I don't remember anything else."

"You could have been killed," Celia repeated.

"I could," Jonathan said quietly, the realization only beginning to sink in. He barely made it to the bathroom before he began to throw up.

10

"J ESUS CHRIST Almighty, place looks like a fuc . . . like a slaughterhouse."
Diane Williams ran her fingers through her shaggy blond hair, pushing it back off her face.

Frazer glanced sidelong at her. "It's a bit of a mess," he agreed. There were glass fragments from the shattered lights everywhere, covering everything in a fine glittering white sand, crunching underfoot as they moved.

Diane smiled. She was wearing purple-black lipstick to match her eye shadow, and he found the whole effect rather startling. "That's a bit of an understatement."

Where the dog had been butchered was a bloody mess. Long tendrils of thick-crusted brown gore were spattered high on the walls, speckling the ceiling, dappling every single object within a six-foot radius. There was a large dark brown stain on the concrete floor where the carcass had continued to bleed.

Jonathan and Diane stood looking at the floor for a few moments and then they both turned away without a word, each absorbed in their own thoughts. Looking at the bloody pool made Jonathan realize that could very easily be his blood on the floor.

Diane was beginning to have second thoughts about working here. She turned suddenly; she had seen something moving from the corner of her eye. But when she looked there was nothing.

Christ, but she was on edge!

Hardly surprising was it? Some madman wandering around butchering animals. The police were treating it very seriously, it could just as easily have been one of the officers. She glanced quickly at Frazer: could just as easily have been her boss.

Diane Williams turned slowly, eyes drawn to stare at the mirror, hands on her hips. She was wearing all black today, partially in mourning for Tony, whom she genuinely liked, though he could be an irritating old bastard, but principally because she usually wore black. She could just about make out her reflection in the warped glass. The young woman turned her head to one side, staring hard at the glass. There was something . . .

"What's wrong?" Jonathan asked quietly, startling her.

"Nothing, nothing really. Have you made any decision about the mirror, Jonathan?"

"No, not really. I haven't had a chance to even think about it."

"I'd like to work on it."

Frazer blinked at her in astonishment. "But I thought you said . . . ?"

"That was then and this is now. I was upset, I wasn't thinking clearly. I'd like to work on it as a sort of a tribute to Tony. Putting everything he taught me into practice, completing the last piece he worked upon. Do you think he'd like that?"

Jonathan swallowed away the sudden swelling at the back of his throat. "I think . . . I think he would have liked that very much."

Diane stepped forward and rubbed her hand down the length of the mirror; it came away covered in thick grimy soot. "Hey, I cleaned this mirror before I left the other day."

"I've noticed that about it too. It seems to attract every particle of dirt and dust."

"I'll see what I can do about it," she murmured. "I can put some anti-static polish on it, but let me start with the mess in here first though."

"I can call a cleaning company, you know, people who specialize in taking care of this kind of thing."

"No, it's OK. I'd rather do it myself. I was born and raised on a farm, blood doesn't bother me."

Jonathan looked around the room again, trying to put the pieces together in his mind from the moment the alarm had gone off, to the death of the dog and the attack on himself. Someone had been here last night, someone strong enough and brutal enough to kill the dog. And, whoever had done this had possessed tremendous strength. But what had they been looking for? Granted there were a lot of valuable objets d'art and antiques around, but disposing of them would have been particularly difficult and a cursory examination seemed to suggest that nothing had been taken. The police had dusted for fingerprints but had found none. Jonathan briefly wondered if it might have been some local kids breaking in just for the hell of it, but the police had said that was unlikely; if had been full of electronics, then it might have been something to consider. And they would have run scared from the dog.

He stood up and dusted off his hands. He could understand killing the dog—if he'd had a weapon to hand when he'd first seen the creature, he'd have taken a swing at it himself. But slicing open its throat and breaking its neck was . . . what? Unnecessary?

And that reminded him . . .

He returned to the mirror and looked deeply into its grimy surface. When he'd been standing with his back to it he could have sworn he'd felt a hand on his shoulder: ridiculous, of course, but it had been so real. Real enough to make him jump with fright. He touched his left shoulder, wincing as his fingers touched bruising. He was almost tempted to push down his shirt to examine his flesh. Would he find the impression of fingers?

Maybe it had been a real hand. Maybe the intruder had crept up behind him and had been preparing to grab him or attack him when the police had walked in and ruined his plan.

"It's only since that mirror arrived," Diane Williams said quietly, coming up to stand beside Frazer.

That thought had already crossed his mind.

"It could be cursed," she said dramatically.

He attempted a laugh, but the sound caught in his throat. He was glad he was disposing of it. It made him—in some vague way—uncomfortable.

"Yes, can I help you?"

He turned at the sound of Diane's voice, the strident quality in it bringing him back to the present. There was a figure standing in the doorway, one of the biggest men Frazer had ever seen, though with the sun behind him, it was almost impossible to make out his features.

"I'm looking for Jonathan Frazer." There was a curious accent, a lilt to his voice: English, Australian, South African perhaps?

"I am Jonathan Frazer." He stepped forward, his sense of unease growing. No one was allowed down to the guesthouse. "Can I help you? Can I ask how you managed to make your way back here?"

"I was given your name," the man said, not answering the question. "I understand you have a mirror here for sale, Mister Frazer," he said directly, stepping into the room and looking around. And Jonathan knew, beyond a shadow of a doubt, that this was the same man who'd been in the guest-house the previous night. He looked at the man's size and obvious strength, and his unease turned to fear.

"I'm afraid you're wrong, nothing here is for sale, it is all under . . . re-pair. However if you would care to visit our retail store, I'm sure we . . ."

"I was told you had a mirror here for sale," the man repeated doggedly. He took another step into the room, looming larger over Frazer. Now that he no longer had the sun at his back, not only his size, but also his physical appearance was intimidating. His cheeks were deeply scarred, his nose had been broken and badly set, long horizontal lines cut into his forehead. His eyes were coal-black and penetrating, and his mane of pure white hair seemed to make the disfigurement all the more shocking.

"May I . . . may I ask who told you?" Jonathan asked, turning the tremor in his voice into a cough.

"Anthony Farren."

And Jonathan immediately knew he was lying. Tony had never been known as anything other than "Tony."

"It is a family heirloom," the man continued inexorably, and Frazer was beginning to wonder what was going to happen when he refused him. "It should never have gone up to the auction in London."

"I'm afraid the mirror is not for sale."

The big man leaned forward. "Make it for sale, Mister Frazer." The threat was unmistakable.

"I must ask you to leave now," Jonathan said, as quietly as possible, attempting to keep his voice from shaking.

Diane Williams appeared by his side with a hammer in her hand. The big man looked at the hammer and laughed quietly.

"If you don't go now, I shall be forced to call the police," Jonathan said more forcefully, encouraged by her presence. "You are trespassing."

The big man glared at Frazer and then stared long and hard at Diane, his dark eyes moving slowly over her face as if committing it to memory. He turned and left, moving surprisingly quickly for such a big man. Jonathan and Diane turned to look at one another: they both knew that this was the intruder from the previous night.

And they both knew he would be back.

11

DIANE WALKED the length of the guesthouse, glass fragments rasping beneath her sneakers—she thought she'd cleaned them all up—checking that all the windows were locked. Frazer had gone back to the house, scampering along the graveled path like a frightened rabbit to phone the police. The phone in the guesthouse no longer worked for some reason. She'd locked the heavy door behind him and ensured that all the skylights were sealed.

Maybe she'd ask Jonathan Frazer for a few days off. She could go away, she had some savings put aside. She'd been wanting to buy a red Vespa Scooter she'd found at a nearby dealership, but she thought that a little vacation right now might be a much better idea.

The way that guy had just looked at her!

The scarred man had scared the shit out of her. The size of his hands, and he hadn't got those scars on his face playing chess. Give him the fucking mirror if that's what he wanted. Gift wrap it too with a big bow.

But it looked like Frazer was going to try and play cute with him; the only problem was, people like the scarred man didn't know how to play cute.

No, she'd take a couple of weeks off and maybe by the time she got back, this mess would have sorted itself out. And what would have happened if she'd been here on her own, she wondered. Her eyes scanned the workbench looking for something that she could use as a weapon. The hammer was too cumbersome. Rummaging through the clutter she eventually found a long crosshead screwdriver and a needle-pointed awl. She tucked them both in the back pocket of her jeans, one to the left and one on the right. So what if she felt ridiculous: she felt a little safer.

Diane moved the heavier items of furniture away from where the dog had been killed so she could bleach the floor. She carefully removed some of the antiques that Tony was working on before his death. A lot of them were in a poor state of repair—which is why they had been here in the first place—but she was wondering if there was anything more useful than a screwdriver and awl, like a .45 magnum for example.

Then she remembered Tony had once kept a BB gun in the guesthouse. He had demonstrated for her how accurately he could fire the weapon by taking the flower heads off a hibiscus plant in the garden. She smiled, remembering his delight and Frazer's horrified expression when he saw the devastation and knowing he would have to explain it to Celia. Jonathan had then banned guns of any sort, antique or modern, from the property.

Tony had known so much and yet there had still been a playfulness in his character. What a waste. What a way to die: killed by a fucking mirror.

Diane walked back down the room to stand before the huge slab of glass, staring at its grubby surface. She pulled a cloth from the workbench and worked it in a circle, grimacing at the amount of grime that came off the glass. She knew she must have cleaned this mirror every day since it had arrived: where did all this shit come from?

A glint of silver on the floor suddenly caught her eye. Squinting, she bent down and just underneath a small round side table she found a butcher's knife. This must be the knife Jonathan said he'd been carrying the night before. "Now that's more like it."

Carefully placing the knife on the ground within easy reach, she lifted a bottle of cleaning fluid from the top shelf. Starting at eye level, she rubbed furiously at the grime on the glass. Ten minutes later, with a fine sheen of sweat on her forehead and an aching arm, she stepped back to examine her handiwork. There seemed precious little result for so much effort. Bringing her face close to the glass, she rubbed at a patch she'd just cleaned with her fingertip. The glass was slightly greasy, clammy to her touch.

Movement caught her completely unawares, sending her stumbling backwards with a scream. She whirled around, swiftly picking up the knife and holding it before her with both hands. The room was empty. The door was still closed and bolted, while dust motes spiraled undisturbed in the air.

"Fucking hell . . ." she breathed. "Scared the shit out of me."

Feeling slightly foolish, she lowered the long blade and turned back to the mirror, grinning at the unexpected picture that presented itself: faded black jeans, blond hair, white face, the purple-black lipstick and eye shadow lending her a skull-like appearance. She laughed shakily; Tony's crazy death, the funeral—she hadn't been to a funeral in years—and now this strange business had her on edge.

She saw movement, definite movement, a twisting shifting flicker reflected in the glass.

Heart pounding she spun around, bringing the knife up again. She had glimpsed the movement behind her right shoulder, which would have put it there! Behind a sleek white bookcase still encased in its plastic wrap with a large sold sign attached. Behind it were three curved leather dining chairs. There was no place for anyone to hide. And yet she wasn't alone in here, she knew that. She opened her mouth to call out . . . and then closed it again. She didn't want them to know that she knew they were in the room with her. Maybe if she turned away, they would appear. Still clutching the long knife, she turned back to the mirror and looked into the glass.

There!

The temptation to turn was almost irresistible, but she continued staring at the mirror. She frowned, attempting to make sense out of what she was seeing, but the mirror was distorting the image. Transferring the knife to her left hand, she rubbed at the glass with the palm of her hand.

And yelped!

Something like a spark had leapt from the glass to her flesh. She rubbed her hand furiously against her thigh: static. She sometimes sparked when she touched metal, door handles, some cutlery, especially motorbikes, but never glass. Reaching out, she tentatively touched the glass again, but this time there was nothing. The surface of the glass felt unpleasant, slightly greasy, vaguely damp.

The flickering was still perceptible over her left shoulder. A twisting, shimmering movement, like a heat haze on a summer's day, but with some darker, deeper thread inside it, like coiling smoke.

Diane glanced back over her shoulder, but there was nothing moving except the twisting dust motes. She turned back to the glass, frowning and looked again. And then she realized . . . the disturbance was *within* the glass!

She drew back in shock, heart thumping. She leaned forward, forefinger touching the slick surface. With her finger still pressed to the glass she turned her head again: there was still movement within the glass, but nothing behind her. OK, so it was an imperfection in the glass, after all it was five hundred and more years old, some trick of the light, refraction or reflection or whatever it was called.

She was about to turn away when the flickering seemed to intensify, becoming even more agitated, the twisting, coiling smoke seeming to speed up. Diane watched it, mesmerized by the movement, fascinated by the way the colors ran along its length, like oil on water.

It was . . . it was the mirror, she thought, magnifying the whirling dust motes behind her . . .

That's . . .

That's . . .

. . . all it was.

She blinked, and then blinked again, realizing that she'd been daydreaming, watching the spiral dance. The shimmering was hypnotic.

Diane straightened, attempting to pull her hand away. And couldn't. Cold fire ran up the length of her arm, tingling into her shoulders, down into her breasts, deep into her stomach. Black spots danced before her eyes and her breath came in great labored gasps.

She was asleep and she was dreaming and there were pins and needles in her arm and she was going to wake up.

Except . . .

Except that she was awake.

Diane dropped the knife, gripped her right wrist with her left hand and pulled. But it was firmly stuck, fingers splayed . . . and yet she could only remember touching the glass with her forefinger.

There was a rational explanation for this . . .

There was . . .

No rational . . .

Her hand was becoming warm, pleasantly so. The warmth rushed up through her arm—she could actually feel the movement—across her shoulders, down into her chest, into her belly, through her groin, along her thighs and into the soles of her feet. She shuddered, abruptly conscious of the weight of her breasts, her nipples hard against the smooth fabric of her T-shirt, the buzzing tingle in her groin. Another shudder rippled through her, and she felt her legs grow tremulous. She dropped to her knees, her hand still stuck to the glass as another spasm rippled through her body, more intense than any orgasm. This was pleasure so intense it was almost painful.

And then ice-cool flesh touched her hand.

The scream caught in her throat as she attempted to stagger to her feet, hauling herself upright, using her trapped hand as leverage.

There was flesh beneath that hand. Soft, rounded flesh, like . . . like a woman's breast.

She could barely catch her breath now, and her heart was pounding so hard her ribs were vibrating.

The shimmering in the glass had become almost frantic in its intensity . . . and then Diane realized it was throbbing in time to the beating of her heart. As she watched, the coiling, throbbing threads coalesced into a face, smoky, intangible, the planes of jaw and forehead and cheeks moving, sliding together into a pale mask. A dark circle appeared for a mouth, two more for eyes. The mouth opened, smoke coiling from the maw, matching the wreathing steam that took the place of hair.

Diane reached for the knife on the floor by her side, fingers sliding across the cold metal before catching the wooden handle. The figure in the glass copied her, holding a knife of its own. Mesmerized, Diane moved the knife from left to right in a slow sweeping movement. The figure copied her every move . . . and then with a sickening revelation, Diane discovered that her arm was mimicking the movement of the figure in the glass. She was no longer in control. Her arm was being dragged left and right, up and down . . .

The image in the glass raised its knife and Diane's arm jerked upwards. She attempted to scream, but her throat was clenched tight. Struggling to resist, she tried, and failed, to pull her arm away from her face.

Diane felt the tip of the knife touch the soft flesh of her left cheek, lightly twisting and turning, tracing the length of her cheek bone, until it stopped abruptly. Then the tip pierced the skin. A ruby of blood gathered, trembled, then ran down her face. There was no pain. Not yet. Her fingers clenched around the knife's wooden base, knuckles white, as she attempted to jerk the knife away. The blade dug deeper. Then the vaporous image in the glass pulled the knife downwards and the blade in her hand mimicked the movement. The blade slid down the side of her cheekbone parting the tender skin underneath.

The pain was exquisite.

And it brought release. Suddenly she found her voice. The scream that tore from her throat was audible even up at the house.

And in the mirror, the mouth shape opened wider and wider . . . and then a second face appeared within the black gaping maw, smaller, the features sharper, clearer because of its tiny size.

And it was Tony Farren.

Tony: mouth and eyes wide in terror or pain.

Tony: older than she had ever seen him, lines etched into his forehead, skin like parchment, eyes filled with blood . . .

The knife in her hand sliced her throat open, slowly, carefully, deliberately moving from left to right cutting through muscle, nerves, the trachea, eventually severing the jugular vein. Dark crimson spurted onto the mirror, spraying across the glass with every pulsing heartbeat.

There was no pain now.

There was just an icy coolness seeping out from the glass, up along her arm and across her throat.

She focused on the glass, trying to make sense of the shape within the mirror. She needed to know what—or who—was killing her. But there was nothing, other than the vague shape, the outline of eyes and mouth and gossamer hair. Diane gulped for air, her body jerking uncontrollably as she slumped, hand still stuck to the glass, cheek pressed to the mirror as she slid downwards. Her body continued to twitch and spasm until the last drops of blood leaked from her torn throat. Finally, when she had nothing left to give, her hand released from the glass and her lifeless body slid to the ground at the base of the mirror.

12

P OWER.

    Raw coursing strength.

  Confusion, pain, anguish. It had felt these before, but these sensations were stronger, much stronger now. This was no animal. This was a human. A human soul in mortal agony.

  The colors in the Otherworld now were bright. Sharp, clear, clean colors slicing through the grayness.

  The quickening was upon it. The past was returning, memories of promises made, oaths sworn and broken.

  For ever and ever.

  This was a petty life, a female life, not a virgin, but responsive. It savored the life, a foretaste of the feast to come.

  Blood dripping.

  The tang of it in the dust of the Otherworld.

  Color and with the color came life and memories, sensations and emotions.

  The blood was the life.

13

ONE DEATH was messy, but two—and obviously connected—meant piles of paperwork. And she hadn't joined the police force to be a secretary.

Detective Margaret Haaren leaned forward, peering between the front seats, looking at the impressive facade of the Frazer house. In real estate terms she wondered what she was looking at: three and a half million, maybe four? Without knowing a thing about the Frazers, she guessed there'd be two cars, one child, probably with an exotic name, and a dog, the small fluffy kind. She knew the type.

"Hmm, not dissimilar to my place," José Pérez murmured, as they drove through the large ornate wrought iron gates and up the long graveled driveway.

"I thought you lived in a box on Skid Row, José," Margaret Haaren murmured.

"It's a very expensive box."

Both detectives laughed, and Haaren caught the startled look from the rookie in the passenger seat. Her smile faded: she hated babysitting rookies. Although Carole Morrow had done her obligatory four years as a patrol officer when she graduated the Police Academy, this was her first murder investigation. And it didn't help that she was clearly in awe of Detective Margaret Haaren, whose reputation was fearsome and terrifying.

"OK, so what do we have, Detective Pérez?" Margaret asked, sitting back into the seat, picking up the report again.

José Pérez had spent twenty-five years on the force starting as a patrol officer, then working in some of the LAPD's toughest precincts before joining homicide. While much had changed over the years: the types of crime, the frequency, the violence, the sort of people committing them, there were still some things—like motive—which remained satisfyingly the same.

"I think we've got a case of money problems."

Margaret Haaren sat forward, listening intently. She had known José Pérez since she had joined the force a lifetime ago, and when she moved to homicide, eight years previously, she had requested him as her partner. She respected his advice and intuition.

"Talk to me," she said quietly. She tapped Carole on the shoulder. "Listen. You'll learn something."

"Yes, ma'am."

"And don't call me ma'am."

"First we have the accidental death of one Anthony Farren, employee of Jonathan Frazer. Mr. Frazer then reports a break-in to the same property, and we have the savage killing of one of our K-9 dogs. Next, Mr. Frazer reports the appearance of a scarred man, followed, almost immediately by the death of another of the employees, Diane Williams." He smiled ruefully, looking into the mirror, catching the eyes of the woman in the back seat. "Assuming that Mr. Frazer is not lying to us. And I do not think he is," he added, "then someone is leaning on our man."

Haaren nodded. "Makes sense."

Detective Pérez caught the look of puzzlement on the rookie's face, and explained patiently. "Mister Frazer is obviously very wealthy. Now let's say someone wanted to make him pay a little insurance, a little protection, and he refused, then what better way of gaining his attention than by knocking off two of his employees, terrorizing him in this way."

"But two people are dead," Carole Morrow said, horrified. In her disgust, she forgot her fear of the detective and half turned in the seat to look at her. "No one would kill for that reason—just to threaten someone. Would they?" she asked plaintively.

"You're assuming that other people place the same value on life that you do, like most normal people do," Margaret Haaren said gently. "I think you'll find that's not always the case. I've seen people killed for the price of a packet of cigarettes."

"Yes . . . yes . . . err . . . thank you, ma'am. Detective Haaren."

There were two police cars neatly parked in the graveled driveway, and a BMW rather more sloppily parked closer to the door. As they pulled up, the front door opened and a short stout man, who looked like a doctor even if he hadn't been carrying a bag, walked out onto the step. He was talking to a slender blond woman sporting a deep golden tan that looked too good to have come from a tanning salon. The doctor reached over and patted the woman's hand reassuringly, then walked down the steps to the BMW.

Haaren leaned forward and tapped officer Morrow on the shoulder. "Stop him. Find out what's wrong. He's probably sedated someone, if so find out how long it'll be before I can ask questions."

"Yes, ma'am.

Detective Pérez stood on the brakes, scattering stones, but effectively blocking in the BMW, allowing the young woman time to hop out of the car and hurry across to the doctor. Margaret Haaren popped the back door and strode up the steps to where the woman remained standing in the open doorway. Their dislike was instinctive and almost palpable.

"Detective Margaret Haaren, LAPD Homicide." She flashed her gold shield. She heard gravel crunching behind her and without turning around, she said, "My partner, Detective José Pérez. And that's Officer Morrow." She looked at the younger woman, waiting for her to introduce herself.

"Celia Frazer," the woman said eventually. "We have some police officers here already," she added impatiently.

"I know and I am here to take charge." She walked past Celia Frazer into the tall, wide hallway. "May I come in?"

Margaret Haaren had turned forty-eight last birthday, and looked older. A tall broad woman, with a square mannish face, emphasized by hair cut straight across over her eyes, curling around by her cheeks. There were strands of gray in her brown hair which she didn't bother disguising, but her strength and determination showed most clearly in her startlingly bright green eyes. She was dressed in a black two-piece suit that seemed almost a size too small for her large framed body. A white shirt with frilled collar softened the suit's rather severe line. Her nickname in the force was Mata Hari, for no real reason that anyone could remember. The last officer who had used it in her hearing had ended up with a desk job for the best part of a year. There was some talk that she might even be in the running to become the first female Chief of Police.

"You will not be able to speak to my husband for some time I'm afraid," the woman said curtly, obviously resenting the intrusion. "He was quite distressed by the death of Diane and the doctor had to sedate him."

"When can we speak to him?" the detective asked, glancing up the broad curved stairway.

"Tomorrow."

"Tomorrow," Haaren repeated slowly. "Tomorrow's too late. He might have seen something which might be of immediate use."

"He saw nothing," Celia Frazer said quickly.

"So you were with him when he discovered the body?"

"Well no, but . . ."

"We'll take your statement shortly, Mrs. Frazer." Haaren turned to Carole Morrow who had stepped into the hallway, and raised her eyebrows in a silent question.

"A mild sedative, valium in liquid form to relax him, the doctor said. You should be able to talk to him for the next thirty minutes before it kicks in and makes him drowsy."

"Thank you. Is your husband up here, Mrs. Frazer?" Margaret Haaren started up the stairs.

"Yes, but I don't think he'd want to be disturbed. In any case shouldn't you have a search warrant?" Celia demanded.

"Mrs. Frazer, we are here to ask your husband a few questions, that's all, we do not need a search warrant." Margaret Haaren smiled sweetly. "And I'm sure he won't mind."

"Shouldn't he have a lawyer present?"

"Any time he wishes."

"I'll call one."

"Do that. And I'll talk to your husband."

MARGARET HAAREN FOUND Jonathan Frazer lying on an enormous bed in a room that her entire apartment could have been squeezed into. He was fully dressed, except for his shoes, and appeared to be dozing.

She tapped on the open door. "Mr. Frazer, Jonathan Frazer?"

He opened his eyes, blinking sleepily at her. "Hello?" he murmured.

"Detective Margaret Haaren, LAPD Homicide." She stepped into the room and showed her badge again. She quickly crossed the room to the bed. "I'd like to ask you a few questions, Mr. Frazer, if you don't mind. I know you're tired, and you've had a terrible shock, but I want to speak to you now while the memories are still fresh."

"Of course . . . of course . . ." He started to sit up and swing his legs out of bed.

"No, no, please stay where you are." She wanted Frazer in the bed; it gave her a certain psychological advantage, and the fact that he'd been sedated meant that his defenses would be down. She pulled over a high-backed plain wooden chair and sat down on it. "Now Mr. Frazer . . . may I call you Jonathan?"

"Yes, of course."

"In your own words, Jonathan, try and remember everything that happened, no matter how trivial."

"Either he's not telling us everything or he knows nothing," Margaret Haaren said to Jose Pérez thirty minutes later, as they approached the guesthouse.

The detective nodded. "From what I can gather from the gardener and the housekeeper, the wife's a cool enough bitch. They all like him, he's a gentle sort apparently, but she's one of these rich Beverly Hills wives, likes to think she's above the rest."

Haaren stopped at a bend in the path and turned to look back at the house. She could make out the kitchen door and part of the bedroom, so that part of Frazer's story was borne out. "Anything else?"

"There's a daughter, Emmanuelle, Manny for short. She's been staying with friends. She just got back from some fashionable school in Paris. Last year it was Rome and undoubtedly next year it'll be New York."

"Little jealousy, José?"

He grimaced. "Hardly. At least my wife and I have a good, solid marriage."

Two LAPD officers were standing outside the door to the guesthouse chatting to Officer Morrow. They straightened as Haaren and Pérez approached.

"Anything to report?" Pérez asked.

"Nothing. No one's been around since forensics finished and the coroner took away the body."

"Anything else?"

The second officer, younger, round-faced, red-cheeked, looked from Haaren to Pérez. "We did hear noises at one point though . . ." He continued despite his partner's disgusted face. "But when we investigated, we found nothing."

"What sort of noises?" Haaren asked.

"Sort of moaning, groaning sounds." He looked desperately at his partner for support, but found none.

"Can you be more specific?"

The color in the young man's cheeks intensified.

"Cries of pain, of agony, panting . . . ? Be more specific."

"Sort of . . . of pleasure."

"Pleasure?"

His eyes flickered from Morrow to the older detective. "We thought . . . we thought there was someone inside . . . engaging in some sort of sexual activity."

"But there wasn't?" Margaret asked seriously.

"No."

"OK, then keep your eyes open." Ducking under the yellow crime scene tape she stepped into the relative darkness of the guesthouse, blinking to allow her eyes to adjust to the dimness, desperately resisting the urge to burst out laughing. She could tell by Pérez's expression that he was controlling the same impulse.

"Where do we get them from, José?"

"I really don't know, and that's no mistake. It's the twenty-first century: surely people should be able to talk about sex and drugs and rock and roll openly."

"*Sexual activity*," Haaren repeated wonderingly. It had been a long time since she'd heard that phrase. Her smile turned rueful; it had been a long time since she indulged in any sexual activity herself.

Their noses led them to the spot where the young girl had died, the peculiar once-smelt, never forgotten, odor of blood and excrement pervading the dry atmosphere.

"OK, José let's talk it through," Margaret said quietly. She stood back and folded her arms across her broad chest, her left arm raised, chin cupped in the palm of her hand, fingers rubbing back and forth against her cheek.

"Well, as I see it, the big guy with the scars appears and frightens the shit out of both Frazer and the girl, Diane Williams. He was talking about a mirror . . ." He nodded to the slab of glass. "This mirror, which he said he wanted to buy. When he was told that it wasn't for sale, he became vaguely threatening. Frazer says he's going to call the cops, the girl picks up a hammer, the scarred man leaves, and the pair relax, thinking they've frightened him off."

"A little something like that wouldn't frighten someone like that," she murmured, and he nodded in agreement.

"Frazer goes up to the house to phone our guys because he's convinced that it was the intruder from last night."

"So why did he have to go to the house? There was no phone here? He didn't have a cell phone on him?"

"No, it seems that the phone on the wall behind you wasn't working. I checked it out myself: the wire's been cut. And Frazer's cell phone was back in the house, charging. Story checks out. Phone was plugged in on the kitchen counter, with a fifteen percent charge showing."

"Frazer told me he waited until Diane had locked herself in before he left here," Haaren said.

"Frazer phones us from the main house when he hears the deceased, Diane Williams, scream."

"So the call came from the main land line?"

"Yes. We have the transcript, but we're in the process of accessing the 9-1-1 call. The scream may be audible on the call, and hopefully we'll hear his reaction."

"And then he rushed back to the guesthouse?"

"I guess so, yes. The housekeeper also heard the scream and she described it as blood-curdling; she said it sounded raw and terrified."

Margaret looked around. "So Frazer races down the path. He would certainly have seen someone coming out of the guesthouse, but he claims he saw no one."

José smiled grimly. "And here's where it gets sketchy. The guesthouse is locked from the inside. When he looks in through that window there, he sees the girl lying on the floor, blood everywhere. He had no doubt from the quantity that she was dead."

"How did she die?"

"Her throat was sliced open by the same butcher's knife that Frazer had been brandishing the night of the break-in. Her left cheek had been cut open down to the bone."

"So the implication is that the big man who threatened them returned, gained entry somehow and killed the girl?"

"Yes," he said.

Haaren shook her head firmly. "It just doesn't make sense: we have one murder weapon, one victim and no forced entry. Diane Williams worked with Anthony Farren as his assistant, maybe they were close to one another, maybe they'd been having a secret affair? He hasn't been dead more than a week, maybe she was depressed over his death?"

Detective Pérez nodded. "Suicide?"

"That's how I would read it." She stopped. "You've got that look on your face . . ."

"Anthony Farren was quite active in the gay community."

"OK, so scratch that theory."

"But we do have a murder weapon with Mr. Frazer's prints on it."

"We do."

A puzzled look crossed her face. "So the door was locked on the inside. When our guys arrived, they had to break their way in with a sledgehammer."

"OK, then," Pérez stated. "Let's keep it simple. One accident we could believe, but two deaths on the same property and in the same place? That's stretching it."

"Motive?" she asked.

"Putting pressure on Frazer for money."

"How valuable are these antiques?" Haaren looked around the cluttered room, finally stopping before the tall, ugly mirror. "And this is the mirror the scarred man talked about?"

"Said he wanted to buy it."

"What do we know about it?"

"Frazer bought it very recently at auction in London. The big guy said it should never have been sold."

"Ugly looking thing," she murmured, staring at the grimy surface.

"That's the sort of thing they put on the ceilings of those cheap love motels in Vegas," José Pérez remarked, "for when the couples are having wild sex."

"When did you last have wild sex in Vegas?"

"I was eighteen and it wasn't that wild," he admitted.

"Well you certainly wouldn't get it on the ceiling of my apartment . . . doubt if you'd even get it in the door."

"What do you want to do now?"

"Let's take a closer look at Mr. Frazer and his interior design business. Pull his phone records and let's see if we can get a look at his financials." She strode towards the door. "And God help him if anyone else turns up dead!"

14

TRACING THE mirror had been easy enough. There was a stink to it that anyone with half a talent could sense. Recovering it would be a lot more difficult.

The mirror had been purchased by a man named Jonathan Frazer of Frazer Interiors. He didn't know the man, didn't know the name, but he obviously needed to be looked at, and he would have to do some research into Frazer's background. There might be no connection, it might simply have been a coincidence, but Edmund Talbott didn't believe in coincidences. Frazer had been lured to the mirror, drawn to it, like a bee to pollen. And he was prepared to gamble that somewhere in the man's past—in previous generations even, for the mirror did not know the concept of time—the mirror's path had crossed with one of Frazer's ancestors.

The big scarred man moved restlessly around the tiny rented studio apartment. The rundown building was situated in a rough neighborhood just off Sunset Boulevard. The room was shabby and it suited Edmund Talbott perfectly. There were fourteen units in the building, each one as anonymous as the next, and most of the tenants appeared to be out of work. They spent their empty days getting stoned or drinking around the dried up swimming pool. No one took any notice of him and, when he left, no one would even remember he was here.

Before settling in, he had taken some basic precautions. He'd removed the spotted mirror from the bathroom, and covered the windows with newspapers for privacy. He was doomed never to look upon his own reflection, never to allow himself to be aware of his own image in a mirror.

Because sometimes when he looked into a mirror, something *else* looked out.

He had been in danger from the mirror before, mortal danger. It had come close to claiming him, but he had always managed to defeat it . . . but now? This was the first time in generations that the mirror had been uncovered for any length of time, and already it was gathering its strength.

It had taken one life, the man's, almost immediately.

Talbott had been asleep when he had felt the cry of a soul in torment. He had been drawn to it, pulled from a deep dreamless sleep into the shadowy Astral Otherworld in pursuit of the cry of the lost soul. But before he could get close to it, the soul had vanished, leaving behind no echo, no resonance, as if it had never existed. Although he had searched through the Otherworld until he endangered his own body's energy reserves, he found nothing. He knew then that the mirror had swallowed it, trapping it within its ancient core.

It had fed off the dog next, but that had been his doing.

He had traced the mirror to Frazer's house by fixing on the last location of the death cry in the Otherworld. Using crystals, scrying, and dowsing over a large scale map of Los Angeles, he had gradually closed in on the precise position of the glass. Once he was close to it, he could actually feel the insidious chill of the glass, though now he noticed that the residual trickle of power he always associated with the mirror was sharper, slightly stronger.

It was growing more powerful.

Time was running out.

He hadn't thought the guesthouse would be alarmed, and that had been his first mistake. And he rarely made mistakes; he was usually the most meticulous and careful of men. His predecessor's mistakes had cost him his life and his soul. Sometimes, in his darkest nightmares, Talbott would hear his predecessor's cries of unending agony.

Edmund Talbott hadn't made a mistake of this nature for a long, long time. Unless, of course, his reason had been clouded, his judgment awry. And if so, then he had every reason to be afraid, to be terribly afraid, because it spoke of the mirror's increasing powers.

He had been close to the glass when he had become aware of Frazer's approach. Instinct had driven him deep into the furthest corner of the guesthouse. When Frazer had thrown the light switch the bulbs had overloaded, sputtering and exploding with sharp pops along the length of the room.

And that had been none of his doing either.

He should have known then that the power was gathering in the guest-house, that the mirror was drawing in its defenses.

Then the cops had arrived with the dog.

The dog had been alarmed, frightened, aware with that residual sixth sense that was once part of human kind, that something was wrong here. It sensed a presence, and it had been torn between orientating on the mirror or on him. Eventually, it had latched onto him as being a tangible, human target.

Talbott knew that the animals were not trained to kill, but as the beast had loomed up out of the darkness, teeth bared, saliva running in ropes down its jowls, eyes wide with terror, he knew it would tear his throat out.

There were implements to hand, hammers, crowbars, screwdrivers, electric drills. His questing fingers wrapped around the rubberized handle of a nail gun just as the crazed animal leapt. He pirouetted, moving surprisingly swiftly for such a large man. As the dog blundered past, he had triggered the gun, launching a trio of brad nails, embedding them into the creature's head. The beast screamed once, a terrifying sound, human-like in its intensity. Even then it had turned on Talbott, snapping furiously, disoriented, bloody saliva spraying everywhere. What was even more frightening now was that it was snapping at him in silence, its front paws scrapping along the concrete floor. And he knew then that something else was controlling the dying animal. With one swift movement Talbott pulled the dog's head back forcefully, snapping its neck before slicing its throat open with a box cutter.

The stench of blood—tart and metallic—suffused the air.

He hated having to kill so close to the mirror but he had no choice . . . or had he? Was this further evidence that his judgment was clouded?

He had made another mistake when he had gone back and asked about purchasing the mirror. Neither Frazer nor the girl—especially the girl—had seemed intimidated by his presence. Indeed, that little ruse had gone badly wrong. The girl was killed shortly afterwards, and naturally, suspicion had fallen on him.

He was unsure what his next move was. He couldn't go back to the Frazer house, not with the police still investigating. But he didn't think Frazer would be offering the mirror for sale in the immediate future. The man's interest in the antique had been aroused. Frazer was frightened, but intrigued.

But if he couldn't buy it, and stealing it was out of the question, then what was left? Could he try to break it? Edmund Talbott immediately dismissed the idea. The mirror itself had its own battery of protections and defenses; it had survived a very long time. It would not allow itself to be harmed.

His only choice now was to wait. But time would only allow the mirror's strength to increase and grow. It would have time to feed. That was its nature.

Talbott stripped naked and washed himself as thoroughly as was possible with the small cold-water sink. His mind was elsewhere, and he didn't feel the chill water raise goose bumps on his arms and shoulders, the cold flesh tightening around the extraordinary network of scars that began on his face, patterned his shoulders and ran down onto his chest and back. Many of the nerves beneath the skin had been damaged during the accident and both heat and pain were dull, vaguely perceptible feelings on his flesh.

Edmund Talbott would be fifty soon, but looked far older. He had reached that age when he should be instructing his own son, Edward, in the legend of the mirror. But his son was gone now, and he would never have another. The Talbott line would die with him. Edward had been dead ten years, destroyed in the same accident that had shredded his own body. He'd been strong, he'd survived, but the child hadn't, nor had his wife, dearest Elizabeth, five months pregnant at the time. There had been an accident, terrible and tragic, it made front page headlines for exactly one day, and merited a brief mention on the television news headlines. The subsequent court case ran for three years and paid a record amount of compensation that warranted five lines on the back pages of some of the newspapers.

It had taken him the best part of a year and a half to recover from his terrible wounds, and when he had finally been released from the London hospital, he had returned to Oxford. His first stop had been in the tiny graveyard close to the house where the bodies were buried. Squatting on the damp ground beside the simple graves, he had wept, the first tears since the accident. Kneeling between the graves, a hand on each, he had finally acknowledged, admitted, that it had been no accident. But what could he prove? And what could he do about it? Who would believe him?

Talbott rubbed his face vigorously, squeezing his eyes shut as the cold face cloth rubbed across them. If he wanted to, he could convince himself that the moisture on his face came from the cloth.

TEN YEARS AGO.

The first week of June. Glorious, warm and sunny.

The details were etched into his memory. The three of them had spent a wonderful weekend in London; he had renewed some old acquaintances, while the heavily pregnant Elizabeth had shopped on Oxford Street. Later, they had taken Edmund to see his first musical, *Billy Elliot.* His young son—his glorious little boy—had spent the entire performance transfixed, his eyes wide and bright with excitement. And when the performance was over, he announced he was going to become a dancer.

Edmund, Elizabeth, and Edward had been happy.

Later, much, much later, Edmund realized that his defenses must have dropped.

The elevator was bullet-shaped, a tube that crawled up the exterior of the building, the view over the city absolutely breathtaking. Little Edward had watched it move up and down the building with all the focus a ten-year-old could muster, and had begun to pester his parents with that same concentration and determination. He wanted to ride in the elevator, right to the very top. To see over the city.

Eventually, Edmund had agreed.

Initially, Elizabeth wanted to stay on the ground. Pressing her hands to her swollen belly, she said that the twins were kicking even with the thought of the elevator. But Edward had insisted. He wanted all of them to see the city together.

The journey up was uneventful.

Edmund had been sure his son was going to be terrified, but the boy had been fascinated with the view through the heavy tempered glass walls, ceiling, and floor. Elizabeth had felt slightly nauseous and even Edmund had to admit that he felt slightly off-balance. The view from the top was spectacular and London had never looked lovelier. Edward announced that he might become an artist or a photographer—as well as an actor—so that he could photograph the city every day.

They were alone in the elevator as it began its descent. The sensation of dropping was pronounced and even the boy fell quiet.

"Look straight ahead, don't look down," Edmund had advised, and of course, everyone had looked down, seeing their reflections in the floor.

Beware the image, it will steal your soul away.

Edmund Talbott opened his mouth to scream a warning, his hand scrabbling for the emergency stop, his eyes locked onto the reflected images.

The elevator immediately ground to a halt, lurched and settled. As he watched, he saw their reflections in the fortified glass change, alter, become something else, something hideous, flesh slewing off muscle, muscle liquefying away from bone, hair lengthening, falling out, features twisting, turning, changing.

Skeletons.

One reached out and touched the wall, mimicking his movement, mouth opening in a parody of a cry. Another, the female—Elizabeth—pressed both hands to her stomach, the bony fingers disappearing into the cavity, her dress folding in around them.

Beware the image . . .

And the elevator fell.

It plummeted twenty-seven of the thirty stories, pulling free of its moorings almost immediately, smashing the frail cocoon off the heavy office windows. Glass—supposedly unbreakable—shattered, showering the occupants with razor sharp shards. Hands locked rigidly around the handrail—later the rail would have to be cut out of his hands because of his unopenable grip—Edmund Talbott could only watch as his wife and son were smashed repeatedly against the glass walls of the elevator, rolling in the slivers of glass that had burst in through the rent in the glass close to the roof and along one wall. Skin was flayed from muscle, flesh torn open to the bone. At some point, close to the ground, the metal hawsers, which had been hissing upwards as the lift fell, became entangled around the falling elevator tube. They sliced through the fortified glass with ease, snapping it in half, catching Edward's tiny body, mangling it before his father's eyes. Edmund squeezed his eyes shut and when he opened them again, both bodies—Elizabeth's and Edward's—were gone, tossed out like trash. Before the elevator finally exploded across the London side-walk he still had the presence of mind to commend their souls to God and was strangely glad that at least they would all die together.

But he hadn't died, though in the eighteen months that followed, he wished time and again that he had.

It took the London fire department nearly four hours with cutting equipment to free his body from the wreckage. Men who had worked on some of the most horrific accident cases for most of their adult lives turned away at the mangled mess. He should have been dead. The fact that he still lived was a miracle . . . or an evil joke. Both legs were broken, multiple breaks which practically guaranteed that he would never walk again. Only two ribs remained intact, most of them having impacted inwards, puncturing or tearing most of the internal organs, collapsing both lungs. Arms, wrists, shoulders and collarbones were shattered. Jaw, nose, cheekbones, and skull were fractured.

And his flesh, especially around his face, had been flayed by the count-less thousands of pieces of glass.

Months later, one of the plastic surgeons had handed him a jar filled with glittering specks. There was a scrawled note on the side of the jar in red ink, "2234."

"That's how many pieces of glass we took from your flesh," he said simply. He had tilted Edmund's face slightly, looking at the ruin, and then smiled ruefully. "Well, you'll certainly never look in a mirror again."

But Edmund Talbott had made the same promise to himself a long time before that. One moment of weakness had destroyed everything he loved. Then, ten years ago, he had thought revenge impossible. He had been weak and ignorant, but a decade of research had given him certain knowledge.

And he would have his revenge.

He swore it.

15

J ONATHAN BLINKED, rising up from a dream in which he saw himself
reflected in endless mirrors, fading away to blackness in every direction.

"Hi Dad, how are you feeling?"

Jonathan Frazer opened his eyes and looked at his daughter sitting beside his bed. He wondered how long she'd been there, wondered how
long he'd been asleep. The room was dark, hazy, as if it was late afternoon.

He reached out and took her hand, turning it slightly, looking at her
long and slender fingers lying against his soft palm. Her fingers tightened
over his, squeezing slightly. There was sympathy and understanding, too,
in her deep blue eyes, concern without the impatient pity he had seen in
his wife's face.

Emmanuelle Frazer was eighteen. She was a stunning classical beauty,
large-eyed, fine-boned, whose resemblance to her mother was slight, although she was the very image of her grandmother, Jonathan's mother,
who had been a great beauty in her youth. One of Manny's features had
been a mane of thick black hair, and he'd been horrified when she returned
from Paris with her head shaved in what he called a skinhead, but which
she insisted was a Number Two haircut, which left a slight fuzz of hair
across her skull. It was, she had assured him, quite the latest fashion, and
he had to agree that, while he didn't particularly like it, it did emphasize her
high cheekbones, and her huge blue eyes.

"How are you?" she asked again.

"OK. I've felt better. You heard?"

"I heard," she said shortly.

"What did your mother tell you?"

Manny shrugged. "She said there'd been an accident; that the detectives are still looking into it." Her fingers tightened on her father's hand. "It's scary, Dad, two people dead within days of one another."

"It's something to do with that scarred man," he muttered.

"What scarred man?" she asked, frowning, her forehead and the skin on her almost bald head crinkling comically. "Mom said nothing about a scarred man."

"Before . . . before Diane's accident, this big ugly guy came around asking about that mirror I bought in London."

"Hang on, hang on a sec, Dad. What mirror? Remember, I've been away. I don't know what's been going on around here."

Jonathan attempted to sit up in the bed, but every muscle in his body protested and he lay back with a groan. "You remember I told you about the mirror I bought in London at some auction house. Tony was working on that mirror when it fell on him."

She nodded slowly, unsure where this was leading. "You mentioned something about a mirror."

"There was a break-in last night . . ."

"Mom told me about that."

He nodded slowly. "I'm convinced it was the same guy who was here today—he gave me this little present last night." He touched the ugly purpling swelling in the center of his forehead.

"How did he get in?"

"The police think he might have had a set of keys—possibly Tony's."

"Why Tony?"

"His keys were not among his belongings. And you know he's had a long term relationship with a man about ten years younger than himself . . . well the young man didn't attend the funeral, nor has he been seen for the past few days."

"You think something might have happened to him?" she asked, almost breathlessly.

"I don't know. All we know is that he's not around, and that possibly Tony's keys were used to open the door, because the lock wasn't forced."

"And then the dog was killed?"

"That's right. The same person who hit me, killed the dog. The police speculated that it must have been someone of immense strength, because he had managed to snap the dog's head back, before slicing open its throat.

So today, when this big ugly guy—must be the ugliest man I've ever seen, terrifically scarred—turns up at the guesthouse wanting to buy the mirror, you don't need to be a genius to work out that they're one and the same man."

"Could he have killed the dog?"

"No doubt about it. He was tall—six three or four—with huge shoulders, broad chest, massive arms. He could have taken care of the dog without even breaking into a sweat."

"And he wanted the mirror?"

"Yes, he said it was a family heirloom, and it had been sold by mistake."

"Was he English? Did he have any sort of accent?"

Jonathan frowned. "He was English. But I can't quite pinpoint the accent. I'd more properly describe it as posh or maybe studied, as if English was not his first language and he'd learned it later in life. Everything about him was intimidating. I was beginning to wonder what was going to happen when Diane appeared. She was holding a hammer."

"A hammer? And what was she going to do with it?"

"I don't really know. I'm not sure she knew either. The scarred man left then, but we both knew he'd be back. I tried to call the police from the phone in the guesthouse, but it wasn't working. I didn't have my cell on me. So, Diane locked herself in while I came up to the house to make the call." He stopped and swallowed hard. "I was on my way back down when I heard her scream." His fingers tightened on Manny's and she winced. "When I got to the door, it was still locked and all I could do was look inside. I could see her. She was lying on the floor before the mirror . . ."

"Was she dead?" Manny's fingers tightened on her father's damp hand.

"Her throat was sliced wide open."

"How?" she whispered.

"I don't know. The detectives are thinking suicide. But nothing's been confirmed yet, they're waiting for the autopsy report."

"Suicide? That's not Diane."

"I know."

"And you think the scarred man is involved?"

"I'm sure of it. I know the police are certainly interested in him. And the mirror's involved also," he added, almost as an afterthought.

"How? In what way?"

"I don't know. But there is something about it. Something special."

"Is it especially valuable?" Manny asked.

"No. Not really. It's a big ugly slab of dirty glass." He smiled crookedly. "Diane never liked the mirror, she said it was bad luck." He laughed shakily. "I'm beginning to wonder if she wasn't right."

16

THE DOOR had been replaced by a temporary, ugly piece of unfinished plywood held in place by crude hinges and secured by a chunky padlock. The remains of the old door, which had been hammered open by the police, lay propped up against the side of the guesthouse, the shattered timbers bright against the stucco exterior.

Manny lifted the shiny new key she had taken off the ring behind the kitchen door and slid it into the padlock. It popped open. She had already disabled the alarm from the panel in the kitchen, but when she stepped into the long dim room and pulled the door closed behind her, she discovered that the alarm hadn't been reconnected to the new door.

There was a peculiar smell in the room, not the usual sweetly pleasant smells of fresh wood shavings and the newness of leather, but a different, sharper odor. There was the scent of blood, too, the smell heavy and cloying on the dry atmosphere, and she could distinguish the sharper stench of urine and the heavier odor of excrement.

Wrinkling her nose, she made her way to the mirror. It was a tall pale rectangle in the shadows. Having heard so much about it, she just had to see the artifact that had been responsible either directly or indirectly for the death of two people.

And she was disappointed.

She had expected something different, something more impressive, maybe with an ornate, heavy gilt-edged frame with intricate carvings, but instead it looked just like an ordinary mirror—a little larger than most perhaps—in a plain wooden frame with time faded opaque glass.

There was a rust brown stain on the concrete floor close to the base of the mirror, and it took her a few seconds to realize that she was looking at Diane Williams's blood. She was surprised that she could look at it quite so dispassionately.

Moving closer to stand directly in front of the glass, she stared at it impassively, hands on hips, head tilted slightly to one side. Her own reflection was barely visible behind a patina of dirt. There were clear streaks in the glass, bright speckles at the bottom as if the mirror had been washed with liquid; more of the liquid had run down from the top, long clear strips bright against the grime.

Manny stepped forward and peered into the glass.

And then something—no, someone—looked back!

For a moment she thought her heart had stopped. The image had lasted a second—less than a second—a brief flickering that might have been a face or could just as easily have been her imagination. The face had been superimposed over her own, coal black eyes matching hers exactly, the same high cheekbones, though she had the impression that the image was slightly rounder, fuller. Full, red lips, like her own. And hair. Automatically, she ran her hand over her rasping scalp. That was the chief difference: the image had had a full head of wavering, twisting, wreathing black hair.

A deep convulsive shudder ran through her, breaking her concentration, losing the picture. She shivered, suddenly cold, goose flesh along her bare arms and legs. She stepped away from the glass, reluctant to turn her back on it.

Maybe it was some of the marijuana or cocaine she'd done during the college year. She had read that some of that stuff could linger in your system for years, and that something—light, a smell, a sound—could set it off again. A flashback. Maybe that's what it was, some sort of residual after-effects of the drugs.

She was almost at the door when she sensed the presence standing behind her. She felt it as a disturbance in the air, the hint of male muskiness, sweat . . .

She screamed and at the same time flailed back with the point of her left elbow as she'd been taught in self-defense classes. It caught the figure dead center in the chest, dropping him to the ground. She spun, fists clenched, all her fear now transformed into anger, pumping adrenaline . . . and discovered her father, red-faced and gasping on the floor.

"Dad, oh Dad. Jesus Christ I'm sorry. I just felt someone standing behind me, and I thought . . ."

"Its OK," he gasped, taking Manny's arm, allowing her to haul him to his feet. He was ashen, his breath rasping through tortured bruised muscles. "I'm sorry, I just saw the door was unlocked and I thought . . ." He stopped. He hadn't been thinking. He had opened the door purely on impulse—just in time to see the faceless figure coming towards him, barely distinguishable in the gloom. And then he had felt the pain. "At least it's nice to know that the martial arts classes you're taking work."

"Dad, I'm sorry . . ."

"Don't worry about it. But what were you doing here?"

Manny shrugged. "I just came for a look." She shifted her head, pointing with her chin. "At that."

"Curiosity killed the cat," he said, and then immediately regretted it. "So what do you think about it?"

Manny shrugged "It's very ugly, it's . . . plain. And disappointing. I'd been expecting something else." She didn't add that the mirror disturbed her. But the image of the face in the glass had already faded to a vague memory, in which she could barely remember the features on the face except that it had been female, yes definitely female. "And what are you doing down here anyway? I thought you were supposed to be in bed."

"I was."

Manny suddenly noticed the item he'd been casually holding away from her, partially shielding with his body. "Dad, what have you got in your hand? Is that a gun? I didn't know you even had one."

"It came in with a job lot of Second World War militaria. Tony cleaned it up and got it working. It's a Browning Hi-Power. Don't tell your mother," he added immediately.

"But I thought you had banned guns from the property?"

"I did, but I kept this one."

"And what are you doing down here with it?"

Jonathan Frazer lifted the weapon, smiling uncomfortably. "Well, I thought that whoever had come for the mirror might just try again. They've had two tries, their next one might be successful."

"So what do you think you're going to do?"

"I'm going to spend the night here and wait for them."

"No. Fucking. Way. Dad, this is absolutely crazy. Tony's dead; his death was an accident. Diane is dead, and we're not sure how or why."

He lifted the gun. "This sort of evens the odds."

"Dad, please don't do this, don't even think about doing this. Let the police handle it. Call them, they'll come round."

"Manny, I have to."

"Why?" she demanded fiercely, the same look of obstinacy appearing on both their faces.

"Because two people are dead, two people I knew very well, one of whom was among my closest friends. And I want to know why. I owe it to them; I owe it to myself."

Manny glanced back into the darkness towards the mirror. "You're crazy, this is crazy," she muttered. "And all because of a mirror . . ."

"I know. But I have to do it."

"Dad," Manny said finally, "will you do something for me?"

"Anything, you know that, sweetheart."

"Take the gun, and blow that fucking mirror apart!"

"Manny!"

"Do it Dad; destroy it before it destroys you, before it destroys us all."

Jonathan Frazer raised the gun and pointed it at the glass. His finger curled around the trigger. But he couldn't pull it.

17

THERE WERE three text messages from Celia on Jonathan's cell phone, each one becoming increasingly unpleasant. The final message was delivered in person by Manny. She stood in the doorway, arms folded across her chest, head tilted to one side resting against the doorframe.

"And what else did she say?"

"That's all."

"I doubt that very much," Jonathan said.

"She just cannot understand why you won't come back to the house."

"I've already explained all this to her," he said patiently.

"She's concerned."

Jonathan grunted. "She's afraid I'm going to shoot someone and bring more police around. That's what really upset her about the two deaths, you know that. Neither Tony's nor Diane's deaths caused her a second thought: she's more concerned about what the neighbors think, and how it affects her standing in the community."

"And the cost of the house," Manny added.

"That too," he agreed. "So, no." He shook his head. "I'm here for the night. At the very worst, it'll be uncomfortable and I'll probably catch pneumonia. At best, I might just catch this person and finish this, once and for all."

"You left out the bit where you might die."

"I did," he admitted. The thought curled and twisted at the back of his head. If the scarred man had killed Tony and Diane, he would have no hesitation about killing again. "I told you, I've made up my mind." Jonathan Frazer didn't look around. He was busy clearing a free area in the center of the room around a chaise longue. With great difficulty he had maneuvered the mirror to the center of the room, leaving a clear path to the door. Anyone entering through the doorway would be immediately visible, though he, hopefully, would be invisible in the shadows.

"And what happens if someone comes looking for the mirror?"

Her father glanced over his shoulder, his bruised face pale in the gloom. "Then I'll hold him for the police, and maybe I'll ask him a few questions before they arrive."

"And the gun?"

"For personal protection only," he muttered, turning away and not meeting her eyes.

"Dad . . ."

"Yes."

"Be careful, Dad. Don't do anything . . ."

"Heroic?" he suggested.

"Stupid," she said.

Jonathan Frazer straightened, dusting off his hands. "Don't worry. You know I'm a coward."

"Yes, that's why you came charging in here the other night, and nearly got yourself killed. That's the sort of thing cowards do."

"You sound like your mother," he said gently.

"Dad!" she said in disgust, turning and walking away into the evening.

JONATHAN FRAZER SPENT the next two hours wandering around the guesthouse, looking through some of the pieces Tony had been in the process of repairing. Some of them had been there for years and now would never be repaired. There was far too much stuff here: it was no way to run a business, he had certainly overbought. But then he hadn't expected the downfall in the economy and the slump in the interior design business. Although that was no longer his primary source of income, he relied on it for cash flow. His father had made the money, and then secured it with shrewd investments; all he had had to do was to consolidate.

Sitting in a late Victorian basketwork chair, he wondered what he would do now without Tony. Every firm that dealt in retail of any sort had someone like Tony Farren, someone whose knowledge was essential to the running of the business. Without Tony, things would be different; he would try to replace him, but finding someone with knowledge and experience was going to prove extraordinarily difficult and expensive. Also, he'd built up a lifetime of trust and respect for Tony.

Jonathan stood, the chair creaking and crackling beneath him. He would have to start taking a more direct hand in the day-to-day running of the business. And the first item on the agenda would be to sell off as much of this stuff as possible. He'd take it down to the store and maybe have a sidewalk sale. Looking around, he realized that he had tens of thousands of dollars tied up in stock.

He pulled aside a flatiron desk, wincing as glass slivers from the shattered light bulbs stung his hands. Diane had done a good job of cleaning up most of them, but . . . but she'd never completed the job. First thing in the morning he'd get someone in to replace the lights, and check the circuits: obviously something had overloaded them, some power surge from the house maybe, or the alarm. Yes, that was it, the alarm had overloaded, tripping the breakers, though he was surprised they simply hadn't just died rather than exploding so spectacularly.

Then, maybe with Manny helping him, he could close the store for a couple of days and bring Robert, the sales assistant, in to help him clean the place up, do a little re-organization. Maybe he'd give some of the odd pieces of junk that Tony had been working on to a consignment store, see if he could make a little quick money.

He only realized the light was almost gone when he found himself squinting to read the sale label on a bookcase. He looked at his watch, it was late, and he was hungry, but reluctant to go back to the house and possibly have another argument with Celia. And he didn't want to leave the guesthouse.

He maneuvered his way through the mess and lay down on a brown leather chaise longue, stretching out and crossing his feet at the ankles. Lifting the gun out of his waistband, he rested it on the top of his right leg, his hand loosely wrapped around the grip, the barrel pointed away from him where the mirror was a pale rectangle against the shadows. Carefully, deliberately, he turned the gun to point down. He didn't want it going off accidentally and destroying the leather chaise. Or the mirror.

If you dealt with any old, antique or second hand artifacts for any length of time, you soon learned that there certainly were some pieces which came with a history and were *unlucky*—cursed was probably too strong a word for them. Every dealer had stories about cursed pieces. An Arizona dealer he knew had a penchant for knives, he'd been collecting them for years, and had one of the finest collections in the Southwest. A couple of years ago, he'd purchased a second hand Gypsy Jack folding knife online at a bargain price. When it had arrived he had opened the gleaming blade, admiring its finish and as he had closed it, it had snapped back unexpectedly, slicing off the tip of his finger.

An accident.

As he was attending to his wounds, his three-year-old son had somehow managed to open the knife. It dropped from his hands and stabbed him in the foot.

An accident.

Deciding to quickly resell the knife, one of the sale assistants almost severed his little finger while retracting the blade.

An accident.

But three accidents with the same piece? The dealer investigated. It turned out that the knife had belonged to a teenager who had used it to stab both his parents to death. The same day, the collector took the knife and flung it into the Yaqui river.

Such stories weren't unusual, there were many unlucky pieces out there. A lot of antique jewelry had bad luck attached to them and a couple of years ago, he'd almost bought a bed which was reputed to be cursed: a couple had committed suicide in it. Tony had dissuaded him.

So was it unusual that the mirror could be cursed in the same way? Or was he simply allowing his imagination to run away with him?

Tony was dead. But Tony had had accidents before. Jonathan smiled, remembering the time he had become locked in an eighteenth-century sea chest, and then again when he'd become trapped in a fourteenth-century suit of armor. He took risks, he did stupid things . . . and he drank. Who was to say that he hadn't been drinking that day, overbalanced and pulled the mirror down on top of him? Accidental death, the coroner had said.

And Diane?

Well, she knew the rules about playing around in the workshop. You simply didn't do it, you concentrated and focused. She'd learnt that rule a long time ago when Tony had been teaching her how to use a SKILSAW. She had taken her eyes off the piece of wood for one second; had Tony not wrenched the plug from the wall, she would have lost all the fingers on her right hand.

And the scarred man? Why had he broken into the guesthouse—for the mirror certainly—and yet it wasn't exactly hidden the night he had broken in. And even if he had found it, what was he going to do with it? It had taken four firefighters to lift it off Tony Farren's body; how was one man going to haul it away? A sudden thought struck him: hadn't the scarred man mentioned Tony's name? Maybe he'd been involved with Tony, maybe there'd been an argument and the mirror had been pushed down onto him.

Jonathan Frazer sat bolt upright. This was craziness. He could feel his head spinning, his thoughts chasing one another. He was thinking like a madman, curses and plots and murders. He must be still feeling the effects of the valium the doctor had given him. Maybe that's why he was so confused and sleepy.

But what would happen if he fell into a drugged sleep now? What would happen if someone broke into the guesthouse tonight? A pulse started in his temple and he felt his heart begin to pound in a panic attack. All the windows were screened, the skylights secured, so the only way in was through the door and that was bolted on the inside. He climbed up out of the chaise longue and lifted a box of tacks from the workbench and scattered them over the floor. He tied a length of fishing wire across the entrance to the little clearing where he had positioned the mirror so that anyone approaching him wouldn't be able to do it without making enough noise to wake the dead . . .

Frazer began to laugh, a dry hissing sound, at the thought of waking the dead—Tony Farren's and Diane Williams's faces floating before his eyes. The laughter went on for two minutes before dissolving into gentle snoring.

18

THE FULL moon was high in the heavens, the sky clear and cloudless, its light cold and sharp across the dirty streets.

Edmund Talbott stood at the window of the apartment and looked out over the almost deserted street through a tiny rent in the newspaper he had pasted over the glass. The young woman in a too-tight, too-short dress and thigh-high boots had finally left her post on the corner across the road, obviously hoping to pick up a late customer coming out of the 7-Eleven at the end of the road.

The big man looked up into the heavens, gauging the time. He folded his arms and leaned back against the wall, watching the way the moonlight moved across the bare floorboards, the light still distinct even through the newspapers.

Talbott closed his eyes, concentrating, trying to remember the layout of Frazer's guesthouse, orientating on it, fixating on the mirror in relation to the windows, then determining the fall of the moonlight. Finally, he relaxed, shoulders slumping; providing everything had remained untouched, the mirror was out of the direct moonlight—and anyway, there'd be no one in the room to see anything.

SHIMMERING MOONLIGHT MOVED down the length of the long room, gradually illuminating each of the screened windows in turn before moving on. It was close to three in the morning before the luminescence finally reached the mirror. Liquid silver ran down the length of the glass, bringing it to startlingly brilliant life. A trembling shadow drifted down the length of the tall glass.

Jonathan Frazer opened his eyes and looked at a wall of shining light. And then he discovered that shapes moved within, ghostly, flickering images wrapped around with smoke.

They were real enough to touch.

19

S MOKE, THICK, gray, almost glutinous, coiled and twisted around enormous pillars. Lower down, closer to the floor, tendrils of dank mist rose up through the cracked and shattered slabstones. Water dripped in the distance, the sound echoing hollowly through the high-ceilinged chamber. There was water on the floor, large shallow pools washed silver in the vague light, and the walls were streaked green with fetid moisture. The air felt damp, heavy, cloying, tainted with excrement, seaweed, and fish.

The cloaked and hooded figure moved through the swirling mist, seemingly unconcerned with the chill or the odors, moving confidently across the maze of broken stones and the other, less easily identifiable, debris that littered the ground. There were natural potholes strewn around the huge echoing chamber, as well as other, man-made traps. Even if someone managed to breach the outer security defenses without raising an alarm, they would have to be very lucky indeed to make it past this sanctum without succumbing to one or other of its lethal snares.

Moving deeper into the huge chamber there were sounds, distant and indistinct, occasionally broken by a rasping shriek that might have been metal on metal. There was light, too, an archway illuminated by warm golden light, incongruous in this dark and dreary place. A gossamer wind carried newer, though possibly even less pleasant odors, overlaying the stench of the place.

Two men suddenly appeared out of the shadows, the wan light running off their leather jerkins, sparkling on the swords and knives in their hands. Their faces were flat, impassive, eyes wide and unblinking, pupils tiny. Their lips and tongues were black.

The hooded figure stopped and straightened, throwing back the hood, shaking out a mane of thick black hair, coal black eyes regarding the two men impassively.

The two men stared at the woman, their mouths slack, dark saliva running onto their chins, into their beards. She stared them down, knowing that even though they had been trained to accept her, they could still tear her apart if she showed the slightest fear or hesitation.

Without a word they both saluted with their swords and stepped back into the shadows. They were effectively the last line of defense and even if an intruder managed to get this far, it would be impossible to pass them. They were twin brothers, taken from their mother at the moment of their birth and trained in the same way hunting dogs and pit bulls were trained—beaten, starved and tortured—until they were completely loyal to their master. Narcotics kept them docile and obedient, especially the weed that had originally been brought back by the knights returning from the Crusades.

The woman moved into the arched doorway and stopped, unwilling to intrude now, knowing that the work was at a very delicate stage. When he was finished, he would notice her.

There had been some improvements in the place since she had last been here. Equipment had been brought in, there was a table and chairs, a brazier. And the mirror. She caught herself looking at it, staring deep into its grimy depths before she realized what she was doing and tore her gaze away, forcing herself to concentrate on the room. The chamber was actually below the level of the Thames in a rotting wharfside warehouse, surrounded by filthy slums. And even in this overcrowded disease-ridden part of the city, the building remained unoccupied. People who entered its dank interior—homeless people, vagabonds, some of the women who plied their trade on the wharf—had been found dead in the street the following morning.

The building was cursed. As simple as that.

The woman smiled. How primitive these peasants were; how easily controlled. A few dead bodies and they spoke of curses. Yes, the building was cursed, but the only curse on it was the two half-human creatures. This might be the age of discovery and invention, and men might write about the Americas and the Indies as if they had actually been there, they might admire the new weeds, the fruits and the vegetables coming back from the New World, but in all their quest for knowledge, they were ignoring a greater, larger, far more mysterious world: a world of magic and power.

There was a man in the center of the room, tall, thin, a shock of red hair and beard emphasizing his pale skin, highlighting his green eyes. His clothes had once been white and cream, but now his silk shirt and hose and pale doeskin boots were soiled with the filth of the place. His hands were on his hips and he was looking at the floor.

Without turning around he raised his left hand, fingers crooked, calling her forward. She moved through the debris littering the floor to stand beside him, her arm moving around his waist, her head resting on his shoulder. "Kelley," she murmured.

The man ignored her, staring at the floor. There was a pit at his feet, ten feet deep by ten feet wide. Thick iron bars, already speckled by rust even though they were barely weeks old, had been set into a stout wooden frame, which in turn was bolted to the floor.

And deep within the pit was a man.

The woman leaned forward to look down, taking care to lift the hem of her dress and long cloak off the floor. "He is young?" she said. It was difficult to make out his features or age in the dim lighting.

The tall red-haired man lifted the lantern from the table and held it high, shedding yellow light into the pit. There was a quick scrabbling movement as the rats scurried for cover and the young man came to his feet. He was naked, his pale body patterned in bruises and scrapes, covered in filth. His hair was thick—filthy now with grease and straw—but there was a distinctive bald patch in the center of his head.

"A cleric!" she said, delighted.

"A cleric," the big man nodded. "He believes I am the devil."

She smiled, showing long yellow teeth. "He is almost right."

The big man smiled humorlessly. "I wonder what he will make of you." His accent was flat, dull, almost crude.

"And he is a virgin?" she asked.

The red-haired man shrugged. "Who can tell these days? But he is young, fanatical, not the type to give himself to the sins of the flesh."

"Wash him," she said, turning away.

Kelley shouted aloud in a guttural language not unlike Gallic and one of the guards appeared. He pointed to the terrified man in the pit and spoke again in the same harsh tongue. The brute looked into the pit for a moment and then moved away, returning moments later with an enormous bucket of water which he dumped unceremoniously over the man below. The prisoner screamed with shock and surprise: the water had been pulled from the Thames and was freezing.

"*Aris,*" Kelley grunted. Again.

More water was emptied down onto the young man. He was now shivering so badly he could barely stand, and the water had turned the floor of the cell into a quagmire.

Kelley unlocked the heavy hasp lock and pulled back the gate. The dead-eyed guard dropped the ten feet into the sodden mire of straw and filth and hauled the cleric to his feet. Although he was barely conscious, he attempted to strike the guard with his fists. The guard slapped him once, a single blow that rocked his head from side to side.

Kelley lowered a makeshift ladder—a length of wood with pegs set on either side—and the guard climbed up, the cleric tossed over one shoulder.

"*Anseo!*" Here. He pointed to the long wooden table that had been set up before the mirror. The guard dumped the young man onto the table. His head thumped against the wood.

Kelley and the woman stood on either side of the table and looked down, examining him critically. He was perhaps seventeen years old, physically perfect, all his limbs, fingers, and toes intact. His back teeth had gone, but his eyes were unclouded by cataracts, the whites reasonably clear, tainted around the edges by yellow. His armpits and groin were free of growths or nodules and there were no cankers or pustules on his penis. Perhaps this one was a virgin. They had been unsuccessful on two previous occasions: both young men had been diseased.

Kelley looked at the woman. "Well?"

"Well enough." She looked around as she unhitched her cloak. "Fetch me some more water—and not that swill you were drowning him in," she snapped. "Proper water, hot, too, if you have it."

Kelley stared at her for a few moments longer, his long, delicate face impassive. She was just beginning to wonder if she'd gone too far when he suddenly nodded and walked away.

She busied herself preparing the narcotic, a mixture of henbane, wormwood, and hashish from the east, diluted in brandy. Crouching beside the young man, she allowed the mixture to trickle between his lips and down his throat. He coughed once and she saw his throat working as he swallowed the liquid.

Kelley meanwhile had returned and stood behind the woman, a wooden bucket of tepid water and a half dozen rags in his hand. "Well," he said eventually, when she had managed to feed the youth the entire mixture. The woman raised her hand for silence, and then she laid her head on his chest, listening intently for his heartbeat. It was slow, but strong and steady. They had killed two people experimenting with the strength of the mixture. Finally, she looked up, eyes blazing, and nodded.

Kelley handed her the bucket and cloths and stepped back. Not normally an excitable man—he had lived his entire life suppressing his emotions—but he could feel the blood beginning to pound in his veins now. They were close, very close. He could feel it.

The young man opened his eyes.

THERE WERE MEMORIES of fear and pain, of hunger and thirst, of cold and wet and . . . fear. His overwhelming memory was one of fear.

He had been . . .

He had been praying in the Church of St. Saviour in Southwark, when he'd become aware of a cloying stench and then something rough—a burlap sack—was thrown over his head. Blows on his body, kicks . . .

And the pit! He remembered the pit! Adrenaline surged through his body and he sat up straight—only to fall back down again as bruised, stiffened muscles refused to obey him. His head pounded against wood.

The woman came to him then. A beauty, an angel. She had rescued him from the pit and taken him . . . taken him where?

Was he dead?

Had he died and gone to heaven? He was warm and dry and the filth was gone from his body. He felt rested and relaxed, at peace with his surroundings. Floating.

Now the woman was bending over him, raven tresses brushing his face, tickling along his chest. He felt their touch with a strange intensity, and then he realized he was naked.

A man should not show himself . . .

The woman's lips brushed his face, his forehead, his lips, her hair now moving across his skin like trailing fingers.

And then—to his horror—he felt his body begin to respond! No angel this: a demon, a succubus. He attempted to lift his arm, but it barely responded. He opened his mouth to cry out, but the woman pressed her mouth to his, and he shuddered as he felt her tongue against his, licking at his lips. She straightened and allowed the cloak she'd been wearing to drop from her shoulders. She was naked beneath.

The young cleric attempted to squeeze his eyes shut, but he could still feel—exquisitely—the woman climb onto the table beside him, he could feel her breasts against his skin as she stretched herself along the length of his body. He attempted to pray, but the demon was whispering words in his ear, foul, obscene words that managed to arouse him ever further. He shrieked aloud as he felt the woman's moist flesh envelop his, and he knew then that he was lost. He was dead and damned. He was in hell. That is why he could not pray, that is why he could not concentrate on the holy images.

Opening his eyes, he saw the woman sitting astride him, her hands on his shoulders, moving rhythmically, her eyes closed, mouth open, tongue moving across her moist lips. He watched the movement of her breasts, fascinated by the sweat tricking down between them, curling across her flat stomach. She suddenly stopped moving and opened her eyes ... and then he discovered that he had taken up the rhythm, moving inside her. He was lost now; a damned soul. The woman smiled triumphantly. Almost of their own accord, his hands moved up to her hips, across her stomach to cup her breasts. He felt ... he didn't know what he felt. He had never experienced this before. He had never been with a woman before.

And, for the first time in his life, he knew why men sinned.

He was moving frantically now, and the woman had to clutch his shoulders to remain atop him, her nails digging deep into his flesh. His heart was pounding, the veins in his forehead and neck visibly swelling, and his face and chest and thighs were bathed in sweat. He was dimly aware—as the tingle began deep in his groin—that the woman had looked past him, and nodded, but he was too far gone in his passion to stop even if he wanted to.

There was a shadow behind his head. A shape. The glitter of metal. A sickle-like blade.

There was pain.

And pleasure.

He watched blood—his blood—arc from his throat and spatter across the demon's female body. And as his life faded, he watched her rub his blood into her body, licking the drops from her fingertips. Dying muscles relaxed and his head turned and he saw his own blood spray into a wooden goblet, where it gathered like altar wine.

BLOOD-SPATTERED AND SATED, the woman climbed off the cleric's body, picked up her cloak and draped it casually around her shoulders. Timing was essential: the virgin had to be slain when their blood was hottest, but before orgasm. Once their passion had taken them they were useless. She watched as Kelley approached the mirror, holding the cup in both hands like an offering. With careful, deliberate movements, he spilt some of the liquid onto the dirty glass, allowing it to run down the surface, scouring through the dirt.

For an instant the mirror cleared, and images flickered within.

The red-haired, red-bearded man spattered more of the blood onto the glass, careful not to touch the mirror himself.

The images were clearer now; there were faces, dimly glimpsed buildings, shadows.

Standing back, he threw the remainder of the contents of the goblet at the glass, splashing it at about head height. The steaming gore dripped in long sticky strands down the glass, wiping away the encrusted slime.

The images were clearer now; sharper, brighter. There was a face, a woman's face . . . eyes wide, mouth open . . . and then it faded.

Edward Kelley swore and then he turned back to the woman. "Again; we will have to do it again!"

JONATHAN FRAZER CAME awake as the moonlight slid off the glass. He was freezing and his heart was pounding painfully in his breast. The dream had been so vivid, so real. He had been lying on that table, while the dark haired woman sat astride him, breasts swaying over his face.

He sat forward, head throbbing . . . and then realized that his pants were wet. He was horrified and disgusted to discover that he'd ejaculated in his sleep.

20

T HE MEMORIES *were returning and with the memories came strength and knowledge. It knew now that it was not without power.*

To lure, with images and shadow shapes.

To court, with desires and promises.

This was its power.

This was its strength.

This was its skill.

And now the trap had been baited, the prey sighted.

Now there was the time of waiting . . . but it had waited for so long—forever and ever, unchanged and unchanging—it could wait a little longer.

21

DETECTIVES HAAREN and Pérez pulled up in an unmarked car and parked outside Frazer Interiors in Beverly Hills.

"Impressive," Margaret said.

"Expensive," Pérez added. He looked up and down the street. "Many of these shops are by appointment only."

On either side of the glass-etched front door were large, tall glass windows. The windows displayed a different room, each one dressed with extraordinarily beautiful antiques.

Haaren and Pérez climbed out of the car and stood for a while in the bright November morning sunshine, looking into the windows.

"No price tags," Margaret said.

"If you can afford to shop in this neighborhood, you don't care about price tags." José grinned. "Though, even if I could afford them, I'm not sure if there's any I'd want."

"Not sure any of them would fit in my apartment."

The door was locked and José rang the brass doorbell. "Why don't you move?"

Margaret Haaren had lived in the same tiny apartment in West Hollywood for the past twenty years.

"There's just never enough time to look for an apartment and move," she admitted. "But soon," she added, unconvincingly.

José was reaching for the bell again when a figure materialized from the back of the store. A slim dark curly-haired young man cracked open the door and smiled professionally. "Good morning, can I help you?"

"Yes, we are here to see Mr. Frazer."

Margaret Haaren was wearing her usual dark suit over a white shirt, but she still felt shabby standing before the assistant's two-piece charcoal gray Italian silk suit, slate-blue shirt with a heavy raw silk tie. She tried her usual trick of estimating the value of his clothing, jewelry, tie, and shoes, and then began to wonder how a sales assistant—albeit in a place like this— could afford to wear upwards of twenty-five hundred dollars of clothes, shoes, and jewelry to work. She somehow doubted that he'd be paid that well. Maybe he earned a lot in commissions.

The assistant's smile never moved. "Do you have an appointment?" He tapped a small brass sign to the right of the front door. "By Appointment Only."

José shifted slightly, revealing his badge clipped to his belt.

The assistant's fixed smile cracked.

The big woman smiled coldly. "Tell him it is Detective Haaren. He will see me."

The assistant's smiled faded to a bare curve of his lips. "Of course, please come in, I'll let Mr. Frazer know you are here." He stepped aside and allowed the two detectives to step inside, then he locked the door, turned and disappeared in the back of the store.

"I thought it would be smaller," Margaret said, looking around.

The discrete frontage disguised the fact that the antiques store was surprisingly large, with tall ceilings and highly polished concrete floors. The huge space was laid out to show different room arrangements. The walls were covered with modern art, the lighting angled in such a way to pick up the radiant colors of the paintings and prints, while the shelves were accented with glass objets d'art or books.

José Pérez wandered into a bedroom setting. It was dominated by a large black steel framed four poster bed with crisp white linens, accent pillows and a colored throw. Two curved mirrored nightstands with turquoise blue base lamps and black shades stood on either side of the bed. He picked up one of the pewter picture frames on the nightstand and turned it over to check the price.

"One hundred and fifty dollars, I think I'll take two!"

Margaret took it from his hands and set it down. "Bed, Bath, and Beyond have them for ten dollars each," she whispered.

The assistant appeared behind them, coughing gently.

"Mr. Frazer will see you now."

They followed the assistant to the back of the store. The back wall was covered in floor-to-ceiling bookshelves. The young man touched a concealed switch and an entire section of shelving swung out to reveal an office. Jonathan Frazer appeared, hand outstretched. "Detective Haaren . . ."

"You remember my colleague, Detective Pérez?"

"Of course." Frazer shook hands. "Good to see you both again."

"I hope this is not an inconvenient time, Mr. Frazer?"

"No, no, not at all, and please . . . it's Jonathan. Can I offer you some water?"

The detectives nodded.

He looked over her shoulder at the assistant. "Water please, Robert, and I'm not to be disturbed."

"Of course." The young man closed the door, which shut with a smoothly oiled click.

"Interesting door you have," Detective Haaren remarked.

"With space being at a premium—especially the way we use the space—we just couldn't afford the luxury of having a blank piece of wood there. It's taken from an old movie set. Please have a seat." He moved around behind a large glass L-shaped desk and sat in a high-backed leather chair. Behind him, the wall was filled with signed pictures of his celebrity clients. "Do you have any news for me?" he asked suddenly.

Margaret Haaren was watching the man closely as he spoke. The bruising on his forehead was still evident, although he had removed the bandage that had swathed his entire head and now used a small square patch to hide the worst of it. He was pale though, and his skin had an unhealthy cast, his soft brown eyes deep sunk and ringed as if he'd spent a sleepless night.

"Not a lot I'm afraid. Our investigations are continuing. We're trying to trace the scarred man you spoke to. We'd like you to come down to the precinct as soon as possible and we'll have you look through some mug shots. If that doesn't work, we can have a police artist draw up a sketch."

"Yes . . . yes, I'll do that. When?"

"Soon. Today, if possible."

There was a tap on the door, and the assistant entered carrying a tray with three bottles of water, tall glasses, and a pitcher of ice.

"Thank you, Robert."

"Will that be all?"

"Yes, thank you."

Margaret Haaren turned one of the water bottles. They had gold etched Frazer Interiors labels wrapped around them. "Nice touch, Mr. Frazer."

"Thank you, I like to make my customers feel special."

Margaret waited until the door had closed and she heard the young man's footsteps moving away from the door—and she realized that she hadn't heard him approach the door, which probably meant that he'd crept up and been listening outside.

"We would also like your employment records for Tony Farren and Diane Williams . . ."

"Of course."

"Also, we would like some details about the mirror you bought in London; maybe we could trace the scarred man that way. Have you any idea why he might have wanted the mirror?"

Jonathan Frazer shook his head, looking distracted, and after twenty-two years on the police force, Margaret Haaren knew when someone was upset and attempting to conceal it. There was something about the mirror.

"Tell me about the mirror, Mr. Frazer."

He shrugged. "There's not a lot to tell. I bought it at auction in London. I go there at least once a year to look for unusual pieces that I can sell here at the store. My clients love the idea that some of the pieces have a history behind them or come from exotic countries. With Thanksgiving and then Christmas just around the corner, it's a good time for antiques and objets d'art. I'll make about forty percent of my sales between now and Christmas Eve."

"What about your wife, she doesn't travel with you?" Pérez interrupted.

"No, she prefers the luxury type of vacations, surfing, skiing, that type of thing. She hates business trips. No fun."

"So, back to the mirror you bought." Haaren nudged him back on track.

"It was my last business day. I wandered around just seeing the sights and then went to my final stop, the auction house in South London. There was an auction in progress, trash mostly, but the mirror was there. And no one bid on it, I think because it was so big. But I recognized its age and I bought it for five hundred pounds—came to around around thirty-five hundred dollars if you count the shipping."

"And it's worth a lot more?" she asked.

"I thought it was worth a few thousand, but Tony Farren—who knew a lot more about these things than I did—estimated it around twenty thousand dollars."

Margaret Haaren looked up in surprise. "Twenty thousand dollars! So it was quite a find then?"

"It certainly was. A sort of once-in-a-lifetime find."

"Then what happened?"

Detective Pérez lifted a discrete black leather notebook from his pocket and began to make notes.

Jonathan shook his head. "The mirror was shipped back here . . . and that's when the trouble started." He looked up suddenly. "Was Tony's death an accident?"

"There is no evidence to suggest otherwise," José said, "but we shall be re-investigating the circumstances in the light of Miss Williams's tragic death."

Margaret leaned forward, the sudden movement focusing attention on her. "Mr. Frazer—and I must ask you now to be honest with me—do you owe anyone any money, do you have any gambling debts, or have you done anything which might leave you open to blackmail?"

The shock on his face was genuine enough, and she knew the answer even before he said, outraged, "No! Absolutely not. I don't gamble and I don't . . . leave myself open to blackmail. This is a reputable business and I have an A-list clientele."

"I'm sure, Mr. Frazer, but you will appreciate that we have to look at every angle."

Frazer sipped his water in angry silence. He was obviously insulted that they should even think . . .

"Tell me about your assistant, Mr. Frazer," Detective Haaren continued as if nothing had happened.

"Who . . . Robert?" he asked, surprised.

"The young man who let us in."

"He is Robert Beaumont; French mother, American father, and a friend of my daughter's. His references were excellent and while he doesn't know a lot about design, he's a superb salesman."

"Is he wealthy?"

Frazer shook his head. "No."

"So how did he end up working for you?" Jose Pérez asked, puzzled.

"My daughter Manny met him when she was in Paris studying fashion.

She was new to the city and he showed her around and they became close friends. She treats him like a big brother. When he returned to Los Angeles, he needed a job. Manny knew I was looking for someone for the store. I interviewed him and found him perfect."

"Do you pay your assistants especially well, Mr. Frazer?"

"Detective Haaren . . . I really don't see what this has to do with . . ."

"Just answer the question, Mr. Frazer."

"He is paid two thousand dollars a month, plus two and a half percent commission of any sales he makes or initiates during the month."

"That's not a particularly enormous salary."

"Is that payment under the table?" Detective Pérez asked, eyebrows raised.

"Absolutely not, he is paid by check, it's all very legal," he said coolly.

"I notice he dresses very well," Margaret said.

"Very well."

"Would he wear the same suit to work every day?"

"No, quite the contrary. It's something of a running joke that he has a larger closet than I have."

"And is he living in an apartment, a house?"

"I believe he lives with his mother in Pasadena. I know his parents are divorced."

"We'll need his address."

"I have it here . . ." Jonathan pulled open the file and pulled out a single sheet of paper, then added photocopies of letters to it. "These are his references," he said. "May I ask why you're interested in Robert? Surely you don't think he has anything to do with the current situation?"

"Is he honest, this Robert Beaumont?" Detective Haaren pressed on, ignoring the questions. "Have you ever had any suspicions about him?"

Jonathan Frazer stared at her for a few moments and then he smiled. "I underestimated you, Detective."

She smiled innocently, but said nothing.

"Well, yes . . . yes. I have suspected him of . . . of irregularities. We had an occasion recently where there was a shortfall in the cash, but he explained it away by saying he had sold certain items at a discount but had then inadvertently entered the full amount into the register."

"But you did not believe him?"

"Not entirely."

"Has he the authority to discount items?"

"There would be leeway on just about everything, yes. In order to make the sale, he would have the authority to reduce it slightly, but to do it in such a way that the customer thinks it is being done as a personal favor to him or her. I would rather sell the item at a reduced price than lose the sale altogether."

"Any other times you suspected him?"

"On occasion small items have gone missing . . . picture frames, small objets d'art." He shrugged. "Well, there are only the two of us in the store." He waved at the small security monitors discretely recessed into the shelving. The images flickered from picture to picture at ten second intervals. "Anyone coming into the store shows up on the monitors."

"But you're not always here."

"No."

"So we have a young man who by his own admission has no money, earning very little, plus commission, living with his mother, who obviously has very expensive taste in clothes. It probably has no bearing on the present case, but I'll look into it just the same."

"What do you think I should do?"

"Probably find another assistant, Mr. Frazer."

22

ROBERT BEAUMONT scuttled away from the door as soon as he heard the conversation come to a close. His heart was pounding and his fine silk shirt was stuck to his skin. He had heard most of the conversation: the important parts anyway. He had heard that bitch do the number on him with Frazer. How could she have caught onto him so quickly?

Because he'd been stupid. It had happened before for exactly the same reasons.

Robert Beaumont was a small time con artist and thief with big ideas of his own worth. He had made a career out of working the better class shops first in Paris, and then later in Deauville, Marseille, and Lyon, before moving onto the Riviera, where his good looks and charm found him employment in some of the best establishments. He preferred boutiques, either men's or women's, where the pickings were easy, light, portable, and resalable. Chic interior design stores were a new thing for him: again some of the goods were portable, pocketable, but more important expensive, and it wasn't difficult to find someone to take them off your hands.

Since moving back to Los Angeles with his mother, this job had proved a real dream. Frazer was rarely in the store; he was a simple trusting sort, good-natured, good-humored; in other words, a fool. Beaumont almost felt guilty taking the few bits and pieces from him, but some people deserved it, some people almost asked for it. And Frazer was one of them.

Most of what he stole went to support his great passion: clothes. He had grown up on the backstreets of Paris, wearing rags and hand-me-downs, cast-offs from his brothers and sisters. He had stolen his first item of clothing—a shirt—off a clothes line when he was seven years old. With the realization that these things were out there for the taking, he had embarked on a life of petty crime, hampered only by his greed and his stupidity. He stole from his employers too often, and he couldn't resist wearing his fine clothes, flaunting a wealth he should not have. He had been caught that way too often before.

But he had never been lucky enough to have any warning before. Maybe he was getting smarter in his old age.

He folded his arms across his thin chest—and then immediately allowed them to drop to his sides, unwilling to crease his suit. He looked around the store, wondering what little "going away" present he might give himself. The problem was everything here on display was labeled, and itemized.

There were voices behind him and he moved quickly through the store, hurrying away, so that when Frazer and the detectives came back into the store, he was busily re-arranging some accessories.

He glared at Margaret Haaren. Bitch! His dark eyes flickered over her. Badly-dressed bitch.

And all because that Farren bastard and his stuck up assistant had had a stupid accident at the guesthouse they used as a storage . . . fuck 'em, they deserved to die, he never liked either of them . . .

It took long moments for the idea to trickle through to his subconscious, and he stopped, frowning. He had never been in the Frazer guesthouse, but from what he had heard, it was crammed with furniture, artifacts and trinkets which were all unmarked, unlisted, and destined for the store at some point. They were there for the taking, with little or no record of them ever existing in the first place. Tony knew everything, but had kept it all in his head. Why, Frazer wouldn't even know they were gone.

Keys. He'd need keys. He glanced at the fake Rolex on his wrist: close to twelve-thirty. Frazer would be on his way to lunch soon; the weak fool would probably need to fortify himself before he came back to "let him go."

He checked his pocket: he still had the key to Frazer's office he'd stolen weeks before. There was sure to be a key to the guesthouse in there.

23

E DMUND TALBOTT spent the day in the Beverly Hills Public Library reading rooms. It was not far from the Beverly Hills Police Department and was very probably the last place the police would think of looking for him.

Now that the mirror had become active again, he needed to renew his knowledge of its history. In the past he had researched the history of the mirror in the British Library which, outside of the Vatican, possessed one of the finest collections of books on occult and related subjects in the world. And while the Beverly Hills library had none of the books he needed, it did have a fast internet connection.

In the past, the Talbott family had been the keepers of the mirror, although how it had come into their hands in the first place had been lost in the mists of antiquity. Fear: fear of the unknown, of the devil, of evil, had nearly always prevented even the most foolhardy from prying too closely into the mysteries of the glass. But now, in this secular age, when these fears had been dulled and almost forgotten, now the danger had assumed terrifying proportions. He had to destroy it. The time for simply guarding the mirror had passed, it was time now to destroy it.

Talbott had attempted to disguise himself, stooping to shield his height, while wearing a loose-fitting voluminous coat to conceal his size. There was nothing he could do about his scarred face. The doctors had given him the option of plastic surgery, but he had rejected it. He wore his scars proudly and as a constant reminder that his wife and child had been taken from him. It was a reminder, too, that he must never look in a mirror again.

The library was almost empty, sunlight slanting in through the tall windows, the atmosphere still and slightly too cold from the air conditioning.

He sat down at a long wooden table and pulled the slip of paper from his pocket. Jonathan Frazer. Anthony Farren. Diane Williams. Was there some connection between the three, something in their past? And yet they were from widely differing social classes, age groups, and backgrounds. What could they possibly have in common? Nothing immediately came to mind, but possibly there was some connection in previous generations? The mirror seemed linked to certain families, certain lines and clans. But what sparked it from its quiescent state? His father had told him that it was nothing more than moonlight on the surface of the glass, but was there something more?

Was the key to its ultimate destruction somewhere in these meager clues? He would find it: he had to before it killed and killed and killed again.

Every death fed it, made it stronger. Deadlier.

24

MARGARET HAAREN was convinced that the police should police and desk clerks at least should be competent to keep up with the work. She had once attempted to work out how many hours she spent filling in forms, making reports, and generally doing desk clerk things, and had eventually given it up in disgust and despair. Then the ratio was running at two to one: twice the amount of desk work to police work. Outside her office, she knew, there were at least three able-bodied police officers sitting at desks tapping at keyboards when they could have been gainfully employed elsewhere.

There was a knock on the door and José stepped in, scores of printer paper bundled loosely in his big hands. "I thought you'd want this immediately," he said, by way of an apology.

"I thought we went paperless?" she grumbled.

"We did. This is the paperless version."

Margaret Haaren shoved the monthly report forms to one side, making space in the center of the desk for the ream of paper.

"It's the report from the Metropolitan Police in London about the auctioneers who sold Frazer the mirror."

"And?" Margaret asked impatiently, aware that Pérez was leading up to something. "Are you going to tell me that they don't exist?"

"Oh, they exist all right; that's not the problem. They hold an auction every week, sometimes twice a week if they have a lot to clear. Apparently everything they have for sale is cataloged on computer, which explains this mess of paper." He rested his hand flat on the stacked pile. "The auction house checked their records for the past eight weeks . . . and while they've sold a couple of mirrors in that time, they certainly have not sold anything like the one we described to them."

Margaret Haaren sat up straight.

"Furthermore, they checked their accounts and they have no record of ever having dealt with Jonathan Frazer or indeed Frazer Interiors." He glanced up and smiled. "It gets better."

"Tell me."

"I then checked with the shipping company—just in case there was an oversight. Again, they checked their computer records and they never made a delivery from London to Los Angeles for a Jonathan Frazer."

"Why did he lie?" Margaret Haaren wondered.

"And such a stupid lie."

"Surely he knew we'd check with London; why did he give me names and addresses?"

"Maybe he didn't think we'd check." Pérez grinned. "He's smart this Jonathan Frazer, you know that, far smarter than us cops," he added sarcastically.

"I didn't think he was that type," she admitted. She thought that Frazer had some respect for the police; far too often people of his class thought that their money and connections made them some sort of superior being. Maybe she'd been wrong.

"Did he ever show you any documentation from the auctioneers or the shipping company?" José asked.

"No." She smiled, showing her teeth in a fixed grin. "I think we should go and pay Mr. Frazer another visit."

"When?"

"Right now."

25

FUCK HIM, Robert Beaumont decided.

Fuck him. That was his considered opinion. He decided he wasn't going to hang around until after lunch so that Frazer could build up a head of steam to fire him. He was going to be long gone by the time he got back.

Sitting at Frazer's computer, fingers moving slowly over the iMac keyboard, he carefully composed a letter, then printed it out on Frazer's laser printer. He liked the idea of using Frazer's computer, printer, ink, and paper to write his resignation letter.

Monsieur.

I got a call from my mother. She has been rushed to hospital, something to do with a possible heart attack.

I need to go to the hospital now and be with her.

I don't know how long or how serious it is but I hope you understand. Please allow me a few days leave.

Respectfully,
Robert Beaumont.

Frazer was such an idiot that he'd believe him, too. He was tempted to take what cash there was, but that would give the lie to his story. What he needed to do was to give himself a couple of days' grace before Frazer decided to contact the police. It wasn't something he could do with someone cleverer, but Frazer was such an idiot. Well, fuck him!

Carefully locking the front door so that he couldn't be disturbed,

Beaumont made his way back to the office. He could still smell the woman's perfume on the heavy dry air, something inexpensive, whorish too, he had no doubt. There was nothing feminine about her, everything about her was cheap, from her mannish suit to her common haircut. He knew the type; he had met them before, worked for them. Women pretending to be men. She thought she was so clever, detecting his little secret. Well, he'd show her.

Sitting in Frazer's chair, he opened the file drawers. There was a set of keys in the first drawer sitting on top of a pile of mail. Beaumont looked at them in dull surprise: he couldn't be so lucky, could he? Well, perhaps he deserved a little luck. Pocketing the keys, he picked up the mail and looked through it. Most of it was circulars, subscriptions for magazines, but the last envelope was from an auction house in London, a computerized invoice for *Lot 69: A large antique wooden-framed mirror, approximately seven feet tall by four feet wide.* Pinned to the back of it was another computerized receipt from a shipping company for transporting the mirror from London to the house in Los Angeles.

There was something about a mirror . . .

Wait a second! That woman and Frazer had been talking about a mirror he had bought at auction. Added to what he had been able to pick up over the past few days, he realized that this must be the same mirror the mysterious scarred man had offered to buy before Diane Williams's death. Frazer had warned him that if a large, particularly ugly man with a shock of white hair entered the store, then he was to phone the police immediately.

Frazer had told the detectives that the mirror was valued at more than twenty thousand dollars. Twenty thousand was a big payout; far better than the few hundred he could get from small bits and pieces of artifacts.

Beaumont tapped the envelope against his lip. This letter contained the evidence which proved he had bought the piece and therefore owned it. And suppose *he* wanted to sell the mirror—maybe to the scarred man if he could make the connection—then this piece of paper would prove the legitimacy of the sale. Sliding the envelope into his inside pocket, he returned the letters to the file drawer and closed it. He glanced at his watch. Just one-thirty. Frazer would be back soon, and Robert had no intention of being around when he arrived. His thin lips twisted in a smile as he surveyed the office for the last time. Frazer would be forced to stay in the store for the rest of the afternoon, or close early, and Robert didn't think he'd do that. Maybe now would be the perfect time to visit the guesthouse. If everything went according to plan he'd be well away before Frazer arrived home.

JONATHAN FRAZER STROLLED down the street arguing with himself. He was a soft-hearted fool. He knew that. He'd always been soft, and curiously, he didn't consider it a character fault. The alternative was to be someone like Celia—hard, unyielding, caring only for oneself—and he was definitely sure he didn't want to end up like that.

So Robert Beaumont had taken him in; well it wouldn't be the first time he'd made a fool of himself, nor would it be the last. He'd paid the young man reasonably well, and in return, his Mediterranean looks and charm had wooed some customers, especially the female ones. And if Robert'd stolen from him, well . . . what was done was done and could not be undone. He would dismiss him now—immediately, even though that was going to mess up the store for the next few days. Maybe Manny would stand in until he found a replacement: she should, seeing Robert had been her recommendation.

Jonathan turned into Rodeo Drive and straightened up as he walked towards the shop. As he pressed the bell, he decided on the spur of the moment that he was not going to give Beaumont a reference. He pressed the bell again.

Nothing moved within the shop.

Jonathan pushed the bell for the third time. Leaning against the door, he shaded his eyes with his hands and peered inside. There was no movement within. He looked at his watch: it was just gone a quarter to two. Where was Robert? His heart began to pound. Was something wrong? Had there been a robbery; was he tied up in the back of the store someplace . . . or . . . or . . .

He took a deep breath and attempted to calm himself. Maybe the young man had just popped out for something—he'd done it before, even though he'd been warned never to leave the premises unattended during working hours.

Pushing the bell again, he rapped sharply on the glass with a quarter.

"Is there a problem, Mr. Frazer?"

Jonathan whirled, startled. "Detective Haaren!"

"Is there a problem?" she repeated, her face hard and expressionless. She hated to be taken for a fool and so far as she could see, this man had done nothing but.

"I don't know . . ." He turned to look back into the store, hoping to see Beaumont appear. "I've just come back from lunch and I've discovered that the store is locked." He rattled the handle for emphasis.

She continued to stare at him, saying nothing.

"Well, Beaumont should be there." He lowered his voice. "I was wondering if there'd been a robbery, or something."

Margaret Haaren looked back over his shoulder, and Detective Pérez immediately stepped out of the unmarked car.

"Yes, ma'am."

"Mr. Frazer's store appears to be locked, and he's concerned there may have been a robbery. Anything on the radio?"

"Nothing."

"Do you have a key, Mr. Frazer?"

He handed it over without a word.

Detective Pérez turned the key in the lock and stepped inside, followed by Haaren and Frazer. Pérez walked swiftly around the store, his gun drawn, moving surprisingly quietly for so large a man. He returned moments later, placing the gun back in its holster, shaking his head. "There's no one here. But I did find this on the desk in his office." He handed Frazer the single sheet of paper with his name scrawled across the top. Jonathan read it aloud, and then glanced at Haaren. "This man thinks I'm a fucking idiot," he said angrily.

"It's not a nice feeling is it, Mr. Frazer?"

The tone of her voice caught his attention. "Is there something the matter, Detective Haaren?" he demanded, transferring his anger onto her.

"I think it's you who has been taking me for a fool, Mr. Frazer. You told me you purchased the mirror—the cause of all your recent problems— at auction in London. That does not appear to be the case. Neither the auction house nor the shipping company have any record of ever having dealt with you."

"That's nonsense, absolute crap!" he snapped.

"You will, of course, have all receipts and invoices from both sources then?" she demanded.

"Of course! And I must say I find your attitude and your suggestions offensive."

"Just show me the proof, Mr. Frazer, and I will apologize," Margaret Haaren said, suddenly turning away.

"I'll get them now," he snapped.

"Is there another way out?" Margaret asked quietly, as Frazer disappeared behind the swinging bookshelves.

"Not that I could see. Anyway, where's he going to go?"

They wandered around the main showroom, not talking. The detective had warned Pérez about the security monitors and they were both aware that Frazer could see them, although they weren't sure if he had an audio pick-up. Five minutes later, Margaret Haaren looked at her small-faced wristwatch and glanced at Detective Pérez. "How long does it take to find an invoice?"

They had both started towards the office, when the section of shelving swung back and Jonathan Frazer, wide-eyed and white-faced, stepped out.

"Let me guess, Mr. Frazer." Detective Haaren smiled. "You can't find them at the moment. They've been misfiled, misplaced."

"No, no." He shook his head violently. "They were in the front section of the filing cabinet. But they're gone," he said wonderingly. "They must have been stolen!"

"How very convenient," Detective Pérez said. He glanced at Haaren. "We often have people stealing invoices from filing cabinets, there's a big market in stolen invoices." He took Frazer by the elbow and steered him towards the door. "I think it's time for a trip down to the precinct for a somewhat more serious conversation."

"Do I need to call my lawyer?"

"Well," Margaret Haaren said, "what do you think?"

26

I T HAD been easy, pathetically easy.

Robert Beaumont parked on a side street and walked past the Frazer house twice just to make sure that neither Jonathan nor Celia Frazer's cars were in the drive. Finally, he boldly walked right up to the front door and rang the bell long and insistently. Then, with his hands folded together in front of him, he turned his back on the door and looked out over the expanse of manicured garden. Like everything else about Jonathan Frazer, it was unspectacular, conservative.

Robert Beaumont had no appreciation of gardens, but he appreciated land and property prices and Frazer's property was certainly in the big leagues. The man was obviously doing very well for himself. And he did it by paying his assistants a lousy five hundred a week. If Beaumont needed an excuse for extracting a few things—which he didn't—he had it now. Frazer wouldn't even miss them, fuck him. And he deserved everything coming to him.

The door clicked open behind him and he turned, smiling automatically, until he discovered that it was Emmanuelle, and the smile turned genuine.

"Bonjour, mademoiselle," he murmured, bowing elegantly. When they had first met in Paris, she had mocked his too-elegant old world manners.

"Robert," Manny said, blinking sleepily. She had been out until the early hours of the morning, and she'd drunk far too much and smoked a little more than she should. She'd been dead to the world until the persistent jangling of the bell had awoken her. Idly wondering where the housekeeper was, she pulled on a long candy-striped T-shirt that came down past her knees and padded down the stairs. She peered out through the fish-eye spy hole, but the caller had his back to her. She glanced at the clock—two in the afternoon—and debated ignoring the caller. Of course . . . it might be the police. She looked out through the spy hole again and noted the caller's short haircut and neat suit. Probably a Jehovah's Witness she decided, as she turned the lock and swung back the door. She discovered then that the suit was far too smart and far too expensive for a Witness. It took her a second to recognize the smiling young man. "Robert," she said, digging the heel of her hand into her eyes, and smothering a yawn. "What are you doing here?"

He smiled ruefully and ran his fingers back through his slick coal-black hair. "Business I'm afraid." He showed Manny the key ring he had taken from Robert's desk drawer. "You father asked me to come out and collect a few things from the guesthouse."

"Sure. Come on in."

She stood back and allowed him to walk past her into the hallway. He caught a hint of her perfume—now heavy and musky with sleep—and the sour, sharper odor of stale alcohol.

"You were partying I take it," he murmured, glancing surreptitiously around the hall.

"I did have a late night, or an early morning," she admitted, and then added philosophically, "and now I'm paying for it, I'm afraid. And I'll pay for it tonight when Dad gets home."

"He doesn't know what you got up to in Paris then?" His dark eyes caught and held hers.

A touch of color appeared on her cheeks and then she threw back her head and laughed aloud. "No, thank God, and don't you even think of telling him. It's our secret remember?"

"Mademoiselle!" he said in mock outrage. He pressed his hand to the flat of his chest over his heart. "It is—as the saying goes—more than my job's worth."

"Have you got time for a coffee?" she asked, moving past him.

"Not really, but maybe I'll have a small one." He watched her move down the hall, the realization that she was completely naked beneath the T-shirt exciting him. He had seen her naked many times when they had been lovers, but that had been a long time ago, and he wondered if he had time . . . Shaking his head from side to side, grinning at the very idea, he followed her down the hallway into the kitchen.

"How are you enjoying working for my dad?" she asked, as she pulled open cupboard doors looking for coffee. *Where was the housekeeper?* "I can't find a thing in this place," she admitted. "I'm sure the housekeeper rearranges things every week to make herself indispensable."

Robert went to stand by the back door looking out over the back garden, across the paved patio and down through the trees to where the edge of the guesthouse was just visible. "Your father is . . . well, he's fine really. I don't see him often enough to form any opinion. The store isn't really his main business as you know, and despite the economy, we're ticking over nicely I think. There aren't many walk-in customers. Most of the business is down to our list of special clients."

"You always had the trick of not answering my questions." Manny glanced over her shoulder and grinned. "Come on, be honest: what's he like to work for?" She suddenly pulled out the coffee. "Success!"

"He's a bit of a—how do you say?"

"Robert, your English is better than mine, so don't give me any of that French 'how do you say' shit."

Beaumont laughed. "It was your sense of humor that first attracted me to you, you know that, don't you? Anyway, your father is too picky. He is old-fashioned, slow, unimaginative, and uninventive. How he has survived in this business so long eludes me." He was watching Manny's reflection in the window and saw the smile fade from her lips, and realized that he had gone too far. "And yet," he added brightly, "just remember, I am working for him, so if there is a last laugh going around, he has it." He suddenly changed the conversation. "Is that the guesthouse down there?"

Manny glanced over at him and nodded. "That's it. Mom hates it, she wanted it as her personal gym," she added. "She hates the very idea that Dad turned it into a workroom and storage area. She had a landscape architect come in and gave them specific instructions to hide it. They planted the trees and bushes. Eventually they'll screen even the small corner of the guesthouse you can see."

Robert glanced at his watch. "I'll tell you what. While you're preparing the coffee, I'll go on down and see if I can find the few things you father asked me to get for him."

"Sure. I'll give you a call when it's ready."

Robert opened the back door and stepped out onto the patio. There was a rich scent of flowers and herbs in the still air. Fall in Los Angeles: eighty degrees in the sun and flowers were still in bloom.

First the guesthouse, and then a quick cup of coffee. The thought of it appealed to his sense of irony. It was another way of thumbing his nose at Frazer. Then he'd drive straight to his mother's, pick up some clothes and head to the Burbank airport, grab a last minute ticket to somewhere, anywhere—Colorado, Arizona—just somewhere, out of state. All nice and neat and effective. It was a pity that he didn't have a little more time: he would have enjoyed taking Manny Frazer to bed again, to make love to her. No, not that. They had never made love. It had always been a far baser emotion. It was lust, pure and simple and they had fucked. Wouldn't that be the ultimate insult: take Frazer's goods, drink his coffee, and fuck his daughter on the same day? It was a nice idea; however, discretion being the better part of stupidity, perhaps not now . . .

His first shock came when he realized that the guesthouse was bigger than he'd first thought. There was no way he was going to be able to conduct anything like a proper search in the twenty or thirty minutes he'd allotted himself. He'd just have to count on striking it lucky.

He got his second shock when the key he'd taken wouldn't fit the lock fixed to the surprisingly crude-looking door. He stood, looking stupidly at the hasp padlock, and then turned the keys in his hand to read the names on their sides. None of them matched. Well, he hadn't come this far for nothing . . .

MANNY WAS SURPRISED to find Robert back so quickly. "Get what you came for?"

He spread his hands in a typically French expression, his head tilted to one side. "I can't get in." He held up the key ring. "None of the keys fit the lock."

"Oh, he's given you the wrong key ring," she laughed. "The locks were changed after . . . after the accident," she added, the smile fading from her lips. "He's been so addled lately he's probably forgotten." She plucked a key ring from its hook behind the door and handed it to him. "It's one of the new keys on that ring, but I'm not sure which, you may have to jiggle it a bit."

"You are an angel," he smiled, clutching the key ring and heading out the door, moving quickly now, eager to make up for the time he'd lost. Ten minutes; he'd give himself ten minutes and not a second longer. He was looking for small, highly portable items of worth. And, of course, the mirror. That was the prize.

27

THE THIRD key on the ring opened the lock, and he stepped into the dim, musty interior of the guesthouse and pulled the door closed behind him.

Afternoon sunlight shafted in through the windows and the dusty skylights, catching the silently whirling dust motes, glinting off the wood and metal, glass and leather piled high around the room. There was a long workbench running along the length of one wall. Beaumont moved his way swiftly along it, figuring that this was where Tony Farren would have been working on pieces destined for the store in the immediate future. Valuable pieces. He was surprised at the disarray. He found nothing immediately. He looked around the room, large items of furniture placed at very odd angles. Where were the objets d'art, the pocketable expensive accessories?

"Merde," he whispered.

He had been stupid, why had he thought that the guesthouse would have been laid out like the store, with everything on display? He should have taken the goods from there and now it was too late. Moving swiftly, he made his way down through the center aisle, but everything here was too big, chairs, tables, ugly ornaments, clear bags containing throws and cushions piled high on either side. There was obviously a fortune stored here, but none of it interested him. Where was the mirror he had heard Frazer talk about? At one point the center aisle had been blocked and he had to retrace his steps around by the walls back to the door. Standing with his back to the door he looked around the room for a last time, cursing at his own stupidity.

He had missed it the first time round, because he had turned right at the door to follow the bench, but there, directly in front of him was an opening into the center aisle. He could see a chaise . . . and the mirror.

Robert Beaumont wove his way through the piled up artifacts, realizing that this was what had blocked up the center aisle. A clearing had been created in the center of the room, a leather chaise placed facing the huge mirror. Beaumont walked right up to it and grinned, and his reflection, shabby, twisted, and distorted by the dirty glass, leered back at him. "Merde," he whispered again. This was not his lucky day; there was no way he was sticking this mirror in his pocket. When Frazer and the detective had been talking about it, he had formed the impression that it was a small object, probably jeweled or something like that, but he'd never imagined this monster. Craning his head, he looked up, trying to gauge its height: no wonder it had killed Tony Farren when it had fallen on him, it must weigh a ton.

When he looked down again, Emmanuelle Frazer was standing behind him.

He opened his mouth to speak, but she raised a finger to her lips, shaking her head. He was about to turn when she pointed her index finger at the dirty glass.

With a smug grin, he folded his hands across his chest, not thinking of his fine suit now, and he turned back to the glass, concentrating on the image in the mirror.

Without saying a word, Emmanuelle lifted the long T-shirt over her head, holding it in front of her body, barely covering her breasts and groin for a few tantalizing moments, before allowing it to fall to the floor.

Beaumont felt his breath catch in his throat.

She was even more beautiful than he remembered, and he felt himself becoming immediately aroused. He reached out and brushed his hand across the mirror, attempting to wipe it clean at face level—although her body was clearly reflected in the glass, her face was smudged and in shadow. Through the dirty glass, it looked as if Manny had a thick head of hair. His hand came away filthy, and he fumbled in his pocket for his handkerchief, his eyes still locked on the glass, roving over the reflected woman's body. It had filled out a little since he had seen it last; her breasts were fuller, heavier, though her nipples seemed smaller than he remembered. Her stomach was slightly rounded too, and her groin was now covered in a thick mat of hair, whereas formerly she completely depilated her entire body, leaving her skin soft, silky, and smooth.

With his breath stuck somewhere at the back of his throat he watched Manny run her hands down her body, slowly caressing herself, catching and cupping her breasts, fingers pulling and tugging gently at her nipples. She brought her right arm across her body, her hand pressing itself flat to her left breast, her forearm across the nipple of her right breast. Her left hand moved down across her rounded belly, fingers splayed, fingers probing deep into the thick hair.

With his right hand, he reached for his belt, fingers fumbling with the buckle. His left hand went to the mirror again, rubbing at the grimy, greasy surface with the handkerchief. . . .

The shock that lanced through his system was like an intense orgasm. His heart was pounding, his breathing ragged as he rubbed at the glass, almost *feeling* the touch of her skin beneath his fingers, moving down to brush the silk handkerchief across her reflected breasts.

It was a game now. An intensely erotic game, voyeurism taken to another degree. She was behind him, he could almost feel the heat radiating off her body, could smell the heavy musk of sex in the dry air. And yet he wouldn't touch—not yet anyway. That was part of the game.

He was stroking himself now, a faintly ridiculous figure with his pants down around his ankles, his eyes fixed on the mirror.

Manny's head was thrown back, the smooth column of her throat taut, nostrils flaring, lips wet and parted as her fingers worked deep inside her.

And still with no sound.

Beaumont was aware of his own harsh, ragged breathing, his rapid gasps as his own orgasm approached, but there was no other sound . . . no other sound. His concentration faltered . . . and the image flickered. For one brief moment the woman behind his back was not Manny Frazer, but another, older woman, full-bodied, long-haired . . . long-haired . . . long . . . hair . . .

His hand slowed its pumping as the realization struck home. It wasn't Manny Frazer standing behind him. He was almost afraid now to turn around while behind him the woman continued to arouse herself with complete abandon. He leaned forward, resting his forehead head against the cool glass, supporting himself with his left hand . . .

And screamed!

Agony tore through his body, lancing across his face and up through his hand. There was fire before his eyes . . . inches before his eyes.

Fire in the glass.

Fire *on* the glass.

The glass was burning.

His flesh bubbled, blistered, scorched, and then cracked. It fell in blackened strips from his hand, flesh and fat bubbling in the intense heat. His hair crisped, then ignited, the styling gel running in boiling liquid strips down his back. The silk suit melted onto his body as the flesh burnt off his face and neck, his eyes sizzling, boiling in their sockets, tongue shriveling in his mouth. He sucked in breath to scream—and swallowed flame—and his shout was accompanied by a vomited ball of fire.

And his last conscious thought before the agony totally consumed him was the sudden jerking throb of ecstasy as his orgasm took him.

28

T HE HOWL of triumph ripped through the Otherworld.

Raw power, naked energy, bright coruscating colors rippled across the gray landscape, the vibrations taking a long time to die away.

Another soul, trembling, afraid, and in agony had been dragged into its trap.

It savored the pain. It fed off the agony. It drew strength from the terror.

It had taken the creature's death, accepted it as its due.

It was close now, so very close.

It needed a little more sustenance.

It craved blood. For blood was the life.

Just a little more.

29

T HE SMELL brought Manny running. The sickening, cloying, foul smell of burnt meat and leaves, of dried wood and leather. Oily black smoke was curling from the guesthouse, twisting in the still afternoon air.

She couldn't imagine what Robert had done, probably dropped a cigarette onto an expensive upholstered chair. But he hadn't smoked when she'd known him, well not the ordinary kind.

She slowed down when she reached the guesthouse, the nauseous smell troubling her already delicate stomach. She felt her gorge rise. The greasy smoke coiled around her, making her eyes water, clinging to her T-shirt, adhering to her skin, coating her lips, her mouth.

"Robert? Robert? Are you there, Robert?"

Where the fuck was he?

"ROBERT!"

Ducking beneath the billowing smoke, she ran to the nearest window and, pressing her face close to the glass and cupping her hands over her eyes, she peered inside. The thick white smoke blanketed everything, but she could see no flames. Nor was there any sign of Robert. Maybe he'd been overcome by the smoke . . .

Manny ran back to the house, heart pounding as she picked up the phone, fingers trembling as she punched in the numbers.

"Nine-one-one, what is your emergency?"

Manny looked out the back door of the kitchen as the smoke thickened and intensified. Her words, breathless, "Smoke, fire, there's a fire."

"Ma'am, I need you to calm down, what is your location?"

Manny ran back towards the guesthouse, the phone clenched in her right hand.

"Ma'am, are you still there?"

Manny reached the door of the guesthouse, breathless, and cracked it open, the air sucked out billowing smoke, engulfing her face, making her cough and splutter.

"Ma'am . . ."

"Robert, where the fuck are you, ROBERT!" She held the phone back to her ear and blurted out the words before dropping the phone. "You need to hurry."

She ran back to the outdoor cold-water tap hidden in amongst the bushes at the edge of the path. There was the curl of a green hose half hidden in the bushes. Turning on the tap, she attempted to drag the hose towards the guesthouse, but the hose was kinked and a dribble of water leaked from the head. She tried to rip a strip off her T-shirt, but the material refused to tear and she ended up soaking the hem of the shirt with water, then bringing it up across her mouth and nose. Then, squeezing her eyes almost shut against the smoke, she ducked inside the guesthouse.

The smoke was everywhere, thick and white at eye-level, dark and slick closer to the floor. It twisted and curled like fog, but she found if she stood to one side of the door, it was possible to make out a little detail.

"ROBERT!" Her voice, muffled by the wet T-shirt, was lost in the swirling smoke. Rubbing her streaming eyes, blinking away the tears that clung to her long eyelashes, outlining everything in glistening rainbows, she pressed forward, looking for the source of the fire. Goddammit: where were the fire extinguishers? As far as she could recall, they were somewhere close to the workbench which ran along the wall. Her father had refused to install a sprinkler system, saying that if there ever was a fire—which was extremely unlikely—the water would probably do more damage than the flames.

She scraped her bare shins on the side of a chair and hopped back, swearing, tears of pain springing to her eyes. Where the fuck was Beaumont?

She caught movement out of the corner of her eye and turned quickly, moving forward. The smoke twisted up, thicker now. "Robert?" she mumbled, moving closer.

The fire was around here somewhere. The smoke was thick and cloying, the stench appalling. She swallowed hard, bitterly regretting the amount she'd drunk and smoked the previous night.

Again the movement . . . a flicker . . . a face?

"Robert?"

The smoke cleared and Manny screamed! She staggered back, heart pounding, legs beginning to tremble with reaction. Then, realizing what she'd seen, she attempted to laugh, but the sound caught at the back of her throat: she had been looking at herself in the mirror. She hadn't recognized herself in that sudden, brief glimpse of a pale-faced, wide-eyed, semi-naked woman.

The smoke seemed to be coming from directly in front of the mirror. She stepped forward, frowning. There was a pile of smoldering rags on the floor.

Manny stooped to look closer at them.

On some deep subconscious level, she had already recognized the incinerated man-like shape on the floor, but refused to accept what she was seeing. She poked at the seared cloth with her forefinger, cinders spiraling upwards to dance briefly in the air. Metal glinted, gold against the blackened mess and she touched it, hooking it out of the ash.

It was a watch, a fake gold Rolex watch. The face was cracked, the casing melted to sludge in the intense heat, the enameled face bubbled and warped. Engraved on the back, barely visible beneath the patina of soot was the line, "Robert Maurice Beaumont."

And she suddenly recognized, she suddenly *accepted* what she was seeing.

The watch dropped from her nerveless fingers, falling onto the burnt meat, sinking into the chest cavity, a tiny blue flame dancing about the hole.

She scrabbled away, wrapping her arms around her knees, hugging them close to her body, swallowing again and again, bile flooding her throat and mouth. She closed her eyes, squeezing them shut, but the images—vivid, bloody images, of whitened bone and blackened flesh, a charred skull, strips of crisped hair clinging to it, of an arm that ended in a knotted stump—all the images remained.

And the smoke.

The smoke coiling sinuously from the body, flowing upwards, crawling across the surface of the mirror, clinging to it, wreathing across the surface, forming shapes, forming pictures, forming faces.

Tony Farren . . .

Diane Williams . . .

Robert Beaumont.

Face upon face, image upon image. Eyes wide, mouths open in sound-less agony.

Calling to her . . .

Pleading with her . . .

Enticing her . . .

Emmanuelle Frazer opened her mouth and screamed until her throat bled.

30

Tᴴɪꜱ ɪꜱ ridiculous, absolutely ridiculous. Your insinuations are absurd."

"Maybe you might want to wait until your lawyer arrives, Mr. Frazer . . ." Margaret Haaren suggested quietly.

"I don't see why. Your allegations are unfounded. I am innocent of these ridiculous charges," Frazer continued, almost trembling with rage.

"There have been no charges, Mr. Frazer. You are merely helping us with our investigations." She looked up as José Pérez came into the small office, his broad face completely impassive, a manila folder in his hand. Without a word he came around the desk and placed the folder before her, and then took up a position at the door, arms folded, eyes fixed on her face. Even before she opened the folder, she knew it was bad news.

"You must appreciate our position, Mr. Frazer," she continued, speaking to him while her eyes ran down the single typed sheet. "You told us you bought a mirror in London, the same mirror which inadvertently caused the death of one of your employees, the same mirror which a mysterious scarred man offered to buy, the same mirror another employee died guarding. And yet the auction house in South London has never heard of you, they have no record of ever having dealt with you before, and there was no mirror of the size you describe sold at the auction that day. We contacted the shipping company; the people whom you said delivered the mirror have no record of ever having dealt with you. We are left with one conclusion," she finished softly, having absorbed the impact of what she had just read, "that you have lied to us, Mr. Frazer."

"But why," he began, almost desperately, "what possible reason would I have to lie to you?"

The phone on Margaret Haaren's desk rang, interrupting the already tense atmosphere; she picked it up and listened intently to the voice on the other end, her eyes never moving from Frazer's face. "That's all you have at the moment? I see . . . thank you."

Margaret Haaren stood up and reached for the jacket draped across the back of the chair. "I think you had better come with us, Mr. Frazer."

"Why? Where are we going?" he demanded, not moving.

"We're taking you home. There has been . . . an accident."

Jonathan leapt to his feet. "An accident! What sort of accident?"

"We're not sure. A fire in your guesthouse. Your daughter seems to have been injured."

Frazer looked at her in horror, the color draining from his face.

"I've no further details, I'm afraid," she lied, not telling him about the grisly carcass that had been discovered in the guesthouse.

SIRENS HOWLING, THEY drove across Los Angeles in the unmarked police car. José drove, while Margaret sat in the passenger seat, half turned to look at Frazer, sitting wide-eyed, white-faced and trembling in the back seat. She could smell the rancid odor of his fear leaking from his pores, and this, more than anything else, convinced her that Frazer was not their culprit.

It took fifteen minutes to reach the house. A paramedic unit screamed out of the driveway as they turned in, while two fire trucks, their red flashing lights reflecting off the exterior of main house, were parked directly behind one another in the driveway. Lines of deflated yellow fire hoses led around the side of the house down to the guesthouse.

The detectives parked their car alongside a coroner's vehicle just as a black body bag was being loaded into the back. Frazer gave a scream of anguish and leapt from the still moving car, screaming as he ran across the drive towards the startled coroner's aides. Still shouting, he managed to pull the zip of the body bag down and revealed a burnt and tattered eyeless face before Detective Pérez grabbed his arms and physically hauled him away. "That's not your daughter. She's alive. She's alive, she's OK."

Frazer collapsed onto the ground, his head buried in his hands, sobs racking through him. José Pérez sat down beside him and put his arm around Frazer's shoulder. "It's OK, it's OK, it's not Manny. She's fine, she saw the body and fainted, we think. The paramedics say she wasn't injured; maybe a mild concussion, some smoke inhalation, nothing more."

"I thought . . . I thought . . . I thought . . ." Frazer hiccupped.

"I know what you thought. I've a girl about Manny's age myself. I know what you were thinking."

Frazer rubbed his hand across his eyes and attempted to stand, but his legs felt like water and the detective helped him to his feet. As the coroner pulled away, he looked at Pérez. "Well if that wasn't Manny, who was it?"

"We don't know yet. The body was found in your guesthouse, burnt beyond recognition, all identity burnt with it. All we have left is some rags and the remains of a gold watch."

"A watch? Whose?"

"We don't know yet, forensics will take care of that."

"But if the fire was that intense, what about the guesthouse . . ." Frazer gasped.

"Untouched."

Frazer looked at him uncomprehendingly. "How?"

"I've seen it once before, many years ago when I was a patrol officer. I was called in to investigate an old man who hadn't been seen for days. We found him in his apartment sitting in his chair. But although he was burnt to a crisp, the chair he'd been sitting on had only been scorched. The pathologist told me it was called spontaneous combustion. Happens to maybe twenty people a year; they just burst into flames, from the inside out as it were." He shrugged. "No one knows why or how it happens; just one of life's little mysteries, I guess."

"I'd like to see the guesthouse please."

"I'm not sure. . . ." José Pérez caught Margaret Haaren's nod, and then smiled. "Sure. Why not? Let's go."

The two men walked around the side of the house. Haaren trailed along discreetly. As they neared the guesthouse they could see police officers and the fire fighters milling about, while from inside, light flashed at regular intervals as the scene of the death was recorded. Frazer moved through the crowd, shouldering his way into the darkened interior, blinking quickly to restore his sight. He walked right up to the mirror, looking closely at it before realizing he was standing on the remains of some damp ashes.

Haaren looked at Pérez. Neither of them had told Frazer where the body had been discovered. And the guesthouse was large, the body could have been anywhere.

Frazer abruptly turned away, his face set and expressionless. When he stepped out into the sunlight, he was breathing quickly and his face had an unhealthy cast to it.

"What was that all about? A touch of guilt?" Pérez whispered to Haaren.

The woman shook her head. "Not sure, but it's significant." The detective strode forward and caught up beside him, touching his arm. "Slow down Mr. Frazer . . ."

"There!" he hissed. "There." His voice rose to a shout. "THERE!"

She followed the direction of his stiffly pointing arm. There was a tall, broad man standing at the end of the driveway among a small crowd of curious neighbors, his face in shadow, only his shock of white hair visible.

Frazer's fingers closed painfully on her arm, his eyes wild with excitement. "That's him! That's the scarred man."

"I'll get him," José Pérez murmured, hurrying past them, drawing his gun, crunching stones beneath his shoes. The stranger turned away and faded back into the crowd. "Shit," Pérez murmured, putting on a spurt of speed. He was too old for this. "STOP!" he shouted.

Haaren turned, pointing to the two officers who had come to investigate the shouting. "Go with him. Quickly."

José Pérez pounded down the driveway. The crowd of onlookers scattered quickly. He raced around the corner and had time to register a looming shape before he was grabbed by the arms and hauled off his feet. He was slammed against the ornate wrought iron fence, the back of his head snapping off the metal, dazing him.

"What happened back there?" The voice was hard. The huge man began shaking him, holding him inches off the ground, rattling him from side to side. "Answer me," he grated.

"F-f-f-fuck you . . ."

"Hey you!" The two officers rounded the corner and were almost on top of the white haired man before he—or they—realized it. The younger of the two men fumbled for his gun and shouted aloud before the big man—still holding Pérez pinned to the fencing—kicked the officer high in the chest with the flat of his foot. The force of the tremendous blow snapped ribs, driving them deep into the lungs and actually lifted the young man off his feet, punching him back into the second officer. Both men went down in a tangle of limbs.

Pérez saw a faceful of scars.

"Answer me," the big man snarled.

"Fuck you!" the detective spat. *"Que te jodan!"*

The white haired man kneed him in the groin. White hot pain blossomed in the pit of his stomach and flowed up into his chest. Suddenly he could not breathe.

"Tell me. Or I will hurt you."

José Pérez attempted to double over, but he was still pressed to the fence. He could feel moisture on his head, running down into his neck, had seen—dimly—what the man had done to the officer, he had felt the incredible fire in his groin. He was forty-seven years old . . . too old for this. He was going to throw up.

"Last chance: answer me."

"There was a fire, a man, burnt to death."

"Where?"

"In the guesthouse," he whispered.

"Where?" the big man demanded, raising a huge fist.

"I've told you. In the guesthouse . . ."

"Where. Specifically."

"Before a mirror."

The fist descended, smashing his head against the iron fencing.

31

IN THREE separate hospital rooms at Cedars Sinai Hospital, three families kept vigil.

Jonathan and Celia Frazer sat in a private room on the top floor, watching over the sleeping form of their daughter, Emmanuelle. Outwardly, she was unmarked and the only piece of hospital equipment in the room was the respirator to assist her breathing which was slightly labored due to smoke inhalation. Celia Frazer had fallen asleep, curled up in the large comfortable chair, a hospital blanket thrown over her shoulders. Jonathan sat perched on the edge of a chair, watching his daughter intently, not thinking, not daring to think, only grateful that she was still alive.

On the floor below them, José Pérez's wife and two teenage daughters sat awake and alert, unable to sleep, holding each other's hands, muttering prayers while they watched over the sleeping body in the bed. In the stillness of the room, a heart monitor blipped softly, the respirator hummed and, although the drips were silent, the three women all imagined they could hear each drop thundering into the IV feed. José Pérez's principal injuries were a cracked skull and concussion. A portion of the skull had been depressed inwards and the doctors had initially feared that it was pressing on the brain, but a series of emergency MRIs and CAT scans had removed that worry. There was extensive bruising to his face, and the red imprint of finger marks were clearly visible on his upper arms. There was a flat ugly weal on his forehead where the palm of a hand had struck him with tremendous force. The doctors had also found extensive bruising around his testicles.

In the ICU was the more seriously injured of two officers, Martin Moore. He had only just graduated from the academy a few weeks prior.

He had received a tremendous crushing blow to his chest, which had impacted several ribs into his lungs, collapsing them both. He had actually stopped breathing before the paramedics got to him and there was a grave possibility of brain damage. Sitting in the corridor outside the room, his aged parents sat still and silent, hands locked together. A polished black rosary moved through the mother's tiny fingers.

Even though her manpower was stretched to the limit, Margaret Haaren had placed two officers outside each room with strict instructions that no one was to be allowed in unless they were family or medical staff—and they could prove it. Frazer's description of the scarred man, now backed up and improved by the additional information furnished by the uninjured officer, had been circulated to police within the Los Angeles area. Margaret Haaren's orders were precise and succinct: anyone even vaguely matching the description of the man in the vicinity of the hospital was to be held for questioning.

The situation had now changed dramatically: in the *them and us* attitude held by both police and citizens in most modern cities, the police tended to look upon an attack on one of their own with far more seriousness than a similar attack on a citizen. The attack on Pérez and young Moore had been cold-blooded and brutal, possibly murderous in its intent, and the description of the scarred man had warned that he was "violent and dangerous, approach with caution."

32

A CROSS THE city, in the empty smoke-and-meat-stinking guesthouse, moonlight washed across the mirror, seeming to cling to the surface, swirling along its greasy face, creating patterns, shapes, images.

And faces.

Wide-eyed, open-mouthed, the face of Robert Beaumont peered from the mirror, soundlessly screaming. The image seemed to rush from the distance to explode against the glass. Within its open mouth, a smaller face appeared, distorted by fear and pain, barely distinguishable as the face of Diane Williams, and within her open mouth a smaller face again, that of Tony Farren, eyes like stones, mouth agape threatening to split his face in two. Within his open mouth there was movement, coiling smoke-like figures.

Then faces appeared again and again, writhing in a lunar dance as the moonlight flowed down the mirror. When the glass was completely bathed in silver light, turning its surface brilliant and opaque, the shadow faces vanished and were replaced by the Image. Pressing itself against the glass, it peered out into the night, eyes and mouth wide with hunger.

Soon.

Soon.

Soon.

33

J ONATHAN FRAZER came suddenly, startlingly awake, arms flailing, surfacing from a dream in which he had been drowning, unable to breathe. In his semi-conscious state he realized that he still couldn't breathe. There was pressure on his throat.

When he opened his eyes he looked into the implacable scarred face of a white-haired madman.

"I can kill you." The eyes—black as coal, glittering like polished stones, with only the barest thread of white visible—bored into him. "Remember that," the big man hissed, "I can kill you. And I will—without a second thought." Abruptly the pressure was gone from Frazer's throat and he slipped from the chair to the floor, gasping, hacking for breath.

"Silence!" the man snapped. He walked away from Frazer and went to stand by the bed, looking down at the sleeping Emmanuelle. A muscle twitched at the corner of his eye, and when he turned back to Frazer there was something approaching pity in his eyes. "It is always the innocent who suffer," he muttered.

"Who . . . who are you?" Frazer croaked, massaging his injured throat. The man was even bigger than he remembered, taller, broader, and the scars that crisscrossed his face were even more pronounced. "What do you want?" he asked.

"The mirror," the scarred man said shortly. He bent to look at the sleeping Celia Frazer and nodded slightly. When he glanced up a smile had twisted the corners of his lips, thinning them to lines. "If you'd given it to me when I'd first asked for it, your young woman would still be alive, another man would not have lost his life and this tragedy would not have happened." He turned to look at Manny again.

"But she's going to be alright!" Frazer said quickly, briefly forgetting his fear of the big man as he came to his daughter's bedside.

"No." He shook his head sadly looking down. "At first she will seem to be fine. She will act as she normally acted, but then, if you watch closely, you will notice changes."

The two men faced one another across the hospital bed. "What sort of changes?"

"I don't know. It affects different people differently. It brings out something in their characters."

"What does?"

"The mirror," the big man whispered and walked away from the bed. He stopped with his hand on the handle of the door. "You should have given it to me when you had the chance, Jonathan Frazer. Now it is too late."

"Who are you?" Frazer asked again, his words abruptly slurred, his tongue thick in his head.

"We'll talk next time," the big man said, opening the door and walking out of the room.

"Wait!" Frazer raced to the door and jerked it open.

The two police officers surged to their feet.

"Can we help you sir?"

"That man. The one who just came out . . ." He glanced up and down the corridor, but it was deserted. "Where did he go? Why didn't you stop him?"

The two men looked at one another. "No one came out of the room, Mr. Frazer."

"No! He came out a moment ago. The man, the big man, with the scarred face, white hair . . ." He looked at them both, seeing the disbelief in their eyes replaced by anger.

"No one went into your room and no one came out."

He touched his throat. "He grabbed me here, there must be some marks . . ." He tilted his head back for inspection.

One of the men dutifully looked at Jonathan Frazer's throat. "There's no mark on your throat, sir."

"Perhaps you were dreaming," another suggested, not unkindly.

Frazer looked from man to man, suddenly feeling chilled. There *had* been someone in the room with him, he had felt the man's fingers around his throat, smelt the strange spicy muskiness that clung to him, seen his scarred and torn flesh. There had been someone there. "No marks," he muttered, touching his throat again.

"No sir."

He turned away, aware of the police officers' eyes on his back. "Maybe it was a dream," he whispered.

"A nightmare," one of the officers agreed.

34

EDMUND TALBOTT lay naked on the thin mattress in his room, his hands by his side, breathing easily. To the casual observer he was sleeping peacefully, though if that same observer had looked closer, they would have seen that the man's broad chest was barely moving and that behind his slitted eyelids his eyes were moving frantically. Although the room was hot, muggy with the stale smells from the outside street, his flesh was cold to the touch, bathed in an icy perspiration.

Edmund Talbott suddenly opened his eyes and began to breathe again, great gasping breaths, filling his lungs with the warm air. He started to shiver and when he swung his legs out of the bed he had to wait while the room stopped its crazy spinning. Reaching for the towel that was draped into the sink, he rubbed it briskly across his body, drying himself.

He had only mastered the skill of astral projection with the greatest of difficulties. Although the ability to shift the spirit out of one's physical body was inherent in most people, and occurred naturally while the body slept, controlling the spirit, directing it to a specific location, required great skill and concentration. Now Edmund Talbott used it to track those associated with the mirror, but never the mirror itself. Perhaps the astral body was the soul—he didn't know, he wasn't qualified to even think about it—but he wasn't going to risk it by going anywhere near the glass.

Visiting Jonathan Frazer had been dangerous, making contact with him, actually impinging on the sleeping man's consciousness, had been an even greater risk. The man's association with the mirror, his prolonged exposure to it, and especially Emmanuelle's contact with it at the time of a violent death—when it had been feeding—meant that they had been tainted. He wasn't sure how far the mirror's influence extended. He used to think one had to be very close for it to have any effect, but now ... now he didn't know the extent of its power or influence. He was aware though that it was gathering its forces, flexing its muscles.

He had been shocked when he had first entered the perpetually gray, usually formless astral world. Snaking lines of power, tainted with electric colors, principally reds and deep purples, were clearly visible flowing across the landscape. Fully conscious of the danger, he had followed the twisting, coiling lines across the astral equivalent of Los Angeles, until he had seen the swirling gray whirlpool that marked the presence of the mirror in the physical world.

The customary silence of that desolate landscape had been breached too: a thin high keening emanated from the midst of the whirlpool. In the gritty dusk, he had been able to make out figures trapped in the maelstrom, faces, shapes, the newest souls closest to the surface, the souls it had taken previously now lost deep in its twisting core.

And he knew then that the haunted mirror had awoken from its century old slumber.

To survive, to remain sentient, it needed souls and blood. The killings had only just begun.

35

IT WAS close to midnight before Margaret Haaren reached home. She was exhausted, the adrenaline rush of the attack on her men and the emotionally draining process of informing wives and families, the mentally demanding procedure of gathering and preparing reports while the events were still fresh, had all conspired to completely sap her vitality.

And tomorrow promised more of the same.

Her tiny apartment was stale and dry, close after the heat of the day. Without bothering to turn on the light, she draped her jacket over the back of the chair and kicked off her shoes. She padded through the front room and into the kitchen. In the darkness, the answering machine light blinked red. She thumbed the play button as she reached for a glass and the bottle of scotch.

"Hi, Aunt Margaret, it's Helen. Just to let you know that my plane gets in at twelve-thirty tomorrow. There's no need to meet me, I'll get a cab. Can't wait to see you. Happy early Thanksgiving!"

Margaret Haaren closed her eyes in dismay. She had completely forgotten that her niece was due in this week for a few days vacation over the long Thanksgiving weekend. She had started coming eight years ago, when she was ten, and over the years it had become something of a ritual. Thankfully, as she had grown older, they had already covered most of the tourist sights: Disneyland, Universal City, Six Flags, Walk of Fame, and now at the age of eighteen her passion was shopping for clothes especially on Rodeo Drive. To be truthful, Margaret Haaren enjoyed the company . . . well, most of the time anyway. However, at least this year the girl was eighteen, so she shouldn't be too much of a burden. Anyway, she could explain that she was under pressure at work. Helen would understand; her father was a detective, too. The tradition of police work was strong in her family: her father and his brother, and her two older brothers had all entered the force. When she'd left school, there really hadn't been anything else she'd even thought about doing.

There were days—like this one—when she wished she'd done something else.

She was forty-eight years old, unmarried, unattached, unpursued by male companions, and likely to remain so at this stage. She had the disadvantage of being a successful professional woman and a police officer. A lethal combination in any man's eyes and, while there were many relationships made within the force with like-minded souls who understood the pressures and were aware of the difficulties of police work, the fact that she was a senior female detective precluded that.

She took a large swig of scotch, appreciating its smoky, earthy flavor and then debated whether she'd have a bath or take a shower. The shower won out simply because it was easier to stand under the water and let it do all the work.

She walked back out of the kitchen, through the front room, into the hall and turned into the bedroom. She could have afforded to rent a bigger, better apartment, but what was the point, she reasoned. Even if she bought herself a house, she'd never use it—and an empty house was simply an open invitation for burglars. Once it became known that she was a police officer and out all day, she could almost guarantee that it would be turned over with monotonous regularity. In the condominium complex she allowed people to think she was a simple filing clerk in the local sheriff's department and because she was a woman, they believed it. It also meant that they didn't make a point of being nice to her, thinking that one day they might need her or that she might be able to do them a favor, like fixing a speeding ticket.

Without turning the light on, Margaret Haaren stood before the half-closed vertical blinds and stared out onto the noisy side street. Police sirens wailed in the distance and she wondered if she knew any of the officers on duty. West Hollywood had seen a surge in violent crimes in the last year and Haaren was certainly privy to all the locations within her area where they'd taken place. Even in the quiet safety of her apartment she never felt she was off-duty.

Finally, closing the blinds, she undressed and padded naked into the bathroom. She climbed straight into the shower, turned the water on as hot as she could bear and then simply allowed it to flow across her shoulders and down her back. She consciously refused to even think about the day's events, they would still be there in the morning, the same questions looking for answers.

She stood there for about five minutes until the water abruptly turned icy cold, sending her leaping from the shower with a muted scream. That was always happening! If someone upstairs turned on their hot tap, it "stole" the hot water from her! Dancing on the bathroom linoleum floor—why didn't she get tile—she toweled herself dry standing before the square mirror above the sink. Maybe it was time to have something done about the hair, she decided, it was looking a little on the butch side, and a little color in it wouldn't go amiss, there were far too many gray hairs there for comfort. Tucking the towel in around her heavy breasts she stepped closer to the vanity mirror and began to apply cold cream to her face. She knew her nickname in the force was Mata Hari—it came from Margaret Haaren, and because Haaren was Dutch. Her parents had met close to the end of the Second World War, her father had been in the Dutch resistance, her mother had been his American contact; they had spoken together via radio for three years before they actually met. Margaret Haaren wasn't sure if she approved of the nickname or not: Mata Hari although reputedly beautiful, had apparently been quite plain. And of course had been shot as a spy!

She blinked: her image in the glass was becoming fogged. She ran her hand down the moist glass . . .

The mirror image appeared for a second: a woman's face, pretty, with strong rounded cheekbones, full lips over yellowish teeth, black, impenetrable eyes and thick black hair.

Frowning, Haaren reached for the mirror. And it suddenly split right down the center. Jagged splinters of glass tore into the soft flesh of the palm of her hand. The larger pieces shattered into the sink, tiny flecks stinging the bare skin of her arms and legs.

The detective staggered back, shaking with fright and reaction, cradling her torn palm. The remaining pieces of glass in the mirror were smeared in her blood, and there were bright red droplets on the sink and floor. Already her conscious mind was beginning to rationalize the event—she had pressed too hard on the glass . . . the heat of her hand against the cold glass . . .

And the face, the woman's face?

Imagination or even the scotch perhaps.

Just that. Nothing more.

IN A HOSPITAL bed two miles away, Emmanuelle Frazer twisted and turned in a nightmare in which she was trapped in a block of ice. No matter how she hammered or shouted or screamed, she couldn't get out, couldn't attract attention of the people looking in.

36

D AWN WAS breaking when Jonathan Frazer returned to the house in the Hollywood Hills. The street was quiet and completely deserted; this was one of those rare mornings with no trash services and no gardeners.

Although Detective Haaren had told him that she was assigning officers to keep an eye on the house, it was still a shock to find an unmarked police car parked in the street opposite the house. The doors opened and two men moved out of the car when they saw the Volvo slowing to approach the gates. One of them must have recognized him, or the registration of the car, and they returned to their car with a wave. From the corner of his eye, he saw one of the men talking into a radio, obviously noting the time of his arrival.

He parked the car neatly in front of the garage and then sat for a few moments, listening to the engine tick quietly. He had come back to the house to pick up a few things for Manny. He also badly needed a shower to clear the sterile hospital odor from his clothes and body.

Frazer stepped out of the car, breathing in great clean lungfuls of air. There was a definite feel of autumn in the chill morning air and the grass was dew-damp. His footsteps sounded extraordinarily loud as he crunched across the driveway. He walked around the side of the house toward the rear garden. It felt colder here and tendrils of white mist coiled across the grass, wrapping and twisting around his ankles. The sprinkler system was on a timer and came on just after sunset and just before dawn, damping down the garden in anticipation of a fine day. They had obviously just switched off. The air smelt sweet and earthy and water droplets glistened everywhere, dripping off the overhanging branches and leaves.

He walked down the pathway to the guesthouse, his breath pluming before his face, digging his hands deeper into his pockets, suddenly conscious of the chill that clung to the garden, but unable to distinguish if it was simply a natural phenomenon of the pre-dawn chill or . . . or something else . . .

He stopped in the middle of the path, abruptly realizing that he had accepted—*had actually accepted*—that something very strange, that something very different, that something very frightening was happening here.

And it was all somehow connected to the mirror.

People had died around that seven foot tall piece of glass. He was forty-five years old and he had never seen a dead body before. In the past week he had seen three.

The crime scene tape had been removed and the padlock on the door was cold, slick with the morning's dew. The lock was stiff and his fingers were so cold that it took him several moments before he finally got the plywood door open.

When he stepped into the guesthouse, he was immediately aware of the smell, a strange, almost sickly sweet odor that was tainted with burnt fabric and human flesh, and another stink, something sweet, something rotten. After the chill of the garden, it was warm and close in the large room and he pulled off his jacket and draped it over his arm. He stood for a few moments, absorbing the atmosphere of the place, almost frightened by the change that had come over it.

This had always been his favorite place. It was his sanctuary. Whenever he had wanted to escape from Celia's insistent nagging, or simply to be alone with his thoughts he would retire to the guesthouse and walk along its narrow aisles, looking, touching, handling the objects of the past and absorbing the peace and tranquility of the room.

Now the warmth, the comfort he had taken from the room was gone: it had been replaced by an atmosphere of menace, of death.

He breathed deeply, gagging slightly on the tainted air and walked directly towards the mirror. He could see his reflection in the glass, not distinctly and in detail, but far clearer than he had seen it before. He thought that the glass seemed brighter, and certainly some of the distortion and bubbling effects had vanished. However, as he drew nearer, he could see that a layer of grime still clung to the mirror.

Frazer walked right up to the edge of the mirror, putting his face close to the surface and attempted to stare *into* the glass. Only his own frightened, hollow-eyed face stared back at him, ghostly pale, deeply shadowed in the dirty glass.

"What are you?" he whispered.

The silence mocked him.

"What are you?"

Jonathan Frazer backed away from the glass and sat down in the chaise longue he had set up before the mirror, draping the jacket over his legs, wrapping his arms across his chest.

High above him, still perfectly visible in the paling morning sky, the full moon shone down through the grimy skylights to illuminate the mirror.

37

THE WOMAN stood naked in the small wooden tub while two women
moved around her body, rubbing the soft flesh with pumice stones,
massaging scented oils and unguents into her skin. Her rich dark hair had
been bathed in dew skimmed from the grass in the last moments before
the dawn. She had been told it was of the purest quality and certainly her
hair now glistened like burnished metal. The slightly abrasive touch of the
pumice had brought the blood flushing to her skin, giving it a rich glow,
and expensive and exotic oils had soothed the slight irritation that was an
unfortunate by-product of the volcanic stone.

There was a chill draught as the door opened and the tall, red-haired,
red-bearded, green-eyed man stepped into the room. He shook snow from
the shoulders of his cloak, brushed it from his beard and strode to the
fire to kick off his boots. He looked at the woman dispassionately. "Are
you near ready?" he demanded.

She turned in the tub to face him, spreading her arms wide, a smile
twisting her full lips. "Do I not look ready?"

"Clothes?" he grunted.

"I wasn't going to wear any," she leered.

"Then you'll catch your death. It's freezing. There were folk walking
on the Thames earlier today. The queen complained that she was so cold
that they actually began to burn some of the old wooden furniture, and
that was fine until they began chopping up an oak chest that had once belonged to Henry, and you know how fond she was of her father."

The woman laughed dutifully. This was as close as the dour Kelley ever
came to humor. "You have found someone else, someone suitable?" she

continued, ignoring the two women servants, both of whom had been deafened by having their eardrums punctured.

The man known as Kelley suddenly looked evasive. "Yes . . . no . . . possibly."

She knew better than to mock him, but she found this sudden indecisiveness a little frightening.

"Get dressed," he commanded. "We can talk then."

"We can talk now; my nakedness doesn't bother me."

Kelley strode over to her and gripped her small face in his large hands, squeezing along the line of her jaw and cheekbone. "You may think what you wish of me, but I am still a man, and I would be less than a man if I were not aroused by the sight of your nakedness, so cover yourself, you wanton. We have much to discuss." He turned away, to stand before the fire.

The woman swallowed hard and stepped out of the tub. The two women, who had retreated before Kelley's approach, returned with towels.

"How is your master?" she asked, exacting a little revenge for his treatment of her by reminding him that he was little more than an employee.

"The good doctor is well. He had prepared yet another horoscope for the queen, which delights her no end, and he has promised her further delights when he has mastered the art of crystallomancy."

"You told him!" she accused.

"I had to give him something," he said defensively. "It was a hint, nothing more. I spoke to him about scrying."

"But it is a gamble," she said, climbing onto the high-soled wooden shoes, while the two maids fixed the ornate ruff around her neck.

"He has some art, you know that, but no talent. He has some mathematical and alchemical knowledge and he has the contacts at court, not only with the queen, but also with Sir William Cecil and Sir Francis Walsingham. Now, we can never oust him from that position—he is too close to the queen—but if we can control him, it places us in an extraordinarily powerful position. We will have power without the danger."

"What would you have me do?"

"Dismiss the women," Kelley commanded.

"They are deaf."

"But not fools. Dismiss the women."

The woman turned, and waved her hand to attract the attention of the two servants who were busying themselves around the tub, mopping up the water splashed onto the wooden floor. When they looked up, she pointed to the door.

One—the older of the two—indicated the tub and raised her eyebrows in a question. The dark-haired woman shook her head and pointed to the door again, her face tightening into a frown. Both women scurried from the room.

When they were alone, Kelley turned to the woman and grabbed her forearms, pulling her close. "How badly do you covet immortality?"

"To live forever?" she asked dreamily.

"In saecula saeculorum. For ever and ever," he promised.

"I will do anything. You know that."

"Even marriage?" he asked.

"In light of what I have already done, marriage would be the least of my crimes," she smiled.

"And to conceive a child?"

She looked into his mad, bright green eyes and frowned.

"And to conceive a child?" he repeated.

"If it was necessary," she said cautiously.

"And to give that child, unbaptized, to me."

"Why?" she whispered.

"To allow me to fulfill my promise to you: to grant you immortality, to enable you to live for ever and ever . . ."

"But surely we could buy a child on the street?"

"It would not have those especial gifts from its parents. It would lack your own power, your consummate skill, your devotion to the carnal senses."

"And the father? What of his skills?" She almost expected him to nominate himself as the child's father. Though they had never slept together, and at times she thought him a catamite or a eunuch, she knew he was prepared to do almost anything in the pursuance of his art.

"The father is a mathematician and an astronomer of some note. He possesses a little knowledge of natural magic and the arcane arts and much of alchemy."

Realization flooded through her, and she suddenly laughed, almost with relief. She had thought he was going to suggest union with a demon.

"That's right," Edward Kelley smiled. "I want you to wed John Dee, our noble Queen Elizabeth's Astrologer Royal."

38

J ONATHAN FRAZER's eyes snapped open and he came to his feet with a
shout, his jacket dropping to the floor. He stood swaying before the
mirror, his heart tripping in his chest.

The dream had been so vivid, so clear . . . and he abruptly remembered
his previous dream. That too had been clear, vivid, alive. And he had experienced that whilst sleeping before the mirror.

And the nameless woman and the man Edward Kelley had been in both.

With a growing sense of elation, he realized he was close to something.
He had clues now, clues he could pursue. He had another name: John Dee,
Queen Elizabeth's Astrologer Royal. To solve the mystery of the mirror
he would have to trace those references back to their source.

And soon.

Before the mirror exerted its baleful influence on anyone else.

39

JONATHAN FRAZER met Detective Haaren at the hospital. He would have avoided her if he could; he knew she held him responsible—indeed, he held himself responsible—for the injuries to the two officers, and he knew that she suspected his involvement with their attacker ran far deeper.

"Mr. Frazer, may I talk to you privately?" Catching his arm by the elbow, holding it in a vise-like grip, she directed him down the long corridor away from his daughter's room. She led him into an empty private room and pushed the door closed behind them. Then she turned to face him.

"I just received a report from forensics. It seems the watch they found was a fake gold Rolex with the name 'Robert Maurice Beaumont' engraved on the back."

Frazer stood frozen in horror. "Robert? That was his body?"

"May I ask what he was doing in your guesthouse Mr. Frazer?"

"I have no idea, I swear." Frazer's shock turned to anger. "I was with you, remember."

"We know he went to your house, Mr. Frazer. We can only assume that he heard us talking in your office that day and decided to get out before you confronted him. We think he went down to the guesthouse to steal something."

Jonathan nodded. Beaumont had taken him for a fool. And had paid the price. But no one deserved to die like that. "I keep wondering how much Manny witnessed," he whispered. "Did she see him burn to death?"

"I don't think so," Margaret lied. She had no idea what his daughter had witnessed. "How is she doing, Mr. Frazer?"

"The doctors have kept her sedated. We haven't really had a chance to talk to her."

Margaret Haaren nodded.

"And your men, Detective?" he inquired. "How are they?"

She shrugged. She had just been in to see both men and while José seemed to be improving, the younger officer in ICU was now in a coma.

"Detective Pérez will pull through, but the other officer . . ." She let the sentence trail, and then stopped, her hand on Frazer's arm. "Are you sure there is nothing you can tell us about the man who did this?"

"I've told you before. I don't know the man. I never met him before . . . and even if I did know him, don't you think I'd tell you? I've seen what he's done and I'm scared to think what'll he do to me and my family if he doesn't get what he wants."

"And that's the mirror," she stated flatly.

"That's what he said he wanted. But you don't believe me."

"I do," she said, surprising him.

"But you don't even believe I bought the mirror in London."

"Actually, I do. I believe the scarred man may have intimidated the auctioneers in London to say that they had never dealt with you and possibly bribed the couriers to say the same."

"Thank you," he breathed. "That you for that. For a moment, I thought I was going mad."

"Mr. Frazer," Haaren said seriously, "I want your assurance that you'll contact me if you see or hear from this man again."

"You have my word," he lied.

Margaret Haaren looked into his eyes, knowing he was lying to her, desperately wondering what he was trying to hide. "Give my regards to your daughter, Mr. Frazer."

"I will. Thank you, Detective . . . and . . . I am sorry, truly sorry, about what happened to your officers."

"There was nothing you could do, was there?" she said, almost in an aside. In her experience people usually apologized when they had something to hide.

"I suppose I feel responsible because it happened on my property."

"Well, I'm sure you are already aware I've placed a twenty-four-hour surveillance on your house, Mr. Frazer," she said. "That should give you some measure of security." What she didn't tell him was that as well as the unmarked police car parked in front of the house, there was another very discrete watch being kept on the house from across the road, where the owner—a retired FBI agent—was a personal friend of the Chief of Police and who had been only too delighted to do his friend a favor.

Jonathan Frazer watched the woman stride down the corridor, her gait long, quick, and decisive, almost like a man's. But there was something else about it—and then he realized that she was moving in complete silence. She was wearing rubber-soled shoes that made no sound on the linoleum floor.

A squeaking sound made him turn and he saw Manny in a wheelchair pushed by a nurse. Celia walked by their side. "Dad, they think I'm a child. I can walk to the car by myself."

"Hospital regulations," the nurse said primly, "we have to see you off the premises safely."

Jonathan stared into his daughter's large blue eyes. "Are you sure you're fit enough to come home? I really would prefer if you would stay another day or so."

"I'm fine Dad, really I am. And I know if I stay here another hour, never mind another day, I'm going to go insane."

"Let's get you home and to bed," he said sternly.

"To bed," she agreed. "I'm looking forward to sleeping in a comfortable bed," she added, glancing up the nurse, who ignored the jibe.

THEY DROVE HOME in virtual silence. Manny dozed in the back of the car and Celia—for some reason unknown to Jonathan—was giving him the cold shoulder. He had more than enough on his mind at the moment and ignored her, and this only served to infuriate her even further. When they drove past the unmarked police car before turning into the driveway, her reserve finally collapsed.

"This is stupid!" she snapped. "What do they think this is—a police state? I'm going to call the sheriff's department and talk to the chief straight away."

"I'll bet you don't even know who the chief is, do you?" Jonathan teased her. "And anyway, the police are there for our own protection. In case that maniac comes back."

"But what must the neighbors be thinking?" She glanced out at the houses, clearly visualizing the neighbors gossiping over the sudden police activity around the Frazers'. "We'll never get a dinner invitation again."

"To be honest, I don't give a flying fuck what people are thinking!"

The obscenity stopped her cold. Jonathan rarely swore; he prided himself that he didn't need to resort to foul language. "Three dead bodies have been taken from this house," he said coldly, glancing in the mirror, checking that Manny was still asleep. "Two men have been very seriously injured, one may not make it, a police dog has been butchered and I've been attacked. Oh, and our daughter almost lost her life." He had been speaking slowly and clearly, but it suddenly rose to a shout. "So don't give me any fucking shit about the neighbors!"

"Jon . . . Jonathan . . . you're tired, you're overwrought . . ."

"And don't fucking patronize me," he snapped, standing hard on the brake, bringing the car to a stop in a shower of pebbles, gouging long straight lines in the gravel. He swiveled in the seat to face her, his face pale, sheened with sweat, eyes sunk into his head. "I'm tired, very tired. Unlike you I didn't sleep very well last night, nor did I sleep the night before. I've got things on my mind, it's been hell for me the last few days." He took a deep breath and visibly controlled himself. "Leaving aside everything else, let me put this in a context which you may be able to understand: Tony Farren, Diane Williams, and Robert Beaumont are dead, I'll repeat myself: dead! Dead on our property. I'm going to have to close down the store, I have no one to do the repairs and now I have no sales assistant. No store means no money. It's as simple as that. And need I add that we've a lot of money tied up in stock in the store, and even more tied up in the guesthouse. And what you have failed to realize, is that I do not have bottomless pockets . . ."

Celia bit her lips and turned to look out the window.

"So you see, dear, I do have one or two things on my mind at the moment."

"Mom . . . Dad . . ." Manny Frazer came groggily awake. "What's wrong?"

"Nothing's wrong dear, we're home. And you, young woman . . ."

"I know," she smiled, "straight to bed. You'll get no argument from me. I really need to get some sleep."

"You slept in the hospital," Celia said.

"It wasn't good sleep," Manny said quietly.

"Why not?" Jonathan asked.

"Filled with nightmares."

40

IT WAS great to be home. Manny walked around her room, drawing strength from its peaceful familiarity. Jesus, but that hospital—even though she'd been in a private room and all that—it had been grim. And the bed; that bed was unbelievable. And she couldn't get the idea out of her head that other people had slept in that bed, that they had died in that bed. That had been her one abiding thought in the hospital during her lucid hours. She'd been troubled by extraordinary nightmares in which she actually heard the voices of those who had passed away in that room, crying out to her, calling her name, begging her to help them, to ease their suffering, to help, to help them, to *helptohelptohelptohelptohelphelphelphelp* . . .

She could rationalize it away; she was tired, distressed, filled with sedatives and she'd just seen her first dead body, or what was left of it. Robert had been her friend, her lover. It was only natural she'd think of death, especially now, in a hospital, but the dreams had been frightening.

She needed a shower and bed and in that order. Stepping into the large en suite bathroom, she undressed quickly and dumped her clothes into the tall wicker basket. They stank of the hospital, and she imagined she could smell the same sharp odor of chemicals and disinfectant from her own skin. Stepping into the shower, she turned it up as hot as she could bear and allowed the water to run off her shaven head and down onto her body. Rotating her head, she could feel the knotted muscles in the shoulders and at the back of her neck finally relaxing. She scrubbed at herself with a harsh sponge, bringing the blood flushing to her skin . . .

. . . *the rasp of pumice stone against her skin, across her sensitive breasts* . . .

. . . and then rubbed in supposedly odorless shower gel, but the air was abruptly flooded with the sickly sweet scent of a heavy perfume.

Manny stopped, head tilted back, smelling the moist air. What was that smell? Like dead flowers or beeswax.

A cold wind suddenly wafted across her moist body, as if a door had been opened, and she shivered. She peered through the frosted glass door of the shower, trying to see if she'd left the bedroom door open, but she could see nothing. She blinked moisture from her eyes and rubbed at the glass door . . .

. . . *a tall, red-haired, red-bearded man, cruel faced, green eyed, in a heavy snow-capped cloak* . . .

The scream caught in her throat, and she floundered backwards against the icy tiles, hands automatically covering her breasts and groin. The figure seemed to be looking directly at her through the glass, his mouth opening and closing as if he spoke. Water splashed into her eyes and she blinked rapidly. When she could see clearly again, he had gone.

Manny flung open the door and stared wide-eyed out into the empty bathroom. The door leading into the bedroom was still locked, the bolt thrown across from the inside.

Hallucinations . . . the residue of drugs in her system.

Shivering almost uncontrollably now, she staggered from the shower and wrapped herself in a thick chenille bathrobe, rubbing at her head with a towel, hearing the lengthening hair rasp against the cloth. She opened the door and stared out into the bedroom, feeling like a child checking for the bogyman beneath the bed. Three quick strides and she jumped in, and scrambled beneath the covers, only tossing away the dressing gown when she was safely tucked in. She snuggled down beneath the duvet, luxuriating in the feel of the fabric against her naked skin. She was tired . . . over-tired. That was all. A good night's sleep was what she . . .

MANNY AWOKE ONCE during the night, and that was close to two in the morning. Moonlight streamed in through the window, the harsh light turning her skin alabaster. Eyes blinked open, and they were featureless silver discs, then she turned over and closed her eyes against the glare.

And her dreams were terrifying.

41

JONATHAN FRAZER settled back against the chaise longue, folded his arms across his chest and stared at the mirror. This time he knew what he was doing. This time he was conducting an experiment.

Twice before he had experienced something in front of this mirror, he had dreamt dreams, seen images, learned *something*—clues perhaps—to the mirror's past. This time he had come prepared.

He had positioned a camcorder on a tripod directly behind the chaise longue facing the mirror, and he had set it to shoot one frame every five minutes. A digital voice recorder was on the floor beside the mirror. It was voice activated and would start recording as soon as it heard sounds. His Canon digital camera lay on the chair beside him.

Tonight he would have some answers. And proof. Tonight, he would have proof.

But proof of what . . . ?

42

S HE IS magnificent," the tall gray-haired, gray-eyed man agreed, turning to look at the woman.

"And she desires you, lord," Edward Kelley said eagerly in a thick brogue. Gone was his previous air of authority and learning; now he was nothing more than an Irish servant, fawning, ignorant, and ill-educated.

They were sitting in a smoky tavern on a side street just off London Bridge—the bridge that was much frequented by alchemists and others who dabbled in science and the occult. It was often used as a meeting place by those wishing to join a Circle or by a master looking for a servant with arcane knowledge. Doctor John Dee had met Edward Kelley here, four years previously, in 1569. Dee's previous assistant, Barnabas Saul, had turned out to be nothing more than a charlatan, foisted on Dee by his enemies, jealous of his privileged position with the Queen. Saul had promised much and delivered nothing, and come close to destroying the doctor's reputation in the process.

Dee considered himself fortunate indeed in stumbling upon Kelley, an itinerant Irishman fleeing the grinding poverty in his homeland with nothing to his name except some skill as a medium. The Irishman had been hoping to find his fortune in the big city, but had found a similar poverty in London. But London—inhabited by some of the brightest and most dangerous men of the age—had something which Ireland had not: opportunity. Kelley's natural talent as a medium and scryer, enhanced by some less scrupulous additions, soon attracted the attention of several of the city's wealthiest men and women. Within six months of arriving in the city, he had become Doctor John Dee's assistant, and very quickly an integral part of Dee's life and work. The man's knowledge of the occult was extraordinary, far surpassing Dee's, although curiously, this knowledge was only in evidence when Kelley was in a trance, under the influence of his spirits.

"Tell me about her," Dee said, glancing sidelong at the woman again. It was not unusual to find beautiful women in this tavern, though women of such beauty and presence were certainly rare indeed.

"She is a natural talent, neither witch nor sorceress, a practitioner of some natural magic. Look at her, lord; tell me her age," Kelley urged him.

Dee looked at the woman again, and then shook his head. "Hair is without silver or gray, skin smooth and unpoxed, a full set of teeth. One-and-twenty, two-and-twenty?"

"She was born in 1491, the same year Henry VIII, the queen's father, was born."

Dee looked at the woman in astonishment. Why, that would make her eighty-two! He turned to look at Kelley, his thin eyebrows raised in a silent question. The red-haired man nodded. "Kept young by her magic. Ever young. Perhaps immortal."

"And she wants to speak to me?" Dee sounded almost surprised.

Edward Kelley lowered his eyes. "You have a reputation, master. That has drawn her to you."

"I'll speak to her, of course," Doctor John Dee said decisively.

"But not here, master. Too many eyes, too many ears."

Dee nodded. He trod a particularly dangerous path; he was a known occultist close to the queen, he had prepared the horoscope that had shown that the young princess, Elizabeth, would indeed be queen and had then prepared the horoscope which decided upon the most auspicious day for the coronation. Although his travels in Europe had discovered much that had been of military or economic use to the queen's advisors, he had also made many enemies, and the church especially despised him, labeling him a practitioner of black magic and a heretic. He was in little danger while the queen still lived, but should anything happen to her, then his position could turn quickly perilous. And there were always those eager to report his every movement to Elizabeth's enemies, looking for signs of weakness, trying to blacken his name.

John Dee made his way through the crowded room and stepped out into the street, pulling his cloak up around his shoulders. The night was bitterly cold, the frigid air tainted with the stench of the streets and the pungent effluence from the river. He lived in Mortlake, a village on the edge of London and so was particularly conscious of the difference in the air of the city and the country, but he knew that Londoners were rarely aware of the stench of their own city.

Kelley came out a few moments later, with the woman following close behind.

Sensitive to odors, Dee caught the scents of herbs and spices from her, expensive bath oils sweetening the foul night air. She had pulled up the hood of her heavy cloak and now the oval of her face stared at him from shadow, her eyes huge and dark against her pale face.

"I am Doctor John Dee," he said formally.

The woman curtsied before him, but did not extend her hand and did not proffer her own name. Dee glanced at his assistant, but Kelley shook his head slightly, warning him to say nothing.

"You have an interest in Natural Magic," she said suddenly. Surprisingly, her voice was uneducated, her accent placing her somewhere to the north of the Thames.

"I am used to dealing with people with names," Dee said shortly.

"Names are symbols with which we chain others; the knowledge of names grants power."

"That is a superstition and applies only to magical names. To know a person's magical name is to have power over that person."

"Untrue. A name—any name—conjures the image of that person. Knowledge of the name—any name, be it true or false, so long as it is used consistently to represent that person—grants power."

Dee bowed slightly, conceding the point. Her accent may be that of an uneducated woman, but her knowledge was evidence of learning and education, and that was a privilege of the wealthy.

"You have an interest in Natural Magic," she repeated.

John Dee smiled. "I have." He nodded to Kelley. "My assistant tells me you were born in 1491."

"It is true. On the first day of the autumn equinox of that year."

"And you have preserved your youth through this Natural Magic?" Dee asked, keeping his voice carefully neutral. As an alchemist, he had heard of the Philosopher's Stone, the magical formula which granted eternal life to the user.

The woman looked up suddenly. "We should not talk here. Follow me."

She turned and walked away, her wooden heels clicking loudly on the few pieces of paving that still remained this close to the river. Dee looked at Kelley and shrugged. The doctor touched the knife on his belt and he was relieved to find that Kelley was wearing his sword. This was a particularly unsavory part of London.

The woman led them down through the warren of side streets and alleys running parallel to the docks. Rats scurried across their path, huge creatures that could easily be confused with a cat or a dog. Dee was horrified to discover that even though it was after midnight on a bitterly cold winter's night, there were still women and children on the streets, begging and selling themselves for the price of a meal. If he could truly discover the Elixir of Life then surely he should be able to put it to some use to ease man's suffering?

He was becoming nervous now. They were in the heart of the docklands, a vicious, no man's land, where even the Watch rarely ventured. He clutched at Kelley's arm. "Where are we going?"

"She has some sort of base close by," he said carefully. "Her Natural Magic draws its power from the river."

Dee nodded, not completely satisfied with the answer. His every instinct warned him of danger, but his desire for knowledge, his thirst for information, was greater.

They stopped outside a rotting wharfside store and the woman produced a brightly shining key from the depths of her cloak. The key turned easily in the lock and she stepped into the darkness. After a moment's hesitation, Dee and Kelley followed her.

Flesh touched his, and Dee stifled a shout as he recognized the woman's hand on his, her soft fingers wrapping around his wrist pulling him forward. Kelley's heavy hand dropped onto his shoulder as they moved into the darkness. He wondered how she could see in the dark, and supposed that it might be a side effect of her Natural Magic; perhaps the senses grew more finely tuned as one aged, rather than degenerating as they did at present.

Or perhaps she was a demon leading him to hell.

They moved down into the bowels of the rotten building. The smell of decay, or ordure and corruption, was stronger now, and there was a ripe dampness in the air that caught at the back of his throat, eased its way into his lungs. Still in total darkness, the nameless woman led them across an echoing chamber, boots splashing through water that had been long stagnant by the smell it exuded.

And then there was light.

Dee didn't realize he was holding his breath until they reached the lighted chamber, and then he took a great sobbing breath that he turned into a cough.

The room was set up as an alchemical studio, a long table laden down with instruments occupying one wall, a broken chair beside a rough cot in the corner. There was a second, completely bare wooden table shoved up against another wall.

But the room was dominated by the mirror.

The woman walked into the center of the chamber and threw off her cloak, while Kelley took up a position at the door, arms folded across his chest. Dee walked up to the mirror, mesmerized by its size: he had never seen a glass so big.

"Do not stare into its depths," the woman advised.

Dee immediately whirled around. "Why not?"

Her lips moved in a smile. "It has certain . . . properties."

"Properties?"

"Properly activated it can be used as a scrying glass for example," she said, repeating the words Kelley had tutored her in earlier.

Dee turned to look at the glass again. Scrying—the ability to see the future in a glass—had always been one of his especial interests. "And how does one activate it?" he asked, running his long fingers along the smooth wooden frame. Yet again, he cursed his lack of any Talent or Ability. He glanced over at Kelley, wondering why he didn't approach the glass. Did he know something, did he see something with his second sight that disturbed him? "How does one activate the glass?" he repeated when the woman didn't answer him. He glanced over his shoulder—and stopped.

The woman was naked.

She looked at him, lifting her arms, running both hands through her thick black hair, exposing herself to him. "Blood will bring it to life," she said, "clean blood, with the proper incantation from the Key of Solomon. Semen too, will enliven it. Seed and blood, the building blocks of all life."

Dee turned from the woman and stared at the mirror again, watching it from the corner of his eyes, his agile mind evaluating these snippets of knowledge. He had heard of such glasses—though never on such a scale before—and they too had to be fed with the body's sacred fluids, blood, semen, or tears. But once fired they showed many, many wondrous things, the future, the past, Heaven, Hell.

"But we did not come here to discuss the glass," she continued, "we came here to discuss Natural Magic."

Dee dragged his gaze away from the mirror and turned back to the woman. She was now wearing a blood-red cloak over her nakedness, though the cloak hung open down the middle, and he found the tantalizing glimpse of flesh even more arousing than the sight of her fully nude.

"Natural Magic," the woman said, walking past the man to stand with her back to the mirror, hands on her hips. "We are all of us vessels of power, repositories of magical energy. But few realize that, and fewer still can tap the unlimited power of their own bodies."

Dee nodded slowly. His own theories ran very much along these lines.

"I have developed a system of Natural Magic that can access the un- limited power of the human body," she continued, her large dark eyes now locked on Dee's face. As she spoke, her right hand had moved off her rounded hip bone and slid into the dark patch between her legs. "This is the oldest magic in the world," the woman continued, her fingers mov- ing, probing, "sacred in some parts of the world, shunned in others. The druids knew of its power and the witches, their successors, knew a little also. The Egyptians knew the secret of this special magic, and we know the savages conduct their ceremonies naked."

Dee said nothing, mesmerized by the sight of the woman arousing her- self so brazenly. He was conscious of the odor of the woman's body in the room, aware of his own arousal.

"The power is only evident at moments of great emotion: pain, anger, desire, arousal, orgasm. These are the most potent of all the emotions . . ." Her fingers were moving swiftly now, delving deeply into her body, and her breath was beginning to come in great gasps.

And suddenly Dee was aware of the mirror behind her. Rainbow hues were flickering down its length, shimmering tints that hinted of pictures. He started forward, his gaze fixed on the glass.

Edward Kelley bent his head to hide his smile. They had Dee now. Much of what he had instructed the woman to tell Dee had been true, and the display on the glass was an almost natural phenomenon, triggered by the proximity of the woman and the intensity of her growing orgasm.

She had started to pant. "At the moment . . . of orgasm for example . . . the natural magic of the human . . . human body is available. All one needs to do . . . is to . . . to capture that magic, utilize it. I have used . . . the magic of my own . . . body to remain young. Properly employed there is no limit to its . . . POWER!" The last word was a scream as the woman collapsed into a writhing heap on the ground, her entire body shuddering in the throes of orgasm. But Dee's eyes were not on the woman; he was watching the undulating display of rippling colors on the glass. There were pictures in the glass, images, half seen, barely glimpsed. But they were there.

And what would he see if he were to properly apply the laws of Natural Magic to the glass, he wondered. What would he see if he fed the glass with blood and semen and tears?

MANNY FRAZER WRITHED on the bed, the duvet a tumbled ball on the floor. Her hands were busy at her groin, her breath coming in heaving gasps, her entire body covered in a sheen of sweat.

She dreamt she was standing before a huge glass mirror, masturbating before a gray-haired, gray-eyed old man . . .

43

T HIS ONE *was perfect.*

Such power, such passion. It fed off her sensations, savoring their intensity. It was one of the mysteries of the human body. Such a frail delicate shell, and yet it was capable of such response. It was a mystery that had never failed to intrigue, a paradox.

There had been others, women always.

The image of the naked woman was one of the most potent symbols of power it possessed in its armory. It had experimented with the men, but men were tools, to be used, useful to bring the offerings and to perform the petty mundane tasks necessary for keeping the gateway open and safe. Perhaps because it had once worn a female form, it felt happier in that guise, and in truth, it never trusted the male species since the betrayal.

But womankind.

Since time immemorial they had kept the secrets, fed the fires, given freely of themselves and their great passions to honor the mysteries.

And yet it could not dismiss the male.

There were always two, male and female, one was never enough: a male to feed the symbol and a female, made in its image.

Across the Otherworld, colors flickered and the seething column of power trembled with anticipation. In its core, the souls of those who had fed its hunger down through the countless centuries screamed their agony.

44

IMAGE.

   The mirror, the topmost left-hand edge touched with moonlight.

Image.

The mirror, the moonlight now further advanced down its length.

Image.

The moonlight now completely bathing the tall length of glass.

Image.

A solid rectangle of white light, flat and featureless.

Image.

A twisting strand of reddish-purple color about three quarters of the way down the length of the mirror.

Image.

Patches of oily color on the glass, irregular circles dotted around the mirror, clustered close to the top and middle, reds, purples, blues, and greens predominating.

Image.

A face.

Image.

A face.

Image.

The moonlight sliding off the glass, the topmost corner washed in darkness.

Image.

A blank slab of glass, revealing nothing except the night.

JONATHAN FRAZER CAREFULLY examined the photographs he had downloaded onto his computer. The pictures had been taken every five minutes, the ten frames representing the vital forty minutes when the activity had occurred on the glass. The digital voice recorder had been useless, he had one hundred and twenty minutes of hissing static, and—despite his best intentions—he had fallen asleep, so the Canon had been useless.

He had transferred the video data to his movie program, then fast-forwarded through the sequence, stopping and rewinding to watch moonlight run down the glass and off it again. He missed it the first time, and it was only on the second viewing when he slowed the machine to a frame by frame examination at the point when the moonlight began its inexorable slide down the glass, that he spotted the shifting swirls and circles of color on the glass.

And then the face in the glass.

Freezing and zooming, he stared at the grainy image of the face before him. It fascinated him. It was a fragment, nothing more, the shadowy outline of a nose, the twist of a mouth, indentations of eyes, a blur that might have been hair. He placed some glossy photo paper in the printer, pressed print, and waited for the eight by ten photograph to appear.

And it was familiar. But familiar in the way that any such photograph would have been, the features could have been almost anyone's. The video image, because of its fractionally better quality, was slightly sharper, but the image was no more distinct.

Finally, he pulled away from the computer screen, rubbing dry, sticky eyes. There was a dull pounding at the back of his head, and when he looked at the clock, he was surprised to find that it was close to one-thirty.

There was a yellow legal pad by his side, and he looked at the notes he'd made. They were little more than ideas and random thoughts gathered from the images he'd remembered from his dreams. And what if they weren't dreams; what if they were more?

John Dee.

He recognized the name: a magician or something in the court of Queen Elizabeth I. He'd been her spy in some of the continental courts.

Kelley.

He didn't know the name, though if he was associated with Dee he shouldn't be too hard to trace.

The woman.

Nameless, though he had a perfect image of her: long face, up-tilted black eyes, rounded cheekbones, yellowish teeth, full lips. And then there was her hair, thick and black, that was her distinctive feature, and he was a little embarrassed when he realized that he also knew that she had full, heavy breasts with small dark nipples and thick dark pubic hair.

The mirror.

That was just as important a player in this game. The mirror was the key . . . either the mirror or the woman. But in his own mind they were interchangeable.

45

THE BEVERLY Hills Public Library was quiet, afternoon sunlight streaming in through the high windows, catching the spinning dust motes. This portion of the library was virtually deserted, only two other people besides Frazer and the librarian in the enormous long rectangular room. The atmosphere was dry, the odor of leather and aged paper and the slightly sickly sweetness of preservative on the air. The librarian nodded to Frazer, who was a regular visitor to the library where he researched into the history and background of some of his more expensive artifacts. Although it would have been far easier to do research online, he preferred having solid paper references when he sold a piece.

Ignoring the computerized catalog, which he still found totally bewildering, he began to work his way down through the bookshelves, not sure what he was looking for, picking titles at random, checking the indices for references to Dee, and finding several, but nothing of any real use. There were some listings for Dee's own works, which he noted, but wasn't sure if there was any point in looking for them: they seemed to be mathematical or astronomical texts.

He was considering going back to the catalog when he rounded a bookcase and almost collided with an old man, white-haired and stooped with age. A heavy leather-bound book slid from his grip and clattered to the floor. "I am so sorry, excuse me." Frazer stooped and lifted the book, brushing his hand down the length of the spine, surreptitiously checking it to see if the ancient-looking binding was cracked.

Majister Johannes Dee.

The title stopped him cold. Ignoring the old man's outstretched hand, he opened the title page.

Majister Johannes Dee, Wim van den Berg, Antwerp, MDCX.

He quickly translated the Roman numerals into 1610. That meant it was written two years after Dee's death in 1608. There was a wood engraving of Dee facing the title page and Frazer felt his heart begin to pound. It was the man in his dream. The same long face, the same tall, thin man.

"How weird. I was just . . ." he began excited, and then he stopped, looking at the old man in horror. The bent back had straightened, the tired, slack, and wrinkled face seemed to become animated and when he had stretched to his full height, which was fully four inches over his own six feet, Frazer found himself staring up at the scarred face of the nameless man.

"The book is full of lies and half-truths," the scarred man said easily, smiling at Frazer's surprise. "In reality, Dee was far more interesting than many give him credit for. The occultist tag has somewhat tarnished his reputation."

"Who are you?" Frazer whispered, anger beginning to replace his fear.

The big man grabbed him by the arm and pulled him to one of the small tables. "Sit down, Mr. Frazer. I did say we would meet again," he said pleasantly.

"Who are you? How did you come to me in the hospital that night? What do you want the mirror for, what did you mean about it affecting my daughter?"

"So many questions." The big man smiled. "I suppose you are entitled to answers." His coal-black eyes stared into Frazer's face. "I would ask you not to go to the police with the information I am about to give you. But once I tell you what you want to know, I don't think you'll be going to the police, anyway." He placed a broad hand in the center of his chest. "I am Edmund Talbott, which might not mean very much to you. However, you might be interested to know that an ancestor of mine, called Edward Talbott, changed his named to Edward Kelley, also spelt Kelly, and was employed by Doctor John Dee. So you see, the mirror is an old friend of the family."

"What do you want?" Frazer asked quietly.

"The mirror. What I wanted from the beginning."

"Why?" Frazer was gazing at Talbott with fixed intensity.

"Because it is mine by right of inheritance if nothing else, and because only I can control it."

Frazer continued to stare at him, saying nothing, realizing that Talbott would tell him more if he wasn't pressed.

"Let me tell you what you saw, Mr. Frazer . . . was it last night, or the night before? You saw Doctor John Dee, and his assistant Kelley—though Kelley was more than just an assistant—and a woman, a mysterious dark-haired woman. Did you see Kelley and the woman feed the mirror with blood? If you didn't then you will at the time of the next full moon. That is when the mirror is at its strongest. Its power waxes and wanes with the moon, when the moon is full the images are at their clearest, then they fade as the days pass. Although I should add that once moonlight had touched the glass, it remains active even at the dark of the moon or when the moon is occluded."

"How did you know what I saw in the mirror?" Frazer asked in a whisper, glancing around. There was a young man at the end of the aisle, but he was absorbed in a book.

"Because I have seen them, too. It is one of the most powerful images in the mirror, it is always the first to surface. When I first looked into the mirror, that was the image I saw. The more often you look, the more sights you will see. Paris during the Terror, Florence during the Medici reign, Rome during the days of the Roman Circus. There are said to be other, stranger sights to be glimpsed in its surface, but I have never seen them."

"What is this mirror? Who is the woman?"

Talbott's smile was bleak. "The woman appears in most of the images. She changes in small and subtle ways, although she is usually nameless and long black hair is common to all images of her. I think perhaps she is an ordinary woman whom the mirror has taken over, absorbed, possessed, if you prefer. I don't know what the mirror is: but it is powerful. Men have died to possess it, men have died to protect it."

"And you, what is your interest in the mirror?"

"My family have—with some exceptions—protected the mirror down through the centuries. Edward Talbott-Kelley was one of those exceptions. He attempted to exploit the mirror's powers. And its powers are tremendous. Once it is fed with human emotions, with blood, sweat, tears, semen, then its powers are limitless. It can show wonders—or terrors."

Jonathan Frazer looked up suddenly, aware that the young man had moved closer and was staring openly at the two men, his head tucked unnaturally into his jacket. When he looked back there was a twisted smile on Talbott's lips.

"Company, I see." The big man stood up, his chair scraping on the industrial carpet. "We will speak again, Mr. Frazer." The young man was moving purposefully down the aisle, a walkie-talkie now clearly visible in his hand.

Edmund Talbott rested both his huge fists on the table and leaned across to stare into Frazer's wide eyes. "Beware the image, Mr. Frazer, it will steal your soul away!" He turned as the young officer grabbed at his right arm with his left hand. Talbott pivoted, his left hand coming up, fingers straight, locked and rigid. They caught the young man in the precise center of his chest, delivering a tremendous blow. He collapsed forward onto Frazer without a sound, driving them both backwards onto the floor.

By the time Jonathan Frazer climbed out from under the young man, Talbott was gone, and the young officer was dead.

46

PEOPLE DIE around you Mr. Frazer," Margaret Haaren said tiredly. She glanced up at the clock on the wall of her office. It was twenty to ten. "Let me tell you about the man who died today," she continued, when Frazer said nothing. "He was twenty-eight years old, married with a two-year-old little girl."

"He only hit him once," Frazer said wonderingly.

"That's all that was needed. A massive blow to the solar plexus can kill. In this case, it ruptured both sets of ribs, driving them into the lungs . . ."

"I tried to give him artificial respiration . . ." Frazer whispered, tears starting to leak from his eyes.

"I know that Mr. Frazer," the detective said, her voice softer. "And the officer's last radioed report said that you seemed to be held against your will," she added. What she didn't add was if the dead officer hadn't said that, she would have held Frazer as an accessory to murder. "And you have nothing to add to your statement?"

Jonathan Frazer shook his head. He had told the police that the man had demanded money, threatening to burn down his house and his store unless he received a hundred thousand dollars. He still wasn't sure why he'd told the lie—except perhaps that he didn't want Talbott captured just yet.

He wanted answers, and only Talbott could provide them.

Or the mirror.

Frazer abruptly realized he had stopped breathing.

The mirror could provide answers: if it was asked the correct questions.

The idea was so obvious.

So simple.

He looked up at Margaret Haaren. "If you're finished with me, Detective, I'd like to go home. I'm very tired."

"Go home, Mr. Frazer. Get some rest; tomorrow is apt to be a long day."

But Frazer was staring through the office window at the thin sliver of moon that was just visible behind rapidly moving clouds. Talbott said that the mirror would remain active even if the sky was clouded over.

"I don't need to tell you to stay in town, do I, Mr. Frazer?"

"I am going nowhere. Except home."

As he hurried down the police station steps, he found his desire to experience the mirror's images almost frightening in its intensity.

What was it Talbott had said: beware the image, it will steal your soul away! Looking up at the sliver of moon, he realized that he was glad he didn't believe in such things.

Well, maybe he hadn't. But now . . .

Now, he was beginning to believe.

47

JONATHAN FRAZER stood before the mirror, fascinated and fearful.

A couple of days ago he would have laughed at Talbott and then suggested he see a psychiatrist. But that had been before he'd seen vivid images of sixteenth century London, before he'd talked to a man who wasn't there, before three people he'd known had died before this mirror, one of them burnt to a crisp. Spontaneous combustion might be what they were calling it, but only a supernatural agency was capable of reducing a man to charred bone, and he didn't care what anyone else said.

He reached out tentatively, running his fingertip down the greasy glass, staring hard at his shadowy reflection in the mirror.

He had never been an overly religious man—he attended church at Christmas and Easter—but he didn't think he believed in a God or a Devil or Good and Evil. Myths and legends, culled together from a dozen other myths and legends. Nothing more. But over his years in the design business he had come across curious artifacts and relics which reputedly had the power to perform miracles. He had handled a Russian icon which visibly trembled with power and was almost too hot to hold, even on the coldest days. He had seen a blind Italian boy open his eyes and see for the first time when Padre Pio's bloody glove was placed on his forehead. He had attempted, but failed, to buy the glove. Some things were not for sale.

There was evidence aplenty of evil in the world, so was it quite so difficult to imagine that an object should become associated with darkness? There was the infamous Spear of Longinus, the blade that supposedly pierced Christ's side on the cross. It was notorious in the antiques trade, with "genuine" spears being offered for sale with surprising regularity. But lots of people believed in its power to do good or ill; even Hitler had made every effort to obtain the spear when his troops invaded Austria.

Jonathan recalled an ugly black-handled knife that Tony Farren had once bought amongst a job lot of Victorian cutlery. The handle had been crudely carved into the likeness of a man and woman copulating. The man was horned, tailed, and cloven-hooved. Within minutes of displaying it in his father's shop it had been purchased by a collector, who subsequently informed him that the knife had belonged to a famous North of England black magic coven, and there were rumors that it had been used in sacrifices. The collector had gleefully informed Jonathan that he would have paid ten times the price for it.

But one of the reasons he had put the object out for sale so cheaply and quickly was because he had found it difficult to touch the object without feeling cold, and almost physically ill.

So, yes: Frazer could accept that the mirror was a focus for something, some power, some sort of negative energy . . . but that didn't necessarily make the mirror evil. Surely it was the intent with which the mirror was used? Could it not be used for good as well as evil?

Talbott had said that it was powerful—he hadn't said that it was evil.

Jonathan Frazer brushed at the glass with the palm of his hand, scraping off the black gummy coating. What exactly had Talbott said about the mirror?

"Once it is fed with human emotions, with blood, sweat, tears, semen, then its powers are limitless. It can show wonders—or terrors."

It can show wonders.

Jonathan reached into his jeans pocket and took out a slender Victorinox Swiss Army knife. Choosing the larger of the two blades, he locked it open. He stared at the blade for a moment and then, gritting his teeth, he jabbed the point into his index finger, hissing with the sting. A tiny bead of blood appeared.

His hand was trembling as he reached for the glass . . .

48

S HE REMEMBERED the last time she had made love to Robert Beaumont. Emmanuelle Frazer twisted on the bed, caught up in the erotic dream. She was half asleep, *aware* that she was dreaming, yet still conscious of the fact that she was lying in her bed, naked beneath the cool cotton duvet, her left hand resting flat against her breast, the fingers of her right hand moving across and down her belly, teasing herself.

She had met Beaumont shortly after she had first moved to Paris to study fashion. She was not so naive that she didn't recognize him for what he was—an opportunist probably, a gigolo occasionally, a con man certainly. But he was also her entrée to a segment of Parisian society that she would never, in normal circumstances, have been able to experience. And if she had to pay for that privilege, then so be it.

That they should end up as lovers was almost inevitable. She was fascinated by him, the way he looked, the way he moved, the way he dressed. She had never known a man who paid so much attention to his clothing, and he was one of the very few men who delighted in going shopping with her. He took an especial pleasure in choosing underwear for her. He had been the first to comment on her fine bone structure and to suggest that she should shave her head, and although she had initially resisted, they had gotten drunk one night and when they had woken, they had discovered her head had been completely shaved—although neither of them could remember it happening.

She had never loved him, and he had never loved her. That was an accepted part of their relationship. They got on well together, they eventually lived together, they slept together, and when she had left Paris they had kept in touch, Skyping each other every weekend. When Robert came back to live in Los Angeles with his mother he had asked Manny if she could do something about getting him a job.

She wasn't a virgin when she met him, but she was still inexperienced. Her previous boyfriend had been unimaginative and the night she and, as it transpired, he also—lost her virginity, it has been a painful, messy, and altogether uninspiring event.

But Robert had taught her how her body could respond, he had shown her how to bring herself to orgasm, how to give of herself freely. Often he would just sit opposite, watching her arouse herself with two fingers, and then, when she was close to orgasm, he would come over to her, and press his lips to hers while his fingertips trailed down her body, until they finally closed over her hands.

And she felt him.

Had she fallen asleep; was she dreaming?

She felt his hands on hers.

She was still in her semiconscious state, she was aware that she was dreaming.

But she could feel him.

She dreamt that she lay on her bed with her eyes closed while Robert Beaumont bent over her, pressing his lips to hers, squeezing her fingers with his free hand, urging her on. She was aware of his hairless chest against her breasts, his breath on her face, his lips and tongue, moist and damp against her lips. His hands spread her legs and he moved atop her body, mounting her smoothly. She lifted her legs, wrapping them around his buttocks, pulling him deeper inside her, her long fingers digging into his shoulders . . .

49

J ONATHAN FRAZER's finger left a single dot of blood on the glass.
Before his eyes, the crimson bead was absorbed into the mirror,
leaving a brown flaking spot in its wake.

Frazer squeezed more blood onto his fingertip and smeared it down
the glass, the thin liquid cutting a stripe—like a window—through the
grimy coating, revealing, for an instant . . .

His wife, Celia Frazer, and a naked muscular blond man.

Dried flakes of blood seesawed to the floor.

Jonathan Frazer stared in horror at the glass. What had he just seen?

Almost without thinking he drew the razor sharp blade across the palm
of his left hand. The flesh parted like an unfolding leaf, blood welling into
the wound. With his fingers splayed, he pressed his hand to the glass, and
rubbed it in a circle, smearing the surface of the mirror with his blood.

*The couple was naked. He was sitting in an armchair, his legs spread and she was
between his thighs, his manhood in her mouth, his hands grabbing at her hair, setting
the pace, pushing and pulling.*

Dragging his gaze away from the couple, Frazer tried to focus on the
surroundings, noting the room's furniture, the ocean view, a bikini and
beach towel tossed carelessly on the thickly carpeted floor. And then he
recognized the location.

It was a physical effort of will to draw back from the mirror.

Sinking onto the chaise longue, cradling his torn hand, he stared at the
glass, his thoughts in turmoil. He had known—deep in his heart and soul—
that Celia was having an affair. He had just never admitted it before.

But what exactly was he seeing in the mirror; surely it was nothing more
than his imagination?

But he knew it was not.

Becoming aware of the burning in the palm of his hand, he raised it up to look at it in the bad light. The flesh was filthy with the dirt from the mirror, the edges of the long cut encrusted with the slime that coated the glass. But then, as he watched, a scab formed along the edge of the wound, it thickened and hardened before his eyes, and then the edges began to peel and flake away. When he carefully picked away the crust, he found that the cut was completely healed, leaving only a thin black line in its wake.

His head was buzzing with questions and possibilities as he started for the mirror—and then something stopped him. If he wanted to see anything else, he would need to feed the mirror again. He looked at his hand again: he could feed the glass his blood . . . but what were the dangers, what were the consequences?

Only Edmund Talbott could answer those questions. He needed to find Talbott.

50

IN THE Otherworld, the astral body of Edmund Talbott watched the silent whirlpool of power circling above the mirror. Suddenly a shudder, a crimson twitch, rippled through the spinning tornado.

Red: it had tasted blood.

Deep in its core, he could see the white threads that ran its length, like thick worms, now pulsating with an ever increasing rhythm.

White: it was feeding off sexual excitement.

Someone was feeding the glass, with blood and sex.

Deeply troubled, Talbott glided away from the area immediately surrounding the whirlpool. Even though he was separated from it by an enormous gulf, he was aware of its tremendous pull, and he knew that it was growing incredibly powerful. It had shown that it was capable of influencing events in the real world, and now it looked as if someone was consciously feeding it.

It could only be one man.

Even in sleep, Talbott's lips peeled back from his teeth in a savage grin. He would kill Frazer without a second thought in order to stop the mirror.

51

MANNY COULD feel him in her body, his stomach flat against hers as he strove to drive himself even deeper into her. Sweat trickled down her body and into the valley between her breasts. She was aware of him licking it off, his tongue rough against her skin. His fingers teased at her nipples, brushing, touching, squeezing, pinching—hurting—even as his pounding intensified, swamping the pleasure with the pain.

Manny Frazer opened her eyes . . . and looked into horror!

It was Robert Beaumont who made love—who was still making love!—to her. But this was not the smooth-skinned handsome young man, this was Beaumont's charred and incinerated corpse, flesh hanging in strips from his skull, his moist tongue a curled stub in his mouth. The fingers that had played with her hard nipples were burnt down to bone, filthy, blackened stumps, some still leaking ichor. His smooth and hairless chest was a slab of raw meat, and his manhood—which had been so deeply inside her—was bloody and fire-blackened.

And even as she opened her mouth to scream, a part of her mind was attempting to calmly rationalize the fears away. But it was a very small voice, and her fears were very great.

And when she screamed herself back to wakefulness, she could still feel the rasp of blackened flesh against her skin, could still smell the stench of burnt meat in the air. Her breasts were red, nipples swollen and her groin was bruised raw.

52

IN THE Otherworld the whirlpool marking the occult presence of the mirror spun, drifting from side to side, shifting off its axis, tendrils of ragged power spinning out across the astral, dipping down into the physical world . . .

BAD BILL HAD been living on the streets for nearly ten years. He'd survived so long because he took care of himself, rarely mixed with the other down-and-outs, and didn't drink or smoke—except in huge binges. He was a quiet unassuming man, good-humored, good-tempered, except when he drank, and then his personality underwent a complete change. And when he was bad he was very bad: and that's how he got his name. He was forty-two years old, looked twenty and more years older and didn't confidently expect to live to see forty-four. Nowadays he couldn't remember why he'd gone on the streets, and that bothered him, but shit, nowadays he sometimes couldn't even remember his own name.

Today wasn't so bad though. It was dry, sunny, and there was no wind, and he found a large discarded cardboard box behind a Ralphs store on La Brea. It hadn't taken him long to flatten it but now he had to decide where he was going to camp down for the night. There were a few daylight hours left and he remembered a small park just off Curson Avenue: it closed to the general public at sundown. It had been a while since he had slept there, but he'd fallen into the habit of never staying in the same place for more than a couple of nights in a row.

It had taken the best part of an hour and a half before he reached the tall gates to the park, mainly because the walk was uphill and he had stopped several times to rummage through various trash bins on the way. He'd got some empty bottles and cans, so it hadn't been a complete waste of time.

Exhausted, Bill sat on the low stone wall beside a leaf-filled pool and thought about the best spot for the night. It needed to be somewhere he could shelter from the cold and away from any wandering coyotes. There were a few people still in the park, playing with their dogs in the open grassy area. He'd wait for them to go, hide while the park ranger glanced around making sure no one was about, and then, when it was quiet, he'd search quickly through the trash bins. There was always food in park trash—discarded lunches, half-finished drinks. He was confident he'd find something to eat. Then he'd set about finding some place to stay for the night. He knew that the park was an odd shape: a long corridor of lawn, wider at the bottom, narrowing as it rose and then fading into brush and dirt. Giant palm trees and large overgrown bushes surrounded the sloping perimeter. An old drunk he used to hang out with told him that it had once been a beautiful Japanese garden complete with a tea house, shrines, and lanterns. But times changed and everyone and everything got old. All that was left of the beautiful gardens was the dilapidated water feature. It was a good place to stay though; no junkies, no pushers, and far safer than sleeping on a bench or in some dark alleyway.

Wandering around, he found a perfect spot to set up his box. Back off the track, behind a solid wall of bushes, he'd be invisible and the box and hedge would keep him warm. He took his time searching along the dusty track, but could find no coyote prints, so he reckoned he'd be safe from them, too. Usually, they didn't bother him, but there were rumors of rabid ones on the loose.

But when he finally got set up and climbed into the box, he found he couldn't sleep. He twisted and turned, tense and aching, listening, his senses buzzing. There was an ache in his stomach, a tightness in his chest, and the pain went down into his left arm. Bad Bill staggered to his feet, clutching his left arm with his right hand. He made his way through the bushes, knowing from experience that a walk would ease the pressure.

He kept to the shadows. It was unlikely that the park ranger would return, but there was no point in taking unnecessary risks. He followed the path that led back down to the fountain. The water had been turned off so there was no misting spray to wet him, and he sat down on the low stone

wall, forearms resting on his thighs, head drooping between his knees, attempting to catch his breath. He sat up, breathing deeply, and turned to
look into the pool. The water was smooth, polished, a perfect mirror.

It took him a few moments to realize what he was seeing, and then his
rheumy eyes opened wide with something approaching delight. His heart
began to trip alarmingly, but he was barely aware of it. His lips curled back
from his almost toothless gums as he bent his head to kiss the brackish
water.

The image lured him down, the image of his long dead wife, killed a
month after they married. Her death had set him off on the long road that
ended on the streets, starving and diseased, but he'd never forgotten his
wife. She was then and had always been the love of his life. He frowned,
struggling to remember her name. Her name. She'd been called . . .

Icy water enfolding his head like a lover, sucking at his mouth, his
tongue, lapping at his cheeks, his eyes, pulling him in, pulling him down.

Bad Bill grew aware of the sensation, the powerful eroticism of the
water, the enfolding warmth, the pulse pounding rhythm. It reminded him
of . . .

Helena! That was her name.

Bad Bill looked at the water and the image looked back.

And he remembered the last time he had made love to her, twenty-two
years ago.

Helena.

ABBEY MEYERS HAD been a widow for ten years, since her husband, a
retired army general had died suddenly and spectacularly at a regimental
reunion. He had been honoring those who served in the war, when he'd
simply fallen down, a massive heart attack taking him in a manner and at
a time and place which she thought he would have totally approved. He'd
been buried with full military honors. Ten years was a long time, but she
still thought of him, especially now, coming up on Thanksgiving and the
holidays. The holidays had been their most special time; they had met
during the holidays just after the war, they had married the following
winter, their first child had been born just before Thanksgiving, and finally,
the general had died a few days before the Thanksgiving holiday. There
were some nights—like now—when the evenings were chilly, the dark

nights drew closer, when she could almost feel his presence around the large house in Beverly Hills.

This had always been his favorite residence. After his death she had sold off the weekend home in Santa Barbara. She hadn't regretted the decision; she got out with a spectacular price just before the market collapsed. And there had been no way she could have looked after the large second home, the upkeep would have drained their resources. Maxwell, her son, had suggested that she also put the Beverly Hills house up for sale and move to somewhere smaller. There was no mortgage to pay off and she would get a handsome price for it, but she didn't really need money at the moment, whereas she knew that Max did and as soon as she sold the house, he'd ask for some. Anyway, it would all be his when she was gone.

She'd gone through a phase when the very idea of death terrified her. Now, she supposed she almost looked forward to it. She was eighty-four years old, she had achieved all that she was ever going to achieve and, if she were being perfectly truthful, she had really lost interest in most things since the general's death.

Abbey Meyers turned the key on the small book-lined study that had been her husband's favorite room. Here his presence was very strong; sometimes she imagined she could still smell the pipe tobacco he favored. She hadn't deliberately kept it as a shrine to him—he was far too practical, and so was she. But she had kept it the way she thought he would have liked it. There was still the wall of leather-bound books, still the army trophies, the medals, the awards, the framed photographs. There was his collection of swords and knives in their decorative displays on the end wall above the fireplace. His desk was very much as he had left it, an old Royal typewriter—a collector's piece now she supposed—still taking pride of place. He had been working on the definitive story of the fall of Berlin when he'd died. It remained unfinished and although she had often thought about completing it from his notes and references, she imagined that other, far more competent historians had already done that work.

In the top right hand drawer of the desk were the photographs. They were mostly wartime snaps, but there was one which was her favorite. It showed Geoffrey as she like to remember him, tall and proud, in his full general's uniform, wearing his Medal of Honor, President Eisenhower shaking his hand. He had always refused to have the photograph framed, saying it was too much like boasting, and when he had died, she had respected that wish.

Abbey stared at the image, concentrating on Geoffrey's face, remembering the young man she had known, and later the hero. He never talked about his wartime exploits, and she never asked, but she had seen a boy go away to war and watched a man come home, and when he had started awake at night, shouting and crying, she had held him until the terrors had faded.

She looked at the image on the paper . . .

. . . *and the image looked back.*

She had never noticed how the eyes in the photograph seemed to follow her every move, how the lips twitched as if they were about to smile. Why, looking at it, she could almost imagine that she could see the chest rising and falling, the material stretching across his chest.

Ten years a widow, and she still missed him. She missed the touch of him, so strong, so gentle, the smell of him, leather and tweed and tobacco, the feel of his skin, so soft, surprisingly soft for such a big man. And the way his moustache would tickle her face, her throat, her breasts . . .

She missed him.

But it wouldn't be long now. She would join him soon. She wasn't a deeply religious person, but she believed in an afterlife. She believed that they would be reunited one day soon. She believed she'd feel his arms around her, feel his breath on her face, the tweed of his jacket, hear his graveled voice.

Soon.

Abbey Meyers sat down at the desk in a creaking leather chair and propped up the photograph of her husband against the typewriter.

Abbey looked at the photograph and the image looked back.

The knife on the desk was a commando knife, made by the Ek Commando Knife Company for the American Commando Units. Geoffrey Meyers had brought it back from the war as a souvenir and had used it as a letter opener.

Abbey looked at the photograph and the image looked back. And smiled. And called her name.

She removed the long razor sharp knife from its sheath. It was cold and heavy in her hand as she pressed it in below and to the left of her jaw, her eyes still riveted on the image, a smile of complete satisfaction on her face as she pushed . . .

MARTIN STEPHENS HAD really wanted the new HP TouchSmart all-in-one computer, 6GB memory, 1TB hard drive with all the bells and whistles: touch screen, Blu-ray player, wireless internet. He'd also given his parents a list of the accessories he needed. He'd been quite specific about his wants, giving them the exact make and model numbers he wanted. His parents, who knew shit about computers, and had balked at the price, had opted instead for a completely different make and model made by someone he'd never even heard of before. It had half the features and programs he'd wanted and had cost a fraction of the price.

He was disappointed, and he let them know it. He was fifteen years old, he deserved a little respect!

Martin had sulked in his room for most of the day and eventually, when his parents went out to some gallery opening, he had settled down to remove the computer from its box and began to set it up. He was still smarting that they hadn't gotten him what he'd wanted, when another grand or so, maybe fifteen hundred, would have been enough to buy it. For Christ's sake, some of the kids in high school were already carrying the latest laptops, notebooks, and tablets: but that was going to be his Christmas request!

He set up the computer and linked up the cables to the printer and then inserted the keyboard plug into the USB port in the back of the computer. The better machines now had bluetooth capabilities, and the keyboard and mouse were both wireless. He plugged in the power cable and turned on the switch. It came to life with an ascending whine, and he spent the next hour setting up the various colors and choosing the right wallpaper. Then he set about syncing files from his six month old machine to the new one. Most of what he put onto the new laptop were games, some of which he'd bought, others which he'd been given or swapped with his friends. He put them onto a directory buried a few levels down so they wouldn't be immediately obvious to his parents should they ever look at the machine—which was highly unlikely anyway, since they weren't really interested in him as was immediately apparent by the cheap present they'd bought him.

However, at least now he'd be able to run some of the games that wouldn't run on the old machine. Some of them, he knew, his parents wouldn't fully approve of.

Right now, his favorite was an interactive game of strip poker. High resolution girls behaved as if they were real, commenting on the game, smiling, laughing, even getting angry. A large bosomed female appeared on the screen whom he'd played against before. When she lost a hand, she removed an item of clothing and although he'd gotten her down to just her bra and panties on friends' machines, he'd never had the chance to take her any further, principally because to take her that far took about two hours, and time had always been against him. However, he had heard lurid stories about what happened when she removed all her clothing. There were a couple of other programs which he'd heard of, but not gotten yet, which showed couples actually doing it in different positions, and now that he had an HD screen, the online porn sites were going to look so much better.

It was close to ten when he began to play strip poker. He had changed into his boxers and a T-shirt and now lounged back in his tilting desk chair with the keyboard directly in front of him, his total concentration on the screen.

By twelve-thirty he was beginning to pull ahead. She was again down to bra and panties and he was holding a winning hand. His eyes were also beginning to buzz and there was a throbbing headache at the back of his skull, but he couldn't give up now, not now, not when he was so close.

He played on, and won the hand.

Onscreen the woman removed her bra, revealing huge breasts tipped with large erect nipples.

Now this was more like it!

Martin felt himself becoming aroused, more with the tension and excitement at coming so close to winning the game than anything else.

At one-thirty he paused the game, freezing the image on the screen, while he pressed the heels of his palms into his eyes. He hadn't progressed anywhere in the past hour and he was down to his last twenty dollars. It would be absolutely frustrating to come so close and lose now.

He stared at the image on the screen. Big, blonde and busty—his type, he nodded smugly. He'd watched a lot of online porn and he'd decided he was definitely a breast man; not that he'd ever seen a breast in real life, or should that be a real life breast? But he'd a good idea what they were like.

Martin Stephens looked at the image and decided that she was close enough to his ideal woman. The way her eyes looked directly at you, the way her mouth was slightly parted, and the way her breasts swung. He reached out and touched the screen with his forefinger, tracing the curves of the image's breasts. He could almost feel the flesh beneath his fingertip.

Martin looked at the screen and the image looked back.

And a static charge snapped from his fingertip onto the glass.

The screen exploded.

Red hot slivers of glass, metal, and plastic ripped into the young man, shredding his skin, peeling back the flesh of his face, his eyes, his mouth. A chunk of molten plastic caught him in the throat, burning through the skin, severing the artery, blood jetting high into the room, up the walls and across the ceiling.

And his last conscious thought was of the smiling eyes of the blonde, busty image watching him. Yes, definitely busty, that was his type.

53

Tired and dispirited, feeling hung over even though she hadn't finished the glass of scotch last night, Margaret Haaren read through the reports, barely paying them any attention.

The accidental drowning of a homeless man in a small park.

The suicide of a lonely widow.

The bizarre death of a teenager when his computer screen exploded.

She was putting away the attending officer's report on the last incident when she stopped and looked at it again. It took her a while to figure it out . . . and then she suddenly realized what had caught her attention: the house numbers of the second two tragedies were the same number as the Frazer house. And then she discovered that the coroner had put the time of death for all three within a couple of minutes of each other.

Coincidence?

Haaren had been too long on the force to believe in coincidence. She was reaching for the intercom button when there was a tap on the door and Detective Stuart Miller stepped into the room. She immediately knew by the expression on his face that something was wrong.

"We've just had a call from the hospital . . ."

She came slowly to her feet, heart suddenly pounding. "The young officer, Martin Moore?" she began.

"It's the two men," he said carefully, his voice suddenly husky. "José Pérez went around three this morning; and Officer Martin at four."

"Both of them?" Margaret Haaren sank back into the chair, ashen faced. The reports before her eyes swam in unshed tears. "Thank . . . thank you Stuart."

"I'm sorry," he said lamely, backing from the room.

When she was alone she allowed the tears to fall. José Pérez had been a good friend for too many years; she was godmother to one of the girls. When a woman officer had been a curiosity, a rarity, something of a freak, he'd accepted her for what she was, and when she made Senior Detective in the Homicide Division, she'd requested him as her partner.

There was a knock on the door and Stuart Miller reappeared, a mug of coffee balanced precariously on top of a sheaf of reports. The detective accepted the coffee gratefully.

"He was a good man," Stuart said respectfully.

"He was a fine detective and a good friend," Margaret said slowly. "And now we can lay three deaths at this scarred man's door."

"Yes, ma'am."

When she looked up her green eyes were cold, implacable. "I want the man who did this. And Jonathan Frazer knows him!"

Silently Stuart Miller handed over the sheaf of brown folders.

"What's this?"

"List of possible suspects, cross referenced with José's old and present cases, further cross-referenced with Jonathan Frazer's friends and business associates. The latter list is by no means exhaustive, but it's the best we can do."

"Any matches?"

"Nothing at the moment, ma'am."

She looked up into Miller's brown eyes. "Frazer's dirty, I can feel it. I want an exhaustive check into his background. Bank accounts, tax records, everything. He's a material witness and possible suspect in a multiple murder case, we should have no problem getting the clearances." She drank her now tepid coffee in one quick swallow. She knew what she was doing now, she had done it before: she was using work to ease the pain of her friend's death.

The detective leaned forward and took the mug from her desk. "We could also try leaning on him, ma'am," he suggested quietly.

Margaret Haaren nodded slowly. "Trust me, I haven't ruled that out either."

JONATHAN FRAZER WENT through his wife's clothing with a fine tooth comb, and then proceeded to meticulously check through her chest of drawers, cabinets, on top of her closet, and the dressing table. He was looking for evidence of Celia's infidelity. He was aware that if he stopped to think about what he was doing, the madness of it would strike home, and he would begin to question his own sanity.

What was he doing?

Why was he doing it?

After an exhausting day, he had imagined he'd seen something in the mirror—a fantasy—and on the basis of that he had allowed all his repressed fears about his wife's fidelity to come flooding to the surface, and now here he was pawing through her things like some cheap private investigator.

But it had been so real. The image had been so real.

Was it true, or just some bad-minded wish?

Where was Edmund Talbott?

MANNY FELT LIKE shit.

The only time she'd ever felt like this before was when she'd had a hit of bad hash in Paris. She dressed slowly, black T-shirt over black jeans, her every joint aching, her breasts heavy and painful, her stomach feeling bloated. On impulse she checked her calendar, but her period wasn't due for another two weeks, so it wasn't that . . . unless it was coming early, brought on by the trauma of the last few days. That was a possibility and she hadn't had sex in about six weeks so that was out of the question.

She stopped and looked at herself in the mirror. She looked ghastly, her face pale and wan, her eyes sunk back into her skull, dark-rimmed and bloodshot. She ran her fingers across her head. The stubble rasped loudly. She'd only had it cut a few weeks ago, and yet it seemed to be growing very quickly this time.

She had no clear memory of her nightmare the previous night. She remembered waking as her mother, drawn by her screams, had come running into the room and turning on the light. But even then, the horrors were fading and she'd been unable to remember anything from her nightmare. She had insisted that the light be left on, and it took her a long time before sleep finally claimed her.

She met her father in the hallway and he stopped, obviously surprised by her wretched appearance.

"I think you should go back to bed, sweetheart," he murmured, kissing her forehead.

"I'm OK, Dad, just a bit whacked out after the last couple of days." She attempted a smile. "You're not looking so hot yourself."

"I didn't sleep so well. Nightmares," he explained.

"So did I. Didn't Mom tell you?"

"I haven't seen your mother this morning. I haven't seen much of your mother since she came back from her surfing vacation, and when I did see her it was at your bedside at the hospital."

Manny stopped. "Then she didn't tell you?"

He looked at her in surprise. "Tell me what?"

"Last night she told me she was going up to that skiing resort in Lake Tahoe first thing this morning."

"She said nothing to me." He shook his head slowly. "I didn't know it was snowing there already."

Manny linked her arm through her father's as they walked slowly downstairs. "Do I get the impression that all isn't sweetness and light between the two of you?" She caught the blank look of dismay on his face, and continued ruefully, "I am eighteen, you know. I'm not a fool. And you don't need to be a genius to guess that you're both going your separate ways. And have been for a while."

"It's true," he admitted. "In the last couple of years, our differences and interests have become more and more pronounced. I'll be forty-six next birthday. It doesn't bother me, aging never has, maybe that's because I worked with old things all my life. But your mother . . . well your mother will be thirty-eight next birthday, and she dresses and acts as if she's ten years younger."

"That's not so unusual. It's a last-ditch attempt at retaining her youth," Manny said with all the seriousness of an eighteen-year-old.

"Thirty-eight is not over the hill," Jonathan gently reminded her.

"No spring chicken either," she laughed. She stopped at the bottom of the stairs and turned to face her father. "But you still love her don't you, Dad?"

"Yes," he said seriously, "yes I do." He was surprised to find that he meant it.

"Well, if you still love one another, surely you can sort out your differences," Manny said, looking into his troubled eyes.

He nodded. "If we both still loved one another," he agreed.

"But you're not so sure if she still loves you?" Manny asked.

"I'd like to think she still loves me," he said.

Father and daughter looked at one another. They both knew it was a lie.

54

D**ON'T TURN** around, Mr. Frazer."

Jonathan froze, his hands locked onto the wheel of the Volvo Estate. He had just climbed into the car and the garage door behind him was humming upwards, flooding the garage with morning light. He recognized the voice immediately. "I was wondering when you'd get in touch," he said, glancing into the rearview mirror. Edmund Talbott's coal-black eyes regarded him unblinkingly.

"Things have become very difficult, Mr. Frazer," the scarred man said quietly.

"I know. It was all over the news this morning. Both officers you struck died," Frazer said coldly.

"I will not be taken into custody," Talbott said simply.

"Why not?"

"Mr. Frazer, perhaps I have not explained myself fully. My family have been the guardians of the mirror for generations. It was our task to keep it inert, to keep it safe from the world, not to allow it to feed its hunger for souls and blood and human emotions. It needs those for nourishment, it needs those to survive. Eventually it would have *died*—if you can apply that term to it—of hunger. And we were so close, so close. It wouldn't have happened in my lifetime, but in the next generation perhaps. It was weak, so weak."

"What happened?" Frazer asked, without turning around, watching the man's eyes in the mirror.

"It was my fault. I had to go away to a site meeting in Saudi. It should have taken no more than forty-eight hours, but it took the best part of a week. When I returned to Oxford, England, I discovered that the house had been burgled and that the mirror and a few other antiques were gone. The burglars were local lads, who knew that the house was empty. One of them did odd jobs around the garden and knew there were some antiques inside the home. That's the official story."

"And unofficially?"

"I am inclined to think that the mirror exerted its influence on the youths; paradoxically it can most easily influence the strong-willed and the weak. Ordinary people, with ordinary lives and ordinary worries crowding their ordinary minds are quite safe from its extraordinary powers. The rest of the story, I think you know."

"Tell me."

"The thieves took the mirror, wrenching the heavy cloth covering from it, exposing the glass. Once uncovered it began to feed. It took the life of your male assistant first, and then the female, and since then it has been feeding on the blood and energy of those all around it, growing stronger with every soul it takes."

"The police say the auctioneers have no record of having sold the mirror to me, nor is there any record with the shipping company."

"The records are probably computerized. The mirror probably deleted the records," Talbott said simply.

"That's impossible . . ." Jonathan started to say and then realized how stupid that sounded. "But I did have a printed-out record, a copy of the receipt and shipping details."

"And what happened to them?"

"They . . . disappeared." He found himself wondering if Beaumont had stolen them. "But what about the people who sold me the mirror? The assistant I was dealing with; the auctioneer, the truck driver who delivered it? Surely they must remember it?"

"You have no conception of the power of the object you're dealing with," Talbott said quietly.

"But what you're suggesting is impossible . . ." Frazer said again.

"Everything is possible. Do you know anything about astral projection, Mr. Frazer," Talbott asked suddenly, "or the astral plane?"

Jonathan shook his head.

"When a body sleeps, the spirit—the astral body—leaves the physical body and moves onto the astral plane. This plane may be a 'physical' place or it may be a state of mind, I don't know. I merely accept its existence, and use it. There are various levels on this astral plane, and with skill and practice and determination, it is possible to move from plane to plane, to move one's physical body through space—as I did when I visited you in the hospital room. You weren't dreaming, Mr. Frazer, I really was there.

"On another level, a higher level, it is possible to see the souls of the newly dead leave their bodies. Some hover uncertainly about the corpse, others fly away to freedom, others are trapped.

"The astral plane is disturbed at the moment, Mr. Frazer. There is a presence, a force rippling through the usually placid domain. It is like a giant whirlpool, sucking everything around it into its circle. I have stood on the very edge of the plane and watched this *thing*. It is the non-physical manifestation of the mirror, Mr. Frazer, a whirlpool of all the emotions, the energies, the blood and sweat and semen, the pain and anger, that has fed the glass down through the ages. It is enormous, ravenous and ravening.

"And it is moving.

"People died around you last night, Mr. Frazer. Innocents. A woman in Beverly Hills with the same house number as yours cut her throat to be with her husband who had been dead ten years. Fooled by the image.

"A young boy, his face shredded by the glass from an exploding computer screen. Entranced by the image on the screen.

"A vagrant drowned in a small park just off Sunset. Beguiled by the image.

"And do you know what else I saw last night, Mr. Frazer? I saw the mirror feed. I saw it drink the blood of sacrifice. I saw it accept the emotion of passion."

"Does the mirror only show the truth?" Jonathan wondered.

"Invariably. It rarely needs to lie. It counts on the fact that truth, like most things, is addictive. And the images on its surface are the ultimate narcotic; people return to them again and again."

"Do you want me to destroy the mirror?" Frazer asked, not sure if he could.

"NO!" Talbott shouted. "Break it, and you have a thousand mirrors, each one complete and whole in itself. Anyway," he chuckled, "I doubt if you'd get within a dozen yards of it with evil intent. The last person who even thought about that paid a terrible price . . ."

Frazer suddenly knew he was talking about himself.

"I cannot come and take the mirror from you now," Talbott said, suddenly sounding distant and tired, "but cover it, for God's sake, cover its surface with a heavy black blanket and turn it away from the moonlight. It will begin to weaken almost immediately, although it will take it a long time to return to some sort of quiescence. But when all the police activity has died down, then I'll arrange to take the mirror from you and have it shipped back to England."

"And then?"

"Then?" Talbott asked, puzzled. "What do you mean?"

"What happens when you take it back to England?"

"Then the whole process begins again. I don't even know how or why it was created. The mirror is ancient, and the glass, its method of construction, and the materials are older still. I don't know what magic, what natural forces went into its creations. But this is one of the most potent occult forces remaining in the world today; there is no way to hurry it along. In a couple of hundred years time, perhaps someone will have figured out some way of destroying it. But I doubt it."

"But what happens if it continues to feed?"

"Every soul makes it stronger. It will kill and kill and kill again, and no one knows to what end. Maybe it is significant that it has always been the most active during the bloodiest events in human history. Do those periods of history awaken it . . . or does it cause them? I have no idea. But it has to be stopped Mr. Frazer, and only you or I can do that . . ."

As Frazer watched, the eyes in the mirror closed as the voice faded. He swiveled around in the leather seat . . . and discovered that there was no one in the back of the car.

55

WITH INFINITE care, Doctor John Dee removed the cork stopper from the glass jar. Blood flowed from the glass and ran along a series of metal coils which fed it into a series of narrow branching glass tubes that were positioned directly over the seven foot tall mirror. The liquid, thick and glutinous, ran down the length of the glass.

It congealed about half way down into a sticky mess.

"It needs human blood," Kelley remarked.

Dee nodded distractedly. Animal blood had no effect on the glass, which meant that there was some element unique to human blood which activated it. And yet his own researches into human and animal blood had shown that there were minimal differences between the two. So the difference had to be metaphysical.

In the dim and warped reflective surface, Dee saw the door behind him open and the woman approach. She was naked as usual and as she neared him, he saw the ripples of power flow down the mirror's surface, sparked by her proximity.

"Feed it with human blood," she whispered, her breath tickling his ear, "then it will show you wonders."

Dee stepped back away from the mirror and put his arm around the woman. Her flesh was chill and damp.

"I've been walking in the gardens," she explained before he could ask the question.

"The villagers and staff will think you're a witch," he said softly.

"Do they not already think you are a witch?" she murmured.

Dee bowed in acknowledgement. Some weeks ago he had finally persuaded the woman to move to his home at Mortlake on the outskirts of

London. She had travelled in the dead of night, bringing the mirror with her. The huge slab of glass was carefully swathed in sacking, packed between sacks of feathers and strips of leather. It had taken six strong men to maneuver it up the narrow winding stairs to Dee's own study at the top of the house.

Since then he had experimented endlessly with it, attempting to recreate the fleeting images he had glimpsed on that first occasion.

And with little success.

The mirror became active in the woman's presence, he knew that. And she was the most exciting, the most erotic women he had ever encountered. Perhaps it was her natural magic firing his lusts, or perhaps it was simply that she rarely dressed, and usually wore little more than a cloak to cover her nakedness. At times he ached for her, and yet, despite Kelley's assurances that she desired him, she had shown no signs of it. She touched him often, pressed herself against him, crowded him, but never with anything other than seemingly innocent intent.

And he still didn't know her name.

He had asked for her name countless times, but all she would say was that when there was a time for names, he would know hers.

The only other way to activate the mirror was to use human blood. He had experimented with animal bloods and found them to be useless: in fact, they were worse than useless because they befouled the surface of the glass, clinging to the sticky black grit that covered the face of the mirror and were difficult to remove, but he was still reluctant to take that final step of smearing the glass with human blood. It smacked too much of witchcraft, and he was not a witch: he was a scientist.

The problem was that he had mentioned to the queen that he was in possession of a scrying glass of extraordinary powers, and she had pointed out to him the obvious potential for observing England's enemies. He cursed himself now; he had never been so indiscreet before. Now, she was beginning to put pressure on him to produce results . . . and he knew from experience that her patience was not limitless and that often the favorite of today was the villain of tomorrow.

He needed to be able to show something to the queen.

John Dee looked over his shoulder at Edward Kelley. "Can we get some human blood?"

"My lord, in London, one can buy anything."

"Pure blood," the woman murmured. "Neither diseased nor tainted, preferably the blood of a virgin or a child."

Kelley nodded again, bowing this time to hide the smile that twisted his thin lips. He had coached the woman well, but she was also a natural actress. And this was the role of a lifetime. If this was successful, then her reward would be great indeed.

THIS TIME THE blood had an immediate effect.

John Dee stood three feet away from the mirror, the woman standing at his left shoulder, Kelley in the background, while the blood slowly flowed down the length of the glass, slicing through the grime to leave long sparkling clean ovals in its wake. For the first time, Dee saw himself clearly in the mirror, tall and thin, gray-haired, great-bearded, the voluptuous raven-haired woman standing behind him, Kelley standing off to one side.

And then the glass clouded.

The gray-haired, gray-bearded image in the mirror had been replaced by a tall dark-haired man, with sharper, harder features than Dee's. His short goatee beard was jet black. Standing beside him was a young woman, ragged, dirty, no more than a child . . . except for her eyes, which were cold and cunning. Behind them stood a tall, gangling youth, with a shock of fiery red hair, his head bent, his eyes squeezed shut in what looked like fear.

Dee turned slowly, beginning to realize what he was seeing. He looked from Kelley to the woman and then back to the glass . . . these images were from the past, this was Kelley, the woman, and himself as youths, decades ago.

But the image had changed. The glass clouded, and strange images, blood and fire, the flash of a knife blade descending, arising bloodied, writhed across the glass. Now it no longer reflected, it showed . . .

Dee: naked and aroused, sitting in a chair while the woman made love to him with extraordinary abandon.

The woman: naked, though now her belly had swelled and her breasts were full, the nipples dark. Dee was standing behind her, his hands on her shoulders.

Doctor John Dee started forward, trying to make sense out of what he was seeing: was this the future definite or the future possible?

The woman: lying on the ground, her legs spread wide, her body sheened with sweat, her head thrown back. A bloody head appearing between her legs, and then Dee reaching in and drawing out a girl child, raising her high as if in triumph or offering.

Dee looked at the woman by his side, saw that she too was staring intently at the glass. He glanced back over his shoulder, but Kelley was crumpled on the ground, his head buried in his hands, obviously terrified by the pictures flowing across the glass.

A child: perhaps four or five years old, naked, with hair flowing down to the base of her spine. Her hands were raised high above her head and were visibly glowing with twisting energies. She straightened, dropping her hands, pressing downwards with her palms, and then she shifted, rising upwards . . .

Dee looked at the woman and she turned her large dark eyes on him. The girl had the woman's eyes and Dee's long face. He gripped her shoulder, ignoring the mirror in his excitement. "It is our child. The child of a new generation of man—a race in tune with the natural magic of the universe."

The woman smiled. "It is our destiny." She turned to point at the glass. "Watch," she whispered.

There were new images on the glass, images of blood and fire and a face. Wavering, indistinct, the face assumed a demonic cast, teeth drawn back from stained teeth, curling black hair spiked with grease, eyes wide and staring. He was dressed entirely in black with a broad ruff stained with blood and the knife in his hand was thick with gore.

"An evil man," the woman whispered, "who brings evil to the queen."

"It's Essex," Dee whispered. "but it cannot be, he is one of her most loyal subjects."

"But ambitious?" the woman suggested.

"Ambitious," Dee agreed.

"He should be taken away from the queen," she said softly.

Dee nodded his head in silent agreement. He turned abruptly from the mirror and almost stumbled over Kelley who was still crouched on the ground, his head buried in his hands, his face screwed up in terror, tears on his cheeks. He had bitten through his lips and the blood had run down his chin. Dee kicked at him, cursed him for a coward, and staggered from the room.

As soon as the door closed, Edward Kelley rolled over onto his back, a broad smile on his lips.

"Well?" the woman asked.

"You were magnificent," Kelley said. "I might almost say possessed," he added with a smile.

"He's leaving," she said.

Kelley rolled to his feet and joined the woman by the window. They watched the carriage sway across the rutted track towards London. "The good doctor hurries to bring ill news to the queen," Kelley said.

"What happened?" the woman asked, "where did the first images come from, those of Dee and me and you, too, I think, many years ago."

"That was before I could take control of the images," he muttered, rubbing the palm of his hand to his head. He had a pounding headache—the effort of projecting the images onto the mirror had been agony, and what Dee had taken for cowardice and an expression of fear, had been intense concentration and effort.

He had lost control of the mirror at a couple of points, when it had shown the blood and fire, but in the main the experiment—and the gamble—had worked spectacularly. Previously he had only projected pictures onto the glass, simple images that lasted only fleetingly.

Kelley had stumbled on the process by chance. When the mirror had been in the wharfside den, he had taken an old women in off the streets on the pretext of feeding and clothing her. Instead, he had dragged her unceremoniously down before the glass and cut her throat, spraying the glass with her thin blood. The results had been disappointing. The glass had cleared for brief moments to show a few strange and terrifying images—disembodied faces howling in what looked like agony—before clouding over again. He had been standing before the glass idly wishing that he had caught the woman's blood in a goblet of some kind and allowed it to flow more evenly down the surface of the mirror, when he had suddenly seen an image of the goblet in the glass. It had lasted no more than a heartbeat, but Kelley had been an alchemist for long enough to immediately recognize the signs. He had dragged the lifeless body of the old woman to her feet and sliced open her ragged bodice with his knife, exposing the dirty pallid flesh. He had cut through the empty dugs, and snapped the ribs beneath with his bare hands before finally wrenching the heart from the chest. Allowing the woman's body to fall to the ground, he smeared the mirror with the bloody organ and then stepped away, the remnants of the heart still clutched in his left hand, the knife in his right. He looked down at the knife, and then brought it up before his face, looking closely at it, concentrating on the triangular Italian blade, the plain wire wrapped hilt.

And then he allowed the knife to fall to the floor.

But the image remained in the mirror.

He stared at it for five pounding heartbeats until the smeared blood dried on the glass and flaked away and the image faded.

But by then Kelley knew that he could project images onto the glass with his mind.

He thought the plan to remove Essex was his master stroke. With the queen's favorite out of the way, she would obviously come to rely more and more on people like Dee for advice and guidance, and Dee was malleable.

Edward Kelley threw back his head and laughed aloud, even though the sound pounded through his skull, threatening to split it. Everything was coming together nicely.

And once they had Dee's child and had sacrificed it to the mirror then everything would be complete.

The trap was baited.

56

THE TRAP had been baited.

With images that preyed on the fears of the humankind, it had successfully survived through the Dark Times, and the times of Imprisonment.

It had come close on occasion to escaping, to shucking off this crystal shell, but it had always been thwarted.

But these were better times, more complex times, and that suited it. The belief in its kind and its sisters had faded, they had been relegated to petty tales used to frighten children.

Ignorance now was its greatest weapon.

It had grown in strength since it had been uncovered and had started to drink of the myriad complex emotions of the humankind. And whereas before it had been a shadow in the Otherworld, a fetch, now it was an elemental force that swept all before it. The souls of the newly dead were sustenance to it, the dreams of the innocent and the insane fed its hunger, but its thirst could only be fed with blood and tears and semen.

It had started to extend its influence into the world of men, to hunt, taking those closest to its core, calling them with images from their own minds. It relished their fear, their terror, it clutched them to its bosom, draining their lost souls of all emotion, leaving the husks to be twisted on the whirlwind of its power.

But there were irritations.

The last scion of the old enemy was at large, it had felt his presence on the very edges of the Otherworld, a thin, cold spark of hatred, carefully shielded from all influences. But as its powers increased, then so too did his vulnerability, and soon, soon, it would reach out and snatch his immortal soul from its cowering place, and that was a morsel it would enjoy.

But now it thirsted. It needed blood and sweat and semen to satisfy its craving.

The trap had been baited with subtle and beguiling images. Soon it would drink its fill.

Soon.

57

MARGARET HAAREN walked away from the graveside and picked her way through the headstones to where Jonathan Frazer was standing sheltering beneath a large black umbrella. She was wearing her full uniform and Frazer thought this lent her a dignity which her otherwise rather matronly figure denied her.

"I'm surprised to see you here, Mr. Frazer," she said quietly, stepping under the umbrella, deliberately bringing herself close to him.

From a distance, the minister's voice carried through the still wet air. "Ashes to ashes . . ." The thud of wet clay onto the wooden coffin sounded like a gunshot across the bleak rain-swept cemetery.

He looked past her, his soft brown eyes unfocused. "I suppose I felt I had to come. I felt responsible."

The detective said nothing. She was a great believer in allowing people to talk themselves into trouble.

"I mean it happened on my property . . . and he was investigating a crime that had happened in my . . ." he trailed off, realizing he was talking nonsense.

"I'm going straight on to another funeral, Mr. Frazer. Another officer killed on your property. And tomorrow I'm attending the funeral of the officer slain in the library. I didn't really know those men, but they were police officers under my command, and I have a duty to find their killer." Margaret Haaren glanced back over her shoulder. Without turning her head, she continued. "But José Pérez was a friend, a very good friend. He was twenty-five years a policeman. That's his wife and two daughters over there. They married the year he joined the force: they would have been twenty-five years married this year . . . next month in fact. He was going to take her to Hawaii for their anniversary. The tickets are in the top right hand drawer of his desk." When she turned back to Frazer, her face was a hard mask. "I don't have a duty to find José's murderer. I have an obligation. I want the man who killed him, and my other two officers. I know you know this scarred man Mr. Frazer; I know you know more than you're telling me. But unfortunately I cannot prove it—yet." Her voice was now little more than a whisper. "I'm going to catch the man responsible and he's going to jail . . . and I've a feeling you're going along with him. Accessory to murder, Mr. Frazer, is a very serious charge and doubly so when the victims are police officers. Remember that, Mr. Frazer, the next time you meet your scarred friend."

"Aunt Margaret?"

With a hiss of anger, Margaret Haaren turned around, and Frazer looked over her shoulder at a tall, dark-haired, blue-eyed beauty. "I'll be with you in a moment, Helen," she snapped. "My niece," she explained to Frazer.

"I don't blame you for your suspicions," he said tiredly. "But I am the innocent here. I am truly sorry for the deaths of your officers, but I can assure you that I had absolutely nothing to do with them, nor did I know anything about them. If I knew where this scarred man was I would tell you; remember, I'm the one he's been threatening."

"Perhaps you should surrender the mirror into our keeping until he is caught: at least then you can tell him the police have it." She was watching him closely as she made the suggestion, and she'd already guessed the answer before he spoke slowly, obviously picking his words carefully.

"I'm not sure if I could do that. I already have some interest in it . . . from collectors of glass . . ." he added absently, and then he abruptly wished her a good day, turned and walked away.

Margaret Haaren nodded slowly. The mirror was the key. It linked the scarred man and Frazer. Frazer had lied about the mirror when he said he had purchased it in London; the company there had denied all knowledge of it. It was time to take a closer look at this mirror. She wondered if she'd be able to confiscate it as evidence? She watched the man disappear through the trees, head bent, umbrella low on his head. He was in this up to his neck . . . the only problem was she wasn't sure what he was up to his neck in. Extortion? Smuggling? Theft? And murder . . . don't forget murder. But whatever it was, Jonathan Frazer was making her life miserable. Maybe it was about time she returned the compliment.

JONATHAN FRAZER SAT in the Volvo parked across from the graveyard, his hands locked in a white-knuckled grip on the steering wheel. Through the ornamental iron rail surrounding the cemetery, he could see the mourners beginning to drift away from the graveside in ones and twos. He did regret the policemen's deaths, but there was nothing he could have done about it, was there?

Was there? He could have given the mirror back to Talbott when he had first asked for it. He could have done that . . . and Tony and Diane and Robert and those three police officers would still be alive.

And why was he now protecting Talbott? The man was a murderer, a cold and callous killer with some sort of occult power. Why didn't he tell the police what he knew?

And what was he going to tell them: the man appeared to me in a dream; I saw the man in the mirror of my car and when I turned around, he was gone? Oh, and by the way, he tells me my mirror is haunted?

Yes, he could see them believing that! He was already in enough trouble as it was. They believed he was involved with Talbott, and Detective Haaren had accused him of being implicated in the death of the police officers. He wondered if she had enough evidence to hold him for questioning or, even worse, to confiscate the mirror. That thought filled him with a strange—almost overpowering—terror.

He savagely turned the key in the ignition, the engine screeching, then slammed the car into gear and took off with a squeak of rubber just as the last of the mourners left the graveyard.

Margaret Haaren stood at the gate of the graveyard and watched the Volvo exceed the speed limit as it disappeared down the road. She wondered where he was going in such a hurry. She turned in time to see the black and white Chevrolet Caprice pull out from the curb and take off after him. She nodded in satisfaction: she'd read the report later on.

58

T HE DRY dust and leather smell of the guesthouse was overlain with a sharper, bitter odor, a rich metallic copper tang. In the silence, the maddened buzzing of a fly sounded unnaturally loud. And then another sound broke the silence, a sharp hiss of pain.

Jonathan Frazer knelt on the floor before the mirror. He was wearing a T-shirt and jeans, his jacket flung carelessly on the floor behind him. He had used a surgical scalpel, which he'd disinfected in alcohol beforehand, to open one of the small veins in his wrist, and blood was dribbling onto the thick bath sponge he held in his right hand. He didn't even want to think too closely about what he was doing; he preferred to regard it as a scientific experiment, and if it failed then nothing would have been lost and he'd review his alternatives. But if it succeeded . . . well, he preferred not to think about that, either.

When the sponge was sodden with his blood, he reached out and rubbed it across the mirror. The grime wiped away cleanly and he was able to see himself clearly in the mirror for the first time.

He grinned at his reflection. He looked ridiculous: no, worse, he looked like a junkie who'd just shot up, kneeling here on the floor, blood snaking along his arm. He reached out and rubbed at the glass again, squeezing the sponge, blood trickling through his fingers and running down the glass, cutting through the filth.

So, that part of the experiment had been successful: blood did clear the glass. Must be something in the liquid . . .

But Talbott had also said that the mirror showed images. He stared into the glass, wondering what it would show. He had seen things in it before, dreamt dreams, seen faces . . .

He blinked as his vision blurred, or maybe it was a distortion in the glass. He rubbed at it again with the blood-soaked sponge, but the ghosting around his features remained, the planes of his face, the curve of his chin, the shadows of his eyes seeming to shift, to move, to blur.

To change.

There was shadow and shape and finally, a face.

A woman looked out of the mirror at him!

A dominant, powerful face, strong cheekbones, slightly up-tilted black eyes beneath curving eyebrows, full lips, a thick mass of hair.

The image moved.

Jonathan Frazer fell backwards onto the floor, supporting himself on his arms, as he stared horrified at the moving shapes.

The woman was moving, drawing away from him even as the background behind her became clearer, like a stage set coming to life. The image of the woman was combing her thick luxuriant hair, staring *into* the mirror while behind her a man, bald, short, corpulent with a huge hook of a nose, sat naked sat on the edge of an enormous drapery-hung bed. The room was magnificent, the walls frescoed, hung with ornate tapestries and there were numerous rugs on the marbled floor. Two tall bronze doors, each one worked in fabulous detail, were barely visible at the far end of the room.

The woman walked away from the mirror, and Frazer could see that she, too, was naked, and he watched the sway of her buttocks, the trembling of her mass of hair as she approached the fat man. His arms went out to encircle her as she spread her legs and climbed onto his lap, deftly working him inside her.

Aware of his own arousal, Frazer watched as she moved swiftly on top of him, her hands clasped on either side of his head, her mouth locked on his with a savage passion. And then the man's hands—heavily beringed, Frazer suddenly noticed—began to tighten on the woman's back, clutching at her flesh, leaving red weals in their wake. They scored long lines down her back as he gripped her buttocks, fingers digging into the soft flesh.

Frazer saw the woman moving more quickly now, pounding up and down on the man. And then she stopped. She stretched her hands out and her back arched, her head tilting upwards, face to the ceiling, the long mass of her hair falling almost to the floor behind her. Frazer saw that the fat man's eyes were squeezed shut, tears squeezing out from beneath the lids.

And then the woman's hands were at her hair. Frazer saw the pin—at least eight inches long, tipped with what looked like a single ruby. He saw her hands come back around the man's head, brushing past his jowls, his tightly cropped gray hair, cupping his ears. She bent her head to kiss him, her mouth opening wide, fixing onto his, and Frazer saw her left hand move away from the man's head—and then back in again, plunging the pin deep into the man's ear. He thrashed in agony, but the woman still clung to him, holding the pin firmly in place, her mouth still locked over his— preventing him from crying out, Frazer suddenly realized. The fat man's struggles abruptly weakened and the woman, who was still astride him, pushed him back, forcing him down onto the bed. His hands beat feebly at her, but she kept twisting the pin, turning it, forcing it in deeper. There was a sudden spasm and the fat man's struggles ceased.

When she was sure he was dead, the woman climbed off him, and hurried to the low marble-topped table. There was a heavy goblet and two glasses standing on the table, and Frazer immediately identified them as fifteenth century Venetian glass. Dashing the wine from one of the goblets she hurried back to the corpse. Dragging the bloody pin from his ear, she plunged into the jugular, twisting and turning the pin to enlarge the opening. Blood spurted and then almost immediately died to a trickle. Holding the man's head, she tilted it to one side, catching the trickling blood in the goblet. When she had collected enough of the sluggish liquid, she walked slowly back to the mirror.

Toward Frazer.

Jonathan Frazer felt his mouth go dry, his breath catch in his throat. He had become aroused as she had made love with the man, but that arousal had passed as he watched in horrified fascination while she killed the old man and collected his blood in the goblet. Now he felt himself becoming aroused again as she walked towards him and he saw her fully exposed for the first time: the large and heavy breasts, the small nipples puckered and erect. Her belly was smoothly rounded, her navel deeply indented, and the hair between her thighs was as thick and dark as the hair on her head.

The image crouched before the mirror, seemingly no more than a foot away from Frazer. She clutched the goblet in both hands and her lips were moving as if in prayer. Dipping a hand in the liquid, she rubbed it across her breasts and down over her belly. When her hand touched her groin she shuddered in sudden orgasm. Then, she looked up, straight into Frazer's eyes—and threw the contents of the goblet directly into his face.

He shrieked aloud and fell backwards, his arm across his face. When he opened his eyes and looked at the mirror, he saw that the mirror was clouding over *from the other side.* The greasy grime had returned and there was no sign of the image in the glass.

It was only when he sat up that he realized his white T-shirt was speckled in blood.

59

THERE WAS too much glass, too many mirrors around for him to be comfortable, and bitter experience had taught him that as the image gained strength, it could work through any reflective surface.

House music throbbed, a deep base vibrating through the walls, pulsing in the air and the arched ceiling and orange glow from the lights gave the nightclub interior an eerie inferno feel. As the music intensified the lights flashed intermittently from blue to orange along with the beat. Edmund Talbott reckoned that hell had a chamber very much like this. Scantily clad, sweaty bodies gyrated to the beat of the deafening music.

He had initially thought he was going to be very much out of place, but he was surprised by the number of older men cruising the nightclub, lounging at the bar, obviously watching the women. He was even more surprised at the number of young women who were dancing, drinking, and flirting with them.

He shouldered his way through the crowd, making for the bar, already regretting coming in. He reckoned his chances of finding Manny Frazer here were slim indeed.

He'd spent the day sitting in a stolen blue Toyota Corolla, watching the Frazer house through binoculars. He had seen Jonathan Frazer drive up in the Volvo and hurry into the house at around one, but there had been no activity since then, and Frazer was still in the house . . . or was he in the guesthouse?

He needed to get to Frazer, but with the police surveillance outside the house he couldn't simply walk up to the front door, and he was too close to the mirror to even think about using astral projection. Even this far from the glass, he could *feel* the coldly pulsating core of the whirlpool battering against his unconscious.

He was going to have to get into the house. He knew that the mirror was already exerting its influence over Frazer. He had seen it in his eyes, had felt it, and he knew he couldn't count on Frazer to cover the glass with a black cloth. But he had two cans of aerosol black lacquer paint in his pockets and if at all possible he was going to spray the surface of the glass. He wasn't sure how effective that would be, but it should cut down the mirror's ability to show the images it used to entice its victims.

And Jonathan Frazer was an obvious target.

Edmund Talbott was becoming concerned for Frazer's mental health. He had encountered disturbing signs on the astral that someone was feeding the mirror with blood, and yet Talbott hadn't heard of any deaths, hadn't *felt* any souls entering the Otherworld. So that meant the feeding was deliberate. Was the mirror more powerful than he'd thought: had it taken Frazer several steps further than he imagined? If he discovered that Frazer was feeding the mirror with blood then Talbott would kill him with no more compunction than he would a dangerous insect.

Day turned to evening and fell into night and, around ten, just when he was contemplating giving up, a yellow cab arrived. Talbott saw a brief flurry of activity in the unmarked police car as the cab drove up the driveway to the Frazer house. The door opened almost immediately and light shafted out into the mild night air. Manny Frazer appeared, wearing a long loose coat, and climbed into the cab. Talbott immediately started up the Corolla and drove out onto the main road, timing it so that the cab ended up directly behind him. The light turned red and he used the opportunity to glance around—he had removed the rearview and side mirrors—and saw Manny pulling off her coat. He pulled in to the curbside, allowing the cab to move past him, and then pulled out behind it. He had followed it through the busy evening streets as it cut across Barham Boulevard, the Hollywood Freeway, Highland Avenue and then down onto Sunset Boulevard, eventually pulling outside a nightclub close to Crescent Heights. Talbott saw the brake lights flare and immediately turned right into a side street. The cab stopped outside what looked like a minimalist stone storefront with a single wooden door and Manny Frazer stepped out—and he immediately knew why she'd been wearing a coat when she left the house. She was wearing a tiny black dress. It barely covered her buttocks, a scooped neckline exposed most of her breasts, and when she turned her back, Talbott saw that most of her back was bare.

He parked the car, climbed out and carefully locked it. The narrow street was buzzing, valets busily parking customers' cars in a parking lot that catered to the comedy place next door and the nightclub. Talbott could feel the throbbing in the air as he approached and he cringed at the thought of entering the noisy, hot interior, which was undoubtedly crammed with people. There were two large security people at the door, ridiculous in their black suits; they gave Talbott the once over, nodded, and for a moment, he thought they were going to stop him, but they apparently thought better of it.

The noise inside the room was a physical thing. He imagined he could feel the very air tremble with sound. His head begin to throb immediately and he was conscious of his heartbeat increasing in time to the pulsing of the music. How anyone could come to a place like this for pleasure was beyond him.

It took him ten minutes before he finally got the barman's attention over the noise, and there was surprisingly little change from his ten bucks for his bottle of Perrier. He turned his back to the bar, squeezing through the sweaty bodies before finding a small breathable space, looking for Manny.

The stench in the place was almost overpowering, a combination of a hundred perfumes, both male and female, sweat, alcohol, the sweeter tang of hash and the vaguest hint of rot and damp. How could this be pleasurable, he wondered again.

He sipped the water, his hard cold eyes watching the crowd. The problem was that Manny's outfit was similar enough to scores of the young women present, and he knew that unless she actually passed right by him . . . there! He immediately pushed his way through the throng, following the young girl, using his height to watch her move, relaxed, through the crowd. The pulsating lights were infuriating, making him clumsy, and if there was skill to moving through a crowded room, then he obviously didn't possess it.

Manny was lounging up against a wall when he finally caught up with her. Her right leg was raised high enough to display that she was wearing no underwear, her head tilted back against the wall, a hand-rolled cigarette drooping between her lips. The man standing directly in front of her, his hand high on her thigh, was old enough to be her father—older probably.

Talbott shouldered his way into the couple and plucked the man's hand off the girl's thigh.

"Hey, what the fuck . . ."

Talbott brought his face close to the man's, smelling his aftershave and sweat. "She's my daughter," he hissed.

"She's over the age of consent!" he blustered.

Talbott's hard fingers grabbed a fistful of the flesh that bulged over the older man's waistband and squeezed. The smile on his face was terrifying. "Do you enjoy pain?" he whispered, his voice barely audible above the throbbing of the music. "Now fuck off!" He gave a final twist to the flabby stomach flesh for emphasis, and the man turned pale in agony before backing away from the terrifying figure.

When Edmund Talbott turned back to the girl she was gone!

60

IT WAS turning out to be a shitty night.

It hadn't started out right and it was going to end in tears, she knew that.

Manny had been feeling *off* all day, a little distracted, a little dizzy, like she'd done some grass or speed, but she hadn't done drugs since she'd come back from Paris—well not much really, a few tokes at Amanda's party a couple of weeks ago, but nothing serious.

Maybe it was just all the madness in the air over the past couple of weeks. People she'd known had died for Christ's sake! Surely that meant that she was entitled to feel a little crazy?

She'd planned to stay in, but late in the evening she'd opted for a long leisurely bath rather than a shower, and soaked for the best part of an hour and that had helped to wake her up. She'd climbed out of the bath and dried herself off in front of the full length mirror, curious at the peculiar changes taking place in her body. The hair on her head, for example, was really growing quickly and her pubic hair, which she'd recently had waxed, was now growing in as well. Her breasts, which were full, actually looked and felt heavier, and she was obviously putting on weight, too, because her stomach looked slightly rounded, though when she checked it on the scale, she discovered she'd lost a pound. Must be something to do with her period, she decided again; maybe it was coming early this month. Wasn't stress supposed to bring it on—or did that delay it?

She needed a night out, she decided. On her own: just go out, go wild, drink a few cocktails, maybe toke a few joints, find a nice guy to dance with . . .

And it was a mistake.

She'd realized that about five minutes after entering the club. In the time she'd been away in Paris, the character of the place had changed. It used to be the "in" place to be seen, limousines lined up outside, celebrities would come and hang out, the paparazzi would have a field day photographing the rich and famous as they entered, blocking the entrance and then hanging around waiting for them to leave in a disheveled state, drunk and slightly high. Now the club had turned into a cattle market, with a lot of older guys cruising for girls who couldn't be older than some of their daughters. The music was a lot louder, too, and the colored strobes that she used to find so exciting now only confused and disorientated her. All the old faces were gone—except Miriam, who'd been the coat check girl when she'd last been there and who remembered her. As Manny handed over her coat, Miriam slid her a joint with her ticket, "Help ease the pain," she grinned, nodding to the dance floor.

She'd been relaxing against the wall when this creep had come up to her: short, slightly pudgy, with a shirt open down to his naval. He slid his hand up her leg, saying nothing, concentrating on looking meaningfully into her eyes—which translated as a leer—and she was contemplating kneeing him in the balls, when security had come up and shoved the guy away. She'd wanted none of this, and didn't want to be leaned on by the security guy. God alone knows what he thought with her dressed in this get up. She was sorry she'd worn it now, especially here, where some of the girls leaning against the walls were eyeing the men with a professional interest. She wouldn't be at all surprised if some of the security guys were in on the action, and she certainly didn't want them to think she was a freelancer. In Paris anyway—and Los Angeles too, she assumed—girls working without a pimp tended to end up hurt.

So, while security was having his few words with the creep, she slid away from the wall, ducked into the cloakroom and grabbed her coat from Miriam, promising she'd call her tomorrow, and was out of the place before either man even noticed she'd gone.

The fresh night air hit her with an almost physical blow and she stood swaying on the street for a moment, desperately resisting the temptation to vomit. She'd only had one drink, but whatever had been in that joint had been good shit.

Cab or walk?

Common sense said cab, so she walked, padding barefoot down the street, dangling her heels in her hands.

It was a little after eleven, a cool night in November, and the city seemed almost relaxed, all the sounds were muted, and the pulsing of the club faded rapidly as she walked away from it.

She walked east on Sunset, and ignored the lewd comments from a couple of passing drivers. She wanted to walk a little further to clear her head before making a decision, but there was no way she could go home like this. Her dad would still be up and she didn't want him to see her dressed like this, or in this state. She must have walked for almost a mile when she decided to rest on the stone steps leading to a building. A fountain spat water, white noise drowning out the traffic. Manny sat peering into the rectangular water fountain, drawn by the mixed colors of deep blue and turquoise mosaic tiles. She had been staring into the flat reflective surface of the water for a few seconds before she realized what she was seeing.

There was a face beneath the water. Looking up at her. Manny rubbed her eyes, smudging her brown-black mascara and eyeliner across her cheeks.

An oval face, with prominent rounded cheekbones, full lips, and dark up-tilted eyes.

And it was watching her. The mouth opening and closing, calling to her.

More and more of the body came into view—the shoulders, the chest, arms, hands, fingers, raising upwards, reaching for her, clutching at her, coming closer to the surface, rising up out of the blue waters—and when the body broke the surface Manny knew it was going to pull her in.

And she couldn't move, couldn't scream. Could only watch in horrified fascination as the woman came ever closer.

The mirror image was familiar, desperately familiar, and the portion of her mind that remained coolly practical was trying to work out where she'd seen the face before, but somewhere at the back of her head, she wanted to believe that this was nothing more than the shit she'd been smoking.

But in her heart and soul, she knew that this was something more than a hallucination, this was too real, the image was too powerful.

She was looking down into the water, locked onto the shimmering reflections ... when cool, long fingered hands burst from the surface, locked around her shoulders and dragged her down.

"You were swaying to and fro when I saw you. I knew you were going to fall into the water. You could have drowned."

Manny Frazer looked up into Edmund Talbott's scarred face and then fainted gracefully into his arms.

61

J ONATHAN FRAZER had given blood on dozens of occasions, and it was a simple straightforward task, with absolutely no pain, merely resulting in a mild discomfort in the crook of his arm. So extracting a pint of his own blood should have been no problem—or so he thought.

It had taken him the best part of two hours to get close to three-quarters of a pint. His left arm was one enormous bruise and the ragged puncture in his vein now almost spitefully refused to close. The bathroom sink and mirror were speckled with blood and the stink of his own sweat was heavy on the pine-scented air.

Jonathan looked at the glass beaker full of the viscous liquid, and wondered if it was enough. He looked at himself in the bathroom mirror, surprised at the deep shadows beneath his eyes, the lines on his face. He looked old, he decided, old and tired.

He ran his fingers down through the stubble on his chin, scratching. He hated being unshaven; it was practically the first thing he did each morning, and usually again just before dinner. He had shaved this morning, surely he didn't need to shave again? He stopped, and then stepped out of the bathroom to look at the red glowing figures on the digital clock on the nightstand.

Two minutes past midnight.

He stared at the clock, watching the digits change from two to three. Where had the time gone? It had seemed to slip away while he'd been staring into the mirror watching the naked woman make love to the fat man before she killed him. It was a dream, nothing more, except . . . except that it had been so real. So vivid.

He looked at the bottle of blood again. He must be out of his fucking mind to even consider it!

But he had seen something in the mirror, he reminded himself. And now he was going to see if he could see it again. He was conducting a scientific experiment. If nothing happened he could feel stupid, and he could curse himself for being seven sorts of a fool. But he had seen what blood did to the mirror; this was not going to fail.

Wincing with the ache in his left arm, working slowly and painfully, he cleaned up the bathroom, wiping away all traces of the blood, flushing the evidence down the toilet. As he came out of the bathroom he glanced at the clock again.

Twelve thirty.

He had the house to himself. Manny had gone out, and he doubted he'd see her again before dawn, so he had plenty of time. He'd spend an hour or so with the mirror, and then give it up. He looked at his wife's dressing table, and wondered where she was, whose arms she was in. Well, if everything went according to plan, he'd soon know.

He began to giggle then, the sound high-pitched and hysterical in the empty house.

62

She'd been married about seven years when Celia Frazer had her first affair. Wasn't it men who were supposed to get the seven year itch? Celia had a lot of time on her hands then: the nanny looked after Emmanuelle during the day, Jonathan had been busy building up and expanding the business. She'd been bored and it wasn't entirely her fault: Jonathan was as much to blame.

That first flush of passion that had brought them together had worn off and Jonathan seemed quite content to allow it to bubble along at a simmer. But she needed him to be a little more responsive, a little more demonstrative, in showing his love for her. A peck on the cheek in the morning, another at night when he came in from the store and by bedtime, he was usually too tired for lovemaking, except on the weekends.

But on the weekends she usually arranged a dinner party or organized a night at the theatre with friends or a movie with the result that when they returned home, *she* was usually too tired—or too drunk—for lovemaking.

They had also become a little bored with one another.

So, given the combination of circumstances, was it any wonder that she looked outside her marriage for satisfaction? Her first lover had been a neighbor, a foreign diplomat stationed in Los Angeles. His wife spent much of the time abroad and he'd been lonely. Theirs was a purely physical relationship and it had lasted on and off for nearly three months, and had taken place right under Jonathan's nose—although she was quite convinced that unless he had actually come home and found them making love in the bed, he wouldn't have noticed. The affair ended when her lover was posted abroad, and Celia Frazer was just as pleased, she was becoming bored with him anyway.

It had been a year before she'd had another lover, this time on the first vacation she'd taken on her own. He had been a French student, about ten years her junior, waiting tables to earn money to put himself through college for the coming term. The sex had been unsophisticated but his staying power had been phenomenal.

The following year there had been another holiday romance, and then after that, well, it became almost a habit. Jonathan's idea of a vacation and hers differed tremendously, and once the precedent had been set that they should vacation apart, that became the pattern. Finding a lover for the duration of her two or three or four week vacations was now part of the fun.

This year had been a little different, however. She had met Colin, a young surfer dude who had come to Hawaii to experience big surf. He'd offered to help her improve on her surfing skills, and while she had little interest in surfing, his toned and muscled body attracted her. He had planned to leave a few days before her vacation was due to end, but she persuaded him to stay on as her guest . . . not that he needed very much persuasion. Colin was a glorious and accomplished lover, always careful to ensure her own satisfaction first, before taking his own. They'd flown home together and he had invited her to join him up in Lake Tahoe where he was a ski instructor for the winter months.

It was an invitation she didn't want to refuse, but she couldn't justify taking off on another vacation having just come back from one. Could she?

But when she arrived home, Jonathan had been in shock at the death of that horrible Farren man. He'd been stamping around the place in a foul temper; there'd been police everywhere, and while the social circuit had suddenly rediscovered her, she knew they were only looking for tasty bits of gossip. She needed to get away for a bit, so she finally decided: hell, why not? She could go off to Lake Tahoe and enjoy herself with someone she liked, or she could stay at home, miserable, with someone she didn't really care about one way or another. Maybe that was what was wrong with their marriage: they didn't really care for one another, weren't really interested in one another, they had become too bound up in their own lives, their own petty interests. Where had the sharing gone?

She'd still hesitated about making the final decision to go to Tahoe—because she felt that in some ways it might be *the* final decision. But when Jonathan started actually sleeping in the guesthouse, well then, it was an easy decision to make.

At least with Colin she knew where she stood. Their relationship—if that's what you wanted to call it—was almost purely physical. He was eight years younger than her, and his energy and boyish enthusiasm made her feel like a teenager again.

She was still young. She should be out there enjoying life. Maybe it was time to start thinking about a divorce.

At least while there was still money to be split.

CELIA FRAZER, PLEASANTLY sated by the two bottles of wine they had drunk over dinner, lay back on the bed and watched the young man undress. Colin Mariner was tall, perpetually-tanned, broad-shouldered, and slim-hipped. Nine months on the water ensured toned six-pack abs and his shoulder length hair was bleached golden blond. And Jonathan—skinny, pale-skinned, short, graying black hair, with the beginnings of a paunch—compared very unfavorably with him. In fact, there was no contest.

Kicking off the single sheet, she turned her head to look at herself in the dressing table mirror, running her hands down her naked body. She thought she kept herself in pretty good condition. A good body, maybe a little too slim, small firm breasts, a flat stomach and narrow waist. The muscles in her thighs were clearly delineated now from all the surfing which made her seem slightly out of proportion . . . maybe she'd go to the gym and work on her shoulder and chest muscles. She brushed the palms of her hands up across her flat stomach, aware now that Colin was watching her. Maybe she'd think about slightly bigger breasts, too, the new implants were apparently absolutely amazing.

Celia turned back to Colin, cupping her breasts provocatively. "What would you think if I had them made bigger?"

The young man laughed. "I like them just the way they are," he said, climbing onto the bed between her outstretched legs, leaning forward to delicately kiss each nipple. "Besides," he added with a startling white smile, "anything more than a mouthful is a waste." His mouth opened wide, then closed around most of her breast.

Closing her eyes to the sensation, Celia allowed herself to drift. It wasn't her fault she was having affairs, it was Jonathan's, if he'd paid her as much attention as he'd lavished on his precious antiques . . .

63

T HE BLOOD had already begun to turn sticky and tacky by the time he reached the guesthouse and settled himself before the mirror, squatting about a foot away from the glass. With infinite care he uncorked the glass jar and the dry air of the guesthouse was immediately tainted with the meaty copper stench of blood. Lifting the bottle, he poured the thick liquid—now black and tar-like in the wan light—onto the sponge. The pale cratered bath sponge turned dark and heavy, and he immediately pushed it against the glass, squeezing it when it touched the surface, liquid snaking down the glass in twisting runnels. He rubbed the sponge in a quick circular motion, slicing through the grime, opening a window at about eye level. Wincing with the pain in his left arm, he reached into his jeans pocket and pulled out a small color photograph of Celia and held it up before his face, squinting in the dim light at the vague picture. He dropped the sponge and splashed blood directly from the glass beaker across the glass, creating a shallow arc that dripped blood down its length. Jonathan Frazer vigorously rubbed the blood onto the mirror, concentrating intently on Celia, squeezing his eyes shut in an effort to visualize her clearly, to *see* her face, her eyes, her hair . . . but the picture wouldn't come. How could you live with someone for so long and not be able to visualize their face? When you stopped seeing them, he realized, when you stopped looking at them. He opened his eyes and looked at the photograph again. It had been taken late last year at that skiing resort she'd gone to in the French Alps. She was wide-eyed, smiling, looking tanned and relaxed: the way she always looked after lovemaking.

A rainbow flicker shivered the length of the glass, blue and red and green.

Frazer lowered the picture and quickly threw more blood onto the glass.

The second ripple moved far more slowly down the mirror and coalesced around the spot where he'd rubbed in the blood. The colors and twisting shapes reminded him of oil on water, and then, as he watched, the thick black blood disappeared, absorbed into the mirror, leaving tiny dark flakes in its wake.

There was a small amount of his blood left and he was just about to throw it onto the glass when Celia Frazer's face appeared.

It was the face in the photograph, wide-eyed, smiling, tanned, relaxed, but larger, life-sized, three-dimensional.

It was staring at him.

And then the eyes blinked.

The mouth twisted into an ugly smile, showing long yellowed teeth. The eyes blinked and the head dipped, until all he could see was the top of her dyed ash-blond hair, the roots black and coarse. Then the head came back up again and grinned at him, the mouth working to form his name.

Jonathan.

Frazer fell back away from the mirror, flinging the sponge at the image in the glass. His foot struck the glass jar, sending it crashing against the frame, the bottle shattering, blood staining the wood.

The face in the mirror leered and grimaced. It was still Celia's face, but subtly altered, changed. The tanned skin had assumed a leathery appearance, the eyes seemed deeper in the skull, further apart, the cheekbones more prominent, the teeth longer, the expression mocking, long moist tongue licking lasciviously at cracked lips.

He understood, on some deep unconscious level, that it was still Celia he was looking at, but now he was seeing another aspect of her, as if the mirror had stripped away layers of deceit and subterfuge, revealing her true character.

The face abruptly shrunk in size, falling away from him, drawing him forward, until his face was inches from the glass. The spreading oil of colors obliterated everything and then twisted, and shifted, curling into shapes, resolving into a series of tiny pictures which fluttered past like wind-blown leaves. There were images, faces, pictures: a woman, a naked body, an infant, a face with long waving hair, Celia's face convulsed in ecstasy, Edmund Talbott's, Manny's, a tanned youth, blood, and flames. Abruptly they stopped and solidified into one image on the glass.

He was looking into a bedroom: a hotel bedroom judging by the furnishings and decor. The angle was low, a few feet off the floor, and looking directly onto a bed on which two naked figures writhed together, arms and legs locked around one another. He frowned, wondering what he was supposed to be seeing, and then he heard the high-pitched gasping pants of a woman approaching orgasm.

It was Celia's voice.

A smile of something like triumph locked onto his face, pulling his lips back from his teeth. The experiment had worked . . . was working. He pressed up close against the glass, staring deep into it, wishing he could be closer to the bed, trying to make sense of the angle, wondering how he was seeing them, trying to make sense of it in relation to his own position in the room. He looked around; what was missing from the picture of the room? And then he suddenly realized that he was looking *through* the dressing-table mirror!

The woman's gasps had now been augmented by a man's panted grunts, and Frazer was forced to sit, watching and listening to the couple reach their orgasm together and then finally collapse in a heap on the bed, where they lay breathless and gasping for a few moments, until the woman rolled out of the bed and approached the mirror.

Maybe he had been hoping—desperately hoping—that his mind had been playing tricks with him, and that it wasn't Celia who'd been in the man's arms, making love to him with an abandon and energy she'd never shown with him. But it was Celia, the smile of sated satisfaction back on her lips now, her skin flushed with the after-effects of orgasm.

Bitch, bitch, bitchbitchbitch, fucking bitch.

She sat and peered into the mirror—looking directly at him—and then she stretched out her hand to reach for him.

In his rage, Frazer pressed his hands flat against the cool surface. Then he slapped at the mirror, the crack of flesh off glass sounding like a blow.

64

CELIA USED to think that all the talk about multiple orgasms was so much nonsense, but tonight she'd had several in quick succession. She supposed everything was possible with a considerate lover, and while Colin might be many things—brash and arrogant, ignorant too, not terribly well-educated—he had an instinctive understanding of how to treat a woman, where to touch, when to kiss, how to lick, and what to suck.

Reluctantly, Celia Frazer swung her legs out of the bed, and padded toward the bathroom. She wanted to stay in bed with Colin, to feel his arms wrapped protectively around her, but two bottles of wine and a bout of energetic lovemaking were not compatible: her bladder was about to explode. She made a note: go to the bathroom before making love.

A flicker on the dressing-table mirror caught her attention. She stopped and looked behind her at the bedroom wall, wondering what was reflecting off the glass, making the shimmering rainbow patterns on the surface of the mirror. She could see nothing obvious. She leaned forward, looking deeper into the glass, frowning now. There were shadows in the glass. Shapes. Faces. Dear God—one of them looked like her husband. She was reaching out to touch the surface of the mirror with her fingertips . . .

When the glass exploded outwards!

Celia Frazer screamed, reeling away as razor sharp slivers dug into her naked skin, gouging at the flesh in her face . . .

AND JUST OVER three hundred miles away, Jonathan Frazer howled with delight as his slut of a wife reeled away from the glass, her flesh nicked and torn, four long scratches running down the right side of her face, under her chin and into the soft flesh of her shoulder.

Looking exactly as if someone had clawed at her!

65

A DOT, a spot, a circle of white in the distance.
   Growing.
Expanding.
Moving.
Taking on shape, shadows appearing, planes forming, becoming a face, wide-eyed, opened-mouthed, terrified. Screaming.

EMMANUELLE FRAZER AWOKE with the scream ringing in her ears, and then realized that the scream had been hers. She came bolt upright in the bed, both hands pressed to the side of her face, staring wildly around her.

Where was she?

Her last memories were of leaning over the fountain, feeling herself falling, the hand grabbing her, and the face of the ugly scarred man.

The scarred man.

The scarred man was sitting in a chair facing her, elbows resting on the arms of the chair, fingers laced together. He was wearing a black polo neck sweater with black pants and, with his dark eyes fixed on her face, he looked positively evil.

She scrabbled for the thin blanket that covered her, dragging it up to her chin. "Who are you? What am I doing here? How did I get here?"

"You're like your father," he said quietly, "he asks too many questions, too, without waiting for an answer." He stared at her for a moment, and then he said quickly, "I am Edmund Talbott, and I saved you from falling into the fountain. You are safe here."

Manny wasn't quite so sure about that.

"You know my father?" she asked.

"In a manner of speaking. We have met a couple of times. Has he not spoken to you about me?"

She started to shake her head and then the fragments fell together. "You're the big scarred man who wanted to buy the mirror," she whispered, horrified. "You killed Tony, Diane, Robert and those policemen." She was too shocked to even be frightened.

"I killed the police officers, that is true," he nodded gravely, "but none of the others. The image killed them."

Manny nodded gravely. She was in the presence of a madman, and all she had to do now was to humor him until he fell asleep and she could escape. There was only one door in the dingy room and he was sitting right beside it. There was a newspaper-covered window to her left but she had no way of knowing what was on the other side. It could be a blank wall for all she knew, or they could be six stories high.

She looked at the man—Talbott?—noting the lines of the scars and wrinkles on his face, figuring that he must have been handsome once, before the accident or whatever had so badly scarred him. She wondered why he didn't have plastic surgery.

"The scars are memories," he said suddenly, frightening her. He smiled at her horrified expression. "When people look at me—and I mean really look, not a quick glance—they usually wonder two things, how I got the scars, and why I keep them and not use plastic surgery."

Manny nodded. Keep him talking. While he was talking he was calm and reasoned.

"I got the scars in an elevator accident. I keep them in memory of my wife and son who died in that accident."

"Oh," she whispered, wondering if it were true. "That's . . . that's terrible . . ." She had tried to inject empathy into her voice, but it came out flat and unemotional.

"I attempted to meddle with something I could not control. And it didn't like it." He touched his face. Talbott stared intently into her eyes and then added, "But at least I knew what I was doing . . . or attempting to do. Unlike you."

"Me!"

Talbott stared at her impassively.

"Look, I really don't know what you're talking about!" she snapped. Mistake, mistake, mistake, she thought, always agree with them.

"The mirror," he said quietly.

"The mirror?" She looked at him blankly and then said very softly, "The mirror. What about the mirror?"

"Why don't you tell me about it," he said maddeningly.

"Look mister . . ."

"Edmund Talbott."

"Look Mr. Talbott. I know nothing about this mirror. I've seen it, it's in my father's guesthouse. And three people that I knew have died around it."

Talbott brought his fingertips up to his lips, palms of his hands pressed together. His finely developed senses told him that the girl was telling the truth, and yet he had seen the whirlwind in the Otherworld feeding off sexual energies that were undoubtedly female. Was it possible that the mirror was using her without her knowledge? It was unlikely, and yet not impossible. There was so much about the mirror and the images that it controlled that he did not know. The last person in his family to have a full understanding of the mirror had been his grandfather, whose knowledge of the occult was extraordinary, and who had counted many of the modern figures in the occult revival amongst his students. The stroke that had robbed him of most of his faculties including speech and the power of his hands had been a terrible tragedy, or so Talbott had thought until he discovered that before the stroke his grandfather had been talking of putting down the history and the legends surrounding the mirror onto paper. Then he realized it had been no accident of fate: the mirror had somehow caused the stroke.

"Have you ever seen—or experienced—anything strange or curious around the mirror?"

"What do you mean, strange or curious?"

"Tell me what you think I mean?" he said coyly, unwilling to lead her on.

Manny considered for a moment. "I don't like it, if that's what you mean . . . it's . . . it's creepy. And I saw a face in it once," she admitted almost reluctantly.

Talbott nodded. "What sort of face?" he asked gently.

She closed her eyes, remembering. "A woman's face . . . a . . . a woman's face." She opened her eyes again, shaking her head. "That's all I can remember. Why? What is it about this mirror? Is it haunted?"

He shrugged, a wry smile stretching the scars on his face. "Yes, no, I don't know. It is evil, it attracts evil, it disseminates evil, that is all I know. It is ancient and deadly."

"I don't see what all this has got to do with . . ." Manny began, but Talbott held up a hand, stopping her.

"The mirror works through people, controlling them, using them to feed its appetite. It shows people things, sometimes it shows them what they want to see, more often than not, it shows them what they most fear. You may or may not choose to believe this, but I think you've seen enough over the past couple of weeks to know that what I'm telling you is the truth. And you will also admit that your father has been acting strangely of late?"

Manny suddenly nodded. "I thought this might have something to do with Dad. Yes, he's been a little odd, but then strange things have been happening around him . . ."

". . . ever since he bought the mirror," Talbott finished for her.

"So what are you saying to me? Are you telling me that this mirror has some sort of control over my dad, that it's possessing him?"

"No, I'm not saying that at all," Talbott murmured. He was watching the young woman carefully, wondering how much to tell her, wondering how much she would accept. Usually, the young were always so open to ideas.

"I am saying that your father is seeing things in the mirror . . ."

"What sort of things?"

"Whatever he most wants to see, whatever he fears most. I don't know. He will keep going back to the glass again and again, feeding it, becoming addicted to the images."

"What do you mean *feeding it*," Manny asked suddenly, the significance of the words suddenly sinking in.

"The glass is dirty, grimy, greasy. Only blood will clean the glass, only blood will fire the images. Blood and sex." He saw the sudden coloring on her cheeks, and pressed on. "The intense emotion of orgasm can also fire the mirror. But I think perhaps you know something of this, eh?"

"I think I want to go home," Manny said, suddenly.

"Why, what have I said that frightened you?"

"Nothing. Shit! Everything you said frightened me. Magic fucking mirrors, blood, sex, images; you're a crazy person!"

"I'll not deny that. But everything I've said to you is the truth." He came suddenly to his feet and crossed the room to stand towering over the girl. "Now someone has been feeding the mirror with blood, and if it is not you, then it has to be your father. But someone has also been feeding it with sexual energy—and that is you, I believe." Manny started to shake her head, but Talbott pressed on. "But you see, since you know nothing about the mirror, I can only assume that you've been doing this unknowingly. Have you been having strange dreams lately, erotic dreams?" he asked suddenly. He saw the answer in her eyes and continued relentlessly. "Usually the female is a willing part of the conspiracy, giving freely of herself, deliberately feeding the mirror. But not you. You're so close to your father, so close to the mirror that I suppose it was only natural that you should be caught up in it."

"I have been having . . . strange dreams," Manny admitted in a whisper, "erotic dreams. When I wake up I realize, I've . . . I've . . ."

Talbott patted her shoulder. "I know. I know," he said quietly. He straightened and crossed to the window, peering out through a tiny nick in the newspaper across the silent streets in the general direction of the Hollywood Hills. Even in his waking state, he could still feel the vague disturbance in the Otherworld.

"What can I do? Can you help me? Can you help my father?"

Edmund Talbott turned back, shaking his head slightly. "I don't know," he said truthfully. He looked down at the pale-faced girl, wondering if it wasn't too late for them all.

He glanced at his watch. It was three-thirty. "Was your father going out tonight?"

She shook her head. "He rarely goes out."

"Where is your mother?"

"She got a bit fed up with Dad—or at least that was her excuse—and went up to Lake Tahoe for a little break. She said she'd come back when all this was over and done with."

Talbott nodded thoughtfully. At least that was one less problem to take care of. "You know there are police watching your house. They're watching for me," he added unnecessarily. "Can you get me back to the house posing as a boyfriend?"

"Why?"

"I asked your father to cover the face of the mirror with a black cloth. But I don't think I can trust him to do that." He dug his hands into his pockets and pulled out the cans of black paint. "I want to get close enough to the mirror to do the next best thing."

Manny nodded, looking at the cans in horrified fascination. She didn't tell Talbott that she felt almost physically sick at the thought of spraying the mirror with black lacquer paint.

66

N ow ...
     Now ...
  Now ...
  NOW!

It had tasted his blood, savored it, felt his touch upon the imprisoning crystal. It had turned his dreams, his fears, into reality, allowed him a taste of power, given him a glimpse of possibilities.

And the blood had been good, so good; almost fresh, still bright with energy.

The whirlpool of energy whipping through the Otherworld began to vibrate, to shiver with trembling energy. Vivid reds, vibrant greens, sulphurous yellows, cut across the placid astral landscape and a deep violet stain spread across the grayness, twisting, turning like a coiling cloud, dispelling the Otherworld's drabness. Fragments of the whirlpool began to break away, lurid clouds flashing across the plain, spinning curls of lambent color. But deep within the core of the whirlpool of power the twisting energies latched onto the presence before the crystal cage, feeding it, as it had fed them. It had never been so close to freedom before.

It called up the image from its memory.

67

Jonathan Frazer rocked back and forth on his heels, tears streaking his grimy face.

Bitchbitchbitchbitch.

She thought she could fool him, but he'd gotten her in return. The experiment had been successful.

The mirror was some sort of psychic resonator, he decided. It obviously magnified thoughts or emotions, or possibly the blood was what originally charged it, allowing it to create the psychic link between people or places, translating the image through the nearest mirror, or possibly any reflecting surface would do. When he'd lunged at Celia, he'd obviously overloaded the mirror at the far end of the connection, causing it to break, the glass slicing into her skin.

Jonathan Frazer sat back nodding quickly, rubbing his sleeve across his eyes, convinced that his explanation was at least plausible. He was sitting cross-legged on the floor, staring speculatively at the mirror, mentally and physically exhausted by his recent encounter, when he noticed the flickering deep in the core of the glass. It was a slow, flesh-colored pulse and as he watched, it grew from a tiny spot to an egg shape, and then larger into a pale-colored sphere. Colors, indentations, shadows began to appear on the pulsing ball, and just as Frazer realized that his heart was throbbing in time to the entity in the mirror, it assumed a definite form and shape and substance.

There was a woman in the mirror.

The woman he had seen before: this was Dee and Kelley's mysterious nameless woman, with the long hair and uptilted black eyes.

But he had never seen her so clearly before, never in such exquisite detail. It was almost as if she were standing on the other side of the glass.

Jonathan Frazer came slowly to his feet and discovered that she was about his height. But whereas her legs and groin were clearly delineated, her breasts and head were still slightly shaded. He stooped and picked up the still damp sponge, rubbing it across the glass, squeezing hard, smearing the last of the tacky blood onto the glass, clearing the dirt. Her features immediately came clearer. Her eyes were wide and pleading, her mouth working, her hands outstretched.

She was attempting to communicate with him.

She was a spirit, a ghost, trapped within the mirror, he was convinced of it. And she wanted to be free.

"How?" he asked, mouthing the word clearly. "How can I help you?"

The image's mouth moved slowly, her full lips forming words. But did she say *feed me* or *free me?*

Frazer pressed the palm of his hand against the glass, and the image on the other side did the same, matching his fingers with hers.

Feed me?

Free me?

It didn't matter. He'd do both. ·

68

MANNY HAD first felt it in the cab, the strange tingling and warmth deep in her groin, the itching in her fingertips and toes, the pressure on her breasts. She was conscious of her heart pounding so hard she could actually feel her skin vibrate, and she was acutely aware of her shortness of breath.

And it was Edmund Talbott's proximity.

When the scarred man had leaned over and tapped on the partition separating them from the cab driver, asking him to pull over, she'd been delighted. She needed the air.

Manny stepped out of the cab and into the shadows and watched Talbott pay the driver. She could make a run for it now if she wanted to. She was about a hundred yards from home and she was sure she'd get to the police car parked outside her house before this madman caught up with her. But she didn't run.

She had found that her attitude towards Talbott had changed as she'd approached the house. He seemed genuine, and certainly everything he told her fitted in with what she already knew. She could feel the power radiating from the man; she knew he was dangerous and a killer, and yet she didn't feel threatened by him. He spoke of strange energies, powers, and places with an intimate knowledge which she found fascinating and exciting. And while she had at first doubted his story about his wife and child, as he had continued to speak she discovered she had less and less reason to mistrust him, and now she found the whole idea of him keeping his scars as a memento to his dead family almost romantic.

And of course, she didn't want him to harm the mirror.

Talbott waited until the taxi had pulled away and walked over to

Manny, moving in under the trees that overhung the road, blanketing her in shadow.

"You know what to do?" he asked gently. "Do you still want to do it?"

"I want to do it." She slipped her arm through his. "You are my boyfriend; I've known you for years. You're a little drunk so you're coming home with me for the night. God knows what the cop'll think of me," she said archly.

"Does it matter?" Edmund Talbott's lips curled in a smile that never came close to his eyes. What he hadn't told the young woman was that if the police saw through the ruse, and there was every possibility that they would, he would have to kill them both, and then all thoughts of subtlety went out the window. Killing so close to the mirror would only draw its attention down on him. He would then have to get to the glass as quickly as possible . . . and God help Manny and Jonathan Frazer if they got in his way.

Manny led him down the street, her right arm around his waist, his left arm across her shoulders and her left hand holding his, as if supporting him. They stumbled along the road, her high heels clicking loudly on the sidewalk, the sound unnaturally loud in the predawn silence. He glanced at the glowing green dial of his watch; it was a little before four, the dead time of night. More suicides were committed at this time of the morning than at any other, this was the time when the nightmares held sway, when dreams turned ugly with returning consciousness. This was the time when the astral spirit began to return to its fleshy host. It was a time of memories.

They stopped at the gated entrance. The unmarked police car was still parked across the road. Edmund stared at it for a few moments, but could see no movement inside. He smiled; he hadn't chosen to come here at this particular hour without good reason: this was also the time when the human body's imperative to sleep was at its strongest.

They wove drunkenly up the driveway, Talbott's head dipped low on his chest, stooping to disguise his height, Manny clinging to him, her arm around his broad waist. She could feel the heat coming off the man, she was close enough to smell his strange scent, a curious bitter-sweet aroma of herbs and some exotic orange-flavored spice. She was also aware of the effect he was having on her. Maybe her heart was pounding, her flesh tingling because she was about to do something illegal and dangerous, but she didn't think so. She was becoming aroused, and it was Edmund Talbott's fault.

The two police officers were asleep in the car. Mouths open, they both had their arms folded, one leaning against the left window, the other against the right.

Maybe there was a God after all, Talbott reflected, resisting the temptation to smile.

As they neared the front gate a deep shuddering chill wracked through his body, causing him to stumble. Manny held him as he attempted to catch his breath.

"What's wrong, what's the matter?"

"I can feel it," he muttered through gritted teeth. "It's strong, so very strong." He held his head up, almost as if he were listening and when he looked at Manny, his eyes were wide in alarm. "It's fed recently. I can taste the blood on the air." Blood and the faintest hint of sex. His large hand closed around Manny's arm, almost dragging her up the driveway. "Come on."

"What do you mean, it's fed?"

"Blood," he murmured.

"My father?" she asked in alarm.

"I can't think of anyone else."

The power of the image was strong here. He concentrated on building psychic defenses around himself which he hoped would prove effective. Every element of his consciousness had to be withdrawn into himself; he had to focus on thinking about one thing only, something simple: if even a portion of his consciousness went into the Otherworld then he was lost. This was the very heart of the whirlpool. He could almost *see* it towering over the house—gray and sere, twisting, turning, with faces, both human and demon within it—could almost hear the howling of the ghost wind, hear the wailing of the damned . . .

STOP IT!

It knew he was here. It was attempting to lure him, to beguile him into thinking about the deadly glass. Was he strong enough to withstand the blandishments of the mirror? He had to be. He touched the cans of paint in his pockets. Something simple, he needed to focus on something simple.

Manny let herself in by the front door. It was easier and quicker to make their way through the house and out through the kitchen than it was to go around the side through the garden. She turned as Talbott came into the hallway and then stopped, frozen by the expression of horror on his face. "Mr. Talbott . . . Mr. Talbott . . . Edmund . . . ?"

"The mirror," he whispered, squeezing his eyes shut, "for pity's sake, cover the mirror!" He fell to his knees clutching at his face, covering his eyes with his hands.

Manny whirled around. There was a large freestanding ornate gilt-edged mirror in the hallway at the base of the stairs alongside the coatrack. She could see herself and Talbott reflected in the glass. And then she blinked. Talbott's image had briefly flickered . . . and so had her own. As she watched the glass clouded. Emmanuelle Frazer approached the mirror slowly, touching it with her fingertips, her heart pounding convulsively. She could no longer see herself in the glass. There was a misty gray oval where her face should be.

And Edmund Talbott's reflection showed him lying on the marbled floor, his clothing ragged and shredded, his flesh torn and bleeding.

The scream caught in her throat as she spun around. Talbott was unmarked. "Edmund . . . ?" she whispered slowly.

And Edmund Talbott slowly took his hands away from his eyes. He had caught a brief glimpse in the mirror as the front door had swung open, and in that instant he knew he was lost. That face, those eyes, the soft auburn hair, the gently curved lips. Even covering his eyes couldn't remove the image that had been seared on his brain. Now he could smell her in the room, that eau de parfum she favored, feel the heat from her body, and then—the final touch—her voice. Soft, gentle, husky, her English accent strong when she whispered, "Edmund?"

It was Elizabeth, his wife.

And where was Edward, his son? He must be around here somewhere. "Edmund?"

He'd been away too long, too many business trips, and he'd missed her. She'd missed him, too. She was standing before him, her arms around his neck, kissing him with a passion he didn't ever remember her demonstrating. He could feel her tongue against his lips, pushing, probing, her hands working at his clothes, fumbling with buttons. And he was aroused, so aroused; he wanted her, he wanted her so badly. He tore at her black dress—he'd never seen her wear it before—exposing her breasts, and then pulled the dress down to her groin, ripping it apart. He fumbled at her breasts, her nipples larger than he remembered them, but then she was nearly five months pregnant, her breasts were bound to be heavier, nipples larger than usual, darker. She had almost pulled his shirt off, buttons were popping and skittering across the floor, and now she was working at his belt, snapping open the top button of his pants, dragging them down. And those eyes, so wide, so expressive, so full of love and warmth and need. Her mouth, now flat against the side of his head, whispering obscenities in his ear, urging him to take her . . . take her . . . take her. And his own passion reaching a stage where he simply had to have her here and now on the floor and he knew she was five months pregnant and he didn't care, and then he was inside her and she was wrapping her legs around him, pulling him in deeper, her fingers clawing at his flesh, as she thrust herself at him. She'd never done that before, she'd always been passive in bed, but obviously his absence had fired her blood, and he found himself pounding savagely into her, grunting, savoring her whimpering and her little gasps of pain and pleasure, concentrating now on his own release, feeling it building deep inside him . . .

MANNY WASN'T SURE when it started exactly. She'd knelt on the floor, wondering what was wrong and put her arms around him, and then he was kissing her and the pressure she'd felt building up inside her, the coiled tension, seemed to unwind, and she found herself returning his kiss with a passion that surprised even herself. The tingle of electricity in her limbs continued to shudder through her body, concentrating in her groin, on her breasts, and when he had rubbed his thumbs across her sensitive nipples, the first orgasm had taken her, snatching her breath away, increasing her already racing heartbeat to an almost frightening level. She could feel the power coming off him, raw, primal energy that flowed from his body into hers. When he entered her, a second orgasm had shivered through her and she had clutched at him, wanting all of him inside her, acutely aware of his body against hers. His chin and stubble rasped against the soft flesh of her cheeks. She was speaking to him, shocking herself as she urged him on, encouraging him to take her, guiding him with pornographic detail. He began to pound into her, his large hands tightening on her breasts, twisting and pulling the nipples . . . and hurting.

Everything changed in a single heartbeat.

Suddenly, his pounding became painful, her lubrication suddenly seeming to vanish, and the rasp of flesh against flesh was agony. She attempted to push him off, but his weight was pressing her down. She flailed at him with her fists, but his face was locked into an impassive mask, his eyes blank and unseeing, spittle dribbling from the corner of his mouth. His hands began to convulse on her breasts, digging into the soft flesh, leaving long red weals in their wake, scoring the skin, drawing blood in places. She attempted to scream, but his mouth was on top of hers, his tongue probing deeper, his lips locked against hers. Her groin was on fire now, pure agony as he continued to batter at her, slamming against her pubic bone, attempting to push himself deeper and deeper.

And then his orgasm took him.

Talbott's back arched, and his head went back, his eyes squeezed shut in blissful pleasure as he thrust himself inside her.

And Manny Frazer punched him with all her might in the throat!

Edmund Talbott convulsed off the young woman, his eyes wide in shock, both hands clutched to his throat. She saw his Adam's apple working, his chest heaving, and then his eyes began to bulge, his face purpling as he fought for breath. He staggered to his feet, turned . . . and found he was facing the mirror.

And, in that moment, knew he was a dead man.

The mirror exploded.

In those last few moments of life, Talbott realized what had happened. After all the preparations, all his precautions, he had been trapped by his own stupidity. He discovered now that he'd been made to come here, *here* where the mirror was so strong, where the power of the image was absolute. It had played with him, showing him the image of his long dead wife—he wondered what poor Manny had seen—and then taking his lust and inflaming it. And it had been a long time since he'd slept with a woman. It had fed off the sexual emotions the two of them had generated: what a triumph that was for the glass. And then it had turned the emotion of lust to fear for the woman, making what he was doing no more than rape. It undoubtedly took extra pleasure in that: sex by force was probably a delicacy to it. The link between him and the mirror was lost only in the few seconds after orgasm had wracked his body and he suddenly discovered what he was doing to Manny. A feeling of horror and revulsion swept through him.

And then he'd felt the pain.

It lanced through his throat, impacting the trachea, blocking the air passages and his deflated lungs began to scream for air almost immediately. Coolly, almost calmly, he realized it was a death blow.

He staggered away from the girl, turned . . .

And saw himself in the hall mirror. But now every glass, every reflective surface was controlled by the image.

The mirror exploded.

He watched the freestanding mirror at the base of the stairs dissolve, long slivers of glass erupt outwards, lancing their way towards them, moving almost in slow motion through the air, glittering, sparkling, lethal.

Edmund Talbott's last conscious thought was to throw himself forward atop Manny, wrapping his arms around her, shielding her as the glass tore into his body, shredding the flesh on his head, shoulders, back, and buttocks, cutting down to the bone in many cases, laying open a whole section of his spine, spears of glass penetrating his kidneys, ripping into his lungs.

It had taken ten years, but the image had finished what it set out to do in the glass elevator in London. With his last breath, Edmund Talbott wondered what would happen now to Jonathan and Manny and everyone else who came in contact with the image.

He was surprised to find that he still cared.

69

"Personally gentlemen, I don't give a fuck what your excuses are. You let him walk right past you and then rape the girl in her own fucking hallway! I'm bringing you both up on charges." Margaret Haaren stalked away from the two officers standing at the gate. Neither of them attempted to offer any excuses: they had none. The first they'd known about the attack was when a screaming, naked and bloodied female had hammered on the windshield of their car, jolting them both awake. Her bloodied handprints were still smeared across the glass.

Haaren strode up the graveled driveway, almost shivering with rage. So you did your best, no, you did more than your best because you were a woman in a man's world but the best wasn't good enough. You had to give a hundred percent plus ten. And when the Chief of Detectives had asked for a report in person, you told him you had the situation under control and that you had two of your best men—best men, *Jesus*—watching the house and that there was no way the scarred man was going to get within a hundred yards of the place. And this was only yesterday; this was the chief telling you—warning you—that they needed a result, and fast. The bodies were beginning to mount up and far too many of them were police officers.

And what happened?

The fucking animal waltzes in past the two *best* men on the gate, gets in through the front door and brutally rapes the daughter in the hallway. The only good thing to come out of all of this was that she'd actually killed the guy. Punched him in the throat and then pushed a mirror on him, ripping him to shreds in the process. He was probably alive when that happened, too, his throat completely closed, unable to scream. Well, it couldn't have happened to a nicer guy.

Forensics had finished by the time she arrived and the coroner had removed the body but the hallway still looked like a slaughterhouse. There was blood and glass everywhere, splashed high on the walls, the back of the doors, some of it even speckling the ceiling. It stank, too. The sharp copper tang of blood was everywhere, but the bitter stench of urine and the sweeter, cloying odor of excrement was heavy on the air.

Detective Stuart Miller came up and stood beside her, saying nothing, allowing her to absorb the atmosphere of the place.

"How's the girl?" she asked eventually.

"She's upstairs with the family doctor. She's refusing to go to the hospital. She's hysterical," he added slowly, "and I've seen enough hysterical women in my time to know when it's being put on a bit for our benefit. This is the real deal."

"How is the father taking it?"

"Oh, he's the cool one all right. If I didn't know any better, I'd think he was smoking some weed. I'm not saying he was uninterested in what had happened to his daughter, but it's as if it didn't really affect him one way or the other. He didn't impress me. I only know how I'd react if it was my daughter . . ."

"I don't think our Mr. Frazer is a very nice man," Margaret Haaren agreed. "What about the mother? Where is she?"

"On another vacation in Lake Tahoe; skiing I presume. Neither of them want her informed."

"Just one big happy family, eh?"

Stuart Miller nodded. "How do you want to play this?"

"By the book; I'm picking up flack from upstairs. The suits are looking for a result—well, they got that with the death of the scarred man, but I've a feeling it's not going to be enough. A live body would have been nice."

"What about Mr. Frazer?" Miller suggested quietly. "Nice and live. And definitely dirty."

"Nothing would give me greater pleasure," she said feelingly.

As she began the procedure of working through the exact sequence of events, she tried to establish why she disliked Jonathan Frazer with such intensity. Rarely had she become so emotionally involved—if that was the right word—with one of her suspects. It wasn't a new feeling, but it was usually reserved for rapists or child molesters. What had Frazer done to deserve her ire?

He'd lied to her. He'd looked at her and decided he was cleverer than she was; he'd decided that he could run a scam on her and she wouldn't pick it up. And he was involved directly or indirectly in the death of several police officers, one of whom had been a very good friend. Here was a man who had seemed more upset about the death of one of his employees than the brutal rape of his daughter in her own hallway.

And neither husband nor daughter wanted Celia Frazer informed. "What the fuck is going on in this house?" she murmured.

"I'm sorry, ma'am?" Miller said.

"Did I say that aloud?"

"Afraid so. But I agree with you," he added quickly. "This . . . this death doesn't add up. There's something wrong, but I'm not seeing it."

"Give me a few minutes." Haaren stopped in the doorway and examined the sketch one of the attending officers had prepared of the scene, and then flipped the page to read through his initial notes on the man's injuries.

The scarred man—no identification present on the body—had been in a state of partial undress, coat and shirt lying on the floor—still there—his pants down around his ankles, still wearing one shoe; the other was lying on its side in a pool of thickening blood.

His back had been shredded, glass everywhere, long slivers actually penetrating deep into his flesh.

According to Emmanuelle Frazer she had pushed the mirror over on top of him.

Margaret Haaren looked up.

And what had she done then? Lifted it up and wheeled it back to its position at the base of the stairs where it was now? But there were no wheels.

Skirting the blood on the floor, Haaren stopped in front of the mirror, looking closely at it. The glass was broken outwards, which was consistent with it having been dropped onto the ground. Crouching down she examined the base. The mirror was obviously an antique. The heavy gilded frame ended in four legs, each one shaped like a carved animal claw clutching a ball. Licking her finger, she ran it across the floor directly in front of one of the legs: a faint ring of grime appeared on her finger, with a corresponding white mark on the floor. Surely if the mirror had been moved the legs would have left some marks on the marble tiles. She stood and looked closely at the mirror, and then, clutching it in both hands, she attempted to lift it. It shifted slightly, but didn't move. She knew adrenaline lent strength, possibly giving a terrified woman the strength to push the mirror over on top of her assailant. But to move it back again? The fact the mirror hadn't been moved added more credence to the theory she was developing.

Margaret Haaren walked halfway up the curving staircase, stopped and looked down, visualizing another scene, creating another set of circumstances to fit the facts.

When Stuart Miller, still standing in the hallway, saw her smile, he immediately started up the stairs. "Yes, ma'am?"

"Where is Mr. Frazer?"

"Having a little lie down, ma'am. He looked beat," he added.

"As if he'd been up all night?"

"Something like that."

"Is he still there?"

"There is an officer on the landing, outside Miss Frazer's door—for her benefit of course," he added with a smile.

"Of course." Her lips pulled back from her teeth in a humorless grin. "Let's go, I'd like to talk to Miss Frazer first, see what she has to say for herself. There is something very, very wrong about all this."

70

OFFICER CAROLE Morrow came to her feet as the door opened and Haaren and Miller entered the room.

"How is she?" the detective asked, looking at the girl lying on the bed, eyes closed. In the pale dawn light the flesh on her face looked gray, speckled with scores of tiny nicks from flying glass.

Manny Frazer's large blue eyes snapped open. "She's as well as can be expected having been beaten and raped while your men slept outside. Much fucking good they did me!"

Margaret Haaren immediately sat down, putting herself on a level with the woman. "I know what happened," she said gently, reaching out her hand. "The officers will be dealt with. I'm not making any excuses for them."

Manny Frazer subsided back onto the pillows, turning her head away.

"Do you want to tell me what happened?" Margaret Haaren asked gently.

"I've already told her what happened," Manny snapped, jabbing a finger at Officer Morrow, "and then I told the doctor what happened, and then I told another officer what happened. How many times do I have to tell what happened?"

"Tell me," Margaret Haaren said sympathetically, "I want you to tell me."

Manny sighed audibly, and then she took a deep breath. "There was a knock on the door late last night, early this morning. I thought it was Mom coming home. I shouted through the door, asking who it was, and the voice said, 'Taxi; just dropping a fare.' So, I was convinced then it was my mother. I thought I heard footsteps moving away on the gravel, so I opened the door. It was this guy, big ugly scarred guy. He pushed me into the hall, threw me to the ground, ripped my clothes and raped me. There was a struggle; I punched him in the throat and then I pushed the mirror down on top of him. I then ran out and got your men. They were both sleeping," she added.

Margaret Haaren nodded. "That's essentially the same story you told my officers. But now I'd like you to tell me the truth."

Manny sat up in the bed, the covers falling down, revealing the scrapes and grazes on her breasts. "What do you mean 'the truth'? I told you the fucking truth."

"Tell me again how you dragged and pushed the mirror over onto the man," the detective said quietly, her cold green eyes locked onto the younger woman's face.

Manny looked away. "I . . . I punched him in the throat. He was holding his neck and gasping for breath and . . . and I sort of slid out from beneath him and grabbed the nearest thing, and that was the mirror, and pushed it down on top of him. The glass broke . . . and then I lifted the mirror off just to see if he was still alive."

Margaret Haaren noticed that there was a slight sheen of sweat on her top lip and Manny wouldn't meet her eyes.

"The umbrella stand behind the door was nearer than the mirror," the detective said very softly. "There are a couple of heavy walking sticks in it. Good solid weapons."

"What?"

"The mirror is about eight feet from where the man attacked you. It would take two of my officers all their strength to lift the mirror . . . but then the mirror hasn't been moved, has it?"

Manny Frazer looked from Margaret Haaren to Stuart Miller, and then back at the detective. "What are you saying?" she demanded.

"I'm saying that you're not telling the truth." Haaren smiled humorlessly. "And suddenly, what could be justifiable homicide begins to turn into murder. Do you know what I'm saying?" she murmured.

"Look . . . look, I've told you what happened. Now I'm not saying another word unless my father is here. Or my lawyer."

"You've been watching too many cop shows, my dear." She turned and looked at Miller. "Charge her with accessory to murder."

"What . . . what . . . what are you talking about?" Manny's voice had grown shrill, strident.

"Where was your father last night, Miss Frazer?"

"I don't know."

Margaret Haaren stood up suddenly. "We will make arrangements for you to be taken to the hospital . . ."

"I'm not going to the hospital," Manny said firmly.

"Yes, you are Miss Frazer." Haaren's tone was cold.

Stuart Miller stepped forward. "Miss Emmanuelle Frazer, I am formally charging you as an accessory to the murder of one John Doe. Anything you say will be taken down and may be used in evidence against you later. Do you understand what I am saying?"

"I didn't murder him!"

The detective half turned her head, and Miller looked up from his notebook. " 'I punched him in the throat. He was holding his neck and gasping for breath . . .' " he read.

"Did you get Miss Frazer's statement, Detective?"

"Yes, ma'am. Sounded like an admission of guilt to me," Miller said, face impassive. "Punched him in the throat . . ."

"You're under arrest, Miss Frazer. We will be taking you to a hospital for a sexual assault examination and then you will be brought to the local precinct for further questioning." Haaren turned abruptly and walked from the room.

Stuart Miller caught up with her on the landing. "What do you think?" he said softly.

"Get rid of the rookie officer and substitute someone older, a maternal figure she can talk to. Have her run the 'horrors of prison scenario.' We'll let the girl sweat for a bit and then I'll talk to her later today and we'll see if she still sticks to her story."

"And Mr. Frazer?" Miller asked, stopping outside the bedroom door.

"Suspicion of murder, conspiracy to murder, and whatever else I can think of."

"How do you read it?" he asked, genuinely interested.

"I think the scarred man was attempting to extort money from Frazer. He tried threatening him, killing off his employees, and maybe he tried to kidnap the daughter, or maybe it was rape as an example. Frazer comes in. There's a struggle. The guy is thrown against the mirror, and suddenly he ends up dead. The only problem is," she admitted, "there's not a lot of glass around the base of the broken mirror."

"Most of it ended up in the dead guy's back," Stuart Miller reminded her.

"So we'll have Mr. Frazer down to the precinct as well for a few questions. Let him sweat, too; let's see what happens. This will be a pleasure," she grinned, turning the handle and walking into the bedroom.

The room was empty.

71

S HE WAS a demon, John Dee had decided. Some creature from the pit. And he was fascinated by her—completely under her spell.

They had been married for the best part of a year now, although the priest Edward Kelley had produced had been of dubious antecedents, and he wouldn't have been surprised to discover that the man had been a Papist, so he wasn't entirely sure if the nuptials were legitimate. But he didn't care: he loved the woman.

It had been an extraordinary year in many ways, and he sometimes thought he knew just as much about the woman now as he did on the occasion of their very first meeting. He still had to learn her name. She subscribed to the old pagan tradition—that was still current in some magical circles—that there was magic in a name, and to give that name freely and without thought to another person delivered you into their power.

She rarely spoke, and more often than not he seemed to find her in a trance, her cold black eyes glazed, looking at something only she could see. Often she talked through Kelley when he was in a mediumistic trance. She would speak some alien foreign tongue, that sounded a little like Welsh or the barbarous language of the Celts, and Kelley would translate.

Her knowledge of alchemy however, was profound, deeper even than Kelley's, whose knowledge was impressive. She was also versed in several of the arcane arts, and if some of her craft approached the darker side of magic then he felt that it was worth it in return for the knowledge gained.

But it was whilst working with the mirror that her extraordinary abilities became evident.

He had watched her perform—if that was the word, though it seemed so base a word for what she did—before the mirror every month when the moon was full. Standing naked and proud before the glass, she would arouse herself with complete abandon and then—at the precise moment of her greatest passion—he would spill blood down the length of the mirror.

The resultant images were profound, vivid, terrifying, and completely exhilarating.

And they had brought him recognition at court. Although he was already a favorite of the queen—she had even allowed him to choose the precise time and day for her coronation and he had prepared several natal charts for her—with the virtual banishment of Essex to Ireland, he was one of the few persons at court she asked for advice.

And she believed in magic.

In so many ways she was so practical, so level-headed, so firm in her convictions, it was difficult to believe that she should ever vacillate in any one thing. And yet she was quite prepared to take and act upon advice from outsiders.

But Dee's greatest advantage was that his advice was *good*—so good. The mirror's images were never wrong. Indeed, the queen had been so curious about the quality of Dee's information that he had been obliged to inform her of the mirror's existence, and had promised to show it to her when the time was propitious. She promised to ride out to Mortlake to see it soon.

Married for a year and now Dee's enigmatic wife was pregnant.

They had made love . . . no, that was not the correct term. The had engaged in congress together every night for two weeks, but there was no love involved in it, their coupling had been in the manner of a scientific experiment. She had been in control at all times.

Dee had thought he would have found some difficulty arousing himself as the nights progressed, but when the time came, one look at the woman's naked body had been enough. They had swived in front of the mirror, with the woman on top, and she always ensured that the great passion took them simultaneously. Then the mirror would explode into sights and visions that Dee was sure must emanate from hell. There was so much to see, so many images, from all the ages of man, from times he had heard about, places he had read of in ancient Roman and Greek texts.

He remembered one image in particular. It appeared on the last night of their lovemaking.

The mirror showed the woman and himself standing side by side holding a child by the hands—a female child—raven haired, gray-eyed. He saw the child drop its parents' hands and approach the mirror, stretching out its long-fingered hands toward the glass, and Dee saw the mirror come alive with sights and movement.

"A magical child," the woman whispered, watching the mirror over her shoulder. And then she had crouched lower over Dee, pressing her full breasts against his thin chest. "Husband: I believe this night you have impregnated me."

He didn't need to ask her how she knew; her natural magic would surely have told her. And later, when he worked out the birthdate of the child, he discovered that it was due around the midwinter solstice. Truly, a magical child.

Now when she came to the mirror, heavy with her babe, her breasts and belly swollen, he found he could still watch her with the same satisfaction, feel the same desire. Unselfconsciously, she squatted on the floor before the tall glass and proceeded to arouse herself with her fingers and a carved wooden stick. Colors flowed down the glass, images flickered in rapid succession . . . but one image in particular kept recurring . . . that of a knife rising and falling . . . rising and falling . . . silver when it fell, red with gore when it rose.

He had no idea what it meant.

72

. . . A KNIFE rising and falling, rising and falling, silver when it fell, red with gore when it rose.

Jonathan Frazer came awake with a scream. He sat up in the tiny foul-smelling room and rubbed his face with his hands, feeling his stubble scratch against his skin. He felt—and looked—like shit. Swinging both feet out of the bed, he rested his elbows on his knees and buried his head in his hands. How had he gotten himself into this situation, he wondered dully.

How?

Why?

Why had he run away? He raised his head and looked into the speckled mirror on the battered dresser beside the filthy sink. He almost did not recognize the face that stared back at him. He looked like a junkie, his eyes sunk deep into his head, flesh tight across his cheekbones, his expression haunted.

He'd run away because he was close—so damned close—to solving the secret of the glass. He couldn't afford to be put in jail or taken in for questioning. Not now, not when the answers were within reach.

He wasn't finished with Celia just yet.

And then there was the image. He'd made a promise to her.

Feed me.

Free me.

And he couldn't do that in jail. So what was he supposed to do? Go up to that bitch of a detective and say to her, look, don't put me in behind bars at the moment, I've just discovered through my magical mirror that my wife's having an affair, and by the way, I've also discovered that there's some woman—some creature—trapped within the mirror?

Oh sure, she'd like that, and she'd believe him. She already suspected him of conspiracy or whatever; she'd use any excuse to haul him in, and then use whatever influence she could to keep him in.

They were probably looking for him now. They might even suspect that he had something to do with Talbott's death.

And what was he going to tell them when they finally caught up with him? He'd heard a crash of glass and come down to see his daughter lying naked beneath Edmund Talbott who looked like a piece of meat on a butcher's slab?

And how did the glass get there, Mr. Frazer?

Oh, the mirror broke of its own accord and the glass flew through the air at him.

Tell us the truth, Mr. Frazer?

Well, actually, I believe the woman trapped in the mirror sensed the danger to my daughter and was protecting her the only way it knew.

And you believe that, Mr. Frazer?

Absolutely. Why, less than an hour previously, I'd watched my wife in bed with another man. I scratched her face through the glass. Go and ask her if she's fucking her skiing instructor, and while you're there, see if she has scratches on her face.

Yes, he was sure they'd believe that, too.

So he'd made up the simple story of Talbott raping Manny. It was plausible enough to be true. He was raping her, she struck him a lucky blow that immobilized him and then Manny had dropped the mirror on him. He'd didn't think they'd investigate too closely; Talbott's death tied things up neatly and it would all be over.

Later, when he discovered the police officer posted outside his bedroom door, he knew he had a problem. They were going to take him in, and neither his nor Manny's stories would stand up to serious questioning.

Getting out of the bedroom was simplicity itself. The large double windows opened out onto a small balcony which was positioned directly over the sloping sunroom. The only problem he'd had was making sure he didn't put his foot through the glass panels of the roof. Keeping in the shadows, he'd crept to the furthest point of the garden, scaled the fencing and landed in the neighbor's yard. Staying in the bushes he made his way carefully to the street, then simply walked briskly down the road, away from the house. Dawn hadn't broken yet and the house was full of police activity. So now he was on the run. That brought a smile to his face.

He looked at his reflection in the glass. He was forty-five years old, and his only previous encounters with the police had been for the occasional parking fine, and now here he was a suspect in a murder. He had five hundred dollars cash in his wallet, his credit cards, and his cell phone. He'd used an ATM machine to take out the cash, all in twenties, but he knew if he used his cards again the police would be able to trace him. Also, he couldn't use his cell phone again. He turned it off, and then pulled out the battery; he'd read somewhere that police couldn't track phones that were powered down. He'd already spent twenty-five dollars on a cab and then seventy-five dollars for the night in some seedy motel on Vermont Avenue. So far this evening he'd had three women of various ages and conditions knocking on his door asking him if he was looking for any company.

What he needed now was a plan. Running away had been spur of the moment, now he needed to do something more constructive, more long-term. Obviously, he was going to have to clear his name. He'd need to talk to Detective Haaren, make her listen to sense.

And he needed to get back to the mirror again. He wanted to see the image again.

Feed Me.

Free Me.

Yes, and he was going to have to work out some way of freeing her, releasing her spirit. Talbott would have known . . . but he was beginning to wonder if everything Talbott had told him had been the truth. Maybe Talbott knew of the existence of the woman in the glass and wanted to keep her for himself. He nodded fiercely. Talbott wanted the woman for himself; that's why he wanted the mirror.

Jonathan Frazer stood and crossed the room, swaying slightly, suddenly realizing that he hadn't eaten in more than twenty-four hours. He searched through his jacket pocket, looking for a slip of paper, and a pen, finally finding his twenty-two karat gold Cross pen and two theatre ticket stubs: *Les Misérables*, the last time he and Celia had been out together. He smiled, remembering. It had been a good night. The smile faded as he turned the ticket stubs around in his hand. Unfortunately, there had been far too few good nights in the last few years of their marriage. He stood looking at the stubs for a moment, before he returned to the bed—there was no chair in the room—and sat down.

On the back of one of the tickets he began to list his imperatives.

Clear my name. Clearing his name meant going to Detective Haaren and talking to her, but she wasn't likely to believe him without evidence. And what evidence had he got? He couldn't exactly bring the mirror to her, could he?

And why not?

Why not bring *her* to the mirror, let her see for herself. His hand was trembling so much now that he could hardly write. It was so obvious. So simple.

Return to the mirror.

He needed to feed it some blood again. It would be hungry soon; he could almost feel its craving. He needed to get back to the mirror to have another "look" at what his dear wife was up to. And he wanted—needed—to see the image.

Getting back into the house might prove to be difficult; the police would undoubtedly be watching it. But he didn't need to go back to the house. He could go directly to the guesthouse. Surely they wouldn't be watching the guesthouse? And with Talbott dead would they even be watching the house?

Blood.

He was going to need some blood. He rolled up his sleeve and looked at his left arm. The flesh was still darkly bruised and tender, and he didn't fancy trying the same trick with the other arm. Maybe that was another reason he was feeling dizzy.

What about animal blood?

That didn't *feel* right. Surely it would be wrong to feed the glass with the blood of one of the lower creatures? Was it possible to buy blood, he suddenly wondered, staring blankly at the gaudy drapes. Hadn't he read that you could buy anything on the internet? But he didn't have a computer. Maybe he'd have to kidnap somebody? Or maybe he could buy some from a street person. Were there hemoglobin pushers and plasma junkies?

He began to giggle at the idea.

And what was the going rate for a pint of blood? Was there a set rate dependent on its purity and age, and did the price go up or down according to its age? Younger blood would be pricier.

If one of the street girls cost sixty dollars for an hour and there was eight pints of blood in the human body, did that not work out to seven dollars and fifty cents per pint?

He started giggling again. He loved the very thought of going up to a girl and saying, "Excuse me, could I buy a pint of your blood?" The smile faded from his lips. What was the first thing she was going to do . . . run to the nearest cop and say she'd been approached by some freak. The newspapers would have a field day with that, *Vampire on the Streets of Los Angeles.*

Nonononono. This was going to be done subtly. He wondered if it was possible to work out some way to get blood from a body without the person knowing. That might be an idea: there had to be some way. How did hospitals take blood? He knew how they took blood, the donors were awake, but they could just as easily be asleep. So, he was going to have to put his donors to sleep. Drink? Drugs?

Celia had sleeping pills back in the house: shit, she had a whole pharmacy in the bathroom!

OK, so he'd get these sleeping pills, administer them to his donor, in a drink presumably, and then when she fell asleep he'd take a pint of blood. He'd be gone by the time she woke up, and if he did it properly she'd never even know what he'd done.

He glared at his expression in the mirror opposite. Of course she'd know what he'd done. She'd have a fucking big hole in her arm! The face in the mirror was fierce, twisted, the warped glass giving him a depraved expression. And maybe the sleeping tablets wouldn't have any effect, maybe the pain would bring them awake. And what then?

Why was he giving himself all this grief; why the fuck didn't he just kill one of the sluts? Who was going to miss them? Wasn't as if they were important. Dirty, diseased whores. Spreading their filth, sapping the vitality of honest men like himself. Why not make them serve a higher cause? The bitches should be honored to feed the image.

Jonathan Frazer began to shudder. He pressed both hands to his head, feeling the pressure, the pounding deep in his skull, sure it was going to burst. Not enough sleep, not enough food. He was going crazy, thinking like a crazy man.

. . . A knife rising and falling, rising and falling, silver when it fell, red with gore when it rose . . .

He barely made it to the sink before he retched up a thin bile. He stayed, crouched over the sink, feeling his stomach churn as sickening images and vile thoughts crowded at his mind, pushing their way in, insinuating themselves into his consciousness.

He was tired and hungry, emotionally exhausted. Staggering back to the bed, he flopped on it. He'd sleep. He'd feel better when he awoke.

THE NIGHTMARES WERE terrifying and erotic, dark fantasies of blood and pain. He knew he was sleeping, was aware that he was dreaming, and was conscious of his heart beating, beating, beating.

Feed me.

Free me.

IT WAS LATE in the night when he awoke again. There was no longer traffic on the street outside, or in the corridor outside his door. He turned over on the soft, sagging bed, and found himself staring into the pale oval of the dressing-table mirror. As he watched a pale flickering oval appeared, not quite a face, twisted, misshapen, ugly. It cleared once—for a single heartbeat—and the mouth worked.

Feed me.

Free me.

73

Doctor John Dee moved through the filthy streets, watching the people part before him, acknowledging him on some deep subconscious level as their superior. He could feel the power flowing out of him now, could almost see it. He lifted his left hand and peeled off the leather glove. Yes, his pale flesh was surrounded by a pale bronze aura, shot through with particles of red. He saw one of the women standing in an alley, her ankles exposed, staring openly at him. He glared at her, his thick eyebrows drawing into a straight line across his forehead, drawing his lips back from his teeth in a sneer and she quickly looked away. How easily these animals were controlled.

They were cattle, to be led, to be used.

What visions he had seen in the mirror, what sights. Mysteries beyond comprehension, carriages without horses, birds of metal, boats without sails, glass and crystal buildings standing impossibly tall.

But he was astute; he recognized that what he was seeing was some future tomorrow. Even now, in the Golden Age of Elizabeth, he could see the precursors of those fabulous articles all around him. If he were clever, he would be able to invest in the correct properties, the proper stocks and shares. And that income would allow him to continue his experiments. He had all the time in the world. By feeding the glass he was becoming immortal, he knew that. Already he felt stronger, sharper. He had seen his aura turned from the color of mud to bronze, when it turned gold he would be undying.

And then, of course, there was the image.

Once he had freed her he would have everything he wanted, everything he needed.

One more should do it . . . well, one or two.

74

FRAZER NEEDED blood again.

His mistress hungered.

It was late now, after midnight certainly, but the streets of Los Angeles were unusually busy, and there were no *decent* people on the streets at this time. He wasn't sure how long he'd been walking; lately time had ceased to have any real meaning for him, and he knew that by feeding the glass he was becoming immortal. Did the ever-living appreciate the passage of time? Mankind was intimately aware of time because each passing day brought them closer to death. But if one did not die, then time lost its sting. He stopped suddenly, pleased with the proposition.

His mistress hungered.

He was aware of her hunger as an almost physical ache, and he knew that if he didn't appease it soon, then that hunger would grow into an all-consuming ravening need.

It had been raining all day and the streets were shining and slick, the air cold and crisp. Many of the professional hookers had gone for the night, knowing the weather would keep their customers inside. Those few who remained were likely the ones desperate to make a few more dollars to support their drug habit. They had to be riddled with disease, their blood thin and poisoned.

He turned into a side street just as the woman came out of the squalid club. She was younger than most, mid-twenties he would guess, and pretty in a vulgar sort of way. And drunk.

"How much?" he asked directly, taking her arm, maneuvering her down the street into the shadows. He'd do her the first opportunity he got, some dark alley.

"Hey dude, not so rough, gimme a moment will you?"

He could smell the liquor on her breath, mingled with an underlying stink of unwashed flesh and the sourer scents of sex. "How much?" he repeated.

"Whatcha want, a hand job, blow job, or the works?" The woman took a deep breath, unsteadily placing her hands on her hips. "You look like you could do with the works, and that'll be sixty bucks for you."

He laughed. "Sixty bucks?"

"Make it seventy hon, and you can stay the night. My place is just around the corner."

It would be good to work indoors, out of this teeming rain which might wash some of the precious blood away. "Seventy bucks it is then," he agreed, and then asked, "is there a mirror in your room?"

She looked up at him blearily, her eyes red-rimmed, bloodshot with the alcohol. "Why—you wanna watch us do it? Sure there's a mirror there."

"Excellent." He wondered why he hadn't thought of it before. Fresh blood spilt directly onto the glass, what images would he see then, what visions?

76

MANNY FRAZER stood naked before the mirror, combing her hair, a smile fixed on her face, her gaze vacant. She looked into the glass, idly wondering how long it had been since she'd last had hair to comb. Her tight haircut should have lasted through the holidays and into spring. But it had sprouted with extraordinary rapidity, until she now had what resembled a straightforward short haircut that not even her father could object to. Another couple of weeks at this rate and it would be flowing down her back. The young woman ran both hands through the hair, pulling it back off her face, noticing the way her cheekbones seemed more prominent, her eyes slightly sunken, her lips thicker.

The first thing she had done when she'd come home from the police station was to have a shower, a long hot shower, washing away the grime that clung to her body like a second skin. They'd treated her like shit, she decided, like a criminal, and she'd get her father's lawyer to bring a case against them, wrongful arrest, something like that.

If she knew where her father was.

That woman detective had been very curious about his whereabouts—she'd practically accused him of killing Talbott and being involved in the deaths of the other policemen.

Where was he? Where was he likely to go? Had he a special club he liked to go to? A friend? A mistress? Where was her mother? What was his relationship with her mother? What was her relationship like with her father? Tell us again what happened? Tell us again . . . and again . . . and again . . .

After a while she just refused to answer any more questions until her lawyer was present. She wasn't being charged with anything just yet, the woman told her, she was simply helping them with their enquiries.

Finally they just let her go.

Now the police presence outside the house was much more visible. There was an officer stationed on the gate and the unmarked car out front had been replaced by an official black and white.

Margaret Haaren's last words as Manny climbed into the police car had been, "If your father contacts you, let us know immediately. We are very worried about the state of his mental health."

What shit! What utter shit. They didn't give a toss about the state of her father's health. They were going to try and pin something on him. The woman had more or less said so.

Manny pulled on a heavy bathrobe and wrapped a towel around her still damp hair. She walked around the house, looking into each room, checking the windows, locking the doors when she had finished. She felt tired, a little freaked out, too, like she'd just come down off a trip, but then again, it was the middle of the afternoon and she had been up all night . . . and been attacked, too. Raped. That's what the police had written down on their reports. But somehow it hadn't felt like rape. Even when Talbott was on top of her, she'd always known that she was in charge. He wasn't using her; she was using him.

Or something was using her.

Everything was a little jittery, colors seemed sharper, brighter, edges were more defined, and she had the impression that objects were moving at the corner of her vision. She needed a good night's rest and some food, too, she decided, coming into the kitchen.

She made herself a tomato sandwich and a cup of herbal tea and then sat crossed legged in the living room on the plush cream sofa. Staring absently at the large flat screen TV, she aimlessly flicked through the hundreds of channels. She stopped at her favorite news station just as the female newscaster announced a "breaking news" story about three local prostitutes who had been brutally murdered. Police were reluctant to use the word serial killer, but the press had no such hesitation. There were wild rumors that all the women had been drained of blood and it was only a matter of time before someone would call the suspect the vampire killer. She turned the TV off, not wanting to hear anything else about sex and death. Finishing her sandwich, she wandered around the garden, sipping at the almost cold tea, trying to clear her head and relax, so that she could sleep.

It was a miserable evening; colder than usual for this time of year and quiet, the sounds of the city a very distant hum, and the sunlight coming in over the tops of the trees was a rich warm gold, deepening to purple. The garden had taken quite a beating over the past weeks, with all the police activity: turf was shredded, plants and bushes crushed and broken. With Dad gone and Mom still in Lake Tahoe, she supposed she'd better speak to the gardener . . .

Manny stopped. She found herself standing in front of the guesthouse. And the door was ajar.

Her heart was pounding as she pushed it open, slowly. There was no sign of the heavy lock—perhaps the police had it—and the bolt had been neatly folded back. Just the way her father did it. She stopped. And then a broad smile spread across her face. Of course, where else would he go? She stepped into the room and called, "Dad?"

The heat and musty closeness took her breath away. The skylights were washed with light, diffusing gently into the room, and the air was alive with swarming motes and spots of dust.

"Dad?" The room swallowed her voice.

Maybe she'd been wrong or maybe he had been here and slipped out, and of course he wouldn't necessarily know that she'd be back so soon. Manny made her way into the room, breathing in the dry air. She shared some of her father's interest and enthusiasm in antiques and, like him, she had often found peace of mind in this place. Some of the objects had been here for as long as she could remember. They were always going to be fixed *tomorrow.*

In the center of the room, in the middle of a veritable maze of furniture and artifacts, was the mirror. It had taken the late evening sunlight and darkened it, turning it a deep, iridescent purple, the same shade as a bruise. She stopped before the glass, squinting against the glare from the sunlight, barely able to make out her reflection.

Talbott believed that this was responsible for everything, and she couldn't help but think that maybe he was right. He'd talked a lot of nonsense, asking her all sorts of strange questions about her own feelings towards the mirror, about what she'd seen there . . .

The face.

She remembered the face. A woman's face.

He'd said the mirror controlled people, using them to feed its appetite. She'd half believed him then, but now, standing before the glass, she wasn't quite so sure. She reached out, rubbing her finger along the dirty surface.

"The glass is dirty, grimy, greasy. Only blood will clean the glass, only blood will fire the images. Blood and sex. The intense emotion of orgasm can also fire the mirror."

And she remembered her own dreams, the erotic dreams that left her exhausted.

But it was only a mirror—wasn't it? She desperately wanted to believe that it was just a mirror, just an ugly antique mirror and she was crazy to even think about that madman's words. He'd been insane, he'd killed people, he'd raped her . . . and he'd died with his back cut to shreds protecting her.

She closed her eyes, remembering him crouching before her, both hands clutched to his throat, his face purpling, eyes bulging. She'd been facing him, both hands pressed to her mouth, desperately resisting the urge to throw up. He'd been looking at her, and then *past* her. She'd heard it too, a snapping, popping, cracking sound. She remembered the look on his face, that look of horror, and then he'd thrown himself forward on top of her, covering her entire body with his, his arms cradled around her head.

She'd struggled violently, as she felt him shuddering, gasping, twitching, grunting. She'd thought he was in the throes of orgasm, until she felt the liquid running down her body, down her face, her arms, her legs. And Talbott was unmoving. With one violent heave, she managed to roll him off her, and that was when she saw the blood, the glass . . .

Manny Frazer opened her eyes.

And the mirror image looked back.

Unblinking, dark-eyed, solemn, the woman in the mirror regarded her impassively.

Manny looked at the face and recognized it. No, that wasn't true; she didn't recognize it: she *knew* it. Only the face was visible, the body was in shadow. She knew the face, the lines, the wrinkles around the eyes and lips, the curve of the nose, the point of the chin, the way the teeth indented the bottom lip, the weight of the hair on her head. She knew that face as well as she knew her own.

Manny was surprised that she felt no fear. But looking into those wide unblinking eyes, she immediately knew that there was no evil in them. She reached out, touching the glass, tracing the lines of the woman's face. She wasn't beautiful, but that was part of her allure. Manny would have found it easier to believe that a beautiful creature was evil: surely something powerful would create for itself a beautiful image. Wasn't the devil supposed to be handsome? But this woman, this image, was so ordinary, only the eyes, the extraordinary eyes, uptilted, wide, quizzical, lent it a mystery. And the hair. Yes, the hair was very beautiful: thick, dark, moving slightly in some unfelt breeze. Manny Frazer reached up and ran both hands through her own short hair, pulling her fingers through its sudden thickness.

Why had Talbott hated this woman so? Why had he wanted to cover the surface of the mirror with black paint?

Why did he fear her?

Because he could not possess me.

Manny looked at the face, stark and white, hair black and solid against the grayness. She felt no fear, merely a sense of wonder, of curiosity. She looked deep into the mirror and spoke aloud, "Why did Talbott fear you?"

Because he could not possess me.

"Who are you?" The image closed her eyes, shaking her head slightly, almost sorrowfully.

"Can I help you?"

Feed me . . . Free me.

"How?"

But the image was fading, moving away from Manny, hair swirling around its face as if blown from behind. She touched the glass, feeling a sting as something snapped from the mirror to her fingers, like static, but the image had vanished.

Manny crouched before the glass for the best part of an hour, staring at it, but no further images came. When she began to nod off, she came slowly to her feet and made her way back up to the house, careful to leave the guesthouse door ajar, the way she had found it.

She would see the image again. She was sure of it.

Feed me . . . Free me.

Hadn't Talbott said that the mirror fed on blood and emotion?

Feed me . . . Free me.

Manny fell into bed, still wrapped in her bathrobe, the words running around her head in a monotonous refrain.

Feed me ... Free me.

Feed ...

Free ...

77

Cold, detached, Jonathan Frazer stood in front of the full-length mirror and watched the reflection of the woman behind him undressing. Moonlight streaming in through the skylights turned her hair silver and black, and washed the color from her skin, leaving it alabaster, flawless. Her nipples were dark coins against her flesh, her groin in shadow.

Frazer reached out and touched the glass, tracing his fingers over the reflection of her breasts. The surface of the mirror felt slick, greasy. He spread his hands on the glass, splaying his fingers, and for a single moment he imagined he felt the surface of the glass shift, soften, meld beneath his clammy palms. When he took his hand off the glass, he found no sweaty print on the surface.

The woman—he suddenly realized he had forgotten her name, but no matter, she was cattle—was standing naked with her hands on her hips, watching him, her whole stance suggestive, aggressive.

"What's wrong? Shy?"

"No . . . yes . . . I mean this is the first time . . ."

"It's OK, take your time. You're paying for it." She wandered around the huge room, peering at the numerous pieces of furniture and artifacts that clustered along the shelves, touching the leather of the dining room chairs, running the tips of her fingers along some side tables and then glancing at the workbench, humming tunelessly to herself.

"You could do with a light in here," she said suddenly, reaching for the light switch beside the door.

"DON'T. Don't," he repeated more gently, "I prefer the dark. It's much more romantic, don't you think?"

The woman looked at him, nodding slightly, a smile on her red painted lips. She was twenty-two years old and had been on the streets since she was sixteen: she didn't know the meaning of the word romantic. She had also done it in some strange places, but never in what looked like a converted guesthouse, at the back of some expensive house. It was filled with junk. She wasn't sure if the john worked at the house she'd briefly glimpsed as they'd made their way down through the garden and along the path, or if he rented it out. But he acted like a married guy—you could always tell—and he was used to money, she was sure of that. He'd agreed to the fifty dollars she'd asked without even blinking, even though it had been a slow night, and she'd have taken thirty. Shit, she had done it for ten dollars. He'd also agreed to an extra ten bucks for the inconvenience of taking her off her patch.

All in all, it was going to be a good night.

Frazer watched her in the mirror as he slowly undressed. The moonlight slid off her body, touching it with mystery, lending it a grace it didn't possess, hiding the bruises along her upper arms, the puncture marks behind her knees. She was heavy breasted, no longer slender, and even the makeup didn't disguise the haggard lines in her face. But Frazer wasn't interested in how she looked. He had deliberately chosen one of the more common-looking hookers, the one who didn't have a pimp to look over her shoulder, figuring that it might take a little longer for someone to come looking for her.

He knew what to do. He had done this before: picked a desperate woman, someone who wanted to make a quick buck or two, the raddled, the drunken, the debauched, those who would not be missed, and even if they were, who would care about a whore? He saw her stop before a sixteenth century Venetian goblet, reach out and touch it with a tentative fingertip.

In the mirror the goblet slowly rotated.

Frazer spun around—the goblet was part of a pair and priceless—but the woman hadn't lifted the glass, merely touched it.

His heart began to trip.

She was here.

He swung back around to the mirror, staring hard at the vague reflection of the goblet in the glass. It *was* moving. As he watched, fingers—pale, golden, perfect fingers—appeared around the stem of the glass. The wrist and arm that flowed into the air were also flawless, so detailed he could see the tiny fuzz of hair on the skin. Shoulders, breasts: the image of the body flowing downwards, like frost on a windowpane. The long slender column of a neck and then, finally, the head.

Vaguely transparent, black-eyed and raven-haired, the image raised her head and looked at him. Her long-nailed hand lifted the goblet in a parody of a toast, while her left hand moved lasciviously down the length of her body, caressing her heavy breasts, the palm of her hand moving across one nipple, and then continuing downwards, across her slightly rounded belly, into the coarse dark hair between her thighs. Her mouth opened, teeth strong and yellow against a glistening tongue. She was speaking to him, but he heard nothing, the only sound now the thundering of his heart, the harsh rasp of his breath. The image lifted the goblet, mouthing the words slowly, *"Feed me."*

Ice cold hands wrapped around his body, folding on his stomach and he yelped with surprise.

"I should have guessed you'd be a watcher." The woman—Susan, no *Suzee,* that was it—rested her chin on his shoulder and stared into the mirror.

"What, what do you mean?" he whispered hoarsely.

"You've spent all your time looking into that old mirror. I bet you like to look at yourself. Watch yourself while you do it." She indicated the shadowy room with a jerk of her head. "You've got all these fancy bits of furniture, I bet you've got some fancy clothes, too. I'll bet you like to dress up in them and look at yourself in this old mirror." She looked disdainfully at the plain ugly frame, the slightly warped, speckled glass. Frazer said nothing. Standing directly before them, he could see the shimmering image, the goblet raised in its hands.

"Look, if you want this to be an all-nighter, we can negotiate a new price . . ."

"No." Frazer spun the woman around so that she was facing the mirror, her arms limp by her sides. Standing behind her now, he moved his hands across her stomach, up beneath her breasts, cupping them.

"I knew you'd be a looker," Suzee said, smiling tightly. He was a weird one all right, but harmless.

Frazer pressed his cold lips to the back of her neck, slowly working around to the side of her throat. She tilted her head to one side, closing her eyes, leaning back into him. She could feel the dull pounding of his heart against her back. At least he was gentle. Maybe she'd convince him to fork out for an all-nighter. She'd exhaust him in the first hour and then have a comfortable night's nap.

"Keep your eyes closed," he murmured. His fingers gently pulled at her nipples, stroking, twisting, tugging.

Suzee began to relax. This guy was taking his time: she'd get an all-nighter out of him, maybe even breakfast. Might even enjoy it, too. Been a long time since she'd enjoyed it.

His right hand moved away and she could feel him stretching out. Probably got one of those fancy sex toys. And that meant he had money. Maybe if she was extra nice to him, he'd become a regular, maybe put her up in a little apartment somewhere . . .

"Hey," she began huskily, opening her eyes, "how about . . . ?"

The knife was eight inches of razor sharp steel, double-edged, needle-pointed. As Frazer's left arm locked around her body, holding her upright, the blade tore into the left side of her throat, and then ripped across. Hot dark blood spurted across the mirror, hissing on the greasy glass.

Suzee's scream died in a liquid gurgle. She scrabbled weakly for the blade, slicing through her fingers.

Frazer flung her up against the glass, pressing the side of her face against the surface, pumping blood smearing down the length of the glass, dark and ugly, hissing loudly like water dropped onto a boiling surface.

And then it disappeared: absorbed into the oily depths of the glass, vanishing without trace.

The woman abruptly stopped struggling, and the blood pumping from the wound in her throat slackened. Frazer stepped away from the torn corpse, allowing it to slump to the ground. He pressed the palm of his hand into the bloody stain that remained on the glass, and then lifted it away.

The image appeared.

The figure was close to the surface now, so very, very close, arms and legs spread wide, displaying and giving herself to him. He could just about make out his own reflection through the woman's glorious body. She pressed herself against the glass, her breasts flattening themselves against some unseen barrier.

Frazer reached for her, forefinger tracing the outline of her breasts through the glass, moving upwards along the line of her throat, touching her lips. Her tongue darted out, licking at his fingertips.

And he felt it!

Like a cat's tongue, harsh and rasping, it sent an electric spark through his entire body. He spread his hand on the glass about her face, pressing hard into its surface. It felt soft, almost resilient, palpable, like flesh.

And then the woman began to lick his hand, tiny pointed tongue darting, flicking at his skin, arousing him almost unbearably. He lifted his hand, looking at it in wonder—the blood had vanished, the image had licked it off.

Jonathan Frazer stepped forward, over the body of the hooker and pressed himself to the glass, willing himself *through*. The image mimicked him, molding her body to his, her eyes wide with longing, mouth open, breasts heaving. His own orgasm took him suddenly, shuddering through him, exhausting in its intensity, his fluid splashing onto the glass where it was absorbed into the mirror. The wash of ecstasy was so powerful that he felt the world spin around him and shut down in blackness.

FRAZER AWOKE AS the cold light of day unmercifully illuminated the room. He was stiff and shaking, his body wracked with shivering, and there was an iron bar deep in the pit of his stomach, bile in his mouth.

The woman's corpse was a gray and twisted thing curled around the base of the glass. There was surprisingly little blood, and the body looked like nothing more than an empty sack. Disposing of it would not be a problem.

He came slowly to his feet and approached the ancient mirror, reaching out to run his fingers down the length of the glass. It looked brighter, cleaner this morning, his own reflection in it seemed crisper, sharper. Its surface still felt slick and greasy, but most of the speckling had vanished.

Pressing both hands to the glass, he peered into it, attempting, wanting to see something—anything—out of the ordinary, but all he saw was the dim reflection of the cluttered room behind him.

No matter.

He had established contact—physical contact—with the woman in the mirror, the image. Blood had given her substance: he would give her enough blood to make her whole.

78

EMMANUELLE FRAZER *opened her eyes.*
And knew immediately that something was wrong . . .

THE ROOM WAS dark, cold, the blankets covering her were coarse, rough, and foul-smelling. She sat up with a strangled shout, blankets falling away, revealing breasts that were heavy and painful, nipples large and dark. There was movement beside her and in the wan dawn light she saw an old gray-haired, gray-bearded man roll over and look at her.

This was a dream.

This was a nightmare.

"Mistress?" he asked, his accent strange, guttural, rural.

She had seen this man before, in her dream, this man and the red-haired, red-bearded man.

"Mistress?" he asked again. "Is it time?"

"Aye," she murmured. "Find Kelley."

She could hear herself speak, the words pounding in her head. This was a dream. This was a nightmare. And she had no control over it.

The old man—his name was Dee, she realized—threw back the covers and hurried from the cold room, a vaguely comical figure in his long soiled night-shirt. She swung her legs out of the bed more slowly, gripping the edge of the coarse, rustling mattress with one hand, her left hand resting on her swollen belly, wincing as the child kicked and kicked again.

Aaah, the agony of the past nine months, to feel her body change so, her flesh becoming misshapen as the thing grew inside her like some foul parasite, robbing her of everything she possessed, her rather dubious beauty, her dignity, and her ability to control men. Who would look at a pregnant woman, an ugly deformed creature?

But it would be worth it—it had better be.

Kelley had sworn . . . and thus far he had delivered on all of his promises.

And now the door was opening and the red-haired, red-bearded Irishman was in the room, his eyes aflame, a rare smile on his lips. "It is time," he hissed, "I told you it would be tonight."

He had; he had prepared a natal chart and had been able to predict the moment of the child's birth almost to the hour, but then he had even chosen the night for her to become impregnated by the old fool, Dee.

"Where's Dee?" she whispered.

He jerked his head upwards. "Gone ahead to prepare the room. Can you walk, or will I carry you?"

"I can walk," she hissed. She was not completely helpless. She wrapped a cloak around her nakedness and strode from the room with as much dignity as she could muster. However, half-way up the stairs to the tower room where the mirror was kept, she had to stop as the birth pangs twisted her almost double, and Kelley had swept her up in his strong arms and carried her effortlessly up the rest of the way, murmuring softly, telling her that it would be soon now, so soon, and then they would have accomplished everything they had worked so hard to achieve: absolute power for him, immortality for her.

And there was a price to be paid, but that was only right and proper: everything in this life had to be paid for. That was what had convinced her that Kelley's offer had been genuine in the first instance. If he had told her that he could make her immortal with no cost to herself, then she would have known that she was being used. She was earning that immortality now. She had earned it over the past nine months.

"The child is mine," Kelley reminded her, his breath warm against her ear.

"You think I want it?" she asked indignantly. "What about Dee?"

"Once the child has been given to the mirror, Dee will be ours, a puppet to be used and controlled by our will. There is nothing we will not be able to accomplish. Absolute power . . ."

"And immortality," she added.

"Forever and ever . . ." he said and kicked open the door to the tower room. "Is everything prepared?"

"All is in readiness," Dee said eagerly.

A couch had been positioned directly facing the mirror, water bubbling in great copper pots over the blazing fire, clean linen towels piled on the wooden table beside the couch.

Dee had wanted to bring in a midwife from the local village to assist with the birth, but Kelley had been against it: too many questions, too much gossip, he had argued. What would the villagers say if they heard that a child had been born in the topmost room of Dee's house, in front of a huge mirror, with Kelley in the background, chanting the proper incantations? Not even the queen would be able to save him from the resultant scandal.

Kelley had midwived women before; he would do it.

The contractions were regular now, deep and powerful, and she barely made it to the couch before the waters broke.

Manny Frazer opened her mouth and screamed.

She was the woman, seeing what she saw, feeling what she felt, aware of her thoughts. And yet she was apart.

She felt she was hovering somewhere in the background, behind and to the woman's right, calmly looking on.

The dream and the nightmare inextricably entwined.

The room resembled a scene from hell. Wild shadows capered across the walls. The only illumination came from the blazing fire, roaring up the chimney when Kelley, his hair and beard metallic in the firelight, worked the bellows. Dee hunched before the mirror like some warped demon, muttering incantations.

The ripple that flowed down the glass was like oil on water, twisting, curling rainbowed, vaguely metallic colors.

A flickering began deep in the core of the glass, a twisting, shifting, pulsing ball of light that throbbed in time to the woman's contractions.

On the couch facing the mirror, the woman screamed in the agony of childbirth, copper colored skin bathed in blood red sweat. When the blood came just before the birth of the babe, it ran black in the light. She saw a distorted reflection of herself in the glass. The warped glass had turned her flesh yellow, twisted her legs, turning them into something like an animal's, her full breasts looking flat and wasted, while her face was a parody of a skull. Only her hair was alive, coiling, twisting, turning, winding around her face with some bizarre life of its own.

The woman looked down through her spread legs at Kelley. Hunched before her, he watched her with an expression that was almost feral, eyes wide, lips parted. He was chanting solidly, lips barely moving, grunting a monotonous mantra, calling, promising . . . promising . . . promising. He eagerly reached for the bulbous head when it appeared, his touch surprisingly gentle, pulling the child towards him, turning the body, drawing it out, and then finally—triumphantly—holding it up by its feet. It was a girl; but that was no surprise, they had known all along that it would be a girl. The child opened her mouth and wailed, the sound pitiful, like a seagull's mewling, the tiny noise almost lost in the room, swallowed up in the roar of the fire and Kelley's chanted grunts.

The images in the mirror went wild.

A face appeared, and then another and another and another. Countless faces, some no bigger than a fingernail, others the size of a palm, male and female, young and old, eyes wide, mouths open, silently crying, calling, shouting, screaming, pleading. When the child was finally birthed, sliding out into Kelley's bloodied hands, the mouths closed, the countless eyes fixed on the bloody bundle between the woman's legs. Their terror was palpable.

Kelley lifted the child in his hands, still attached to the mother by the umbilical cord, and turned to face the mirror. The mouths and eyes opened again, and then began to dissolve, fading away, like melting ice or windblown dust until only one face remained, tiny and sexless, close to the center of the mirror. The mirror rippled and the face altered subtly into that of a woman. It was so perfect it looked like a mask with its bronze-gold skin, jet black hair and huge green eyes. As it grew larger, approaching the surface of the mirror, the rest of its perfect naked golden body appeared from a gritty milk-white background. When it was life-size, it reached for the squalling child with both hands, fingers long and slender, black fingernails pointed and curved.

Kelley smiled at the golden image, lifting the child even higher.

Manny screamed in horror when she saw him produce the knife.

Deftly, surprisingly neatly, he snipped the umbilical cord, spattering the mirror with blood. The image touched the score of tiny droplets on the glass, and they vanished, drying to a dry crust and flaking away as she brought her fingertip to her mouth and sucked.

The image reached for the child again, but Kelley shook his head . . .

. . . and her face twisted, turning ugly, beast-like for an instant, hair boiling around her head. And then, abruptly, she was gone.

Kelley turned away from the mirror and wrapped the child in a pure linen cloth, cleaning its face and eyes with the corner. He leaned over the woman. "Your daughter, Mistress."

The flesh was soft against her breast, the babe's mouth opening automatically, and she could actually feel a surge in her breasts before the milk came. The baby girl latched onto her nipple, and the release that followed was almost orgasmic in its intensity.

"I don't want it," the woman hissed.

"For appearance sake," Kelley murmured, eyes drifting up to where Dee had left the fire and was hurrying towards them. He straightened and smiled. "You have a daughter, sir."

Dee looked at his wife with the baby now sucking at her breast. He ran his fingers through his wife's thick sweat-damp hair and kissed her forehead. "Our child," he whispered. "A child of the New Age." When he looked up, his eyes were bright with unshed tears. "A child of magic."

Kelley nodded, face twisting into a parody of a smile. "A magical child indeed." He touched Dee's arm. "Let us leave your wife to rest."

As soon as the two men left the room, the image returned. The golden skinned, black haired woman pressed against the glass, staring hard at the sleeping woman and the child. The hunger in her eyes was almost tangible.

And then she looked *up* . . . behind and to the right of the sleeping woman.

She's looking at me!

The image looked at Emmanuelle Frazer and her lips twisted in a wide smile. Her thick black hair suddenly battered itself against the glass, coils and strands striking hard against the surface of the mirror. Her large green eyes caught and held Manny's, and the young woman reeled back with the almost physical blow. The woman's mouth was working, mouthing words, and she was pointing to the child . . . and to the knife.

Manny shook her head violently. No.

The creature smiled and the planes of her face subtly altered. She was still golden and beautiful, but her burnished flesh was now dulled and tarnished, her eyes seemed to have sunk deeper into her face and her cheek-bones looked sharper. She had been golden and innocent; now she was ancient and exuded a palpable aura of evil. Her mouth twisted and she spat at Manny, green slime dribbling down the surface of the glass.

But by now the nameless woman was awake, staring in horror at the figure in the glass. Instinctively, she clutched the babe to her bosom and screamed, the sound tearing from her throat. The image instinctively spat at her too—and a gobbet of the green fluid passed through glass and splattered onto her face, searing into the flesh to the right of her eye.

Manny screamed with the pain, the fire in her face.

And awoke.

MANNY RESTED HER forehead against the cool glass of the bathroom mirror. She was bathed in sweat, her bathrobe sticking to her skin, and yet she felt cold, chilled through to the bone. She looked at her face again . . .

The skin from the corner of her right eye, almost down to her jaw bone was red and raw, leaking a pale watery pus.

79

THIS WAS only Toni's third night on the street, and she was still terrified. Her two friends who also worked the streets told her that only the first night was the hardest and then after that it got easier. But the second night hadn't been any easier and she was absolutely petrified with the prospect of another customer tonight.

Frankie, who lived in the apartment further down the hall, told her that she should be able to get three or four johns a night and if the clients wanted the "works" at one hundred bucks for an hour, that would mean she was earning four hundred dollars for a mere four hours work per day, not bad. Go for the big bucks while you're still young and pretty, she'd advised, forget the hand jobs or the oral.

The first night she'd managed one guy, a hand job. She'd been shaking, but he'd been drunk and hadn't noticed. She'd been so sick, so ashamed afterwards that she'd gone right back to the apartment and washed herself again and again, imagining she could still smell him—stale sweat and beer—on her skin.

The next guy on the second night had been so nervous that she felt almost sorry for him, and again, she'd washed and washed herself, scrubbing away the smell, knowing she could never erase the memory.

She hated it, she'd never be able to get used to it, not the way Frankie or Joey did. But she had to do it, she needed the money desperately.

It had started when she lost her job—and she'd been lucky that they hadn't pressed charges, but she supposed it would have cost the store more to sue her for stealing several T-shirts. And it couldn't have happened at a worse time: she was four months pregnant and just beginning to show. Maybe that had been another reason the store manager hadn't pressed charges, simply dismissed her on the spot without a reference. Without a reference she stood absolutely no chance of finding another job. And she was too proud to return to her Kansas hometown, she didn't want to see the disappointment in her parents' eyes.

She'd borrowed some money just before the baby was born. None of the regular lending agencies would give it to her, and she ended up dealing with a "private finance company." Later, when it was too late, she realized they were little more than loan sharks. When they'd asked her if she was working, she'd lied and said yes, and they'd never checked. When they discovered that she couldn't pay back the loan, they'd become very upset. Now a guy was coming around every day demanding money, threatening her, and the last time he'd deliberately turned and looked at the baby as he told her that people who didn't pay him always had bad luck.

She'd spoken to Frankie, telling her the story, hoping—but not asking—that she might help her out, give her some money. She knew Frankie had plenty of cash; the older woman had her hair done twice or three times a week, and always wore the latest fashions. Frankie hadn't been any help though—except to make the suggestion that she go on the streets. Toni had immediately dismissed the idea out of hand, until Frankie had started to tell her how much money was to be made from it, and as long as you were careful and picked the right clients and didn't go with any crazy looking guys, never got into a car with more than one person and avoided some of the sleazier bars, you'd be all right. Oh, and you always made sure to take your pill and you didn't do it with guys who wouldn't wear a condom.

Toni owed over three hundred dollars; it had started out at one hundred and fifty, but the interest mounted up rapidly. Frankie had pointed out to her that three nights on the street at three clients a night would take care of her problem and leave money left over to buy herself or baby Stephanie a present. And you never knew, maybe she'd end up liking it. Frankie knew women who only did it on weekends or mid-week, just for a night or two, earning themselves enough money to carry them through to the next week. And yes, some husbands knew about it: but if you were trying to claim unemployment benefits with a couple of kids to bring up and a mortgage to pay and the bills just mounting up, what other way was there to earn money . . . except maybe go out and rob a bank.

Toni knew she'd never like this. She enjoyed sex, but only with someone she loved, or at least thought she loved. But there was nothing pleasurable in this. This was a necessity.

She hadn't even dressed "whorishly" and yet she felt as if everyone knew what she did, and everyone was looking at her. She'd come into the bar tonight with Frankie and though she'd been here nearly two hours—and Frankie had been in and out with three different guys, and she charged fifty bucks—so far no one had shown the slightest bit of interest in her. Maybe she looked just too respectable. No one wanted respectable these days.

80

Jonathan frazer looked at her closely. He'd noticed her the moment he'd stepped into the bar: a slim dark-haired, pale-skinned young woman, maybe nineteen, maybe twenty, looking awkward and out of place here. A tall, stunning African American woman chatted to her for a few moments on a few occasions before disappearing with two different men. He knew what *she* was, but the younger woman was different. He closed his eyes, squeezing them tightly shut, attempting, without success, to call up the figure of the image. He looked at the woman through slitted eyes.

Did it matter what she was? She was still cattle. Flesh and muscle, bone and blood. Especially the blood. She was an animal about to be butchered and sacrificed to the image.

He leaned back against the wall, his left arm extended, feeling the pressure of the knife against his forearm. It was a risk wearing it in case he was picked up by the police, but it gave him such a feeling of power, of control, of authority.

Jonathan Frazer sat forward, and stared into his glass of Coke. Reflected in the dark surface, he saw his own haunted expression, his deep sunk eyes, the lengthening stubble on his chin, the new lines around his eyes.

The image looked at him.

Startled he looked up and around the room.

And saw the beasts.

The people were still there, but surrounded now by thin glowing ovals of light. As they moved, the ovals shifted, moving with them, sometimes hardening to a reflective surface, then dissipating to reveal, not the person beneath, but the flickering image of an animal, a fleshy beast with the attributes of a human, a man with the face of a swine, a woman with the huge eyes of a cow, a small man with the feral features of a rat. The shimmering ovals were wan pinks and delicate greens, pale blues, insipid yellows. But one was different: the woman at the bar was bathed in a warm blood red light that so was intense he could barely make out her features beneath it.

Jonathan Frazer was on his feet before he was even aware that he was moving. The beasts parted before him.

81

Toni watched the guy move through the crowd, and knew instinctively that he was making his way towards her. Tall, thin, with a three-day growth of beard on his face, and a directness about his gaze that she found disconcerting. His clothing was good quality, but looking a little rumpled now, as if he had slept in them.

Watch out for the crazies, Frankie had warned her.

He stopped in front of her, saying nothing, simply staring at her. She attempted a smile, but found she couldn't meet his eyes.

"You shouldn't be here," he said hoarsely. "A girl like you is too pretty, too good to be doing this."

Surprised, she looked up, staring into his eyes. She thought she saw genuine pity there. But Frankie had warned her about this type, too—the type who wanted to save her from herself.

"You're new." The man moved in beside her, and she caught a faintly musty, damp smell from his clothing. "Let me guess: a husband unemployed, the rent due, bills to be met or maybe you've lost your job?"

Toni nodded. Was he a pimp, a social worker, or the police maybe?

He shook his head, drawing his fingers through thin black hair that needed a wash, pulling it back off his face. "It doesn't matter, does it? What matters is that you've been forced into doing this."

"Are you going to tell me there's another way?" she asked boldly.

"No," he shook his head, surprising her. She expected him to give her an answer; everyone had an answer to her problem. "If you see this as the solution to your problem, then so it is."

"I owe money," she said suddenly, surprising herself. "Over three hundred dollars to a money lender. He's grown threatening. I think he's going to hurt my baby if I don't give him the money." She had no idea why she was telling this stranger her story.

"How much do you charge?" the man asked gently. Now the shadows beneath his eyes lent them compassion.

"Forty."

"How long have you been doing this?"

"This is my third night."

"And how much have you earned so far?"

"Eighty," she whispered.

"Tonight?"

"Over the past two nights. I've had two men . . ."

"Come with me then, and I'll pay you two hundred and twenty dollars on one condition . . ."

"What's that?" she asked fearfully, expecting to discover that he wanted her to do something kinky.

"You ask me no questions."

"No questions?"

"None."

"You don't want to do anything . . . odd, do you?"

"Not in the slightest," he smiled. "Just the most natural thing in the world."

Toni slipped her hand into his. "No questions then."

Now, SHE HAD a hundred questions, and she didn't like the answers she was getting.

She had been reluctant to bring him back to her apartment; there was only one room and the baby slept in the crib in the corner, and when he had suggested his place, she had immediately agreed. He gave the taxi driver an address in the Hollywood Hills. She'd immediately thought he owned a place but when he led her past the side of the main house and towards the guesthouse she realized he only rented the place. Standing outside the door of the guesthouse she felt an uneasiness in the pit of her stomach. She heard him muttering when he discovered that the door was already open.

"Do you live here . . . is it OK for you to be here?" The last thing she needed was to be done for trespassing or breaking and entering.

He looked back over his shoulder. "The house is empty; everyone is away. I'm . . . I'm looking after things. I work here," he added as an afterthought.

Toni followed the man into the dark interior of the long room, wrinkling her nose at the dry, musty smell . . . similar to the smell that clung to his clothes. A hand—dry and cold—reached out of the darkness and found hers, pulling her deeper into the shadows. "Sorry, there's something wrong with the circuit breakers, the electrician is supposed to be here tomorrow morning," he murmured, his voice little more than a whisper. There were objects piled high all around, but with an almost uncanny knack he led her deep into the pitch-dark room without bumping into anything. As her eyes adjusted to the dimness, she could make out the vague squares of the windows and similarly lighted rectangles high in the ceiling. The man—she realized he hadn't given her a name, and hadn't asked for hers in return—dropped her hand and moments later she heard the rasp of a match being drawn across sandpaper and a tiny yellow light flared. He put the flame to a tall white candle, creating a warm circle of yellowish light.

There was an enormous mirror in front of the candle that helped reflect the light. She looked into it. The glass was old and warped: she imagined she could see shapes twisting in the darkness behind her. And then she jumped, her hand flying to her throat as a pale face materialized out of the shadows behind her right shoulder. "Jesus! You frightened me!"

"Sorry."

The dancing candlelight lent him a ghastly expression, deepening the shadows under his eyes, shading the stubble to create a skull-like appearance. He moved around in front of her and handed over a thick wad of twenty-dollar bills.

"You can count it; there's thirty there. Consider it a bonus . . . buy something for your child with it."

Toni put the money into her bag without counting it. "I think I can trust you," she said, smiling.

"I think you can," he agreed, his lips drawing back from his teeth in an imitation of a smile.

Without another word, Toni began to undress.

82

S KINNY, FRAZER thought, flat-chested, narrow-hipped, her stomach
still carrying the weight of the child. He watched her undress without
the slightest flicker of emotion, and when she was naked, he came around
behind her and stood with his hands on her shoulders staring into the glass.

"What do you see?" he asked curiously, wondering if she saw the woman
standing *behind* him.

"You . . . me," the young woman smiled.

He urged her forward with his hand in the small of her back. Her flesh
felt cold, clammy. When she was close to the glass, he reached over her
shoulder to touch it, his fingers pointing to the darkness beyond her
shoulders.

"What do you see there?" he asked again.

"Shadows," she whispered. Her skin began to ripple with gooseflesh.
Frankie had warned her about these guys—the crazies. Humor them, her
friend had said, humor them and when you get your opportunity, run
like hell. But make sure you get paid first. "What do you see?" she asked
hoarsely.

"Shadows," he said with a smile. He moved around behind her until
his dim reflection in the glass was almost completely obscured by her body.
With both hands he drew her hair back off her shoulders. "I think candlelight is more romantic, don't you?"

"Yes," she whispered.

"Do you know there is an old wives' tale that if you stand a lighted
candle before a mirror, you will see the face of your lover behind your
left shoulder?" His face suddenly appeared over her left shoulder.

"Does this mean you're going to be my lover?" she asked coquettishly.

"Absolutely," Frazer whispered, his hands at her hair again, then moving down to her throat, across her breasts, onto her slightly rounded stomach. The woman closed her eyes and rested her head back on his left shoulder. Maybe he wasn't that crazy after all, just Hollywood weird.

Frazer drew the knife out of his left sleeve. It was a twelve-inch mid-nineteenth century Japanese tantō. Designed for piercing lacquered armor, it slid effortlessly into the woman's flesh just above her groin. He felt the tremor run up her body and the fingers of his left hand locked around her throat as he savagely ripped upwards, eviscerating her, flooding the mirror with gore. He pressed the wildly spasming body against the glass with his weight, eyes and mouth wide with savage glee. This shouldn't be some nameless whore, it should be his slut of a wife. She was no better than them. They did it because they had to; she did it because she enjoyed the rutting. She was a beast, cattle. She should be in his arms now, with the knife buried between her breasts, her body cut open, slaughtered like the animal that she was. He threw back his head and screamed her name aloud, "Celiaaaaaaaaaaaaa. . . ."

83

CELIA FRAZER awoke in absolute agony.

She opened her mouth to scream, but it was as if an iron band was locked around her throat. The pain in her stomach was so intense, a spear of agony just above her groin.

It was her appendix . . . no it couldn't be, she'd had it taken out.

An ulcer, a burst ulcer, a bleeding ulcer.

She'd made love with Colin earlier that evening. They'd ended up on the floor with him pounding away as they both screamed and grunted their way to orgasm. He'd been buried so deeply insider her; maybe he'd damaged her, ruptured something . . .

Celia threw back the bedclothes and desperately attempted to raise her head to look at her stomach, every movement an agonizing effort. She was bathed with sweat, her hair sticking to her head. She managed to raise her head a couple of inches so that she could look at her reflection in the mirror of the dresser directly opposite the bed.

She could see nothing.

She blinked, not sure if the mirror was fogged or her eyes clouded.

And now she could see a thin red line on her flesh.

The pain was a live thing now, boiling inside her, ripping up through her body, pure and absolute anguish. Her head dropped back to the pillow, eyes squeezed tightly shut, tears squeezing from beneath the firmly clenched lashes and then with a monumental effort she managed to lift her head the few inches to look into the glass again and saw that . . .

. . . flesh was parting, skin folding back almost neatly, to reveal the raw muscle beneath, and then that, too, was peeling back to show glistening organs . . .

With a sudden wrench, her entire stomach burst open, lengths of intestines coiling onto her skin, curling onto the bedclothes. Blood and thick gobbets of flesh spattered everywhere, the walls, the ceiling, the mirror.

The pain took her, wave after wave washing over her body, in surges of ever-increasing intensity, finally concentrating on the spot between her breasts, where her heart hammered so hard it was difficult—no, impossible—to draw breath. A new pain, solid and cold blossomed beneath her left breast, slid up into her shoulder and tingled down along the length of her left arm.

The new pain took her and finally claimed her as she heard something bestial howl her name in the distance.

The bedside clock showed 2:22 A.M.

JONATHAN FRAZER KNELT on the floor of the guesthouse in the blood and tattered flesh of the woman and pressed himself against the glass, staring intently into it. He could see the image of Celia Frazer and her lover lying naked on a bed, arms and legs splayed. He focused on his wife: she had been torn apart from groin to breast.

COLIN MARINER AWOKE with the dawn as usual. His dreams had been particularly vivid—he'd made love to a woman, heavy breasted, dark-eyed for what seemed like an eternity—and he was almost painfully aroused. He rolled over, his arm going across Celia Frazer's breasts.

And then he sat bolt upright recoiling from the chill of her flesh.

Scrambling from the bed, he looked down on the woman. Her eyes were wide open and glassy, her skin clammy, and even before he pressed his hand beneath her breast he knew there would be no pulse. Heart attack?

Colin closed her eyes and attempted to remember the prayers of his Catholic upbringing. He should say something. He was going to miss her; she'd been fun and he had genuinely liked her. But at least she'd died peacefully in her sleep after a night of lovemaking.

That was the way he wanted to go.

84

*A*N ECSTATIC *shiver rippled through the enormous astral whirlpool, vibrating deep in its core. The pulse throbbed throughout the Otherworld, bringing dreamers all across the city abruptly awake, shivering from nightmares, while children awoke crying at shadows.*

One by one, the dogs of Los Angeles began to howl, until the entire city echoed to what sounded like the cries of the damned.

IN LOS FELIZ, Joe Thompson came awake from a startlingly vivid erotic dream. He rolled over in the bed and turned to the digital alarm clock on the bedside table: the glowing green letters read 2:21 A.M.

Jesus Christ! But if he'd told those people once, he'd told them a hundred times that their fucking dog kept him awake howling outside his window. And he'd just done a thirty-six hour straight shift at Walgreens because two of the other managers were sick and they were already short-staffed with cut backs.

When he worked days, the dog kept him awake at night.

When he worked nights their kids kept him awake during the day.

Well, right now, he'd just about had enough.

The big man staggered out of bed and pulled on a pair of ratty jeans over his plaid flannel sleep pants. He hauled on a polo neck sweater and slid his feet into ancient slippers before stamping into the kitchen. Pulling back the drapes he peered out into the high-walled backyard. The fucking dog was running around in a circle in *his* yard—wouldn't do it in its own yard, oh no—howling its head off.

Thompson wrenched the back door open and pitched an empty tin can at the animal. It missed and clattered off into the darkness, but the sudden sound made the animal stop, and it turned to face the big man, a growl beginning deep in its body. The dog was a nondescript mutt, but big and wiry with a mangy black coat that left hairs everywhere. Thompson reached for another can and tossed it at the dog. This one struck it squarely on the nose.

Without a sound, the animal leapt for the man. He saw it coming and slammed the door in its face, seeing his own reflection in the glass . . . but the animal kept coming, exploding inwards through the glass, its teeth finding and locking on his throat even as the shards of flying glass ripped into the big man's face, destroying his eyes, while simultaneously disemboweling the dog. It was 2:22 A.M.

IN CULVER CITY, Kenneth Pearson awoke at 2:21 A.M. with a pounding in his head that was positively frightening. He sat up in bed, holding his head in both hands, imagining he could actually feel it throb.

OK. So he couldn't drink . . . what was it, how much . . . an entire six-pack? Or was it two six-packs? So maybe six had been one too many . . . or seven too many.

Thankfully his parents were asleep when he got in; they would have been less than impressed. Drinking beers was something rowdy teenagers did, not well-educated kids. Mind you, at the time he could see the attraction of it, and he especially remembered the attractions of that girl . . . what was her name?

He shook his head savagely . . . and instantly wished he hadn't. The pain in his head was excruciating, and he needed to puke. Christ, his parents were sure to hear him throwing up. He'd have to use the downstairs bathroom.

The young man staggered out of bed, and discovered that he was still dressed, but his brand new Levi's jeans were stained and the heavy black leather motorcycle jacket hanging on the end of the bed had a long strip hanging off it.

Fuck! That jacket had cost him a fortune.

With his stomach roiling, he hurried down the stairs and ducked into the toilet in the narrow corridor between the kitchen and the stairs. Leaning straight-armed against the sink, he stared into the mirror, squinting against the pain in his head. He felt like he was going to die. Kenneth squeezed his eyes shut, feeling beads of sweat begin to pop out on his skin. He rested his forehead against the cool glass. Why had he ever agreed to go out with the rest of them? It wasn't as if he even liked beer, it wasn't as if he even liked alcohol; good, old-fashioned fizzy Coke was his drink.

The pain had become a regular throbbing, which abruptly intensified to absolute agony. Kenneth Pearson spasmed, his head snapping back and forward and then smashing into the glass. The throbbing instantly eased. Another tremor sent his head into the glass again, and the incredible pulsing agony lifted, though it had been replaced by a cooler, liquid pain. Squeezing his eyes shut, he pounded his face—again and again—into the broken mirror, until there was no more sensation . . . until there was nothing. It was 2:22 A.M.

IN STUDIO CITY, Sandra Lopez was not exactly drunk; she'd only had two, or was it three, glasses of wine. She was mellow, she was relaxed, and humming gently along to one of the golden oldies on the late night radio station. She half remembered the original appearance of the song, but that was no indication of her age. Songs that were only a year old were turning up as golden oldies or classics nowadays. They had a short shelf life.

The lights on Coldwater Canyon turned from orange to red and she slowed the Nissan, allowing it to roll to a stop. She locked the doors. She'd heard of lone women being attacked in their cars while they sat at traffic lights, and while this was not one of the seedier parts of the city, she was still taking no chances.

The lights changed. She was already moving as she glanced in her rear view mirror . . .

And something in the back of her car looked at her with large black eyes. A scream caught in her throat, became a whimper. She tried to look away, but found she couldn't. She tried to stop the car, but couldn't. Her right foot was stuck to the accelerator, pressing it deep to the floor. She pressed her left foot hard on the brake, the engine howling, tires burning against the asphalt as she gained speed.

The eyes crinkled as if someone was smiling.

And the spell was broken.

Sandra Lopez managed to scream once more, as her headlights illuminated the massive plate glass windows of an electrical showroom, hidden behind metal security grilles. The car hit the grille, ripping most of it out of its frame, bringing it down around the car, entangling it as it continued on into the shop front: televisions, DVD players, cameras, and computers, most of which were still plugged in, exploding into showering sparks and acrid smoke.

Several hours later when the car was cut free by the fire department, it was discovered that the falling metal grille had sheared through the windshield of the car, completely severing the woman's head.

Twenty-two people died in bizarre circumstances and freak accidents across Los Angeles. They all died at the same time: 2:22 A.M.

*I*T TOOK NO *more than a heartbeat to regain control. But that had been enough. The overload shivered out across the Otherworld, upsetting the delicate balance between the two planes of existence.*

Little damage had been done, and it had drawn some sustenance from the deaths. But it would have to be very careful now. Very careful. This was the critical time. Freedom had never been so close.

Never had it been so vulnerable.

85

I T HAD been a shitty day. Every so often you got them when one thing just piled on top of the other. By noon, she knew that this was going to be one of those days.

Twenty-two bizarre deaths—suicides, freak accidents—added to the usual night toll of Los Angeles misery. The press was having a field day and the TV and radio were full of experts with increasingly bizarre theories. Government and/or alien mind rays was the current favorite.

Thank God, she didn't have to deal with them. She'd enough to contend with: a serial killer was busy working his way through the street girls and everyone from the mayor down was screaming for results.

But they had nothing: girls disappeared. There was no pattern, no clues, no DNA, nothing except wild theories. They had plenty of those.

MARGARET HAAREN SAT on the edge of the tub, pouring bath salts into the swirling water. She only stopped when the water began foaming up spectacularly and she realized that she'd emptied half a jar instead of a capful. She was tired, dead tired, physically as well as mentally, with an ache that went deep to her bones.

There was a gentle rap on the bathroom door.

"It's open."

Helen, her niece, popped her head around with a large mug of steaming tea in her hand. "Thought you might need this. Chamomile. Help you sleep. You look exhausted."

"I am. Thanks love. I know this hasn't really been much of a vacation for you . . ." she began.

"Don't worry about it. When you're not here, I simply *have* to go shopping and go out and enjoy myself." She smiled widely.

"I was going to take you to some museums, galleries, but it's just been crazy the past couple of weeks . . ."

"I thought LA was always crazy."

"Even for LA in general and Hollywood in particular, this is spectacularly crazy."

The teenager ran her fingers through strands of her brunette hair, pulling it back off her face. "Well, you know, it is such a chore having to explore Los Angeles," she smiled wickedly, "but I suppose I could find it in my heart to forgive you. Look," she added seriously, "I know what it's like; so don't worry about it. Remember, there's a detective or two in my family, too. I know all about the crazy hours. Now, go on, have your bath, relax. I'll see what I can do about making dinner."

"That would be lovely."

"Be a miracle, too," Helen muttered.

THE WATER WAS as hot as Margaret could bear and she almost had to force herself beneath the bubbles covering the surface. Tiny beads of sweat gathered on her forehead and ran down the sides of her nose. Once she was beneath the surface, with only her head showing, the water lapping at her chin, the trick was not to move, because that agitated the water and it stung. Closing her eyes, resting her head against the back of the bath, she deliberately reviewed the day's events before pushing them aside, dismissing them until she returned to the office in the morning.

And adding to the day's mayhem was the news that Jonathan Frazer's wife Celia had turned up dead.

Died in her sleep in the arms of her lover: what a way to go! That had been fine, people died in their sleep every day, until the results of the emergency autopsy she'd requested had come in and revealed that just about every internal organ in the woman's body had ruptured and that her intestines were in pieces—literally!

She'd spoken to the medical examiner who'd performed the autopsy. In a precise Australian accent, the tiny Japanese woman told the detective that in thirty years of practice, she'd never seen anything like it: "It's as if the woman was cut open . . . except that the dermis is still intact!"

That in itself had been weird enough until the body of a young woman had been pulled up out of the Hollywood Reservoir. Her belly had been sliced open. The body had been identified as that of a Toni Kane, a young pregnant woman who'd found herself in financial straits and had gone onto the streets to make some cash. Her friend, who was also working as a prostitute, told them that this had been her third night out.

Third time unlucky.

Then it got downright scary: her internal wounds were identical to those on Celia Frazer's body.

Added to that, a second body had been fished out of the same section of the Reservoir. Although lots of the extremities were gone—fingers, toes—the face was still reasonably intact and one of the guys who worked vice had identified the body as that of Susan—Suzee—Burton, who'd been on the game since she'd been a kid. She'd had her throat sliced open.

So now they had a killer with a pattern: knife, prostitutes, lake . . . and the bizarre connection to Celia Frazer.

Margaret wondered if the Frazer girl knew that her mother was dead. And the father. Where was Jonathan Frazer? He was still at large. Haaren wondered how he fit into all of this. He was connected. She was convinced of that, but she wasn't sure how. Except that she was convinced that he could not be the killer.

86

WHY HADN'T she come?

He'd fed the mirror with blood, why hadn't the image come?

The answer came slowly: because he'd used up the energy, the power in the blood, to strike at Celia.

Yesyesyesyesyes.

The power—the energy—was in the blood.

The blood had called the image the first time, given her substance as well as sustenance. The second time the blood had—what?—given his thoughts substance.

What was it Talbott had said? *"Once it is fed its powers are limitless."*

Jonathan Frazer prowled around the mirror, approaching it, then standing back, almost teasing himself with its proximity and his knowledge that he could bring it to life, that he could call forth the image. That he could make it do his will.

All he needed was blood. And this world was full of cattle, sacks of meat and blood. But he was not going to make do with ordinary blood. He wasn't going to use tainted blood, blood polluted by drink or drugs. He needed fresh blood, pure blood. He needed virginal blood.

The blood of the virgin is powerful indeed.

The thought stopped him cold. He stood in front of the mirror, nervously running both hands through his lank hair, pulling it back off his face and then twining his fingers together around the back of his head.

Yes, fresh blood, pure blood, virginal blood. Surely the power of the mirror was proportional to the purity of the blood? Jonathan Frazer looked up, tongue licking dry lips, eyes narrowing as a smile twisted his lips.

He'd been a fool!

Hadn't Talbott told him everything he needed to know?

The mirror needed a male and a female. The male to feed the mirror, the female to provide the blood. It had been this way since the dawn of time.

And hadn't the mirror already put its mark on Manny, hadn't it saved her from Talbott; hadn't Talbott told him that she would be different?

She was the chosen one.

Moving unhurriedly, Jonathan Frazer lifted the tantō and wiped the blade on his sleeve. Flakes of dried blood and a darker harder substance fell away. He didn't think he'd need the knife, but there was no harm in being prepared anyway.

He slipped out of the guesthouse door and moved silently along the path that led up to the house. There was a light on in the kitchen and he could see Manny moving around the room, wearing a heavy bathrobe. He parted some leaves, peering closely at his daughter. How long had it been since he'd last seen her—a day, two days, three days?—but in that time her hair had grown dramatically.

A broad smile creased his lips. The image's hair was long. Now, it was creating her in its own image.

87

THE PAIN in Manny's face had abated around noon and the red swelling and burn-like mark had gradually faded as the afternoon had worn on. The dream was still vivid though, especially the image of the golden woman or creature, or whatever it had been.

And the baby.

Manny rubbed her breasts. They felt tender, heavy, and the flesh around the nipples particularly was darker and if she pressed, they oozed a thin colorless liquid.

What was that term: psychosomatic? Like when you imagined yourself to be pregnant and your body began to change as if you were, a phantom pregnancy. But could a dream, even such a particularly vivid one, bring on this change in her breasts, and leave the red burn mark on her face?

And what if it wasn't a dream?

Manny Frazer carried the kettle to the sink and stared out into the garden. The evening light was grainy, leeching details and colors, turning the evening sepia like an old photograph.

What if it wasn't a dream?

She shook her head. Maybe Talbott would have been able to explain it to her. The little he had told her just wasn't enough. He'd said that the mirror was evil and that it possessed people . . . like her father, like herself. Was she possessed? She didn't feel possessed, but then if you were possessed, would you necessarily know it, or would everything just seem normal?

Certainly what she'd done with Talbott that night hadn't been normal, something had definitely been controlling her that time. She shivered, and then yelped as cold water poured over her hands as the kettle filled.

Maybe she needed a little vacation. She'd try and contact her mother in the morning. Go and spend a few days with her.

And then she screamed.

A face had appeared at the window.

The kettle crashed onto the tiled floor, spilling water everywhere as Manny just stood there, frozen with horror.

When she looked again, the face was gone, leaving her an impression of wild hair, round eyes, and a fixed, maniacal grin.

Then the kitchen door swung silently inwards and a figure stepped into the room, a sour, damp odor preceding it. She squeezed her eyes shut and opened her mouth to scream.

"Hello Manny," Jonathan Frazer whispered.

"Dad . . ." Manny's eyes blinked open. "Dad?" she said again, looking at the man who bore only the vaguest resemblance to her father. "Oh, Dad." She ran over and wrapped her arms around him, wrinkling her nose at the smell. "Dad, what happened? Where did you go? I've been worried sick."

Jonathan Frazer pressed grimy fingers to his daughter's lips, quieting her. "No time for questions. Come on, we've something to do."

"What? What have we got to do, Dad?" Manny asked in alarm. Her father's hands were busy with her suddenly thick and luxurious hair. Some sort of hormonal change, she realized suddenly, and that would certainly account for the changes in her body, the marks on her face. She twitched her head back away from her father's hands. "Dad, are you OK?"

He nodded vigorously. "I'm fine, I've never felt better."

"Do you want something to eat? You look tired." There was something desperately wrong with her father. His eyes were darting, constantly moving, and he hadn't once looked her in the face.

"I'm not hungry. I'm not tired." He reached for her hand. "Come on, we've got to . . ." He stopped and smiled secretively. "Well, I think you know what we've got to do, don't you?"

"No, Dad," Manny whispered, "I don't know. Why don't you tell me?"

"Come on, come on." His hand found hers and he pulled her out through the open kitchen door and down the path towards the guesthouse. "I suppose I haven't really been thinking, you see. Talbott told me that there would be changes, little things out of the ordinary . . ." His hand went to her hair again. "But I suppose I've just been too busy to notice. And of course I should have realized that there would be two: male and female. He created them in His own image, the yin and the yang, the two making a whole, the two that are one . . ." He was babbling now, making no sense.

"Dad, Dad," Manny whispered, feeling the tears start in her eyes, the burning in her throat. "Come on, you need a rest, a break, you've been working far too hard. I was thinking of heading up to Lake Tahoe to where Mom's staying . . ."

His harsh laugh broke the evening stillness. "Don't bother. Your mother's dead."

She stopped suddenly, and jerked her hand from her father's. Her voice was a hoarse angry rasp. "Dad? What are you saying?"

He turned slowly to face her, and Manny suddenly realized that she was looking at a stranger. "She's dead." Jonathan Frazer's smile became a leer and then the knife suddenly appeared in his right hand. "The bitch was fucking some guy. I cut her from crotch to sternum. Serves her right. Fuck her!"

Manny took three steps backwards, bare feet slipping on the damp grass. "You're not my father," she accused. "My father would never say such things. What's happened to you?"

"Oh, I am your father alright." He moved the knife through the air. "Now, be a good little girl and come on . . ."

"I'm not going anywhere until you tell me what's going on." She took another step backwards.

He shook his head in exasperation. "We need to feed the image." He lifted his head, sniffing the air. "She hungers. I can feel her hunger." He turned to look at her, his eyes like coins. "We need to feed her blood. Your blood. Don't you see: only your blood can make her whole."

Manny Frazer turned and ran.

The police. Were the police still watching the house? She raced across the lawn and then ran on the gravel, the stones cutting her bare feet. She cut across to the grass, feeling it wet with dew, slippery beneath her bare feet. She had to get around to the front of the house. Casting a quick glance over her shoulder, her heart almost stopped with fright.

Jonathan Frazer was loping after her, bent almost double, gleaming knife in one hand. There was a wide grin fixed to his lips, showing most of his teeth, and she could see saliva dribbling down his chin.

Manny raced into the bushes. They caught and snagged her bathrobe, slowing her down, eventually completely entangling her. Her struggles only enwrapped her further in the branches. Finally, she wriggled free of the robe and, naked, scrambled out the other side, the branches tearing at her skin. She made a last desperate effort to reach the house, her naked flesh goose pimpling. She heard her father crash into the bushes, branches snapping and then there was the definite rip of cloth.

Across the patio, footsteps pounding on the grass behind her, now pattering on the stone flags, through the kitchen door, slamming it behind her, turning the key, realizing that this madman was not going to stop, racing out through the kitchen door as he came through the glass door in a cascade of glass and wood, out onto the slippery hall, falling, scrambling to her feet, fumbling with the locks on the front door, hearing the kitchen door snap open, hearing him stumble on the hall floor, and now out the main door and down the graveled drive, screaming, screaming, screaming, footsteps crunching on the gravel behind her, a harsh guttural voice panting, cursing, calling her name and now out onto the road and the white lights close, too close, a scream of rubber echoing her own scream.

And the pain. A starburst of pure agony.

And silence.

Blessed silence.

88

A ND SILENCE.
     Blessed silence.

The screaming had finally stopped and the silence brought her from her sleep. She'd dreamt of a gray landscape and a whirlpool of faces, of mouths opening and closing, their howling like that of the wind through stone, relentless, incessant.

And then silence.

Blessed silence.

WHEN SHE AWOKE Kelley was bending over her, a large hand pressed to her mouth, a forefinger pressed to his lips. His bright green eyes were dancing in the light from the fire which had been built up to keep the winter chill away.

"It's time," he murmured, his Irish accent pronounced now, betraying his nervousness.

"Dee?" she murmured.

Kelley grinned. "Asleep, a little tincture in his ale to ensure he remains that way for a while."

The woman came up out of the bed, only the heaviness in her breasts betraying the fact that she'd given birth in the past three months.

Kelley caught her up in his arms, pressed her naked body against his. "Tonight, I will make you immortal," he whispered. He released her and she went to the cot and lifted out the sleeping form of the baby girl Dee had named Madimi. She looked at the girl without interest: the child had been necessary for the completion of tonight's exercise. Nothing more.

She felt nothing for it; she had deliberately prevented herself from developing feelings for it.

Even though the fire had been kept lit in the tower room, it was still cold, a bone-chill emanating from the mirror. She hung back, loath to approach the slab of glass, touching her face where the *thing* had spat at her the night the child was born . . . or had that been a dream? Sometimes it was hard to tell reality from the dream. Certainly her face had been dappled with a red burn mark the following morning.

She had described the creature, the golden woman she had briefly glimpsed in the glass, but Kelley had dismissed her fears; he knew the history and lore surrounding the glass—after all his family had been its guardians down through the ages—and he had never heard of anything like that in the mirror. He reminded her that she had just given birth to a child and that the body's humors needed time to settle and, he reminded her, she had just consumed a glass of brandy, which had been laced with a soporific to ease the labor, so that it was only natural that she should see something. His words held a ring of truth to them, and he dismissed the mark on her face as nothing more than the blood, which had been excited and agitated by the birth settling close to the skin. It had faded before the day was out as he promised, and she had eventually forgotten about it.

Until now.

She looked at the glass again, and abruptly found she could remember the creature in the glass in perfect detail. She looked at Kelley again, but he was moving around the mirror, preparing for the ceremony that would give him ultimate power, and give her life eternal. He felt her scrutiny and glanced back over his shoulder, brows creased in concentration.

"Second thoughts?"

"None."

"You know what has to be done?"

"Yes."

"You will have to be strong." He turned away and picked up the deep copper bowl, in which was lying a long razor-edged sliver of flint, one end of which had been wrapped in thread coated with tar to form a handle.

"Will there be pain?"

"An instant. Nothing more. Followed by an eternity of bliss." He turned back to the mirror. A deep purplish pulse had already begun deep in the core of the glass. "You see, it knows, it senses our presence. Come, come, bring the child. It is nearly time."

There was an astrological chart spread out on the floor, its edges held down by small copper pots. Months of careful calculation had gone into it to create a web of interconnecting circles with their lines of relevance and reference bisected into neat arcs. The chart had led him to the inescapable conclusion that tonight was propitious. Kelley had been working towards this moment for so long now . . . for most of his adult life, in fact.

And now only seconds separated him from power, incredible occult and magical power.

Edward Kelley stepped back from the mirror and began to strip off his clothing: this ceremony must be performed skyclad, to allow the body's aura to be washed in the mirror's energies. When he was naked, he took the flint knife and scored the palms of both hands in two long crosses, hissing slightly with the pain. Placing the knife back in the copper bowl, he pressed his bloody palms against the glass.

The rippling in the mirror warped and abruptly coalesced into a series of twisting colors, vibrant and vital. There were hints of faces, features, eyes, mouths in the glass.

Kelley stepped back from the mirror, the two bloody crosses on the glass fading, drying to a brownish flake. The woman had come up behind him, placing both hands on his shoulders, her breasts brushing his bare back, nipples hard against his skin.

"It's coming," he whispered. "Get the sacrifice."

The woman turned away and lifted the child from its swaddling clothes, dropping them to the floor. She walked around in front of Kelley, holding the still sleeping child in both hands, offering it to the glass.

The multitude of features on the glass had begun to coalesce, to form hideous masks, with multiple eyes, numerous mouths, teeth, and ears.

She continued to hold the child as Kelley came around and crouched before her, sitting cross-legged on the ground. He placed the copper bowl directly before him and placed the flint knife carefully on the ground to the right of the bowl.

The woman handed the babe down to him. When he placed it in the bowl, the coldness of the metal brought the baby girl wide awake. Bright blue eyes regarded Kelley expressionlessly. Kelley lifted the stone knife. This was the ultimate sacrifice, an unbaptized virginal female, and while it

would have been preferable to find a pubescent virgin on the cusp of men-
ses, where the energies of woman and girl were still in flux and all the
more powerful because of that, the sacrifice of the baby was the next best
thing.

With his eyes fixed on the center of the mirror, Kelley called the image
forth. He lifted the knife and placed it against the child's throat.

"For you," he promised the image.

The mirror came to a blazing, vivid life.

"And what will you give us in return, for this gift, daughters of Phorkys?"

89

THEY WERE the daughters of Phorkys, the third son of Pontos.

Theirs was a terrible power, theirs was an elemental strength. With no conception of time, they had ruled this world before the creature known as man had crawled down from the trees. They had watched it shed its hair, watched it walk upright. They had been old when the first villages had been built, ancient when the first of what the soft-skinned mankind would call civilization arose around the Middle Sea.

The soft-skinned ones knew them and the rest of their kind that the humans called gods, and they offered sacrifice to the Triad as was their due. It amused the daughters of Phorkys to allow the humankind to hunt for them, to feed and honor them, with flesh and blood and seed.

In time, the humankind grew envious of their powers. They turned away from the old gods and began to worship gods created in their own image. And the ancient ones, who had come to depend on the humankind for sacrifice and worship, and who fed off the petty fire of human emotions and the blood of their sacrifices, had felt their powers wane.

This was a Time of Fear.

The mankind had grown strong by then. They had perfected weaponcraft and metal-working, they had mastered the secrets of fire and they knew some of the secret lore.

So the Triad and the others like them, the Ancient Ones, had moved on, leaving the world of men, going into the secret places, the hidden valleys, the floating isles and the barren lands. There they would conserve their waning powers, and wait for the world to change, as it had before and would again.

But still some of the humankind pursued them, drawn by lust or envy, anger or hate. So the Triad created a legend of terror to keep the man-creatures away, but even this failed. The legend drew the foolhardy and the brave, and occasionally, the cunning.

Once there had been three daughters of Phorkys: Stheno, Euryale, and Medusa.

And then the mankind, Perseus, had come and slew Medusa with cunning and a weapon of metal.

The two remaining sisters grew frightened then. They were three, and the three were one, and even though a part of them was gone, they could still survive. But if another part of the Triad were to be slain then they would be lost forever, for all time. So the two creatures the mankind called Gorgons created a vessel that would carry them through time, rightly guessing that with sophistication would come ignorance. And with ignorance, they could become whole again, for within them both, they held the seeds of their sister, Medusa.

But what would entice the mankind, and yet remain unsuspected in their world?

The Gorgons noted that the humans were vain, and liked to admire their reflections, and so they conceived of a huge mirror, a gateway to the Otherworld, where their kind, the Ancient Ones still reigned.

Stheno sacrificed her sister, Euryale, and set her spirit into the glass to prepare the way, and then she flayed the flesh from her sister's bones and spread it out behind the great mirror to keep the magic alive, to allow it to become active when blood was spread onto the glass. The blood—or any human secretion—would seep through the glass and soak into the skin, bringing forth the ancient magic. Stheno then took her own life, spread-eagled across the mirror, allowing her own thin ichor to seep into the mirror, allowing herself to become absorbed. And the two became one.

Then came the Time of Waiting.

In the beginning, they had come close to escape on many occasions. The men beasts were controllable. They needed two: the male to supply the blood to soak the skin, to bring the magic to life. The female was the sacrifice, and the host for Stheno. And once they had the host, once Stheno could come forth, she would raise Euryale and together they would be able to bring forth the Medusa.

But they hadn't counted on the wiles of the humankind. The beasts had always had their magicians, their mages, sorcerers, and witches. Often these were primitives with only the merest trace of power, and of no account. But some had skills or learned fragments and they recorded this knowledge in their grimoires. In time, knowledge of the Otherworld and the astral grew and, in time, some of the human magicians became aware of the mirror with its deadly secret and terrible threat. Too afraid to break the glass, they eventually banished it to a land at the edge of the world, and a single clan was chosen to guard and protect the glass.

So the three who had become two, who was now one—Stheno, alive, alert within the glass—was patient, because she knew that humankind was weak and arrogant.

The passage of years suited it. They lost their faith, they forgot their history, they became arrogant and gullible. They who had once ruled nations, realized they could conquer the entire world. A world of flesh and blood.

All they needed was a host . . .

90

I T's TIME," Kelley turned to look up at the woman. He came smoothly to his feet. "You understand what needs to be done? You will die first, then the child. All your blood must leave your body, for blood carries the corruptions which bring age."

She nodded. She stepped over to the copper basin with its pitiful wriggling bundle and pressed herself against the mirror. The glass was cold against her naked flesh.

She turned her face slightly, pressing her cheek against its coolness, feeling its sensuous touch against her breasts, belly, and thighs. She shuddered, spreading her arms to clutch the edge of the plain wooden frame, opening her legs to the touch of the mirror's moist surface.

She felt her nipples hardening, her breathing quickening.

"Forever and ever?" she whispered. The shadowy figure behind her— barely glimpsed in the mirror's dull surface—moved closer.

"Forever and ever, unchanging, unchanged."

"Yessss," she hissed. Closing her eyes, she visualized herself spread-eagled up against the mirror, face to face, breast to breast, belly to belly with her own image. Her heart began pounding with ever-increasing force, almost as if it were pressing against the glass. Sudden heat bloomed between her legs.

And at the very moment her orgasm took her, wracking through her body, the thin sliver of sharpened stone ripped through her throat.

Ultimate pleasure became absolute pain.

Blood hissed and steamed on the glass. Her mouth opened in a soundless scream and as Kelley's shadowy figure moved closer, bending his head to her face, her lips moved, words forming, bloody froth bubbling on them. "Thank you."

"I love you," he said and, for the first time in his life, he meant the words.

Kelley held her against the mirror as her blood poured onto the surface of the glass, quickly disappearing into the greasy interior of the mirror.

He could barely contain his elation. He knew the secret of the glass. Maybe he could try to remove the back of the mirror to allow him access to the hide of the Gorgon. Though, on second thought, perhaps that might not be such a good idea. Kelley looked at the glass again, a frown creasing his brow. According to his studies, once the blood had drained from the woman's body, the corpse should become animated by the image.

He took his hand away from the corpse and stepped back. The body crashed to the ground, though its reflection remained in the glass. Where was the golden woman?

But this was no reflection, this was the image, naked and complete, its hair waving around its head in a parody of the legend of the Gorgon. He looked at the corpse on the ground and frowned in puzzlement. What had happened? What had gone wrong? Why had the image not stepped through from the Otherworld into the corpse of the just slain woman?

The creature in the glass, the image of the woman he had just slain was mouthing words, repeating them over and over again, until he finally understood their meaning. "The body was impure, diseased. The body must be virginal in every way. We have taken its soul, its reflection, but we cannot use its physical form."

It reached for him, arms outstretched, palms flat against the glass. Kelley pressed himself against the mirror, almost feeling the woman's warm flesh against his. He pressed his lips to hers, feeling her breath, warm and moist against his cheek, her tongue against his lips, probing, opening them.

And then she whispered, "You have failed us!"

The tongue that broke through the surface of the glass and shot into his mouth was rasping, hooked, and forked. It filled his mouth, insinuated itself down his throat. He attempted to scream, but his mouth was full. He attempted to pull away, but couldn't. The foul tongue moved down his throat, deeper, deeper, into his stomach. He could feel it squirming, coiling, moving.

And he couldn't breathe, couldn't even vomit.

Couldn't breathe.

And now the image's hair was changing, twisting, turning, coiling, melding together, tiny heads forming, black polished eyes, tiny darting tongues amongst the strands. The rest of the image was changing also, twisting, altering, her features running, melding together, elongating, a beast-like snout forming, long tusks digging into its own flesh.

It opened its mouth, wider, wider, wider, its tongue still lodged deep in Kelley's throat, its fangs growing, great slab-like teeth coming up from the lower jaw, snapping at his face, scraping against the glass, threatening to break through.

With a final convulsive agonizing effort, Edward Kelley wrenched himself away from the mirror, stumbling backwards across the woman's body. Blood streamed from his mouth and the sounds he uttered were bestial.

In the mirror, the beast devoured his tongue with great relish. "Now, give us the babe," it demanded.

Kelley gathered up the baby in the copper bowl . . . and then turned and ran from the room.

91

So, THE body had to be pure and virginal in every respect. He'd known that, his instincts had been right all along.

Jonathan Frazer crouched before the mirror in the guesthouse, watching the images slowly fading from the glass. He'd been feeding the image with his own blood for most of the evening, and he was dizzy and faint, but now he knew the secret of the mirror.

But even though he had fed her, he could still hear the plaintive cry of hunger, like a distant keening in the back of his mind. His mistress hungered. And he was going to feed her, and at least now he knew just what she wanted, what she needed. She needed a virgin's blood and she needed a virginal body as a host.

He tried to think, but his thoughts had been so confused over the past few days. Which of his friends had teenage daughters and which of them were still virginal? Weren't teenagers supposed to be much more promiscuous these days in any case? How was he going to find a young virgin?

Well now let's see, who says it had to be young? Maybe the image would prefer an older, stronger body when it came back to this world: he just had to ensure that it was still a virgin.

He curled his legs up under him until he was sitting cross-legged. He dropped his head onto his clenched fist, his elbow resting on his knee, and closed his eyes, considering. Maybe someone unmarried, a spinster . . .

Moments later, his head snapped up, his deep brown eyes bright, glittering. He began to chuckle and then laugh, the sound coming from deep within his body. But when it reached his throat it was high-pitched and maniacal. Maybe he might get to kill two birds with one stone. This time the laughter left him convulsed, rolling around on the floor, clutching his sides.

92

In the silence of the hospital room, the regular blipping of the monitors and the gentle susurration of the ventilator sounded very loud indeed.

Officer Carole Morrow looked up as the door opened and then straightened as Margaret Haaren stepped into the room. The detective raised her eyebrows questioningly and the young officer shook her head. Standing at the end of the bed, the woman sighed, looking down at the bandaged form of Emmanuelle Frazer.

The girl was alive: but barely.

She was lucky to be alive, too. Two broken legs, broken hip, shattered kneecaps—even if she survived, and that was somewhat in doubt at the moment—she'd never walk properly again. She also had a cracked skull, concussion, broken ribs, and because she'd been naked when the police car had hit her, she was badly skinned, a mass of cuts and bruises.

What Margaret Haaren wanted to know was why she'd run screaming from the house. Why was she naked?

A search of the house had revealed the shattered kitchen door, but nothing else. The guesthouse had been securely bolted and padlocked and a room to room search from attic to basement had disclosed no one, nor were there any indications that anyone had been in the house. The officers watching the house had seen no one enter or leave.

And there was still no sign of Jonathan Frazer.

Although she had nothing more than instinct to go on, Margaret Haaren knew Frazer had been in the house, knew that he had chased his daughter from the house, where she'd run blindly into the road and been hit by the police car.

Where does a man who is basically a loner go? He'd no real friends to run to; he didn't drink so he couldn't take solace in a bottle, and to the best of their knowledge he was still in the country. He hadn't used his passport, credit cards, or cell phone. She was guessing he was very close by. He had nowhere else to go.

Margaret Haaren picked up Manny's chart and quickly scanned it. Too many years of doing what she was doing now—standing at the end of a bed looking at a victim or a witness or a villain—had made her an expert at reading charts. "Did she say anything?" she asked, without looking up.

Carole Morrow shook her head. "She was mumbling and moaning earlier, but nonsense words, something about a baby, that's all I got."

The detective nodded. "Stay with her; if you've got to leave the room for any reason, make sure the officer outside steps in."

"Yes, ma'am."

"Do not leave her on her own for a single moment."

"Yes, ma'am."

The detective replaced the chart and folded her arms across her broad chest, looking at the young woman.

"Do you think *he* was responsible," Morrow asked, looking at Manny Frazer again. They both knew she was talking about Jonathan Frazer.

"Didn't they teach you never to speculate without facts?" the detective asked, smiling to take the sting from her words.

"They told me to use my imagination," the young officer said simply. "I think she was running from her father."

Margaret Haaren nodded. "So do I," she murmured. "But where is he now?"

The two officers in the police car said they were responding to the sound of terrified screams. They were parked on the road just a few yards away from the driveway, so that they had a clear view of the house. They had driven up fast, lights on, but with sirens off. The screams became louder, more desperate as they neared the Frazer house. And then the naked young woman had run straight out in front of the car, and there was absolutely nothing they could do about it. She hadn't even been looking where she was going, she seemed to be looking over her shoulder.

She was being chased.

"I'm going to the Frazer house," she said to Morrow. "I'll be there if anyone needs me."

"Yes, ma'am." She coughed discreetly. "Can I ask why?"

"Because we've missed something. And I've no idea what it is. But I'll know it when I see it."

93

Tommy Hinge didn't like the term "peeping Tom." It certainly didn't apply to him. He simply walked through the condominium complex where he lived and if he happened to see someone undressing in a window, well, he could hardly be blamed for looking, now could he? After all, he was only human.

He'd lived in these apartments for three years now, a retired mailman—or at least that's what he told people. His discharge from the post office had been anything but honorable. Misappropriation of mail and parcels was the charge and his attorney had suggested that he take the five year jail time knowing he wouldn't serve the full term and he'd probably be out in eighteen months or so. It was a better alternative than the one hundred and fifty thousand dollar fine.

Over the years—because he'd often used their services himself—he'd become expert at recognizing the plain cardboard boxes that came from the companies supplying adult toys and playthings. He knew all the innocuous sounding names by heart. He'd taken the first package out of sheer curiosity, and discovered it held a treasure trove of Swedish porn. And after that . . . well, he was hooked. He never thought anyone would complain: after all, who were they going to complain to—consumer affairs? Excuse me, but I didn't get my blow-up doll . . . my vibrator's gone missing in the mail . . . my Spanish fly seems to have flown. But that's exactly what had happened. Someone had complained—someone who obviously felt no shame or embarrassment. Then someone else complained and since all the thefts had occurred within his postal district, it wasn't difficult to find the culprit. The department's fraud section had sent a few trial packages through the mail and of course he'd fallen for it and lifted them.

And that was that. He'd nearly forty years of service and he lost everything, including his pension for about a hundred dollars worth of not-very-good porn and an impractically large dildo. Even his union wouldn't support him—it was hard to defend a mailman stealing porn and adult sex toys. The meager social security check he got from the state ensured that he couldn't treat himself to any of the glossy new publications or adult toys. Since the internet, porno mags rarely appeared on the second-hand shelves, so he'd had to find new ways to amuse himself.

He'd discovered the pleasures of peeping by accident. He'd been taking out his trash, walking through the complex to the communal bins when he'd chanced to see a young woman in one of the corner apartments undressing. She'd forgotten to close her blinds fully, and he'd spent ten of the most pleasant and exciting minutes in his life simply watching her.

After that it became a ritual, and then an obsession, taking him away from the complex he lived in, finding his arousal in other apartment complexes within the area. He'd even compiled a list and a carefully drawn out plan of the surrounding buildings; half a block down on the right, front apartment, busty blonde, last name: James. Second apartment block to the left, second floor rear apartment, slender Asian woman named Kim.

And now his ambition was to see every single woman in the near vicinity naked or as near naked as possible. High on his list was the woman in the next-door complex, a front unit apartment on the first floor, Haaren was the name listed on the main entry door to the complex. A big woman, mature, masculine—just the type he preferred. And he'd just discovered that she'd got a young one staying with her at the moment. Dark-haired, skinny, but pretty: maybe he could add her to his collection. He wondered if they were lesbians—the thought sent a shiver down his spine.

Tommy was hiding in the small walkway beside the apartment building for nearly an hour before he saw the light go on. From this position, he was able to see directly into the apartment, yet remain concealed by dark shadow from the towering building next door and the bushes. There was nothing visible yet, but there was some compensation in the fact that she hadn't closed the blinds yet. He knew from experience that if the blinds weren't closed the moment a person walked into the room, then the odds were greatly improved that they wouldn't close them at all. It was surprising how many people didn't. Why, just tonight, he'd watched the woman two buildings down from the Haaren woman, dressing to go out. He'd seen nothing he hadn't seen before, but it was the thrill of watching that aroused him now.

Footsteps sounded on the path and Tommy shrank back into the deeper shadows. He knew he was virtually invisible—he'd bought himself some black sweats and then peeled off all the decorations and reflective strips. If he was caught, he was just out for an evening jog.

He watched as a figure moved swiftly by and was suddenly glad he couldn't be seen. There was something about the man—the way he moved, the expression on his face, the smell—yes, certainly the smell, like old decayed meat, like blood. It frightened him.

The figure stopped outside the main entry and consulted something in his hand, finally standing back and looking to either side at the two front units. And then he stepped backwards, standing, staring. The man abruptly grunted in satisfaction and walked briskly away.

Tommy gave a sigh of relief. He turned his attention back to the Haaren woman's apartment.

So how many M. Haarens could there be in the Los Angeles Yellow Pages? And the very fact that it was an initial convinced him that it was the same woman.

Frazer was surprised to find she lived in an apartment; he'd have thought she'd have a house. But then he supposed that an apartment was ideal for a single woman, living alone.

He checked the address again, counting the apartments from left to right. *Yes*, there was a light on in the apartment he had assumed was hers.

The large glass double doors in front of him were locked. To the right was a metal box with the tenants' last names listed, a number beside each name, a metallic push button and a phone. He found *Haaren* on the second line down and pressed the bell. He heard a click and then crackling static. "Yes?"

"I have a delivery for Detective Haaren from Flora International."

"Oh, thank you, come in. First floor, apartment number 2." The door buzzed loudly.

As he pushed through the door he touched the comforting pressure of the knife strapped to his arm.

AAAH, SHOWTIME.

Tommy Hinge smiled broadly as the woman, wearing a towel around her head and another wrapped around her body moved toward the door. She stopped, her head turned sideways as if she were asking a question and listening to the answer.

And then she was stepping back, opening the door . . .

Jesus Christ.

It was him. The man with the smell. He was moving into the apartment, a knife in his hand, pressing it against the woman's throat, his face so distorted with hate it was barely recognizable as human.

THE KNIFE HAD been in his hand, and at the woman's throat before he realized it wasn't Margaret Haaren. It was a teenager, vaguely familiar, though he'd no conscious memory of ever having seen her before.

"The Haaren bitch, where is she?" he snarled.

The young woman looked at him wide-eyed, mouth open in shock.

He pressed the knife against the slender column of her throat, the razor sharp edge parting the skin, blood from the cut snaking down to stain the towel wrapped around her breasts. "Answer me!"

Her throat moved. "Working," she whispered.

Frazer swore. He slashed at the beaded curtain that separated the kitchen from the rest of the apartment, wooden beads and shells scattering across the floor.

"When is she back?"

"I don't know. Later, maybe. Tomorrow, I'm not sure."

All the energy seemed to drain out of Frazer, the knife dropped away from the young woman's throat and his head dipped.

"You're making a grave mistake. Margaret Haaren's a cop."

"I know that," he snarled. And then he suddenly looked up, his eyes bright, glittering. "I know you."

She started to shake her head.

"I know you," he repeated. "I saw you at the funeral." He squeezed his eyes shut, remembering. He'd been talking to Margaret Haaren and this young woman had come up behind her, and called her "aunt" and Margaret Haaren had called her . . .

"Helen," he said, his eyes snapping open.

"Yes," she said, surprised he knew her name.

Jonathan Frazer smiled, lips drawing back from his teeth in an animal snarl. He moved the knife up before her face, allowing the light to reflect into her eyes. "Tell me Helen," he whispered, very softly, "are you a virgin?"

"A what?" she whispered, horrified.

"A virgin."

TOMMY HINGE WINCED as he watched the man speaking intently to the young woman. The hatred in his face was palpable and terrifying. Tommy saw him snatch the towel from the girl's head, exposing damp hair and then wrench the towel away from her body. The girl's head and shoulders were shaking as if she were crying. The man was nodding now, as if satisfied, and then he pointed away with the knife and walked behind her, his left hand on her shoulder, the knife resting against her right shoulder close to her neck.

The light in the bedroom snapped on.

Tommy's heart was pounding loudly. He was transfixed. He knew he should call the cops, but how would he explain his situation, what he was doing outside her apartment at this hour? But he couldn't stand back and allow her to be raped and maybe murdered. He was many things—thief and voyeur, yes—but he wasn't the sort of man to allow a girl to be abused and . . .

The young woman reappeared. She was dressed now, pulling on a T-shirt over pale blue jeans. She lifted a denim jacket off the back of a chair. The light went off in the bedroom. The couple moved through the apartment, and now they were at the door, and while the man's hand was still on her shoulder, the knife was no longer visible. The light went out.

Tommy Hinge watched, desperately wondering what he was going to do. Then the main door opened and the pair stepped out into the night.

They walked right past him, the man's grip so tight on the young woman's shoulder that he could see the whiteness of his knuckles. Tommy's nose wrinkled at the abattoir stench off the man and the sour stink of the woman's fear.

He waited until they had walked down the road and then he stepped out after them, abruptly glad of his black sweats and his rubber-soled trainers.

94

S HE WAS trapped in a crystal, in a huge block of ice. Everywhere she looked there were reflections.

But it was not her own reflection she was looking at.

She raised her arms and a dozen figures—no, a hundred, a thousand—male and female, and obscene combinations of both, raised their arms in silent mimicry. She hammered on the surface of the glass and a thousand arms hammered in perfect syncopation.

Now she was in a glass coffin, and it was growing smaller, constricting, shrinking, contracting. She began to scream, but there was a vacuum within the crystal cage, and there was no sound. She began to pound on the surface of the block of ice, ignoring the mimicking hands, ignoring the slack and gaping faces, beating, beating, beating against the glass, which suddenly . . .

Cracked.

It tumbled down around her in huge razor sharp shards, the glass cutting into her body, slicing into her flesh, hammering into her legs. Dear God the pain in her legs.

Abruptly the pain vanished.

And she could no longer feel her legs.

Emmanuelle Frazer opened her mouth and screamed.

"WHAT HAPPENED?" MARGARET Haaren demanded, tucking the phone under her left ear, trapping it between cheek and shoulder as she locked her car, and hurried back into the hospital.

"She came awake about ten minutes after you left," Morrow said, trying to remain as calm as possible. She could still hear the woman's terrified screams in her ears. She took a deep breath and continued. "She screamed for at least five minutes without a break. The heart machine was going crazy."

"Then what?" She ignored the elevator and raced down a corridor.

"By then the doctors had injected her with a massive sedative. It should have knocked her out completely; it didn't. She grew calm. She looked around and spotted me. I said, 'Hello Miss Frazer, how do you feel?'"

"And?" Haaren said through gritted teeth. Did she have to drag out every particular, word-by-word?

"She closed her eyes first and when she opened them again, she started to cry. She said, very quietly. 'He's got a knife. He was going to kill me. That's not my father.' She started crying then. She's still crying."

"Right." The detective had put her hand on the handle of the door when it suddenly opened and a tall blond-haired, blue-eyed doctor stepped out. He looked about eighteen.

"I'm sorry, no visitors," he said imperiously.

"Don't be ridiculous," the detective said, ignoring him.

For a moment, it looked as if the doctor was going to protest, but the police officer on duty outside the door caught his arm and led him away. "I think we'll leave Detective Haaren alone for a moment."

Manny Frazer had calmed down by the time Margaret Haaren stepped into the room. The young woman was still dreadfully confused, and she hadn't got a clue how she had ended up back in the hospital. She looked up into the detective's broad face and smiled in recognition.

"How do you feel?" Margaret Haaren asked gently. She took the girl's bandaged hand in hers, stroking it lightly with the fingers of her left hand. The girl was eighteen, the same age as her niece, she suddenly remembered, but right now, she looked a lot older than her years.

Manny's mouth worked, but no sound came out.

"Can you tell me what happened? It's important." Haaren's voice fell to a whisper. "Manny, we need to know."

"I'm hurt bad, aren't I? Am I going to die?" Manny's voice was cracked and raw.

"The doctors say you'll be fine," the detective lied. "And no, you are not going to die. You were hit by a car when you ran out of your driveway. What made you run like that?"

Manny's large blue eyes, almost lost now behind the bruises, opened wide and her breathing began to quicken. The now silent heart monitor showed increased activity on its tiny square screen.

"Gently, gently now," the detective murmured. "You were being chased. Who was chasing you?"

The bloodshot eyes opened wide. Her voice was a ragged whisper. "He's got a knife. He was going to kill me. That's not my father."

"Who's not your father? Who is chasing you, Manny? Who is after you?"

"He's got a knife. He's going to kill me."

"You're safe now, Manny. There's no one after you now. Tell me who it was. You know who it was, don't you?" she demanded. "Tell me."

Manny's eyes opened wide. "It was my father."

"So, it *was* your father."

"But it wasn't."

"The man looked like your father," she said patiently.

Manny attempted to shake her head and then stopped, realizing she was restrained. "No. It was my father. But he was different."

"Different? How?"

"Different. Changed. Not the dad I knew."

"He had a knife, Manny. What did he want to do with the knife?"

"He wanted . . . wanted to kill me . . . no . . ." Her breath died away to a ghostly whisper, and Margaret lowered her head to catch the words. The heart monitor began to trip wildly.

"What did he want?" Haaren snapped, and the young woman flinched.

"He said he wanted to sacrifice me. To feed it my blood, to make it whole."

"Feed what, Manny? What did he want to feed?"

"Mother!" Manny's voice rose to a hoarse shout. "My mother. He said she was dead!"

Margaret Haaren stopped, her own heartbeat beginning to trip along in rhythm to the girls'. There was no way Manny could know about the death of her mother. "What did he say about your mother?"

"He said he'd killed her. Said he'd cut her from crotch to sternum, that's what he'd said. Said she was with someone." Her fingers tightened convulsively around Haaren's fingers, blood beginning to seep through the bandages. "Is it true? Is it?"

"Yes, I'm sorry Manny, your mother is dead," the detective said slowly.

"Did . . . did Dad do it?"

"I believe he did," Margaret said quietly. Although she had no idea how he did it.

Manny lay back on the pillows, eyes closed.

"It's not his fault, Manny. He's not well. He needs our help, yours and mine. Now, tell me, who did your father want to feed?"

"Not who—what!"

"What?"

"The mirror."

Haaren frowned. "The mirror?"

"Yes, the mirror. It has possessed him. Talbott said it was evil, and then it killed him. And it would have killed me," she added wonderingly. "He was going to kill me and feed my blood to the mirror."

"Where is he, Manny?" Margaret Haaren said loudly. "Where is Jonathan Frazer?"

"He can hear it, he can feel its hunger. It's making him kill to feed it."

"Where is he, dammit!"

"In the guesthouse. He's in the guesthouse, and he's going to feed the mirror. He's going to kill tonight!"

Margaret Haaren was already moving towards the door when it snapped open and Officer Morrow's pale face looked in. She handed the detective a radio. "Emergency feed, patched through from the station."

"Haaren," she said crisply, turning in the doorway to look back into the room, but Manny Frazer was sleeping again, only the rapid movement behind her closed eyelids evidence that her sleep wasn't peaceful.

"What's wrong?" she murmured, stepping outside the room, closing the door behind her. Carole Morrow stared anxiously at her, until Margaret jerked her thumb and the young officer stepped back into the room.

"We got a report from a member of the public about half an hour ago that a man roughly answering to Frazer's description was seen to kidnap a young woman at knifepoint. The citizen followed them to Frazer's house in the Hollywood Hills, where he was picked up by our men for loitering. Our guys didn't believe his story so we sent a car around to the address where he said the young woman had been taken from."

"And?"

"I've verified this myself, ma'am. Everything checks out. I'm so·sorry," he added, and in that moment, Margaret Haaren knew that whatever she was going to hear now would not be good. "Frazer's got your niece, Helen."

"And do we have Frazer?"

"We've searched the house again. It's empty."

"And the guesthouse?"

"Sealed shut."

She was just about to ask the officers to check inside, but something made her stop. "I'm on the way."

"SWAT is on the way. Detective, the commander has asked that you stand down."

"Understood," Margaret Haaren said.

95

S HE WAS back in the crystal prison, a flat oblong of glass spinning
slowly across a gray and dreary landscape. She was spread-eagled in
the glass, trapped, her mouth open, screaming, screaming, screaming.

And there, in the distance, was a towering whirlpool funnel, lightning
wrapped, shimmering with color. In the gray silence it exuded a barely perceptible hum, a high-pitched keening. Instinctively she knew that herein
were the trapped souls of aeons.

If the whirlpool had a name then it was Agony.

There were faces in the whirlpool, hundreds of tiny faces, from all races,
from all times, mouths and eyes wide, pleading, begging, crying for release.
Close to the top of the whirlpool there were whole bodies of the recently
dead circling around, caught in the great tidal pull of the circle, and further down, nearer the bottom, there were only segments of features, partially glimpsed eyes, mouths, tongues, lips.

She felt its pull, the wrenching deep within her as the crystal prison
bucked and warped. It dragged her forward and suddenly she was within
the whirlpool, sucked into the funnel, and she was spinning, spinning,
spinning, down and down and down, deep into the core of the turgid
grayness.

Now she could hear the song of its captured souls, and this song was
Desolation.

The rectangle of crystal fell further, deeper into the core, and now the
partially glimpsed features were no longer human or even animal, but
something of both. Here were the creatures of myth, of legend, of faith
and fancy.

Abruptly the grayness was broken by a rain of tiny white lights which streaked past her. Vivid, pulsing with their own inner life, the droplets spattered all around her, calling to her, drawing her down even further, even deeper . . . until she saw the opening ahead of her. It was a small rectangle, but growing, growing, growing as she rushed headlong towards it.

There were figures in the rectangle. A man, naked, standing before the opening. A woman, naked, bound and blindfolded lying on the ground behind him. Behind her strange and curious artifacts.

Recognizable artifacts.

Antiques.

The man standing before the opening was . . . Dear God, it was her father. And he was . . . he was masturbating and his seed was streaming past her in long thin streamers and elongated globules, drifting back up into the core of the whirlpool. He was feeding the mirror.

Blood, tears, and semen.

She came to an abrupt jarring halt.

She was on one side of the mirror.

And her father, Jonathan Frazer, was on the other.

And then a figure stepped past her out of the grayness and looked at Frazer.

It was the Image.

96

H E'D MASTURBATED furiously, spilling his seed onto the glass whilst calling up the image. She had appeared at the precise moment of his orgasm and pressed herself up against the glass, staring at him, her eyes wide with desire, long hair battering against the glass.

"I've got something for you," he whispered. He glanced over his shoulder at the bound, gagged, and blindfolded young woman. "A virgin. Unsullied, unblemished."

The image smiled at him, full lips curling against white teeth.

"Tell me what to do," he whispered.

Feed me. Free me.

He remembered fragments of the pictures he had seen of Kelley the night he had sacrificed the woman. The copper bowl, the stone knife. But were they necessary? Surely all the image desired was the blood of the sacrifice.

Frazer stood, leaning forward against the glass, the palms of his hands resting against the glass. In the glass the image mimicked him. He could feel the flesh of his hands against hers, see the way her breasts flattened against the glass. He brought his face close to the mirror, close to the dark-haired, dark-eyed woman's face. "Tell me what to do."

The image's stone-hard eyes flickered to the bound woman. *Feed me. Spread her on the glass. Bring her to the moment of her greatest passion. Then sacrifice her. I will take her life substance, and when she is nothing more than a husk, I shall possess the shell. I shall be made flesh again.* Her tongue flickered out and he imagined he felt it brush against his lips.

"Soon," he promised, "soon, soon, soon." He turned to look at the girl.

"Now, now, now! Feed me. Free me."

97

M ARGARET HAAREN sat in her car and checked the magazine on her .40 Beretta, then she chambered a round and thumbed the safety on. She slid the gun in the holster on her hip under her jacket as she climbed out of the car. She had a very good idea that Mr. Jonathan Frazer was going to be shot while resisting arrest.

The road had been sealed off and the residents of the surrounding houses had been evacuated. A police helicopter whirled above, circling, the strong white beam washing over the house and garden. There were marksmen situated in the homes opposite. Jonathan Frazer was armed and considered extremely dangerous.

The SWAT Commander was now in charge of this operation. His softly-softly approach was famous—or infamous—and she knew he'd more than likely spent the rest of the night in the van talking to the SWAT team before making any hurried decision, and by that time Helen could be dead. Manny had told her that Frazer would kill tonight.

Right now the press were starting to arrive. Of course, she'd forgotten about the press. All the local and national news stations were in place: CBS, NBC, KCAL, FOX. They were kept at bay at the end of the street, but now any chance at dealing with this situation quietly was gone. Also, whatever chances they had of taking Frazer by surprise were going down the toilet right now. She watched the Commander appear from the SWAT truck and stride down the road to give an interview.

Stuart Miller materialized by her side. "What would you say if I told you there was a back way into the guesthouse?"

Margaret Haaren looked at him and then glanced over at the Commander. "I'd say lead the way."

"Shouldn't we tell someone . . ." he asked.

"You just have."

THE TWO POLICE officers moved through the crowd and walked back almost to the entrance of the driveway. Miller stopped, his eyes moving to the left, the detective following the direction of his gaze. It was just another garden . . . no, it wasn't another garden. It was a narrow laneway between the two gardens. The opening was incredibly narrow, barely wide enough for a person to walk in single file down its length. Without a word, she slipped into the leafy darkness, Stuart Miller following her without a sound.

This was how Frazer had managed to get into the house without them knowing! This was how he'd slipped in and out when he'd chased his daughter. The pathway was almost in total darkness, the only light coming from the houses. She glanced back over her shoulder at Stuart. She could barely see him and she almost missed his nod. She heard the snap as he removed his gun from its holster and held it up by his head. Easing her own weapon free, she carefully ran her hand over the rusty iron gate, eventually finding and pressing the catch. The gate swung inwards without a sound. It had recently been oiled.

THE GIRL WAS spread-eagled on the mirror, arms and legs tied to the four corners. She had struggled and kicked until he had laid the flat of the cold knife against her breasts, promising to cut her deeply unless she stopped struggling. When he'd pressed her up against the glass, she had winced, pulling away from the chill, but again Frazer had used the knife to urge her forward.

Frazer stood back grinning widely. From where he was standing it was as if the young woman were embracing the image, breast-to-breast, thigh to thigh, belly to belly. He looked into the image's dark eyes, shivering at the dark hunger he saw there, the longing, the need.

He came up behind the bound girl and ran both hands down her sides; her flesh, though silky soft, still felt harsh to his fingers, her hair coarse and brittle. She attempted to pull away from him and he stroked the side of her face. "Shhh now, shhh now. This will be an amazing experience for you."

Her eyes blazed their loathing.

Frazer grinned. She was a beast. Cattle to be used. He sank to his knees behind her and ran both hands up the insides of her thighs, finally stopping deep in her groin, his fingers probing, stroking, pressing, rubbing. She attempted to squeeze her legs closed, but he pinched her buttocks hard and she relaxed.

In the mirror he could see the image mimicking his movement, arousing herself, her eyes locked on his face, her tongue moving lasciviously across her lips. The invitation in her eyes was almost physical.

Where there had been only dry flesh beneath his fingers, now there was moisture. Deep in the corners of the mirror, he could see the first tentative curls of shifting power begin to twist and weave. He looked at the knife resting by his left hand. At the moment of her greatest passion he would kill her.

Soon. He could feel her muscles begin to twitch of their own accord. Soon.

THE GUESTHOUSE WAS locked—but from the inside this time. Which meant there was someone inside.

The glass panes in the windows appeared to have been recently painted over, the screens removed.

Margaret Haaren pressed the side of her face against the door and listened. For a moment she heard nothing and then, faint, muffled, she heard the quiet sounds of a woman panting, the unmistakable sounds of a woman approaching orgasm.

She stepped away from the door and looked around. She couldn't go through the door, and the windows were covered. There was a tree overhanging the guesthouse . . . and she remembered that there were skylights in the roof. If she got up onto the tree, she could look down into the guesthouse.

Stuart Miller saw her look from the tree to the roof and shook his head. "Don't even think about it ma'am."

"Give me an alternative," she snapped in a raw whisper.

"The SWAT team is back there; let them deal with it. They can blow the door, they'll get your niece out safely."

"Good idea. Go and ask the fucking Commander what he's waiting for.

Go get them now . . . and hurry," she said, and pushed him away into the darkness. Easing down the hammer on the pistol, she stuck it back in its holster. She waited until she heard the gate close softly behind him and then headed for the tree. She hadn't climbed a tree since she was a child, but she supposed, like riding a bike, it was something you didn't forget. Or you fell off.

THE GIRL MIGHT be a virgin, but she was reacting violently to his stroking. Although she was tied to the edge of the frame, she was now actually clutching at it for support while her body bucked and shifted, pressing herself hard against the glass, using its chill as a stimulus.

Frazer guessed that the image had something to do with the girl's extraordinary level of arousal.

And now her orgasm was beginning. Deep shudders were wracking through her body, her buttocks were clenching and unclenching and her stomach muscles were almost rippling. Her breath was coming in great heaving gasps. She started to cry out, short grunting sobs that quickly lengthened, deepened, muffled by the gag. Her head was thrown back and her eyes closed tightly shut.

Jonathan Frazer stepped back and allowed the woman's own passion to do the rest.

He lifted the knife in his right hand and waited. It was only a matter of seconds. But the moment had to be right, it had to be perfect.

MARGARET HAAREN SWUNG from the branch onto the roof of the guesthouse with surprising delicacy for such a heavy woman. She crawled to the nearest skylight. She could see nothing. Gritting her teeth, she crawled, inch by inch to the next. Below her the muffled grunting, moaning sounds had reached a crescendo.

And then silence.

HELEN. THAT WAS her name: Helen.

Gripping her hair tightly, Jonathan Frazer plunged the knife deep into her jugular, and then dragged the blade back across her throat. Helen's shudders continued, but now they were of a different character. She slumped against the glass, and hung there, suspended by the ropes binding her to the frame. The blood from her torn throat gushed onto the glass, warm and salty, steaming, hissing, bubbling.

The mirror exploded into a maelstrom of light. Jagged streaks of color ran from one edge of the glass to the other. The image reached out to match the position of the young woman tied to the glass. Only now when it pressed itself against the glass Frazer clearly saw the glass bow outwards. He saw its fingers stretch the surface like jelly, and then break through one by one, and wrap themselves around the girl's face, pulling her close to the glass to where its lips pressed against the glass around the gaping wound in the woman's throat. Its tongue—long and dark and moist—lapped at the spurting blood.

Frazer stood behind the woman, pressing her slumped head close to the mirror so that the image could suck at the blood. The image looked at him once, and he shuddered with the promise in its eyes, before it returned to licking, sucking, drawing the last remnants of life from the young woman. Frazer watched it for a moment, and then he too bent his head to the wound and tentatively tasted it with the tip of his tongue.

MARGARET HAAREN'S HAND trembled as she lined up the sights. Almost directly below her, Frazer was bent over Helen who was tied up to a huge mirror. There was a dripping knife in his hand and he was licking at her neck where she could see a bloody wound.

She took a deep breath, held it, released it and pulled the trigger.

JONATHAN FRAZER GLANCED up into the image's eyes—and found himself looking at a nightmare.

How dare you taste her blood. She is mine! the beast roared.

Whip-like tendrils of hair shot out from the mirror, as if they were breaking the surface of a pond, and wrapped themselves around his head, holding it tight, pulling it to the glass.

The image's mouth was opening and closing, her teeth lengthening, the upper incisors growing, gouging into the flesh of her chin, scoring through the flesh. Threads of thick dark saliva dripped onto her breasts. Her eyes were changing, the white disappearing, turning black, the pupils length-ening, becoming yellow and slit-like. The face became the mask of a beast, like a boar with curling tusks and leathery verminous skin. The mouth opened and opened and opened, drew back . . . and erupted through the mirror.

The forked tongue lashed at his eyes, destroying the retina, the lower jaws clamped into the flesh beneath his chin, the fangs in its upper jaw tore into the soft flesh behind his eyes and then it bit down, sheering off the whole front of his face.

THE BULLET SHATTERED the skylight, continued down, entered the crown of Frazer's head and blew off most of the lower portion of his face, spattering gore across the glass. He was dead before he hit the floor.

Although another shot was unnecessary, Margaret Haaren calmly shot him in the back of the head as he lay on the floor. The bullet tore off what was left of his face.

EPILOGUE

S TUART MILLER came up and stood beside Margaret Haaren, grinning broadly.

"What's got you so happy?" she asked.

"The SWAT Commander is just about to throw a serious fit. You stole his limelight. He was in the middle of a speech about *a considered response to this delicate situation* when you blew Frazer's head off."

"He'd cut her throat," she said tiredly, watching the paramedics carry out Helen on a stretcher. Light bulbs flashed. "He'd made a puncture in it and was drinking her blood like some vampire."

"I've heard about that. The need for blood is some obscure medical condition, some deficiency," Stuart Miller said mildly. "But the other stuff, the vampire stuff, the black magic rubbish is some sort of sex trip." He jerked his thumb back over his shoulder. "We found some women's clothing over there. Remember those street girls who ended up in the river? I'll bet you my pension we've got ourselves a connection."

"Good." She handed across her gun. "Check this in for me will you? I'm going with the paramedics."

"Give my regards to Helen? Tell her she's a really lucky girl."

"You can say that again."

When Margaret had looked down into the room, she had immediately assumed that Frazer had cut her niece's throat. But when the SWAT team had finally broken down the door, and got her out, the paramedics discovered that there was only a small nick in the side of her throat and that the girl was already beginning to open her eyes.

For one instant they'd stared at Margaret Haaren completely devoid of expression, and then a smile fixed itself to her lips.

"Hello Aunty."

IN HER GLASS prison, Manny Frazer screamed and screamed and screamed ...

AUTHOR'S NOTE

John Dee and Edward Kelly were real historical characters.

Dee, who was Queen Elizabeth's spy, was also one of her closest advisors. He prepared regular horoscopes for her, and did choose the date of her coronation.

It is a matter of record that John Dee married twice: the name of his first wife is unknown, and she died or disappeared mysteriously after only one year of marriage.

Following the woman's death, Queen Elizabeth visited Mortlake, home of John Dee, to view the marvelous mirror she had heard so much about, but she inexplicably refused to enter the house and insisted on viewing the mirror in the gardens.

Edward Kelley or Kelly's real name was Talbott.

Dee's own diaries record that he was advised by a young girl, called Madimi. He described her as "otherworldy" and there is no record of her birth or death.

The mirror, albeit in slightly smaller form than described here, exists to this day. Its face is kept perpetually covered with a black cloth.